Terry Pratchett was the acclaimed creator of the global bestselling Discworld series, the first of which, *The Colour of Magic*, was published in 1983. His fortieth Discworld novel, *Raising Steam*, was published in 2013. His books have been widely adapted for stage and screen, and he was the winner of multiple prizes, including the Carnegie Medal, as well as being awarded a knighthood for services to literature. He died in March 2015. www.terrypratchett.co.uk

Stephen Baxter is one of the UK's most acclaimed writers of science fiction and a multi-award winner. His many books include the classic *Xeelee* sequence, the *Time's Odyssey* novels (written with Arthur C. Clarke), *The Time Ships*, a sequel to H.G. Wells's *The Time Machine*, a Doctor Who novel, *The Wheel of Ice*, and most recently the epic, far-future novels *Proxima* and *Ultima*. He lives in Northumberland.

More details of Stephen Baxter's works can be found on www.stephen-baxter.com

CONCEPTUAL DIAGRAMMATIC SKETCH OF THE FREEMAN DYSON PLANETARY SPIN MOTOR

CLASSIFIED

Magnetic field

Pole-to-pole current loop

Conductive bands

Moon rock

Conductive material

Orbiting 'spacecraft'

THE LONG UTOPIA

Terry Pratchett and
Stephen Baxter

Doubleday

LONDON · TORONTO · SYDNEY · AUCKLAND · JOHANNESBURG

TRANSWORLD PUBLISHERS
61–63 Uxbridge Road, London W5 5SA
www.transworldbooks.co.uk

Transworld is part of the Penguin Random House group of companies
whose addresses can be found at global.penguinrandomhouse.com

First published in Great Britain in 2015 by Doubleday
an imprint of Transworld Publishers

The diagrammatic sketch of the planetary spin motor on p.2 is by Richard Shailer

A CIP catalogue record for this book
is available from the British Library.

ISBN 9780857521767 (cased)
9780857521774 (tpb)

Typeset in 11.75/15pt Minion by Falcon Oast Graphic Art Ltd.
Printed and bound by Clays Ltd, Bungay, Suffolk.

Penguin Random House is committed to a sustainable future for
our business, our readers and our planet. This book is made from
Forest Stewardship Council® certified paper.

5 7 9 10 8 6 4

For Lyn and Rhianna, as always
T.P.

For Sandra
S.B.

1

IN FEBRUARY 2052, in the remote Long Earth:
     On another world, under a different sky – in another universe, whose distance from the Datum, the Earth of mankind, was nevertheless counted in the mundanity of human steps – Joshua Valienté lay beside his own fire. Hunting creatures grunted and snuffled down in the valley bottom. The night was purple velvet, alive with insects and spiky with invisible jiggers and no-see-ums that made kamikaze dives on every exposed inch of Joshua's flesh.

Joshua had been in this place two weeks already, and he didn't recognize a damn one of the beasts he shared this world with. In fact he wasn't too sure where he was, either geographically or stepwise; he hadn't troubled to count the Earths he'd passed through. When you were on a solitary sabbatical, precise locations kind of weren't the point. Even after more than three decades of travelling the Long Earth he evidently hadn't exhausted its wonders.

Which was making him think. Joshua was going to be fifty years old this year. Anniversaries like that made a man reflective.

'Why did it all have to be so strange?' He spoke aloud. He was alone on the planet; why the hell not speak aloud? 'All these parallel worlds, and stuff. What's it all for? And why did it all have to happen to *me*?'

And *why* was he getting another headache?

As it happened, the answers to some of those questions were out there, both in the strange sideways geography of the Long Earth, and buried deep in Joshua's own past. In particular, a partial answer about the true nature of the Long Earth had already begun to be uncovered as far back as July of the year 2036, out in the High Meggers:

As long as they lived in the house in New Springfield, and it was only a few years in the end, Cassie Poulson would always try her best to forget what she'd found when she'd dug the cellar out back, in the summer of '36.

Cassie hadn't been too sure about her new world when she'd first arrived, just a year before that. Not that she was unsure of her own ability to make a home or raise a family, out here in the barely explored wilds of the Long Earth. Or of the relationship she had with Jeb, which was as strong and true as the iron nails he was already turning out of his forge. Nor did she doubt the folks who had walked with them all this way, an epic trek of more than a million steps from the Datum, in search of a new home in one of the myriad worlds revealed just a few years back by Joshua Valienté's pioneering exploration in the very first of the Long Earth airships.

No, it was the world itself that she'd had trouble with, at first anyhow. Earth West 1,217,756 was forest. Nothing but forest. It was all totally alien for a girl who'd done most of her growing up in Miami West 4, which back in those days had been little more than a minor suburb of its parent city on the Datum.

But it had got better as their first year wore away. Cassie had learned to her delight that there were no real seasons here – none of the summers that turned Miami West 4 into a ferocious oven, and no winters to speak of either. You could just kind of relax about the weather; it would never bother you. And meanwhile, aside from the usual suite of mosquitoes and other nibbling insects, there was nothing in this forest that would harm you – nothing worse than a finger-nip from a frightened furball, nothing as long as you stayed away from the rivers where the crocodiles lurked, and the nests of the big birds.

And it got better yet when she and Jeb had cleared enough ground to start planting their first crops, of wheat and potatoes and lettuce and beets, and the chickens and goats and pigs started having their young, and she and Jeb had hammered together the beginnings of their own home.

Yes, it was all going fine, until the day Jeb decreed they needed a cellar.

Everybody knew that a cellar was a sensible precaution, both as a store and as a refuge from such hazards as twisters and bandits with Stepper boxes. While Jeb and the neighbours didn't expect any trouble, well, you never knew, and it would be a comfort to have it in place before they started a family.

So here was Cassie, digging in the earth with the bronze spade she'd carried with her all the way from Miami West 4, while Jeb was off with a party trying once more to hunt down a big bird. The work wasn't hard. The ground had already been stripped of tree cover and the roots dug out, and Cassie was strong, toughened up by trekking and pioneering. By early afternoon Cassie, filthy and sweating, was digging into a hole that was already deeper than her head height.

Which was when her spade suddenly pushed into open air, and she fell forward.

She caught herself, stepped back, took a breath, and looked closer. She'd broken through the wall of the nascent cellar. Beyond was a deep black, like a cave. She knew of no animal that would dig a burrow as big and deep as this looked to be; there were ground-dwelling furballs here, but nobody had seen one much bigger than a cat. Still, just because nobody had seen such a critter didn't mean it couldn't exist – and there was a good chance it wouldn't enjoy being disturbed. She ought to get out of there.

But the day was calm. A couple of her neighbours were chatting over lemonade just a few yards away. She felt safe.

And curiosity burned. This was something new, in the endless unchanging summer of New Springfield. She bent down to peer into the hole in the wall.

Only to find a face looking back out at her.

It was human-sized, but not human. More insectile, she thought, a kind of sculpture of shining black, with a multiple eye like a cluster of grapes. And half of it was coated with a silvery metal, a mask. She saw all this in the heartbeat it took for the shock to work through her system.

Then she yelled, and scrambled back. When she looked again, the masked face was gone.

Josephine Barrow, one of her neighbours, walked over and looked down from above. 'You OK, honey? Put your spade through your foot?'

'Can you help me out?' She raised her arms.

When Cassie was up on the surface, Josephine said, 'You look like you saw a ghost.'

Well, she'd seen – something.

Cassie looked around at her house, which was almost ready to get its permanent roof put on, and the fields they'd cleared for their crops, and the hole they'd already dug to make a sandpit for their kid to play in some day . . . All the work they'd put into this place. All the love. She didn't want to leave this.

But she also didn't want to deal with whatever the hell was down in that hole.

'We need to cover this up,' she said now.

Josephine frowned. 'After all your work?'

Cassie thought fast. 'I struck groundwater. No good for a cellar here. We'll dig a well some day.' There was a heap of rough-cut timber leaning against the back wall of the house. 'Help me.' She started to lay the planks over the hole.

Josephine stared at her. 'Why not just fill it in?'

Because it would take too long. Because she wanted this hidden for good, before Jeb got back. 'I'll backfill it later. For now just help me, OK?'

Josephine was looking at her strangely.

But she helped her even so, and by the time Jeb got back Cassie had spread dirt and forest-floor muck over the timber so you'd never know the hole was there, and had even scraped out the beginnings of a second cellar around the far side of the house.

And by the time they sat down to eat that evening on the porch of their home, Cassie Poulson was well on the way to forgetting she'd ever seen that masked face at all.

And a few years later, in March 2040, Miami, Earth West 4:

It was only a coincidence, historians of the Next would later agree, that Stan Berg should be born in Miami West 4, the Low Earth footprint city where Cassie Poulson had grown up. Cassie Poulson, on whose High Meggers property the primary assembler anomaly proved to be located – an anomaly which, in the end, would shape Stan Berg's short life, and much more. Strange, but only a coincidence.

Of course, in the very year Stan was born the town began to change dramatically, as the first of a flood of refugees from a Datum America blighted by Yellowstone began to show up. By the time Stan was eight years old an increasingly crowded, lawless and chaotic camp had been taken over by government and corporate interests, and transformed into a remarkable construction site – and by Stan's eleventh birthday there was a new 'star' in the sky, stationary above the southern horizon – not a true star, but the orbital terminus of a nascent space elevator that reached down to the local version of Florida, built by a community of hastily recruited stalk jacks that by then included Stan's own mother and father.

But whatever the convulsions that would colour Stan's young life, there was nothing strange about the love that filled Stan's mother Martha from the moment she first held her child. And *she,* at least, saw nothing strange in the apparent curiosity with which, eyes precociously open, Stan inspected the changing world from the moment he was delivered into it.

Joshua Valienté was always sceptical about Bill Chambers's Joker stories. But, he would realize in retrospect, if he'd paid more attention and thought a little more deeply about what Bill was saying, he might have got some earlier clues into the meaning of it all. Such as what Bill told him in 2040 – the same year Stan Berg was born – as he travelled with Joshua in an airship into the High Meggers far beyond New Springfield, a story about a Joker he called the Cueball:

Joshua had actually glimpsed this Joker himself. He and Lobsang had in fact discovered it, nestling in that band of relatively domesticated worlds called the Corn Belt, on their first journey out into the deep Long Earth, during which Joshua had first learned the meaning of the word. 'Jokers,' Lobsang had said. 'Worlds that don't fit the pattern. And there *is* a pattern, generally speaking. But the broad patterns are broken up by these exceptions: Jokers in the pack, as scholars of the Long Earth call them . . .' Joshua already knew many such worlds, even if he'd had no name for the category. *This* Joker had been a world like a pool ball, an utterly smooth, colourless ground under a cloudless deep blue sky.

But even though he'd seen the place for himself Joshua knew better than to take Bill's stories at face value. Bill Chambers, about Joshua's age, had grown up alongside him at the Home in Madison, Wisconsin. He'd been a friend, a rival, a source of trouble – and always a consummate liar.

Bill said now, 'I know a fella who knew a fella—'

'Oh, yes.'

'Who camped out on the Cueball for a bet. Just for a night. All alone. As you would. In the nip too, that was part of the bet.'

'Sure.'

'In the morning he woke up with a hangover from hell. Drinking alone, never wise. Now this fella was a natural stepper. So he got his stuff together in a blind daze, and stepped, but he says he sort of stumbled as he stepped.'

'Stumbled?'

'He didn't feel as if he'd stepped the right way.'

'What? How's that possible? What do you mean?'

'Well, we step East, or we step West, don't we? You have the soft places, the short cuts, if you can find them, but that's pretty much it . . .'

Stepping: on Step Day the world had pivoted around mankind. Suddenly, in return for the effort of building a Stepper box, a crude electrical gadget – and some, like Joshua, didn't even need that – you could step sideways out of the old reality, out of the world and into another, just like the original yet choked with uncleared forest and replete with wild animals – for it was only in the original Earth that mankind had evolved, and had had a chance to shape its world. Whole planets, a short walk away. And, in either direction, East or West, you could take another step, and another. If there was an end to the Long Earth, as the chain of worlds became known, it was yet to be found. After Step Day everything had been different, for mankind, for the Long Earth itself – and, in particular, for Joshua Valienté.

But even the Long Earth had its rules. Or so Joshua had always thought.

'. . . Anyhow this fella felt like he'd stepped a different way. Perpendicular. Like he'd stepped *North*.'

'And?'

'And he emerged on to some kind of other world. It was night, not day. No stars in the clear sky. No stars, *sort of*. Instead . . .'

'Your storytelling style really grates sometimes, Bill.'

'But I've got ye hooked, haven't I?'

'Get on with it. What did he see?'

'He saw all the stars. All of them. He saw the whole fecking Galaxy, man, the Milky Way. *From outside.*'

Outside the Galaxy. Thousands of light years from Earth – from any Earth . . .

Bill said, 'Still in the nip he was, too.'

That was the trouble with combers, Joshua had concluded. They were just expert bullshitters. Maybe they spent too much time alone.

But, he realized, reflecting in February 2052, he'd tended to think even of Lobsang as a bullshitter, albeit a shitter built on a truly cosmic scale. If only he'd listened to Lobsang when he'd had the chance.

Now it was too late, for Lobsang was dead.

Joshua had been there when it had happened, in the late fall of 2045:

He and Sally Linsay had waited by the door of the Home in Madison West 5. It was early evening, and streetlights sparked.

Sally was in her travelling gear, her multi-pocketed fisherman's jacket under a waterproof coverall, a light leather pack on her back. As usual, she looked like she was going to light out of here at any moment. And the longer the Sisters took to answer the damn door, the more likely that became.

'Look,' Joshua said, trying to forestall her, 'just take it easy. Say hello. Everybody here wants to see you, to say thank you for what you did for the Next. Busting those super-smart kids out of the Pearl Harbor facility—'

'You know me, Joshua. These Low Earths are mob scenes nowadays. And places like this. This *Home*, where they lock you up for your own good. I don't care how happy or otherwise you were here, Joshua, with those penguins.'

'Don't call them penguins.'

'As soon as we're done I'm going to get blind drunk, as fast as possible—'

'Then you'll need something stronger than our sweet sherry.' Sister John had quietly opened the door; now she smiled. 'Come on in.'

Sally shook the Sister's hand with good enough grace.

Joshua followed them in, walking down a corridor into what was to him an eerie re-creation of the Home he'd grown up in, the original long ago wrecked by the Datum Madison nuke.

Sister John, her head enclosed in a crisp wimple, leaned closer to Joshua. 'So how are you?'

'Fine. Disoriented to be here.'

'I know. Doesn't quite smell right, does it? Well, give the mice a few decades to do their work and they'll put that right.'

'And you. You're running the place now! To me you'll always be plain old Sarah.'

'Who you had to rescue from the forest on Step Day. When you come back here it feels like we suddenly got all grown up, didn't we?'

'Yeah. To me the superior ought to be a towering figure, and *old*—'

'As old as me?' Sister Agnes was waiting for them in the doorway of the Home's parlour, the posh lounge where the Sisters had always received visitors.

But Agnes, eerily, now looked younger than Sister John. And when Joshua submitted to a hug there was just the faintest hint of artifice, an excessive smoothness in the cheek he kissed – and beneath her practical, slightly shabby habit an alarming, almost subliminal sense of super-strength. After her death, Lobsang had brought Agnes *back to life*, downloading her memories into a lifelike android shell while simultaneously chanting Buddhist prayers. To Joshua it was as if somebody had turned his life's chief mother-figure into a terminator robot. But he had known Lobsang a long time, and he'd learned to see the spirit inside the machine. As with Lobsang, so now with Agnes.

He said simply: 'Hello, Agnes.'

'And Sally Linsay.' With Sally it was a wary handshake rather than a hug. 'I've heard so much about you, Ms Linsay.'

'Ditto.'

Agnes studied her intently, almost challengingly, before turning away. 'So, Joshua, how are your family? Such a shame you're apart from your little boy.'

Joshua said, 'Not so little . . . Well, you know me. I've a split soul, Agnes. Half of me always drawn away, out into the Long Earth.'

'Still, you're home now. Come and join the party . . .'

Sitting side by side on the usual overstuffed armchairs – some of them originals, retrieved from the old Datum Home – were Nelson Azikiwe and Lobsang.

Lobsang, or at least this ambulant avatar, with shaven head and bare feet, was dressed in what had become his trademark garb of orange robe. Sally was briskly introduced to Nelson. South African born, a former clergyman now in his fifties, he was dressed comparatively soberly, in a suit and tie. This ill-matched pair were balancing china teacups on their knees, and plates bearing slices of cake. A younger Sister whom Joshua didn't recognize was fussing around, serving.

And Shi-mi the cat was here. She came to Joshua, favouring him with a brush against his legs, and she glared at Sally with LED-green eyes.

As Joshua and Sally sat down, Agnes joined the circle, and Sister John and her young companion served up more tea and cake. Agnes said, 'Well, this was my idea, Joshua. In this moment of comparative calm – now that the latest global panic, when we all thought we were going to be driven to extinction by super-brain children, has somewhat subsided – my plan was to bring Lobsang here, and to gather his friends together for once.'

Sally scowled. '"Friends"? Is that how you think of us, Lobsang? We're gaming tokens to you, more like. Dimes to feed the slot machine of fate.'

Nelson grinned. 'Quite so, Ms Linsay. But here we all are, even so.'

'Friends,' Agnes said firmly. 'What else is there in this life but friends and family?'

Lobsang, calm, rather blank-faced, said, 'Your own family is making waves just now, Sally. Your father at least, with his ideas of a new kind of space development.'

'Ah, yes, dear old Papa, dreaming of using his Martian bean-stalks to open up access to space. A straight-line path to massive industrialization.'

'Willis Linsay is wise, in his way. We *should* build up again, from this low base we've been reduced to by Yellowstone. As fast and as cleanly as we can, and space elevators will make that possible. After all we may some day need to compete with the Next.'

Nelson asked, 'What *do* you know about the Next, Lobsang? I know they made some kind of contact with you. Is there any more than you've said publicly?'

'Only that they've gone. All those brilliant children, emerging all over the Datum, all over the Long Earth – the next step in human evolution – that our government rounded up and put in a pen on Hawaii. Gone to a place they call the Grange, out in the Long Earth somewhere. I couldn't even speculate where.'

Sally laughed. 'They didn't tell *you*? They just left you to clear up their mess at Happy Landings, didn't they? This is twisting you up, isn't it, Lobsang? The omnipresent, omniscient god of the Long Earth, reduced to a messenger boy, by *children*.'

Joshua made to hush her.

But Lobsang said, 'No, let her speak. She's right. This has been a difficult time for me. You know that as well as anybody, Joshua. And in fact that's the reason I allowed Agnes to call you all together.'

Agnes stiffened. 'Oh, you allowed it, did you? And there was me thinking this was all my idea.'

Lobsang looked at them in turn, at Sally, Nelson, Joshua, Agnes, Sister John. 'You *are* my family. That's how I think of you all. Yet you have family ties of your own. You mustn't neglect them.' He turned to Nelson. 'You, too, are not as alone as you thought you were, my friend.'

Nelson looked intrigued rather than offended at this opacity. 'Textbook enigmatic. Typical Lobsang!'

'I don't mean to be obscure. If you just think back to when we went to New Zealand—'

Evidently frustrated at this hijacking of her party, Agnes interrupted sharply. 'Lobsang, if you've something to say you'd better get to the point.'

Lobsang sat forward, shoulders hunched. Suddenly he looked, to Joshua, unaccountably *old*. Old and tired. 'Yellowstone, and the collapse of the Datum, were hard for me. I suffuse the Long Earth, I have iterations scattered across the solar system, but my centre of gravity was always Datum Earth. Now the Datum itself is grievously wounded. And so, as a consequence, am I.' He pressed his thumbs into his temples. 'Sometimes I feel incomplete. As if I am losing memories, and then losing the memory of the loss itself . . . Yellowstone to me was like a lobotomy.

'Since then I have had – doubts. I told you of this, Joshua. I have had the odd sensation that I *remembered* my previous incarnations. But that is not the accepted norm, under the Tibetan tradition; if my reincarnation has been fully successful I should shed all memory of my previous lives. Perhaps this reincarnation is imperfect, then. Or,' he glanced at Agnes, 'perhaps there is some more mundane explanation. I am after all nothing but a creature of electrical sparks in distributed stores of Black Corporation gel. Perhaps I have been hacked.

'And *then* came the Next, and their verdict on me. Before all this,

I imagined I would become – yes, Sally! – omnipresent, omniscient. Why not? All of mankind's computer systems, all communications, would ultimately be integrated into one entity – into me. And I would cradle all of you in safety and warmth, for evermore.'

Sally snorted. 'An evermore of subordination? No thanks.'

He looked at her sadly. 'But what of me? Without my dream I am nothing.'

Carefully he put down his teacup.

Agnes was clearly alarmed by this small gesture. 'What do you mean, Lobsang? What are you going to do?'

He smiled at her. 'Dear Agnes. This will not hurt, you know. It is just that I—'

He froze. Just stopped, mid-motion, mid-sentence.

Agnes cried, 'Lobsang? Lobsang!'

Joshua rushed to his side, with Agnes. As Joshua held Lobsang's shoulders, Agnes rubbed his hands, his face: synthetic hands on synthetic cheeks, Joshua thought, and yet the emotion could not have been more real.

Lobsang's head turned – just his head, like a ventriloquist's dummy – to Joshua, first. 'I have always been your friend, Joshua.'

'I know . . .'

Now Lobsang looked up at Agnes. 'Don't be afraid, Agnes,' he whispered. 'It is not dying. It is not dying—'

His face turned slack.

For a moment there was stillness.

Then Joshua became aware of a change in the background, the soft, routine sounds of the Home: a ceasing of noise, of the humming of invisible machines, of fans and pumps. A closing down. Glancing out of the window, he saw lights flicker and die in the building opposite. Whole blocks growing dark further out. Somewhere an alarm bell sounded.

Agnes grabbed Lobsang's shoulders and shook him. 'Lobsang!

Lobsang! What have you done? Where have you gone? Lobsang, you bastard!'

Sally laughed, stood up, and stepped away.

Of course even Lobsang had never known it all. Some of the mysteries of Joshua's own peculiar nature were hidden, it would turn out, not in the stepwise reaches of the Long Earth but deep in time. Mysteries that had begun to tangle up as early as March 1848, in London, Datum Earth:

The applause was thunderous, and the Great Elusivo could hear it as he went down the steps to the stage door of the Victoria theatre. His ears still ringing from the din of the threepenny gallery, now he was battered by the sights and sounds of the New Cut: the shop windows, the stalls, the jostling traffic, the street entertainers, the beggar boys tumbling for pennies. And of course there were people waiting for Luis outside, in the dark of a Lambeth evening; there always were. Even young ladies. Hopeful young ladies perhaps.

But this time a quiet voice, a male voice, called from an alley. 'You move very fast, don't you, mister? One might say, remarkably fast. Shall I call you Luis? I believe that is your rightful name. Or one of them. I have a proposition for you. Which is that I shall take you out to dinner at the Drunken Clam – Lambeth's finest oyster-house, if you didn't know it already. Because I do know you're very fond of your oysters.'

The figure was indistinct in the shadows. 'You have me at a disadvantage, sir.'

'Yes, I do, don't I? And the reason I am speaking so rapidly to you, not to say forcefully, is that I know that at any moment you wish, *you may simply vanish*. It is a faculty that serves you very well, as I see. Yet you do not know how you do it. And nor do I. To cut a long story short, sir—'

There was a slight breeze as the man disappeared.

And then appeared again. He gasped and clutched his stomach, as if he'd been punched. But he stood straight and said, 'I can do it as well. My name is Oswald Hackett. Luis Ramon Valienté – shall we talk?'

And in February 2052, in the remote Long Earth:

Overhead Joshua Valienté's own personal stars shone for his benefit alone. It was after all reasonable to assume that his was the only soul in the whole of this particular Creation.

He still had that headache.

And not only that, the stump of his left arm itched.

As something squealed and died in the dark, the spirit of Valienté moved on the face of the darkness. And it was sore afraid to the soles of his feet. 'I'm getting too old for this,' Joshua muttered aloud.

He started to pack up his stuff. He was going home.

2

T HE FUNERAL HAD been held on a bleak day in December
2045, in Madison, Wisconsin, Earth West 5.

At first Sister Agnes had wondered how you could have a funeral
service for a man who had not *been* a man, not by any usual definition, and whose body had not been the usual mass of fragile flesh
– indeed, she had never been sure how many bodies he *had*, or
even if the question had any meaning. And yet he, man or not, had
evidently died, in any sense of the word that meant anything in the
hearts of his friends. And so a funeral service he would have, she
had decreed.

They gathered around the grave dug into the small plot outside
this relocated children's home, where 'he' had been laid to rest – 'he'
at least being the ambulant unit he had inhabited at the moment of
his 'death'. It didn't help the sense of unreality, Agnes thought, that
four of his spare ambulant units stood over the grave as a kind of
honour guard, their faces blank, dressed in their regular uniform
of orange robes and sandals despite the bitter cold.

Compared with that, the prayers and readings murmured jointly
by Father Gavin, of the local Catholic parish, and Padmasambhava,
abbot of a monastery in Ladakh and, supposedly, Lobsang's old
friend in a previous life, seemed almost routine. But perhaps
that was a reflection of the oddest aspect of Lobsang, Agnes
thought: that he had come to awareness as a piece of software in an
elaborate computer system, fully sentient, and yet claiming to be the

reincarnation of a Tibetan motorcycle repairman, and demanding full human rights as a consequence. The case had tied up court time for years.

Now, in his gentle Irish accent, Father Gavin read, "'I know not how I seem to others, but to myself I am but a small child wandering upon the vast shores of knowledge, every now and then finding a small bright pebble to content myself with while the vast ocean of undiscovered truth lies before me . . .'"

Agnes slipped to the back of the group and stood next to an elderly man, tall, white-haired, dressed in an anonymous black overcoat and hat. 'Nice lines,' Agnes said quietly.

'From Newton. Always been one of my favourite quotes. My own choice: a touch immodest perhaps, but you only get one funeral.'

'Well, in your case, that's to be seen. So, "George"?'

'Yes, my "wife"?'

'Good turn-out, even if you don't count yourself. There's Commander Kauffman, looking splendid in her dress uniform. Nelson Azikiwe, as solemn and observant as ever. Always a good friend, wasn't he, L— umm, "George"? Who's that woman over there? Attractive, forty-something – the one who's been crying all morning.'

'She's called Selena Jones. Worked with me years ago. In theory she's still my legal guardian.'

'Hmm. You do come with baggage, don't you? Even Cho-je has turned up, I see, and why *he* hasn't been put out for scrap I don't know. And Joshua Valienté and Sally Linsay.'

'King and Queen of the Long Earth,' said 'George'.

'Yes. Side by side, looking as always as if they belong together and yet wishing they were worlds apart, and that's never made any sense, has it?'

'You've known Joshua since he was a child. You tell me. But speaking of children—'

'The paperwork's all been submitted. It may take some time

before the right child shows up. Years, even. Why, he or she may not have been born yet. But when the adoption clearance comes through we'll be ready. And have we chosen the new world where we'll raise our "son" or "daughter"?'

'As I told you, I've asked Sally Linsay for help with that, when we need it. Who else knows the Long Earth as she does?'

Agnes looked over at Sally. 'She's the only one who knows about you?'

'Yes. Save for you, the *only* one. In fact she said she'd never really believed my end was final; she kind of knew anyhow, before I approached her. But she's discreet. I'll swear she keeps secrets from herself.'

'Hmm. I'm not entirely sure I trust her. Not about her discretion, I accept that.'

'Then what?'

'I don't know. Sally has . . . an odd sense of humour. She's a trickster. And you are sure you want to do this, aren't you? To put everything aside, and just—'

He looked at her. 'Just be human? Do *you*?'

And that was the question that stirred her own emotions, deep in the lump of Black Corporation gel she used as a heart.

Father Gavin read another line, and 'George' frowned. 'Did I hear that correctly? Something about being like a sinner at heaven's gate, and crawling back to me . . .'

She linked her arm in his. 'You have Newton, I have Steinman. Come on. Let's get out of here before anybody gets suspicious.'

3

IF NOT FOR his dog Rio chasing some imaginary furball around the back of the old Poulson place, Nikos Irwin would most likely never have found the big cellar at all. It was a kind of unlikely accident – or maybe not, not if you knew Rio, and the qualities of stubbornness and curiosity she had inherited from her Bernese mountain dog ancestors. But if not for Nikos and his stubborn pet, the whole subsequent history of mankind might have been different – for better or worse.

It was April of 2052. Nikos was ten years old.

It wasn't as if Nikos particularly liked the old Poulson house, or the abandoned township it was part of. It was just that the Poulson place was used as the local swap house, and he'd been sent here by his mother in search of baby shoes, for her friend Angie Clayton was carrying.

So, with Rio loping at his side, he walked out of the shade of the trees, out of the dense green where somewhere a band of forest trolls hooted a gentle song, and into the harsh unfiltered sunlight.

He looked around at the big houses that loomed silently over this open space. Nikos had grown up in the forest, and instinctively he didn't like clearings, for they left you without cover. And this abandoned community was an odd place besides. His parents always told him that the Long Earth was too new to mankind to have much history yet, but if there was history anywhere in Nikos's own world, it was here. Some of these old houses were being swallowed by the green, but the rest still stood out in the light, hard and square and alien, with their peeling whitewash and cracked windows. The place even smelled odd to Nikos, not just of general decay after years of abandonment, but of cut wood and dried-out, dusty, lifeless ground.

All this was basically the work of the very first colonists to come here, the founders. They had opened up the forest to build their little town. You could still see the neatly cut and burned-out stumps where great old trees had been removed, and the fields they'd planted, and the tracks they'd marked out with white-painted stones, and of course the houses they'd hammered together in a few short years, with their picket fences and screen doors and bead curtains. Some of the houses had stained glass windows. There was even a little chapel, half-finished, with a truncated steeple open to the elements.

And in one big old house there was even, incredibly, a piano, a wooden box which somebody must have built from the local wood, and fitted out with pedals and an inner frame and strung with wire, all carried from the Low Earths: a remarkable feat of almost pointless craftsmanship.

Nikos's parents said the founders had been keen and eager and energetic, and when they'd come travelling out to these remote worlds – more than a million steps from the Datum, the first world of mankind – they'd had a kind of fever dream of their past, when their own ancestors had spread out into the original America and had built towns like this, towns with farms and gardens and schools and churches. They had even named their town: New Springfield.

But the trouble was, this wasn't colonial America.

And this Earth wasn't the Datum. Nikos's father said that *this* world, and a whole bunch of similar Earths in a band around it, was

26

choked with trees from pole to equator to the other pole, and he meant that literally: here, there were forests flourishing even in the Arctic night. Certainly this footprint of Maine was thick with trees that looked like sequoias and laurels but probably weren't, and an undergrowth of things like tea plants and fruit bushes and ferns and horsetails. The warm, moist, dark air fizzed with insects, and the trees and the loamy ground swarmed with furballs, as everybody called them, jumpy little mammals that spent their lives scurrying after said insects.

And in such a world, the founders' children had soon started to explore other ways of living, in defiance of their parents, the pioneers.

Why go to all the hard work of farming when you were surrounded by *whole empty worlds* full of ever-generous fruit trees? And rivers full of fish, and forests full of furballs so numerous they were easily trapped? Oh, maybe farming made sense on the more open worlds of the Corn Belt, but *here* . . . The drifters who came through here periodically, calling themselves combers or okies or hoboes, vivid examples of other ways of living, had helped inspire the breakaway. Nikos's parents' friends still spoke of one particularly persuasive and evidently intelligent young woman who had stayed here for a few weeks, preaching the virtues of a looser lifestyle.

Pioneers tended to have their children young; the sooner you raised a new crop of willing workers the better. But the numerous children of New Springfield, growing up in a world utterly unlike their parents', had quickly learned independence of mind, and had rebelled. Most of the youngsters, and a good number of their parents, had given up and walked off into the green. The will to maintain the township had kind of dissolved away – indeed it had only lasted one generation.

Nowadays the Irwins and the other family groups didn't really have permanent residences at all. Instead they had a kind of cycle of living places, which you'd visit according to the fruits of the gentle seasons, and keep clear of fresh brush with a little burning, and repair last year's lean-tos and hearths. So they'd climb Manning Hill on one particular world a couple of steps East in the spring months, when the squirrel-moles came bursting out of the ground to choose new queens and found new burrows, and were easy to trap. Or, in the fall, they'd go to Soulsby Creek four steps further West where the annual spawning run of the local salmon was particularly rich. Nikos had grown up with all this, and knew no different.

As for the old township itself, meanwhile, as they grew old and weary a lot of the founders had gone back to the Datum. A few disappointed pioneers had clung on as best they could, and their relatives had kept an eye on these ageing heroes. Nikos's mother told a wistful story of how she used to hear one old lady play that piano of an evening, and Chopin waltzes would waft out into the silence of the world forest, music written down in a century long gone and in a world very far from here, and sometimes picked up by responsive choruses of forest trolls. But the piano lost its tuning, and there came a day when the music ceased altogether, and now nobody played the piano any more.

Even after it had been wholly abandoned, though, Nikos's group worked together to keep the New Springfield clearing open. It had some uses. Everybody needed a Stepper box, and for that you needed potatoes, and potatoes needed cultivating, so *that* was something useful to do with the remains of the founders' farms. It had taken somebody a lot of effort to build the forge beside the Poulson place, and that was kept functional; you couldn't carry iron across worlds, and preserving the craft of iron-working seemed another good idea. Some of the animals the founders had brought here – chickens and goats and pigs and even sheep – had survived, and bred. Every so often you'd be surprised by a wild descendant of those first porcine colonists bursting out of the undergrowth before you.

And this one house in particular, the old Poulson place, sturdier than the rest, had with time assumed a new role. It had become the swap house, as everybody called it, a place where you could dump and exchange stuff of all kinds.

Which was why Nikos was here today.

He walked cautiously across the clearing, towards the Poulson place.

With one hand on the sturdy bronze knife he carried on his left hip, the other on the Stepper box on his right, he was very aware of his surroundings. He had no real fear of the local wildlife. As far as wild critters went there were only three hazards in the forest: the ant swarms, the big birds, and the crocs. Well, he was too far from water for the crocs, and the big birds were ferocious but were used to chasing little forest furballs and were heavy and clumsy and slow-moving as a result, and if there was an ant swarm around he'd hear it coming long before it came sloshing over the ground like some gruesome corroding liquid, destroying everything in its path. Also the forest trolls would almost certainly sing out any danger, in time for Nikos to step out of its way. *Almost* certainly. Nikos had seen for himself one unwary kid get caught by a big bird, and it had been a terrible sight, and so you kept an eye out because of that weasel word *almost*.

No, the reason Nikos was so cautious was because, among the kids at least, there were stories about this particular house. Legends, if you liked. Legends about *things* that lived in there.

Oh, not just scavenging furballs and such. And not just the familiar monsters of the forest. Something worse yet. An elf, maybe, trapped in there, a Long Earth nasty, broken and bent and old but still vicious and just waiting to feed on unwary children. Or maybe, went one variation of this, it was the *ghost* of one of those very children, waiting to take revenge on those who had forced him or her to go in here in the first place . . .

Of course it made no sense. Nikos was old enough to see the flaws in the logic – if the Poulson house was haunted, why would the adults be using it as a store? – yet he was still enough of a little kid to be scared. Well, stories or not, he wasn't going back without what he'd been sent to get, that was for sure, or the mockery of his buddies would be worse than anything any monster could do to him.

As he reached the porch, Rio sniffed the air, yelped, and went running out of sight around the corner of the house, maybe on the trail of some unwary furball. Nikos paid the dog no attention.

He opened a creaking, unlocked door, pushed his way inside and looked around. Only a little daylight was able to struggle through the green film that was slowly covering the windows. He had a wind-up flashlight that he dug out of his pocket now, so as to see better in the murk. The hairs on the back of his neck prickled with unease. He was used to tepees and lean-tos; never mind ghost legends, it was quite alien for him just to walk into a box of wood, all closed up. Still, he walked deeper inside, treading cautiously.

One main room dominated much of the house. He knew that was how these houses had been built: you started with one big space where the whole growing family lived and ate and slept, and added on others when you could, such as a kitchen, bedrooms, store rooms – but this house, like most of the others, hadn't got that far. He could recognize stuff from the times he'd been here before, under the supervision of his father: the big old table standing in the corner, the hearth under a half-finished chimney stack, the floor covered with a scattering of rugs woven from reeds from the creek and coloured with dyes from local vegetables.

But the room was cluttered with junk, dusty old debris, heaped on the floor and the table and piled against the walls. Yet it wasn't junk, not quite. The people of the forest were always short of *stuff*, because everything they had was either brought from the Datum Earth or the Low Earths, or they had to make it themselves, and either way cost a lot of effort. So if something broke, a bow or a bronze machete or a digging stick, and you couldn't be troubled to fix it, you dumped it here in the swap house, the theory being that somebody else might make use of it, or at least bits of it – the bronze for melting down, a busted bow as a trainer for a little kid. There was a useful store of bits of wire and relays and coil formers, the kind of stuff you needed to make or repair a Stepper box or a ham radio. There was even a heap of fancy electronic goods from the Datum: phones and tablets, all black and inert since their batteries or solar cells had finally failed, their inner parts too fine and fiddly to be reusable. Even these were sometimes taken away to be worn as jewellery, or as shiny gifts for the forest trolls.

And there were always clothes, especially children's clothes: underwear and pants and shirts and sweaters and socks and shoes, much of it brought from the Low Earths, some made here. The adult stuff was generally too worn out to be useful, but Nikos picked out a few colourful scraps for the latest quilted blanket his mother was making; even rough shreds could be used to pack bedding and the like. The kids' stuff, though, was often barely used before the child in question grew out of it. The people of New Springfield were a mobile, nomadic people, and carried little with them. They certainly weren't going to carry around baby shoes for twenty years, on the off chance of some grandchild coming along some day to wear them for a couple of months. And it was baby shoes that Nikos was particularly looking for today, for the benefit of Angie Clayton's unborn.

After some rummaging he found a pair of beautiful little moccasins sewn from the scraped hide of some unfortunate furball, shoes that sat on the palm of his hand like toys.

That was when he heard Rio yelp, and a sound like wood cracking, and a rush like a heavy mass falling into a hole.

4

Nikos dashed outside and ran around the house, the way his dog had gone. 'Rio! Rio!'

At the back of the house, facing uncleared jungle, a row of poles had been driven into the ground, a half-finished stockade, intended to keep sheep in and big birds out. Nikos pushed his way through the tea plants and saplings that choked the once-cleared space between house and stockade – and he almost fell into a hole in the ground.

He took a cautious step back and peered down. The hole was maybe six feet across, and had been covered by rough-cut planks of wood that had evidently softened, made rotten by time. He could see from the remaining planks that they had been buried under soil, with a heaping of forest mulch on top of that. There were even a few hardy ferns sprouting in that skim of earth. But one of the planks had broken now, and fallen into the hole, revealing a deep black space.

Nikos scratched his head. The whole thing was kind of puzzling. Was this a cellar? It could be. As well as a place to store food and other stuff, a cellar was a sensible precaution against attack by bandits and others with nefarious purposes. If you had a Stepper box no wall could keep you out, after all; you just needed to step sideways into a world where that wall didn't exist, walk *through* the location of the wall, and step back again . . . Nobody could step into a cellar, however. Not with the same location in neighbouring worlds blocked off by soil and bedrock and tree roots. There were even shallow cellars under some of Nikos's family's larger, better established encampments, dotted stepwise across the worlds.

Yes, you'd expect a house like this to have a cellar, or at least the beginnings of one. But why plank it over?

And while all this crud on top of the planks might have just gathered there with the years, it *looked* like the hole had been deliberately concealed. Why hide it? Was it actually some kind of trap, rather than a cellar? But a trap for what? Only a big bird or a croc, or a big dog like Rio, or a *human*, would have been heavy enough to smash through those planks – and maybe not at all, back when the planks weren't so far-gone rotten as they were now.

None of this mattered. Rio was missing.

He hesitated, there in the unshaded sunshine. Enclosure under-ground would be even worse than in the Poulson house, because his primary defence, stepping out of any danger, wouldn't be available to him. He nearly backed away. But Rio . . . Carried all the way from Datum Earth as a pup by a trader, she was a Bernese mountain dog, bred, it was said, to pull carts laden with cheese. She was strong, with good lungs, but slow.

She was Nikos's dog. If he had to climb down into this hole he would.

He got down on his hands and knees, cautiously, and peered into the hole, through the broken plank. All he saw was darkness, even when he shone in his flashlight.

'Rio!'

At first he heard nothing at all, not even an echo. Then came a bark, undoubtedly Rio's, from out of the hole – but it sounded remarkably far off – not like it was from a dog trapped just a few feet down. 'Rio! *Rio!* . . .'

And then he heard another sound. A kind of scraping, almost a whispering, like some huge insect. It seemed to move away, as if burrowing deeper down. All the legends and scare stories in his head came bubbling back to the surface. Again, he almost backed off. But his dog was down there.

Feverishly he began to pull away the remaining planks, carelessly tipping dirt into the hole. 'Rio! Here, girl! Rio! . . .'

The pit he revealed was only maybe eight feet deep, crudely cut into loose-packed earth. He dangled over the edge, made sure he could scramble back up the sides before committing himself, then he dropped down to the bottom.

He looked around. If this had been intended to be a cellar it wasn't much of one, the walls bare earth, the floor still showing the spade marks left by the original digger and not smoothed off. It was just a hole in the ground, hastily cut and more hastily concealed. And there was no sign of his dog.

It was pretty clear where Rio had gone, though. There was a breach in one wall, down near the floor.

Making sure he had his pocket knife to hand, Nikos got down on hands and knees, and found himself looking into a kind of tunnel in the earth. It wasn't too wide, just a few feet, but it was a lot more smoothly cut than the aborted cellar, with a circular profile and smooth walls. And, he saw, sweeping his flashlight, it sloped down at a fairly steep angle. Down into darkness, beyond the reach of his light. What could have made *this*? Some kind of burrowing animal, maybe? There were furballs that lived underground, and his mind conjured up a vision of a squirrel-mole the size of a human, with claws on its big digging paws the size of spades. It would be like a kobold, he thought, a human-sized mole-like humanoid that sometimes came by, trying to trade. But he remembered that peculiar rustling, that whispering, scraping noise, like no sound a furball would make, or even a kobold.

Then, in the furthest distance, he heard another bark, a frightened yelp.

He let instinct take over. 'Coming, girl! Just you wait for Nikos!'

He took his flashlight in his mouth, entered the tunnel on all fours, and began to crawl down the slope. Under his hands and knees there was only dirt, smoothed over and close-packed. Behind him the disc of daylight receded, while ahead of him the light of the flash showed another opening at the end of the tunnel, a neat circle that let out into a still deeper dark. Being shut up in this tunnel was scary, and the Stepper box at his belt made it awkward to move. He'd have to back up to get out of here, for he'd have trouble turning round. But he pushed on.

He travelled maybe twenty feet, he figured, a steady descent down into the dark.

Then the slanting shaft ended in an opening to a much larger chamber. Still on his hands and knees, he cautiously peered out, waving his light. His flash picked up a roof and floor, both smoothly worked, maybe ten feet apart, and pillars, like remnants of cutaway dirt or bedrock, regularly placed. He couldn't see any walls, to either side or ahead; his flash wouldn't reach that far. He was evidently entering a much more expansive space, wide and deep.

So much for his ideas about squirrel-moles. What the hell was all this?

It reminded him of what he'd read, in his mother's irregular school classes, about mining back on the Low Earths. He knew there was a seam of iron ore around here that the founders had plundered when the Poulsons had built their forge – the rich seam, unique to this particular world, was one reason they'd settled here. But he'd seen the size of that home-built forge, and the handfuls of nails and such they'd made, the few horseshoes for the exotic-sounding animals they'd meant to import here some day but had never gotten around to (Nikos had never seen a horse). They could never have dug all *this* out in such a short time, and there would have been no need anyhow. But if not them—

The face appeared in front of him.

Face: that was one word for it, a mask that was vaguely the shape of a human face, one side covered by silvery metal, the other even worse, sculpted out of what looked like the black shiny stuff God made beetles out of, as his father might have said. But it was a definite face, mounted on a tiny-looking head that tilted on a narrow neck.

It almost looked curious. Inspecting him, that odd head tilting. Curious. Alive!

The delayed shock hit him. He screamed, and the noise echoed loudly from that big open chamber beyond. He tried to back up, but he lost his hold on the tunnel's sloping floor, and he slid forward, and tumbled out of the shaft—

Right into the arms of the silver-beetle creature. Arms? Did it *have* arms? He felt cold metal under his back, his legs. He yelled and struggled, and was released.

He hit the ground, a drop of only a few feet, but it knocked the wind out of him, and he dropped his flashlight. He rolled to his feet quickly, but in the dark, with the fallen flash giving only a sliver of light, he felt turned around, disoriented.

He saw the beetle thing roll on to its belly and scuttle away, perhaps as alarmed as he was. It looked human-sized, but like a beetle or a locust in its shape and the way it moved and in the shiny black hardness of its body, its multiple limbs.

And he saw, he *heard*, more beetle creatures approach. He grabbed the flashlight off the floor and swung it around.

They were coming at him from all sides, crawling along the ground, like an ant swarm but much larger, more monstrous, and the way those shiny black carapaces were laced with metal, stuff that had been *made*, was somehow even more horrific. When he pointed the light at one it flinched back as if dazzled, but from every other direction they kept on approaching. And when they got close they started rearing up, and he saw soft bellies exposed, with pale grey pods clinging to greenish flesh, like blisters.

Then one of them rose up right before him. He saw a half-face silver mask just like the first he'd encountered – maybe it actually *was* the first, he had no way of distinguishing them one from another – and a kind of tentacle, thread-like, silvery, reached out towards him.

He tried to stay still. But when the pseudopod touched him, cold metal on warm flesh, Nikos's nerve broke.

He ran forward, yelling, waving his flashlight, pushing through rustling bodies that tipped and scrambled to get out of his way. He didn't get very far before he tripped over something and fell on to a hard, compacted floor. Again he dropped the flash, and he had moments of panic in the shifting shadows of the dark before he got it back, moments when he could hear them shifting and whispering and scraping all around him. He had no idea which way the wall was, and the shaft he'd emerged from. Panic rose again, choking him.

And once more one of the beetle things reached out with a squirming silvery tentacle-limb. Without thinking Nikos lashed out with the flashlight. He caught the thing on the dark side of its face, avoiding the metal mask. The black shell cracked, and a kind of pulp, green and foul-smelling, leaked out. As the beetle fell back, another made to grab its wounded companion. But in doing so it came close to Nikos, and again he swung the flashlight—

And the beetle disappeared, with a pop of air.

Nikos was astonished. It was as if the beetle had *stepped*, out of this big cellar, this cavern under the ground! How was that possible?

Again they closed in on him, moving more cautiously now, those strange half-faces with their single eyes following the flashlight as he swung it back and forth. He couldn't get away, and if they rushed him he couldn't get them all.

He tried to think.

That beetle had stepped away. You couldn't step out of a hole in the ground. *But the beetle had.* If a beetle could, he could.

His Stepper box was still at his belt. He turned its big clunky switch left and right, East and West, and tried to step – but both ways he felt the strange push-back you got if you tried to step out of a cellar, or into a space occupied by something massive, like a big sequoia. It was impossible; you couldn't step into solid earth or rock. But that beetle had stepped! There must be some way to do this.

The beetles were still closing in.

With a spasm of fear and disgust he tried again. He twisted the switch of his Stepper box until it broke off in his hand. But then he *stepped*, neither East nor West—

He wasn't in a hole any more.

He was sitting on hard, smooth ground. There was a sky above him, brilliant, dazzling, and the light hurt his eyes after the darkness of the big cellar. But this sky was orange-brown, not blue, and there was no sun or moon – nothing but stars, like the clearest night, with many more stars than he'd ever seen, and some of those stars were *bright*, brighter than any star or planet, brighter than the moon, bright as shards of the sun.

Frozen by shock, he took a jerky breath. The air was thin and smelled of metal, of dryness.

He looked around. The ground under him was like compacted earth. He sat on a slope that stretched down to what looked like a river. On the far bank some kind of pale, translucent bubbles crowded together. They were like the blisters he'd seen on the belly of the beetle beasts, he thought, but these were bigger, the size of buildings, and they were fixed to the ground – or some were, while others seemed to be straining to rise into the air.

And beetle things crawled along paths and roads that tracked the river bank, and crossed low bridges over the water, hundreds of them in great crowds, rustling, scraping.

All this in a heartbeat, a rush of impressions.

There was a beetle right beside him. Nikos hadn't seen it approach.

That half-silvered face hovered in front of him, and a coiling pseudopod reached for his right temple. He felt overcome; he'd seen too much to take in, and couldn't react. He didn't resist.

He noticed one more odd thing about the shining sky: that many of the stars to his left, while bright, were tinged green, but those to his right were pure white.

Then something cold touched his head. Blackness closed in around his vision, like he was falling down another tunnel.

He woke with a start.

He was lying on his back. There was blue sky above him, and around him were walls of dirt, good clean ordinary dirt. He was back in that half-dug pit, under the ordinary sky. Out of the big cellar. Almost in a panic he took a breath, and sweet air, thick with the scents of the flowers of the forest, filled his lungs.

He sat up, gasped and coughed, his throat aching.

Something touched his face. Thinking it was the silver tentacle of one of the nightmarish beetle creatures, he twisted away and got to his feet.

It was Rio. She'd licked Nikos's face. And she'd dropped an animal on the ground beside him: just a dwarf raccoon, unremarkable, limp and dead.

Nikos looked around quickly, and searched his pockets, his pouch. He still had those baby moccasins. He'd lost his flashlight, and he wondered how he was going to explain *that* away.

But here was Rio, safe and sound. She submitted to being grabbed and petted. Then she was first to scramble out of the pit and head for home.

Nikos said nothing to his parents about his adventure in the old Poulson place.

The fear gripped him for a whole day and a night. He couldn't even sleep for thinking about it.

But on the second day he went back to the fringe of the ragged clearing, and inspected the Poulson house from the safety of the cover of the trees.

By the third day he was going back in, with his buddies. Back into the big cellar.

5

J OSHUA VALIENTÉ'S SON Rod called for him at the old family
home in Reboot, in a stepwise footprint of New York State a
hundred thousand steps West of the Datum. Joshua met him on the
porch. It was a little after midnight on May 1, 2052.

'Happy birthday, Dad.'

Joshua shook the hand of his only child warmly. At twenty, the
boy was taller than Joshua, taller than his mother. He had her paler
complexion, his father's darker hair. He wore clothes of treated leather
and what looked like spun wool dyed a pale green. In fact he looked
alien in the lantern light of the Green homestead, but comfortable
in himself, in his own skin. And he looked like he must fit right in
with the shifting, ever fragmenting, kaleidoscopic communities of
the stepwise forests to which he seemed increasingly drawn.

And he's Rod now, Joshua reminded himself. *We named him
Daniel Rodney, the boy was always Dan, and the man is Rod. His
choice.* Joshua simultaneously felt pride in this handsome, confident
young man, and a stab of regret at the evident distance between
them. 'Thanks for coming, son. And thanks for making this trip
with me. Or the chunk you're doing anyhow.'

'Well, we haven't done it yet. And you haven't seen the ship I got
for you to ride in.'

'Your "stepping aircraft". You were kind of enigmatic.'

'It's not a twain, Dad. Nothing like that big old ship we rode to
the Datum when I was a kid. What was it called?'

41

'The *Gold Dust*.' That was Helen, Joshua's ex-wife, Rod's mother; she came out of the house now and wrapped her son in a hug. Helen was dressed plainly, and kept her greying strawberry-blonde hair pulled back in a practical bun. On coming back to Reboot, after her marriage to Joshua had broken up, she'd resumed her profession of midwife, and by now was pretty senior in the stepwise-extended community of New Scarsdale. She was strong, you could see that, strong in the upper body, strong and competent. On such a birthday as this Joshua was very aware of his own age, but Helen herself would be forty next year.

And out came the house's final inhabitant. Helen's father Jack, leaning precariously on a stick, was in his seventies. 'My boy, my boy.' He wrapped his free arm around Rod's shoulders, and Rod submitted with good grace.

Helen bustled around. 'Come inside and let's get this door closed. It might be May but the nights are still cold.' She led them all into the house's main room, the core of the structure and the first to be built, where, as a pioneer family in the years before she'd met Joshua, all the Greens had once lived in a cosy heap . . . All the Greens, except of course Rod the phobic, who they'd left behind in Datum Madison: Helen's brother Rod, to her son a mysterious lost uncle, and whose name he had chosen to adopt.

Rod stood there awkwardly, by a table laden with food, back in a room into which he evidently didn't feel he fitted any more. 'Mom, you shouldn't have gone to all this trouble.'

Helen smiled. 'You knew I would, though, didn't you? Look, I know you two are going to be keen to get away—'

Jack growled, 'Not even stopping by to say hi to Aunt Katie and her girls, and the grandkids? You know how they look up to you, the great twain driver.'

'I'm not a twain driver any more, Granddad.'

'But even so—'

'I'm only here for Dad.'

'Fool stunt!'

'If Dad wants to cross a hundred thousand worlds, all the way back to the Datum, on his birthday, a single day, fine by me. We'll fly most of it. I want to do nine hundred miles to the Wisconsin footprint by dawn, and after that another six hours' flying and more stepping over Madison.'

'If you don't break down on the way. *Damn* fool stunt if you ask me.'

'Nobody is asking, Jack,' Joshua said, gently enough. 'And after Rod drops me off I'll walk the rest of the way.'

Helen rolled her eyes at her son. 'With Sally Linsay! Some birthday treat *that* will be. Two antisocial old curmudgeons stomping across the Long Earth complaining about how fine it used to be when there were no people to mess it up – none but *them.*'

Rod shrugged gracefully. 'It's Dad's choice, Mom. You're only fifty once.'

'Damn fool stunt,' Jack said again.

Helen insisted, 'Well, if you won't see your family, and if you won't let me fuss over you for even one night, then at least you can let me refuel you. You've a long journey ahead. So here, there are homemade cookies with plenty of sugar, and sandwiches – the pork's frozen but it's good – and iced tea, and hot coffee, and lemonade. I know it's midnight but who cares? Sit. Eat.'

Joshua and Rod shared a glance, shrugged as they used to when Rod was a kid named Dan and they'd both known not to argue, and sat at the table. Even Jack awkwardly lowered his bulk into a chair. They filled their plates with food, and helped themselves to drink.

'Too damn late for all this,' Jack grumbled, as he bit into a cookie the size of a small plate, wincing as he tried to lift his hand to his mouth.

Joshua knew that Jack, unfortunately for him, was typical of his generation, the first Long Earth pioneers. The labour he'd put in during those early years building Reboot, after a months-long

43

trek out here with the young Helen and the rest of the family, had bequeathed Jack crippling arthritis in old age. But he had stubbornly refused expensive Low Earth drugs, and turned away even basic help. Even agreeing to come live with Helen had been the end result of a war of attrition mounted by Helen, when she'd come back home from Hell-Knows-Where, and her older sister Katie who had always stayed in Reboot with her own family. Jack still wrote, or tried to, on rough local-made paper, with gnarled old hands holding crude local-made quill pens. Helen had told Joshua he was working on a memoir of the heroic days of Valhalla's Gentle Revolution, when the peoples of the Long Earth had stood up for their independence from the Datum: a brief drama barely remembered now, Joshua suspected, by Rod and his comber friends, as they faded steadily into the endless stepwise green.

Anyhow Joshua knew Jack was right about the lateness of the hour. Even though many of the younger generation were slipping away, the core population in Reboot still made a living off the farms they and their parents had carved out of the native forests, starting around a quarter of a century ago. And, following the rhythms of their animals' lives, they generally retired with the setting sun. Midnight was a foreign country to farmers.

But Helen said now, 'Oh, hush, Dad. When I'm doing my midwifing we're up all hours. Newborn babies don't keep to any clock. Why, *you* get up in the night to make me coffee when I come stumbling in before the cocks crow. And besides, if this is the only time Rod has to be with us, I'm not about to sleep it away. More tea?'

'Not yet, thanks.' Rod looked uncomfortable. 'Mom, listen – I heard you have some news too.'

Helen raised her eyebrows. 'Gossip travels fast, even across the Long Earth. Well, I'm not sure what you heard, Rod, but the truth is—'

Jack cackled. 'She has a new boyfriend. That pasty-faced kid Ben Doak!'

Joshua forced himself not to grin. He was glad he'd had time to absorb this news already himself. By now it didn't feel so bad; it was just another layer on top of the lump of wistful sadness and regret he'd been carrying around inside since his marriage had broken up. And Ben Doak was kind of geeky.

Helen snapped, 'Oh, shut up, Dad. He's *not* a kid, for God's sake, he's only a couple of years younger than me . . . You know him, Rod. He was another of the first settlers, him and his family. We got to know the Doaks pretty well even during the trek. He has a couple of kids of his own, younger than you, and he lost his wife to a forest disease that hit us hard a year back—'

'I've been back since then, Mom.'

'Sorry. And since I lost *my* husband to another kind of disease,' with a glance at Joshua, 'we thought we'd – well – join forces.'

Jack snorted. 'Sounds like a military alliance, not a marriage. You ask her this, Rod, because I've tried and I get no answer. Does she actually *love* this Doak boy?'

Evidently this was an old argument between the two of them. Helen flared back, 'For all the time you've spent out here, Dad, you still think it's like Datum Madison, where *you* grew up. Full of people coming and going, full of choice for company. Where you have the luxury of waiting until you've found somebody you *could* fall in love with. Out here it's different.'

Rod took his mother's hand. 'I do understand, Mom. It's the same for us.'

Jack said, 'Sure. Running around in the forest like Robin Hood and his outlaws. You're not in one of those "extended marriages" we hear about, are you?'

'If I was, I wouldn't blab about it to you, Granddad, would I?'

Jack thought that over, and winked at Rod. 'Fair enough.'

'Mom, I will come back for the wedding.'

'That's good.' But she looked briefly anxious. 'It's not settled yet, the date. How will I contact you? I mean—'

'I'll just know, don't worry.' He added mischievously, 'Actually it sometimes helps being related to the great Joshua Valienté. People take a bit more notice of what you're doing. They pass on messages.'

Helen gave Joshua a dismissive look. 'I know it's his birthday, but don't make him any more big-headed. And he knows as well as I do that I'd much rather he spent this big day with his family instead of going off on yet another dumb Long Earth jaunt.'

'A jaunt with my son,' Joshua pointed out. 'Some of it anyhow. Quality time.'

Jack said, 'It's only because you couldn't manage the trip any other way, you old fossil.'

Rod laughed. 'And speaking of the journey, we need to get going. Mom, thanks – these cookies are delicious, and the sugar will help keep me awake.'

Jack grunted. 'It keeps *me* awake knowing how much we had to barter for that sugar. They use the damn stuff as currency out here.'

'Could I get a doggy bag? . . .'

So the midnight party, such as it was, broke up. There was a final packing up, a stiff hug and handshake for Joshua from ex-wife and father-in-law, a last slurp of strong coffee.

Then Rod, carrying a lantern, led his father out of the little township and down a forest trail to the river, where there still stood a stone commemorating the too-brief life of Helen's mother, Jack's wife.

And where, in a clearing, Rod had landed a small plane.

6

THE AIRCRAFT'S HULL was a smooth white ceramic, unmarked save for a registration number and the inevitable Black Corporation Buddhist-monk logo that marked a capability to fly stepwise. The wings were stubby, the tailplane fat. The main body was a squat cylinder, just big enough for a small cockpit and couches for four passengers.

Inside, the plane had a striking smell of new machinery, of cleanliness – like a new car maybe, Joshua thought, a stray memory from back in the first decades of the twenty-first century when he was growing up, and the Datum was the only world there was, and it had been full of cars, new and otherwise. Once their bits of luggage were stowed, and Rod and Joshua were strapped into the pilot's and co-pilot's seats, Rod passed his hands over built-in tablets that filled the small cockpit with their glow. Joshua didn't recognize a single aspect of the virtual instrumentation.

'You know I'm not really a gadget kind of guy. But this is pretty wicked.'

Rod winced. '"Wicked"? How old did you say you were, Dad? Hold on to your hat, the take-off is kind of sudden.'

With a hum of a biofuel engine and a subdued roar of jets, the craft jolted forward across a grassy sward, bumping a little on the uneven ground. There was nothing like a runway at Reboot; there weren't enough aerial visitors to justify it – and most of them came in airships that didn't need a runway at all. Evidently this little plane didn't need a runway either. After a remarkably short taxi, it leapt into the dark sky.

They didn't step immediately. Rod had the plane bank on autopilot in a wide, lazy circle as he checked the Stepper box at his waist, and then opened up a small pack of pharmaceuticals and began to guzzle pills. As far as stepping was concerned Rod had mixed ancestry: his father, Joshua, was the world's prototype natural stepper, but there were phobics on his mother's side – those unable to step at all, such as his notorious uncle, whose name he'd taken. Rod himself was somewhere near typical. With a Stepper box, Rod could step maybe three or four times a minute, but he'd be hit by nausea each time, and needed treatments to control the reaction. Luckily for him, by the time he was trying to fulfil his boyhood dream of flying the twains – the great stepwise-bound freight-carrying airships – the anti-nausea drugs had reached a pinnacle of effectiveness, and steps coming every few seconds, or even faster, were manageable.

This self-medication went unremarked by Joshua. Although he did wonder if the modern treatments still turned your piss blue.

The cabin windows were big and generous, and as the ground opened up beneath him Joshua was able to see the scattered lights of Reboot, and the neighbouring farms and shepherds' shelters. But they hadn't risen far before the settlement was lost in the continent-spanning forest, a deep green-black sea on this moonless night. 'Makes you think how few we are, on worlds like this, even after all these years. And after all the breeding we've done.'

Rod grunted. 'To me and my buddies this is normal. A planet's not *supposed* to glow in the dark.' He stowed away the pharma kit. 'So you ready?'

'Let's go.'

Rod tapped a corner of another of his glowing screens.

The first step was a faint jolt, like a bump in the road

– and suddenly they were in a rainstorm – and out of it with the second step.

After that, worlds flapped past Joshua's view, one after another, variations on a theme of black, with not a light to be seen on the ground below. From the beginning the stepping was faster than Joshua's heartbeat, which was a little disconcerting, like too-fast music. But as the step rate increased the inevitable juddering sensation soon smoothed out, to be masked, in fact, by the faint vibrations of the smooth-running engines as the plane settled into its run, heading generally geographic west, towards the heart of the continent and the footprints of Wisconsin, even as the stepping continued.

'Nice machine,' Joshua said.

'Sure. "Wicked."'

'I won't ask how much you paid to use it. Or how you earned the money in the first place, living the way you do.'

'I'm making my living my own way, which you know nothing about. Look, here I am for you, just as you asked. You wanted us to spend time. Fine. This ride is my gift to you, Dad. Happy birthday, OK? But why the hell are you doing this?'

'Why the hell not? I'm fifty. I've spent my life wandering the Long Earth. Why *not* cross a hundred thousand worlds in a day? Why not mark it with a stunt like this, while I still can?'

'I hate to tell you, but I'm pretty sure it's not a speed record.'

Joshua shrugged. 'I don't care about comparisons. I never much cared what other people thought of me, as long as they left me alone.'

'Well, maybe you should care, Dad. I mean, like Mom said, you could have marked your birthday with something which wouldn't have involved you being out here all alone.'

'Like what? A barbecue?' Joshua looked at his son sideways. Rod's face was softly illuminated by the glow of the control tablets. 'Now you sound like your mother. Or your grandfather. Once Dan was going to be a twain driver. Now here's Rod the comber, who knows it all.'

Rod replied irritably, 'I wanted to fly twains when I was a little boy, for God's sake. And I got to do it, for a while. But there aren't the opportunities now – you know that.'

It was true enough. Twains still flew locally, especially across the more industrialized Low Earths, but the big Datum–Valhalla route, a 'Long Mississippi' that had spanned a million worlds with a bridge of trade and cultural exchange, had withered after the Datum Earth had been effectively knocked out by Yellowstone. And then, after the catastrophic winter of 2046 and a new wave of emigration from the battered Datum, most Long Earth trade had shrunk back to relatively short-range exchanges.

Still, changing career plans was one thing; changing your name was a different kind of statement.

Joshua hesitated before saying, 'I think it's disturbed your mother that you've started to use your uncle's name, you know.'

'It's my middle name. You gave it to me.'

'True, but—'

'This is the hidden secret of the Greens, isn't it? Jack the great political firebrand, my mother the midwife: once hero trekkers, now the heartbeat of Reboot. But they are only out here because they abandoned their phobic son back on Earth, and look what happened to *him* in the end.'

After Helen's eighteen-year-old homealone brother had played a part in the anti-stepper terrorist nuking of Datum Madison, Wisconsin, he'd spent a lifetime in custodial institutions. He'd died in there only recently, of an infection he'd caught in hospital. Joshua realized with a shock that he'd committed his single, terrible crime when younger than Rod was now.

'OK, but you're kind of throwing this in their faces. Jack's particularly. You shouldn't judge them, Rod. They just couldn't find a way to make it work for everybody.'

'We all make mistakes, eh, Dad?'

'Yes, frankly. You just haven't made yours yet, son. Or maybe you just don't know it.'

'Thanks for that. Now maybe you should shut up and let me fly this thing.'

'Rod, I—'

'Forget it.'

After that, much of the night was spent in not very companionable silence. Long hours of darkness which Joshua spent much of beating himself up for what he'd said, or hadn't said, not for the first time where his family was concerned.

Maybe Joshua slept a little. He suspected Rod napped too, leaving the flying to the autopilot. Even the flaring of an occasional Joker did not disturb them.

The sun came up on all the worlds of the Long Earth.

Some fifty thousand steps from the Datum they were still deep in the thick band of worlds known as the Mine Belt: cooler and less well forested than the Earths of the Corn Belt, which began around the location of Reboot and stretched away to the stepwise West. The Mine Belt worlds were mostly exploited only as sources of minerals of various kinds, either for local use or for export to the Datum and the Low Earths – though even that kind of trade was dwindling now. But there were herds of animals to be seen, drawn to the water courses and lakes, mostly four-legged mammals but not much like anything that populated the human cultural imagination: things like giant camels, and things like elephants with oddly shaped tusks, stalked by things like huge cats. As they stepped, the herds, dark flowing masses, were there and gone in an eye blink.

They had a silent breakfast of Helen's cookies and lukewarm coffee from a flask.

Around eight a.m. the character of the worlds below changed again, subtly. This was the Ice Belt, a band of periodically glaciated worlds, of which Datum Earth – at least in its primordial state, before humanity got to work – appeared to have been a typical example. These Earths were cooler, with open prairie and grasslands, the forests shrunk back to patches of evergreen, and tundra in the far north. As Joshua had learned during his own forays into the Long Earth, and on that first journey of exploration with Lobsang two decades ago, when you crossed the Long Earth it was like flying through the branches of some tremendous tree of possibilities and probabilities. The closer you got to the Datum, the more links in the chain of coin-toss cosmic accidents that had led to the peculiar circumstances of the home world locked into place, and the more familiar the landscapes became. So now, on the sparsely populated grasslands below, they saw animals of the kinds alongside which humans had evolved, even if said animals hadn't necessarily survived to feature in the modern world: mastodons and mammoths, deer and bison. In most of these Earths the epochal collision of the Americas, North and South, must have taken place, for they saw immigrants from the south, such as giant sloths and armadillos the size of small cars.

But, apart from the very occasional pinprick of a campfire, or the even rarer lights of a small township, there was no sign of mankind.

Joshua remarked, 'Nobody at home. And yet you still meet people, especially back on the Datum, who will tell you we conquered the Long Earth.'

Rod shrugged. 'So what? Why do you need to conquer, or not conquer, anything? Why not just accept things the way they *are*? Because even if they do change, you can always just step away . . .'

And Joshua saw that that really was how Rod thought about the world, or worlds: as a kind of endless *now*, an endless *here*, a place where location and time didn't matter – and endlessly generous, a place you didn't need to work at, didn't need to build on, or fix. A place of endless escape. Joshua felt a sudden, intense jumble of emotions. Born in the Long Earth, Rod was of a generation that was forever divided from Joshua's by the great chasm of Step Day, and never could their world views be reconciled.

He couldn't help it. He reached over and grabbed Rod's shoulder, squeezing it hard. But Rod failed to respond.

It was a relief for both of them, Joshua suspected, when noon arrived and the plane banked over an uninhabited footprint of the Madisonian lakes, precisely three thousand steps West of the Datum. A single thread of smoke rose up from a campfire by the shore.

And as the plane began its final approach, a woman by the fire got to her feet and waved.

7

ROD EXCHANGED VERY few words with Sally Linsay. Joshua suspected he had always felt uncomfortable with the tension between his mother and Sally – even though, Joshua supposed, Sally's transient lifestyle was a lot more like Rod's own choice than Helen's sedentary midwifery. Rod said goodbye politely enough, and exchanged a handshake with his father.

Then Sally and Joshua stood side by side as they watched the plane climb into the sky, before it flew stepwise and out of existence. Joshua tried to close the lid on his latest cargo of regret, a feeling of another opportunity missed, somehow.

Sally let Joshua gulp down a lunch of roast rabbit leg and a cup of cold coffee, while she pulled her pack on her back and kicked out her fire.

'No time to lose, eh, Sally? You haven't changed.'

'You betcha I haven't changed. Why would I need to? Anyway you've been sitting on your fat ass in that plane all night, you need the exercise. Happy birthday, by the way.'

'Thanks.'

Sally, fifty-five years old now, only looked even tougher than she had when she was younger, Joshua thought. As if she'd weathered down to some hardened nub. She said now, 'Listen up. You want to get to the Low Earths by the evening, right? Three thousand worlds in six hours or so. We'll need to keep up the pace, a step every few seconds. We'll take regular breaks, we can do it.' She eyed him. 'Always assuming you don't want to cheat and take a short cut.'

'You mean, through a soft place? Not unless we have to.'

'This is your birthday treat. Why the hell would you *have* to do anything?'

'I have an appointment. I'm meeting Nelson Azikiwe for the last leg.'

'That bore.'

'Everybody's a bore to you, Sally. Even me, probably.'

'*Especially* you, Valienté. Don't flatter yourself.' She inspected him more closely, acutely. 'Are you OK? Seriously.'

'I've been having my headaches. That's why I cut short my last sabbatical.'

'Ah. The Silence headaches. Your legendary sensitivity to disturbances far out in the Long Earth—'

'It's no joke, Sally. Lobsang always said you were jealous of me for that.'

'Huh. *That* master psychologist. Well, you've been right before—'

'Right about First Person Singular. Right about the big troll migration back in 2040—'

'I don't need a précis. You have any idea what's up this time, specifically?'

'No,' he said unhappily. 'I never do.'

'Yeah. So is it disabling? Are we going to do this walk, or what?'

Without replying, Joshua dumped the remains of his lunch, got his pack settled on his back, checked his boots, and they began.

Sally led the way on a steady plod around the lake shore. They kept back from the water edge itself where animals were likely to congregate, and away from any crocs or other hazards in the water.

They'd just keep walking around this lake, or its Long Earth footprints, until the evening. And every few paces, they'd take a step East, together. As easy as that. Parallel lakes, and parallel shores.

'You shouldn't worry about your son, you know.'

Joshua smiled. 'You're giving me family advice? *You*, no marriage, no children – a father who abandoned you until he needed you to piggy-back him across the Long Mars?'

She grunted. 'Did you know there are Australian Aborigines up there now? Spreading out across the Long Mars. Their social structures are fit for purpose on such arid worlds, it seems.

'And as for family advice – look, all kids rebel against how their parents did things. It's natural. Your son's generation, lucky for them, are growing up in a completely different environment from you and me. Entirely new challenges, new ethics. Especially since the Datum imploded and the government stopped trying to tax everybody. And for sure, the Long Earth has had a way of imposing a natural selection of the smart over the dumb, right from the beginning.'

'I know, Sally. I was there, remember? And if the selection isn't natural, *you* lend it a hand, right?'

She glared at him. 'Somebody has to, now that even Maggie Kauffman and her flying Navy gunships are rarely to be seen.'

Joshua knew Sally was earning a living these days as a kind of professional survivor. In return for a pre-agreed fee she'd stay a few months, maybe a year, with a new community of settlers, helping them endure the most obvious dangers, avoid the first few booby-traps. For a woman who never suffered fools gladly, Joshua knew this was a tough career choice; the physical challenges would be easy for her, but it was hard for Sally to be supportive as opposed to judgemental.

But Joshua had his own contacts out in the Long Earth, and he'd heard a lot of rumours about what Sally was really up to. She was gathering a growing reputation for vigilantism. He was concerned for her, that she was losing her way. For now, however, he said nothing.

They walked into a world where the animals were comparatively thick on the ground, and drawn to the lake. Maybe there was some kind of drought on in this particular footprint. The travellers paused, sipping their own bottled water. The air felt dusty and hot. A herd of what looked like deer lapped watchfully at the water, and a giant sloth raised itself up to nibble at the curling leaves of a dying tree. Things like big opossums clustered without shyness at the sloth's feet, browsing on the litter it dropped.

'You know, Joshua, you and I are different from the rest. We're not townsfolk, not Datum urbanites. But we're not pioneers either. We're not settlers, like your little mouse Helen.'

'Oh, she's no mouse. And she's not mine any more—'

'We're loners. Loners just survive, they move on. They don't *build* things, like the pioneers. The Long Earth is always going to have room for the likes of us. We don't need any kind of definition. We don't have a *role*. Not even to the extent that the combers have, that self-conscious lifestyle they've developed of deliberately walking on and on, taking nothing save the lowest hanging fruit. We're just – us. Detached from humanity.'

'And detached from human values? Is that what you're trying to say?'

'I'm saying I have my own values – and so, I think, do you.'

He studied her, trying to read her, and failing, as he always had in the twenty-plus years he'd known her. 'Sin or not, you're no avenging god, Sally. You need—'

'I *don't* need you to tell me how to conduct myself.' She hefted her pack. 'We'll come to a glaciated sheaf soon. We need to get to higher ground so we're above the ice when we step.'

'I have done this before, you know . . .'

And here they were bickering, just as Helen had said they would. Sally walked away from the water, stepping as she moved. Joshua had no choice but to follow her, always just a little behind her flickering, stepping presence.

8

SALLY BROUGHT HIM to Earth West 30. On this particular Earth, here on the Madisonian isthmus, there stood a waterfront development with sodium lights glaring in the light of early evening, and golf carts parked up in rows. It turned out to be a sports lodge, a tourist facility. You got this kind of outfit on 'significant' worlds, such as worlds with round numbers: West 30, East 20. And, evidently, volcano winter or not, there were still enough rich folk to support such places.

Nelson Azikiwe, dressed in boots and sensible Low-Earth-type outdoor gear, was waiting for them at the designated spot, just outside the car park.

Sally hitched her pack and looked around disdainfully. '*Tourists.* Outta here. Keep safe, Nelson, Joshua.'

Joshua replied, 'You too—'

But of course she had already gone, in a pop of displaced air.

Joshua shook hands warmly with Nelson. 'Thanks for this, buddy.'

'Well, any friend of Lobsang is a friend of mine – and you and I have known each other a fair time now. It is my pleasure to be your companion on this, the last leg of your long walk. One should not be alone on one's birthday.'

Nelson's accent was soft, pleasing, a clipped South African overlaid with crisper British consonants. He seemed unchanged since Joshua had last seen him, at Lobsang's memorial, save that at around sixty years old he had perhaps a little more grey in that black hair.

Electronic music began to blare from the lodge, half a mile away. Nelson winced. 'I think that's our cue. Shall we take our first step?'

The lodge was whisked away. In Earth West 29 the lake shore was happily virginal.

As he took the impact of the step Nelson managed to stay upright – many poor steppers doubled over with the nauseous reaction, controlled by drugs or not – but Joshua could see discomfort contort his face.

'Hey, are you sure you want to do this? It's only a stunt, after all.'

'Well, Joshua, this is the last stage of your descent from heaven. First you flew like the Holy Spirit through the sky – or like Lobsang's disembodied soul between incarnations, perhaps. Then you strode boldly with Sally Linsay, a super-powered human. And now for these last few steps you must limp along beside an old man like me, a mere mortal. We will complete our remaining twenty-nine Stations of the Cross before midnight, I assure you. Of course we cannot linger in the radioactive ruin of Datum Madison itself, but I am told that the Sisters at the Home have arranged a small celebration for you, back in West 5. Think cake rather than champagne, however.'

'That'll be very welcome.'

'I think I am recovered. Shall we take another step?'

In West 28 it was raining softly, and though the isthmus itself was empty Joshua could see the lights of a township a couple of miles to the south.

Another step, ten minutes later, and on the rise on which, in Datum Madison, stood the Capitol building – or, since 2030, its ruin – a stone pillar had been erected, with plaque affixed.

Nelson said, 'In England – where I had my parish, you know – after the Romans had gone, the first Christian missionaries who attempted to convert the pagan Saxons would raise stone crosses in their sparse villages, as tokens of the churches that would one day be built there. Many of the crosses survive, even today. And thus, in the great days of the Aegis, the US administration has scattered its symbols across significant sites like this, in otherwise largely empty worlds. An echo of the future communities to come.'

'You do see something of the stepwise worlds, then.'

'Oh, yes – though I have never enjoyed stepping myself. I made one journey into the far Long Earth with Lobsang . . . But I do enjoy my jaunts into the Low Earths – to be precise the Low Britains. Even today, even after the great emigrations from the Yellowstone winter, those worlds remain largely wild. The lowest dozen or so worlds, to West and East, soaked up the outflow of an estimated *half* the pre-eruption Datum population, but even West 1 has a population only about the size of the Datum's around the year 1800. Give us a few centuries and we'll fill it all up, no doubt. But for now even the Low Earths are echoing halls.

'And the Low Earths are as the Datum used to be before humans – as they were in the last interglacial, perhaps, before the final Ice Age. Because the trolls and other humanoids stay away from the Datum, even those spin-offs of humanity haven't affected things much. So Low Earth Britain is a place of oak wildwood, grassland and heathland, a place of water and light, where elephants, rhinos and bears mingle with badgers, deer and otters . . . Full of wonders from humanity's lost past. I don't feel the need to go much further.'

Glancing around, Joshua could see no lights in the gathering dusk. 'Getting dark already. I have a flashlight.'

'I also. Let's go on. We may need to light some brands to keep the local wildlife away later . . .'

They put in some distance after that, stepping every few minutes, pacing themselves help Nelson get over the nausea.

By West 11 Nelson seemed winded, and ready for a longer break.

They sat on a low rise, overlooking another copy of the Madisonian isthmus – but here there was a substantial community, the largest they'd seen so far, a sprawl under a gentle haze of wood smoke with the steady glow of electric lights in some of the windows. Joshua even glimpsed a town sign, standing by a dirt track road:

WELCOME TO MADISON WEST 11
FOUNDED A.D. 2047
POPULATION CHANGEABLE
YOU DON'T HAVE TO BE HOMELESS TO LIVE HERE
BUT IT HELPS

The first house to be seen, just down the trail, was a shack, really, festooned with oil lanterns, and evidently put together from scraps imported from the Datum: plasterboard and roofing felt and plastic drainpipes. Behind the house was a fenced-off expanse of farmland, with what looked like a potato crop, chickens and goats, a heap of roughly cut lumber. A rack of some corrugated plastic material had been set up to face the south where the sun would catch it, with clear plastic water bottles fixed to its surface. Joshua knew this was a cheap way of purifying water; the sun's ultraviolet would kill off most bugs.

As the two of them sat there a single vehicle came puttering along the track out of town. Driven by an elderly man who tipped a sun-bleached hat to the two of them, it was a flimsy, open vehicle that ran on a purr of electric motors. Once this had been a golf buggy, Joshua guessed, driven by batteries and manufactured from steppable parts – no steel – to be used on the huge golf courses that, before Yellowstone, had colonized the Low Earth footprints of many Datum cities. But now the buggy had a solar-cell blanket draped over its roof, and its cargo looked like milk churns, not golf clubs. In that farm further down the trail, meanwhile, Joshua saw the silhouette of a more substantial vehicle, what looked like a tractor, but with a kind of fat chimney stack fixed to the rear. That was probably a biofuel solution, a gasifier, a gadget that burned wood to release hydrogen and methane as fuel.

Joshua recognized all this. A colony built out of recycled junk from the Datum, Madison West 11 was characteristic of the second great wave of migration out of the suffering Datum Earth.

The climate as ever had been the problem. By 2046, six years after the Yellowstone eruption itself and the onset of the volcano winter, things had seemed to be stabilizing, if not actually improving. People did continue to die; Joshua remembered a report that in the end Yellowstone had killed more people from lung diseases caused by the ash than had perished in the immediate aftermath of the eruption itself. But then some climatic tipping point had been reached – some had said it was the collapse of the Gulf Stream, but by then the science data-gathering itself had become too patchy to be sure – and the winter that year had been worse than ever. The rivers froze, the ports iced up, and Midwest farmland submitted to permafrost. When the big hydroelectric plants in Quebec began to fail in the freeze, the American national electricity grid collapsed, and such great cities as Boston and New York had finally to be abandoned.

Across America, people who had clung on to their homes for six years finally gave up and walked or drove out of there, either south across the Datum or stepwise into the Low Earth worlds West or East, where refugee camps had overwhelmed communities that were already struggling to cope. With time new towns had started to emerge, like this one in West 11, towns with a new character, using the scavenged remains of the old and scrambling for new solutions. Timber, plentiful on the Low Earths, was used in fuel-producing gasifiers, like the one on the tractor Joshua could see now – a fuel source that was a lot more accessible, for now, than coal or oil or nuclear. Datum museums had been emptied of nineteenth-century spinning wheels and looms and steam engines, for use as models for new kinds of industry. Electricity was got whatever way you could, such as with alternators and batteries from step-capable vehicles like that golf buggy, fixed to windmills or improvised paddle wheels in rivers. Anything resembling a web was still rare outside the larger, older stepwise cities like Valhalla, but in a town like this there would be walkie-talkies and ham radio set-ups, and maybe somebody would be laying down copper wire for a phone network.

Of course agriculture had been the key, as it had been from the day of the eruption itself – the need to feed all those displaced people. There had been a major international incident when in 2047 the US Navy had raided the Svalbard Global Seed Vault on Spitsbergen, a Norwegian island, for its stock of seeds for heirloom crops – the more primitive, hardier strains needed less cultivation than the varieties that had dominated the vast mechanized fields of the pre-Yellowstone Datum.

But Joshua thought it was working, even if these new patchwork Low Earth towns weren't quite like any other: neither like their Datum forebears nor even the raw colonial towns of the Long Earth, like Reboot and Hell-Knows-Where. Madison West 11 was always going to be a jumble of old and new. You didn't drive a car; there were few vehicles on the dirt roads save for farm trucks and ambulances and cop cars and bicycles. You didn't go online any more, but lined up to deposit your money at bank branches, like the manager was Jimmy Stewart in *It's a Wonderful Life*. Yet these quaint 1900-type practices were studded with bits of high tech, such as solar-cell blankets fixed to thatch roofs.

And Datum America itself had not been abandoned altogether, even now. Americans had come to recognize that what they and their ancestors had made of their continent-sized country was a historic monument in itself. So the new worlds had striven to come to the rescue of the old.

Nelson, evidently tiring, had been quiet since they'd sat down here.

Joshua gave him a playful punch on the shoulder. 'Not far now, old friend.'

Nelson smiled ruefully. 'I'm glad to have made the trip.'

'And I'm glad you did too. You always were good company. And you always made me think.'

'Ouch. Even on your birthday? My deep apologies.' He glanced sideways at Joshua. 'Of course, for most of us such occasions mean family and friends. I myself lost contact with my own family in the chaos of the Johannesburg townships, long before Yellowstone. And here you are, Joshua, wandering alone – well, almost alone – on such a significant anniversary.'

Joshua shrugged. 'I am more domesticated now. Even Sally admits that. But, you know – sometimes I miss the alien. The beagles for instance.' Dog-like sapients from a very remote Earth. 'Life gets boring with only humans to talk to.'

'I thought it was a beagle that chewed off your left hand.'

'Nobody's perfect. And he thought he was doing me a favour. As for the rest – well, I do seem to have had trouble building a family.'

'Perhaps because you did not come from a family yourself,' Nelson said seriously. 'Lobsang told me your story, long ago. Your mother, poor Maria Valienté, who gave birth to you alone, and died aged just fifteen. Your father – quite unknown. Of course you were cherished by Agnes and the Sisters at the Home, but that could only be a partial recompense for such a loss, even if you were never really aware of it.'

'Lobsang did find out something about my mother.' And had given him one treasured relic, a monkey bracelet, a silly toy belonging to the kid Maria had been when she'd given birth to him . . . 'Nothing about my father, though.'

Nelson frowned, looking into the distance. 'Which is rather unusual, if you think about it.'

'What do you mean?'

'I mean that if even *Lobsang* couldn't find anything, there must have been deliberate concealment. By somebody, somehow, for some reason.' He grinned. 'I'm suddenly intrigued, Joshua. This is the kind of puzzle that has always attracted me. I found Lobsang himself by following a research trail, you know – even though it turned out that he had engineered the whole thing. And since Lobsang has gone, my world has been rather depleted of conspiracy theories.'

Joshua studied him. 'You're thinking of researching this, aren't you?'

Nelson patted his arm, and stiffly got to his feet. 'Shall we make some more progress? The many candles on that birthday cake won't blow themselves out.'

'True enough.'

'The many, *many* candles—'

'I get it, Nelson.'

'Hmm. But would you *like* me to follow this up? This business of your father. Think of it as another birthday present. If you would rather I didn't—'

Joshua forced himself not to hesitate. 'Do it.'

'And if I do find something – considering the circumstances of Maria's brief life, it could be distressing. One never knows, when pulling such a thread, what might unravel.'

'Well, I'm a grown-up, Nelson.' But he did remember how much Lobsang's revelations about his mother had confounded him. 'Look, I'll trust your judgement, whatever you find. On my count, one, two—'

They winked stepwise together, with pops of displaced air.

9

EVEN AS THE airship dropped its anchor at the summit of the
low hill that dominated the heart of New Springfield, in a
stepwise-parallel version of Maine on Earth West 1,217,756, Agnes
could see the neighbours coming to call. She felt oddly nervous,
as if she had stage fright. This was the moment her new life would
begin, she thought, in this late summer of the year 2054 – nine
full years after Lobsang's 'death' – in her new home, with these
new people.

Ben, three years old, could see the neighbours coming too. If he
stood tall and held on to the rail with his chubby hands, he could
just about look out of the gondola's big observation windows without being lifted up, and being an independent little boy that was
what he preferred. And as winches whirred, drawing the twain
steadily down its anchor cables towards the ground, Ben jumped
up and down, excited.

'Of course they'd come over,' Sally Linsay said, standing beside
Agnes. 'That's what folk do. Check out the newcomer. Welcome
you, if possible. Make sure you're no threat, if necessary.'

'Hmph. And if we are?'

'Folk out here have ways of dealing with stuff,' Sally said quietly.
'Just remember, this is a big world. Almost all of it choked with
jungle, just like this, or thicker. And only a handful of settlements.
An easy place to lose problems.'

'You make an empty world sound almost claustrophobic.'

'These are good people, as people go. I wouldn't have advised you to come here otherwise.'

But Sally said this with a kind of amused lilt in her voice, a lilt that had been there from the beginning, when she'd been approached for advice by Lobsang. (Or rather, she was approached by George, Agnes reminded herself, *George*; he was George Abrahams now and for ever, and *she* was not Sister Agnes but Mrs Agnes Abrahams, George's faithful wife. And little Ben was no longer an Ogilvy but an Abrahams too; they had the adoption papers to say so – signed and dated in this year 2054, having waited so many years until the authorities, horribly overstretched in the continuing post-Yellowstone disruption, had finally approved a child for them to cherish . . .)

Sally had known Lobsang a long time, and she had been some-what bemused by his choice of a new lifestyle. 'Lobsang's having a son? The farming, OK. The cat I can understand. Of course he'd bring Shi-mi. Lobsang and his damn cat. But – a *son*?'

Agnes had protested, 'Ben's orphaned. We will be able to give him a better life than—'

'Lobsang wants a *son*?'

'Lobsang is recovering, Sally. From a kind of breakdown, I think.'

'Oh, I wasn't so surprised about *that*. I suppose he was kind of unique: an antique AI, lots of technological generations all piled up on top of each other. We never ran an experiment like Lobsang before. Complex systems can just crash, from ecologies to econ-omies . . . But most complex systems don't come out of it wanting to play happy families.'

'Don't be unkind, Sally. He has always served mankind in his way, but from a distance. Now he wants to apprehend humanity more fully. He wants to *be* human. So we're going to live in a regular human community, as anonymously as we can. We're even going to fake illness, ageing—'

'He already faked his own death.'

'That was different—'

'I was at the funeral! Agnes, Lobsang's not human. He's Daneel Olivaw! And he wants a *son*?'

There was no talking to her. As far as Agnes could tell Sally had given the matter of her recommendation of a future home for the family conscientious thought. Indeed there were already people living here, in New Springfield, apparently happy and healthy. And yet, why was it that Sally always found the whole project so funny? Even now, the moment they arrived here, as if she was hiding some kind of personal joke?

Lobsang came bustling into the cabin. Locked into the ambulant unit to be known as George Abrahams, he looked in his late fifties or maybe older, with sparse grey hair, a beard hiding much of his blandly handsome face, his skin tanned. He wore a checked shirt and jeans, and even now it was a jolt for Agnes to see him no longer in the orange robes of a Buddhist monk. He said, 'Well, we're down. I'll go unpack the coffee pot before the neighbours get here.'

First impressions were always important. Agnes practised her own welcoming smile, working her cheeks, feeling her lips stretch.

Sally was watching her cynically. 'Not bad. If I didn't know you were a sock puppet too—'

'Thank you, Sally.'

So Agnes, holding Ben's hand, clambered down a short step from the grounded gondola and took her first footsteps on this new world, her home. At least the weather was good, the blue sky all but clear of cloud save for a few peculiar east-west streaks. And a half moon, too, hung silver in the eastern sky, as if to welcome them. This hilltop had evidently once been cleared but then abandoned; the trees here were young, saplings sprouting amid the squat stumps of fallen giants. Abandoned houses stood around, half-built and watchful. Lobsang's plan was that they would take over one of these big old houses and fix it up as their own, use these half-cleared fields for their own crops.

The cat, Shi-mi, scampered down the step, stretched luxuriously in the sunlight, and said, 'Oh, how glorious to be free!'

Agnes turned on her. 'Remember the golden rule, you plastic flea-bucket. No talking! Here you're a cat, a whole cat and nothing but a cat – as far as Ben's concerned, and everybody else. Also you're over twenty years old. Act your age.'

'Yes, Agnes.' The cat was slim, white, healthy-looking, with eyes that glowed green, a little eerily. Her liquid female-human voice came from a small loudspeaker in her belly. 'I'll be good, I promise. It's just that it's such a relief to have nothing to do, now that I've retired from my Navy career with Maggie Kauffman. And now to discover what equivalent of mice and rats inhabit this glorious new world . . .' She darted away into the green.

Ben laughed with delight in the warm late-morning sunshine, and immediately went running off too, into undergrowth that was waist-high for him. Agnes had anticipated this; he'd been the same at every stop they'd made on the way out here. 'Don't go out of sight, mind, Ben.'

'OK, Ag-ness.'

Lobsang/George, meanwhile, was already working at the gondola, loosening the bolts and latches that fixed it to the twain envelope's internal skeleton. The gondola was a brick-shaped block of ceramics and aluminium the size of a mobile home, suspended under a twain envelope two hundred feet long, and was designed to be detached and left behind. Sally, alongside him, was operating controls to draw down some of the envelope's helium, the lift gas, into pressurized chambers, so the ship wouldn't waft away into the air as soon as the weight of the gondola was gone.

The plan was that Sally would pilot the rump of the ship back to its Black Corporation dry dock on a Low Earth. The grounded gondola meanwhile would serve as a temporary shelter for Lobsang and his 'family' in their first days, weeks, months here. It contained tools, seed stock, medical gear and vitamin supplements, pots and pans for the kitchen – even animals, including chickens and young goats and a couple of pregnant sows – everything they needed for a flying start at this new game of pioneering. Also the gondola held a few secrets that would have to remain hidden from the neighbours, locked behind blue doors, such as a workshop for their ambulant android bodies, including a small gel manufactory and a nanotech-based cosmetic facility which would enable George and Agnes to appear to 'age' naturally. There was even a kennel-sized workshop for the maintenance of the cat.

Lobsang, even in his alter ego as George Abrahams, had had the contacts at the Black Corporation to get all this built. 'We don't *have* to ride in on a mule through Death Pass,' he'd said. 'We don't have to rough it. There's nothing wrong with using the benefits of our past civilization, as we start anew. And besides we'll have a little boy with us, remember? A roof over our heads when it rains on the first night will be a good thing . . .'

Maybe it was all necessary, Agnes thought, but she did wonder what kind of impression this gleaming structure was making on their new neighbours, who struck her as a ragged-looking lot as they continued up the trail to this hilltop. But she could see that the children were already entranced by the animals, most of them still inside the gondola: the sheep, the goats, the chickens, the cattle including one youthful bull for breeding, and a couple of muscular young horses. It struck Agnes that these children had probably never seen cattle or horses before.

Suddenly overwhelmed, she felt she needed a moment alone.

Following Ben, she walked away from the airship, climbing a gentle slope to the summit of this low hill. The way was easy as long as she stepped around the fallen trunks and branches that seemed to lie everywhere. The ground was soft under her boots, and covered with what looked like ferns sprawling between the lichen-choked fallen trunks. It all seemed mundane to Agnes, and yet it was not, if you looked closely. What species were these trees, for instance? The trees in this part of the world were mostly evergreens, she'd been told, even here at the latitude of Maine; the seasonal variations weren't strong, on this warm, wet world, and few trees troubled to shed their leaves come the fall. But she didn't recognize the species.

A few paces further on she came to a length of dry stone wall, built by some earlier settler to contain his or her animals. It couldn't be more than a few decades old; it was not yet forty years since Step Day, and humans had been very rare beyond the Datum before then, just a few natural steppers wandering through the emptiness. But the wall was already disappearing into the green.

Agnes could read the history of this place, this hilltop. The first settlers here must have made a start at clearing fields for their crops or livestock, even put up these grand houses. Then, after no time at all, they had evidently given up and wandered off to do – well, whatever it was most people did around here to make a living these days. And now here was the forest already taking back the land, or trying to. This was why Sally had scoped out this abandoned plot as a likely site for Lobsang and Agnes to build a farm of their own; a lot of the grunt work of clearing had already been done.

And all around this low hill with its abandoned farmstead the forest stretched away, dense and green. This was a world of trees, Agnes knew that much. Thick evergreen woodland cloaked much of North America, with exotic kinds of rainforest in southern latitudes, and peculiar broad-leaved deciduous trees growing in the Arctic – even in Antarctica to the south there were trees all the way to the pole, and *that* was a sight Lobsang promised they'd go see some day. It was a world far from the Ice Belt within which nestled the Datum Earth, her own home world: here, it seemed, the forests had hung on since the days of the dinosaurs.

And in these global forests was life unlike anything she'd been familiar with at home. Standing here now, she could hear that life all around her, peculiar hoots and cries echoing as if she stood in some vast cathedral, and the occasional crack as, presumably, some big beast pushed its way through the undergrowth.

Sally Linsay came striding up to her, sweating from her work, sipping water from a plastic bottle. Agnes noted with approval that Sally's first instinct was to check on Ben, who seemed to be fascinated by a kind of termite mound.

Now Sally said simply, 'Neighbours.'

A handful of people, men, women and children, dressed in rather drab colours, brown and green, were clustered around Lobsang and the gondola. One boy, maybe twelve years old, was bending down to tickle a compliant Shi-mi, and Agnes could hear his clear, light voice. 'Cute, ain't you? Wait until my Rio catches sight of you, though. My word, you'll be getting some exercise then . . .'

Sally said, 'The kids are your friends for life if you'll let them brush those horses. Lobsang's already got coffee percolating on the gas stove.'

'Giving away all our luxuries on the first day?'

Sally shrugged. 'Making a good impression on the neighbours. Never hurts. Coffee is *good*.' She inspected Agnes. 'So how are you feeling?'

Agnes thought it over. 'I'm not sure,' she said honestly. 'All this seemed fine in theory. To be uprooted, and chucked across a million worlds. Making the plans and preparations was fun, even the twain ride was fun. And bringing Ben into our lives was wonderful, of course. But now I'm actually here—'

'It's all too strange? You'd be surprised how many people try to cover up that reaction.'

'Well, I'm no faker. I'm a city girl. Why, I used to think I was lost in the wilds when I was out of sight of the gift shop in the Madison Arboretum. And now, *this*.'

'The consolation is,' Sally said, 'people are trying to make a living in worse places. These worlds are kind: they're warm, moist, mostly unseasonal. And safe, relatively. Which is why I chose this place for you. That's because the forest keeps the critters here small.' And, characteristically, she added, 'Well, mostly.'

This was Sally being kind, Agnes reflected. Reassuring, as much as she could be; there was always an edge.

Then a breeze from the west blew up, oddly sharp. Sally turned, frowning, holding on to her battered hat. The forest, the nearby trees, rustled, and the general hooting and cawing seemed to sharpen into cries of alarm. Agnes saw that the sparse clouds were streaky now, long stripes – almost like contrails, but no jets ploughed these skies.

And she saw something else: a flash, from the corner of her eye. She found herself looking at the moon, half full, the familiar features washed out by the blue sky. She'd have sworn that the flash had come from the moon, from the dark half, that shadowed hemisphere. It was probably nothing. A firefly? A bird? Not that she'd seen any birds here yet. Or, more likely still, just something in her eye.

None of this convinced her. Something didn't feel right. That was her immediate, sharp instinct. And from the way Sally reacted, Agnes sensed that she felt the same way.

But Ben was here, tugging at her hand, pulling her back into his life. 'Ag-ness?'

She forced a smile. 'Hello, honey. Come on, shall we go have some lunch and meet some new friends?'

'Lunch!'

10

A COUPLE OF days later, with Sally and the airship long gone, the family were invited to a barn dance. This was to be held in an open space down by the creek that wound its way around the hill where their gondola sat – and, as decided at the last minute, a couple of steps East, as the weather was a little better there that evening. Of course they would have accepted even if it hadn't turned out that the event was being mounted in their honour.

Somewhat nervously, Agnes got herself ready for the evening. Before the journey out here, before they'd been discharged from the Black Corporation laboratories for the last time, Agnes had had her ambulant body set to look as if she was around her middle fifties: a few years younger, apparently, than Lobsang. And a mere forty years or so younger than her calendar age . . . Well, fifties was an age she'd lived through once already; she knew how to make the best of her greying hair, and she'd packed a decent gingham dress that she knew would suit her on the night. Lobsang meanwhile wore a loud checked shirt, jeans and cowboy boots – and little Ben was kitted out in a scale model of exactly the same gear. The outfit wasn't going to last, he'd grow out of it in a few months, but Sally had suggested packing it to make a first impression on just such an occasion as this.

So, prepared, they joined their neighbours.

The barn dance turned out to be just what Agnes would have expected. This field by the stream, roughly cleared and fenced off, was evidently intended for sheep, and Agnes saw a small flock in a pen not far away. Now, in the gathering twilight, the open space was lit by burning brands that gave off a tar-like smell. There was a ribald caller with a couple of fiddlers standing on crates pumping out the music, and the people, maybe fifty in all, men, women and kids, lined up and whirled around. It was a scene Agnes imagined you could have seen anywhere in rural America back on the Datum for decades, if not centuries. The difference here was the in-case-of-emergency Stepper boxes that bounced on people's hips as they danced.

There was a bar at one end of the field, where you could fill up on the juice of some unidentifiable citrus, or water, or on quite good home-brew beer. There were even a few bottles of whisky. A barbecue sizzled and popped, but the food on the grill was mostly unfamiliar to Agnes: strips of red meat, presumably from the little local mammals they called 'furballs', and one monster of a drum-stick that must have come from one of the local 'big birds', there more for show than for eating – it would probably take all night to cook a joint the size of a whole turkey. And there were oat-flour cookies, and slices of pumpkin. A few dogs ran around yapping, or begging for food scraps. Shi-mi, naturally enough, was nowhere to be seen.

Soon they were grabbed by their new neighbours and pulled into the dance.

Agnes had been to enough dances in her misspent youth to have the general idea, but she found herself having to learn new steps rapidly as she went along. Lobsang seemed to be struggling more than she was, and once even tripped over his feet and landed on the deck, only to be picked up again by his neighbours, laughing.

In the heat, noise and laughter, Agnes quickly tired – or rather, emotionless software in her gel-filled head ran programs to simulate tiredness, triggered fake sweat glands, and made her mechanical lungs pump harder at the warm air. She tried to embrace the feeling, and put aside the fact that she was basically living out a lie before these evidently good people.

When she took a break, Lobsang joined her by the rough-and-ready bar. He said, sipping a whisky, 'I will always regret that I now have conscious control over my degree of drunkenness. And we could have been better prepared for this. We spent *nine years* training to be pioneers. We should have just downloaded a barn-dancing application.'

Agnes snorted. 'Where's the fun in that? Or the authenticity? You're a city boy come to learn the ways of the country, Lob— *George*. Get used to it. Enjoy.'

'Yes, but—' He was interrupted, grabbed at the elbows by two burly middle-aged women who hauled him back into the line.

A smiling woman, dark, forty-ish, approached Agnes with a fresh cup of lemonade. 'Sorry about that. We always seem to be short of men at these dances, and Bella and Meg can be a little boisterous when there's fresh meat around. Like big birds on the prowl.'

'Fresh meat? George will be flattered. Nothing fresh about us, I'm afraid.'

'Oh, I wouldn't say that; you're making a fine impression.' She stuck out her hand to shake. 'I am Marina Irwin. My husband Oliver is out there somewhere.'

'Irwin. Oh, it's your boy who's babysitting for us tonight. Nikos?'

'That's right. For a suitable fee, I'm sure. Quite the capitalist, my Nikos, for a twelve-year-old boy who's grown up out in the green.'

'It's kind of him to miss the dance for us.'

'Well, it was a sacrifice for him. But give him another year and we won't be able to prise him away from the girls . . .'

Maybe, Agnes thought doubtfully. She had met rather a lot of twelve-year-old boys during her years in the Home in Madison, and Nikos struck her immediately as a decent enough kid – *but a kid with a secret*, a big one, an observation that had nagged at her since she'd met him.

Marina was still talking. '. . . I wouldn't object if you gave him some work on your farmstead, by the way. It would be good for him to have some experience of that. Not many of us farm any more.'

Agnes pointed. 'Sheep over there.'

'Sure. We keep sheep mostly for the wool,' and she smoothed her own dress, which, Agnes saw in the uncertain light, was knitted, and tinted a pleasant apple-green, presumably by some vegetable dye. 'All you get from the local furballs – the forest animals – are scraps of skin. The feathers from the big birds are more useful, actually.' Her voice had a pleasant lilt, Mediterranean, perhaps Greek, Agnes thought. 'We do raise some crops – mostly potatoes, for the Stepper boxes. And for emergency food reserves, though this world is so clement we rarely need to dig into those.' Though, even as she said that, the breeze picked up again, and Marina pushed loose hair from her forehead with a puzzled frown. She went on, 'The first people here intended to go in for farming – they cleared the forest, marked out fields, the works. The old Barrow place up on Manning Hill, that you've taken over? That was one of them, as you'll have guessed. And the old Poulson house is another – you know, the swap house, our local haunted house! My Nikos spends half his life in there, I think it's a kind of clubhouse for him and his buddies. He'll grow out of that.'

Agnes prompted, 'But the farming didn't stick.'

'No. Now there's a bunch of us spread out over the stepwise worlds. We do have homes, you see, but they're scattered around, seasonal. We work together to maintain the farms for the sheep, the potatoes, a few chickens and such. And we have a kind of rota for when to meet up, for events like this. The rest of the time we just wander. We're not combers, by the way! Oliver takes offence if you call him that.'

'I get it. Just an easier life than farming.'

'Well, that's the idea. These worlds are so rich, why do our kids need to break their backs behind a plough? But,' she said hastily, 'what we choose isn't for everybody. And it's not to say you won't make a go of your farm, if that's what you want. To each his own.'

'That's a good philosophy.'

'I mean, you'll fit right in. If you do grow wheat and stuff we'll be happy to trade for it.' Marina sipped her lemonade. 'And that little boy of yours looks like he'll grow up big and strong, like his . . . father?'

Agnes suppressed a smile; the probe couldn't have been less subtle. 'I'm sure you've heard this already. Ben's not ours. He's adopted.'

'I did hear something – people gossip, you know. But I didn't want to go supposing about something you might not want to tell me about.'

'It's best to be open,' and Agnes felt a stab of Catholic conscience even as those words emerged from her own disguised ambulant-unit artificial mouth. 'His real name's Ogilvy, by the way – just in case something happens to us, and he ever needs to know.'

Marina nodded. 'I understand. I'll remember.'

'Ben lost his parents early. They were both workers on a beanstalk – a space elevator, you know? On Earth West 17. They were in a kind of mobile workshop, outside the atmosphere. There was a leak, a decompression. The kind of accident that would have been entirely impossible a generation ago, if you think about it.

'Their little boy ended up in a kids' home where I used to work. But George and I were already looking to come out to a place like this, and it turned out that Ben's parents had been planning to save their money and leave their jobs behind and strike out on their own in the same kind of way. And we thought, why not give Ben the life his parents intended for him? So we applied for adoption . . .'

And Lobsang, behind the scenes, in the final stages of their desperate wait, had bent a whole slew of rules, while Agnes had gone through agonies of doubt about whether she, a *robot*, could be a fit and suitable mother-surrogate for a three-year-old boy.

'Well, here you are,' Marina said. She clinked her lemonade glass against Agnes's. 'And I for one am glad to meet you. I'm sure you'll get along fine, all three of you.'

'Four including the cat,' Agnes said with a smile. 'Thank you, Marina.'

'Listen, we have an Easter egg hunt. Dawn, the day after tomorrow.'

'An Easter egg hunt?'

'Just what we call it. And I know it's not Easter. Come along and see. Now then, we can't let those men of ours have all the fun out there . . .'

11

THE DAY OF the Easter egg hunt was only Agnes's fifth in the forest.

It was an early start. As Marina had said, the hunt was supposed to get going at dawn of this late summer's day. Farmer's wife Agnes was already getting used to rising early.

But she woke feeling woozy, oddly disoriented.

Her artificial body needed the food and drink she consumed, extracting various biochemical necessities. And it was programmed to deliver what felt like an authentic interval of sleep every night, complete with artfully simulated dreams. She would have insisted on such features if they hadn't already been designed in: how could you even remotely consider yourself human if you didn't eat, didn't sleep? And after sixteen years in this new body and after various upgrades of the hardware and software, she knew herself well enough by now to understand that this peculiar feeling was nothing to do with having to get up at dawn, or with the unfamiliar food she'd eaten since arriving here, or even the moonshine she'd partaken of at the barn dance. No, this was more like jet lag: a modern-life nasty that she'd always been vulnerable to, and she had always avoided long-distance journeys as a result. Or it was like the kind of mild disorientation she got even when a local time zone changed the clocks by an hour.

That, and a faint but persistent sense of unease.

She went through her morning's routine. She showered in the

gondola – another human touch – dressed and had a quick bite of breakfast, trying all the while to ignore that vague disquiet. She was unwilling to ask Lobsang to run her systems through an automated self-diagnosis. She was after all trying to live her life as a full human.

She didn't even want to know the time. Or at least, that was the local rule.

One principle of this community, which they'd been made aware of even before they'd set out to come here, was: *no clocks*. At least, nothing mechanical, and certainly nothing electronic . . . You could build a sundial if you liked. The philosophy was that living so close to the rhythms of sun and moon, the days and the seasons, you didn't *need* to track every picosecond – not unless you were planning to run a transcontinental railroad or some such and needed precise timings, and that, Agnes learned now, was why countries like nineteenth-century America had imposed nationally consistent time systems on their populations in the first place. It was the sort of feature that had actually attracted Lobsang here, a return to a more basic human way of living. He had embraced the idea. They'd brought no clocks! Lobsang had even made minor adjustments to the timers in their own artificial bodies, and in the gondola's systems; such timers were necessary for the machinery that sustained them, of course, but now they couldn't be accessed consciously.

It had been their choice. Now, though, a part of Agnes, nagged by this odd jetlag feeling, longed despite everything just to *know the right time . . .*

Preparing for the walk, she got together her gear: boots, a haversack, a light waterproof coat, dummy Stepper box. And she greeted Angie Clayton, a neighbour, a single mother, who was going to babysit the still-sleeping Ben for the few hours this 'hunt' was supposed to take. As they left the gondola, Oliver Irwin was waiting outside with Lobsang. The party was only a dozen or so, including Oliver and

Marina and Nikos, their bright if oddly secretive twelve-year-old son. Nikos looked to be the youngest of the party; there were no small children here.

Nobody else seemed to be having any problems this morning, most notably Lobsang – or if he did he wasn't sharing them with her. Agnes tried to put all else aside and focus on the moment.

They headed down the hill from the gondola, towards a ford across the creek. Oliver Irwin walked with Lobsang and Agnes, pointing out the sights, of a landscape of dark green under a greyish dawn sky, with mist clinging in the hollows. 'None of us here are first-footers, but we're stuck with the names they gave to places. Your farm is on Manning Hill, and that's about the highest point hereabouts. The river is called Soulsby Creek. The big clump of dense forest we're heading towards, across the creek and a ways north, is Waldron Wood. The features of the landscape persist, a few steps to East and West anyhow. Geography's stubborn in the Long Earth, when you go exploring.' He ruffled his son's hair. 'Right, Nikos?'

Nikos was probably a little too old for that, Agnes thought. He ducked out of the way, grinning sheepishly.

Agnes thought she knew Oliver's type. He and his wife Marina wouldn't think of themselves as leaders in what was obviously a self-consciously leaderless community, but they were a kind of social hub, a go-to contact point for newcomers. Well, somebody had to be.

She asked, 'So which is the old Poulson house, Nikos?'

Nikos looked at her sharply. 'Big old place on the far side of your hill. What do you know about that?'

'Why, nothing. Only that your mother told me you hang out there sometimes. Not a secret, is it?'

'Hell, no.'

'Language, Nikos,' his father said mildly.

'Just a place we hang out. Like you say.'

'OK.'

They reached the creek; a faint, pungent mist hung over the water as they splashed across the shallow ford. On the far side, in ones and twos, they stepped East, the target for the 'hunt' being a short way stepwise. Agnes made sure she worked her own Stepper box convincingly, though Stepper technology was built into her frame. The stepping barely interrupted the conversation. It was just as she'd been told: while the core of New Springfield would always be the founders' community on West 1,217,756, these people slid easily between the neighbouring worlds as and when they needed to, or felt like it.

As they formed up again, Oliver said, 'About the Poulson house. We use it as a swap store. Otherwise it's empty.'

'Save for the local ghosts, according to your wife.'

Oliver grinned. 'Every town needs a haunted house, I guess. Even a town that's barely a town at all, like this one. I suppose you're right to ask about it. If your Ben grows up like the other kids he'll be down there up to no good with the rest soon enough . . .'

His voice tailed off as they approached the thicker forest. To Agnes, still standing in the open air, it looked like a green wall, from which soft hoots and cries echoed.

'OK,' Oliver said, 'this is where we need to start keeping quiet. Don't want to scare the little guys off.'

His companions spread out before the trees, pulling nets and wire snares from their bags, men, women and children alike. Without talking, working almost silently, they began to set traps, or took position under the branches with what looked to Agnes like butter-fly nets. Some went deeper into the forest gloom to check over traps evidently laid earlier.

As the dawn advanced and the daylight brightened, Agnes started to make out a crowded undergrowth beneath the trees, what looked like ferns and horsetails, a dense mass of bushes, and flowering plants around which early bees buzzed. She felt a primitive dread at the idea of going into that thick green.

Oliver murmured to Agnes, 'How's your forest lore?'

'I'm a city girl. I don't recognize most of those trees, even.'

He smiled. 'Well, some are variants of what we have on Datum Earth. Or used to have. Some aren't.' He pointed. 'Laurel. Walnut. Dogwood. That's a kind of dwarf sequoia, I think. The ones with the big flaring roots are laurels. The climbers are honeysuckle and strangler figs, mostly, but we get some grape vines . . .'

A little creature darted out from the tangle of a climber fig and ran across the open ground, evidently heading towards the water. It didn't get very far before Nikos's net slapped down around it.

The boy picked up the struggling little animal and, with brisk, confident movements, broke its neck. Then he fished out the prize from the net and held it up, dangling, before his father. The animal, maybe a foot long, looked like a miniature kangaroo to Agnes, with oversized hind legs. Oliver grinned back and gave him a thumb's up.

It was like a cue for action. Agnes saw more animals emerging now, coming out one by one, clambering up the tree trunks and along the branches or on the ground, and even gliding through the air on membranous wing-like flaps of skin. And the nets flew. Most of the animals stayed out of reach, or scurried out of the way faster than the hunters could react, but a few fell to the nets and to the traps on the ground.

Soon a small pile of corpses built up before Agnes, and she stared at the strange forms. These were the local furballs, as the colonists called them, or a sample of them. Some were like distorted versions of creatures she was familiar with, like squirrels and opossums, and some were entirely different, as if dreamed up as special effects for some monster movie. She was struck by the detail, the striping of the fur, the staring open eyes: each creature exquisite, in its own way, even in death. At least the harvest the hunters were taking was light; the furballs were obviously so numerous that their wider communities would not be harmed.

Now a shaft of sunlight emerged from the mists to the east.

Oliver shaded his eyes and looked that way. 'Sun's fully up. Show's over for now. The dawn's always the best time to catch these critters. You can see they're all tiny little guys, and not too graceful. That's what you get if you've evolved to survive in a dense forest, I guess. And they all go for insects, rather than fruit or leaves. We think that's because these trees are evergreens. They don't discard their leaves, so make them poisonous or foul-tasting so they don't get eaten.

'All the furballs go hunting early, when the insects have started buzzing, but the cold-blooded creatures are still dopy from the chill of night: the lizards, the frogs, the toads. Hard to find a furball in the middle of the day.' He glanced up at the canopy, towering above them. 'We don't know what else lives in the forest, I mean all the species. We only learn enough about their habits so we can trap them. And at night, you know, there's a whole different suite of critters that come out in the dark. You can hear them hooting away. Nobody knows anything about *them*. Anything's possible.'

'And trolls,' Lobsang/George said with a smile. 'I heard them last night, and before. The call.'

'Yeah. Nice to know they're here, isn't it? Now come on, you two, speaking of the big birds – Marina did promise you an Easter egg hunt. We'll need to go into the forest, just a little way . . . Hey, Nikos. You found this nest, you want to lead?'

Entering the deeper forest wasn't as bad as Agnes had feared. The biggest practical difficulty was just working out where to put her feet in the gloom. The ground was covered by a tangle of green, most but not all of it below knee height. She was glad to have Nikos lead the way, expert and silent, and to have Oliver and Lobsang to either side.

They came to a small clearing, and crouched down in the cover, peering out, waiting. On the ground, at the foot of a stout sequoia, Agnes saw a mass of twigs and earth whose function was obvious, even given its size – it must have been six feet across.

'It's a bird's nest,' Lobsang breathed.

'Of some damn big bird,' Agnes said. 'No wonder they're taking their time. Making sure the mother isn't around.'

'Absolutely,' said Shi-mi.

Agnes was startled by the small female voice, coming from the ground beside her. She glanced around quickly; the hunters were far enough away for them not to have heard the family pet speak. 'What the hell are you doing here?'

'I tracked the hunting group. Of course I would come here. I'm a cat. Save for the chickens people imported here, these big mothers are the only birds anybody's found in this world . . .'

Oliver looked their way. He had noticed the cat, though hopefully he hadn't heard her speak. He grinned and called softly, 'Hey, kitty. So you found the nest? Well, this is a world where the birds chase the cats, so you'd better take care.'

Lobsang picked up Shi-mi. 'Oh, she will,' he said. 'She will.'

Nikos said, 'I think it's clear, Dad.'

Oliver listened for a while, peered around in all directions. 'OK. Quick and careful.'

Nikos got to his feet, loped across the clearing to the nest, and after a final glance around he reached into the nest with both arms and extracted an egg. It was maybe two feet long from end to end, and obviously heavy. He bundled this into netting, slung it over his shoulder, and made his way back to his father.

Oliver helped his son bind up the egg tighter, and smiled at Lobsang and Agnes. 'This will make one hell of an omelette. But we're not doing this for the food. You can see that these birds nest on the ground. Every so often we find a nest like this, where the bird has roamed too close to our campsites and hunting grounds for comfort. Gotta keep them away from the kids. So we remove the egg, and with any luck the mother wanders away too. No problem, unless—'

Nikos pushed his father's head down. 'Unless the bird catches us,' the boy whispered.

Now, crouching down as deep as she could, Agnes saw movement in the deeper forest, between the trees: a figure taller than a human walking on two tremendous legs, with a boulder of a body, a strong neck, a powerful beak. Surprisingly small wings were covered with iridescent blue feathers. The bird was a hunter itself, evidently; it was treading astonishingly quietly, round eyes above that cruel beak inspecting the undergrowth, the low branches.

'So,' Agnes murmured, quietly enough for just Lobsang and Shi-mi to hear, 'when the furballs come out to hunt the insects, *this* comes out to hunt the furballs.'

'That looks like a gastornis,' the cat said softly. 'A predatory flightless bird of the Palaeocene—'

'Hush,' Lobsang said. 'I don't want to know about it that way. We've come to live in this world, remember, not to study it.'

Shi-mi said, 'And thereby denying the reality.'

That surprised Agnes. 'Denying what? What reality?'

'I too have had trouble sleeping, Agnes. As if the day is *too short*, subtly. And getting shorter.'

Agnes, startled, said, 'Too short? What could that possibly mean?'

But Shi-mi would say no more.

Now the bird had passed out of sight, evidently unaware as yet of the tampering with its nest. Silently Oliver and Nikos got to their feet, lugging the net with the egg, and started to make their way back out of the forest, gesturing for Agnes and the others to follow.

Lobsang got up. Agnes had no choice but to follow him.

12

IN THE SHADOW of a half-built liquid hydrogen plant, shielded from the intense Miami sun, Stan Berg was playing poker with a few construction workers.

In the year 2056, two years after the arrival of Lobsang and Agnes at New Springfield, Stan was sixteen years old. The purpose of this community, a much transformed Miami West 4, was to construct a space elevator, a ladder to the sky. But the construction of the Linsay beanstalk had been held up for weeks now. There was pretty much nothing to do. And so, at a table full of LETC stalk jacks twice his age or more – some ostentatiously wearing their hard hats even though they hadn't worked for days – Stan played steadily, folding when necessary, winning consistently.

Rocky Lewis, the same age as Stan and his friend, or rival, from childhood, was standing back with a few others, watching the game for lack of anything better to do. Some of the audience leaned on home-made placards that protested about the latest lay-offs and delays.

And Rocky watched uneasily as the shards of spacecraft-hull ceramic that were being used as chips piled up in front of Stan.

The other players were starting to notice. Rocky had seen it all before. Their expressions were turning from kind of patronizing about the smart kid, to resentful at getting beat out hand after hand, to suspicious about some kind of cheating. The dealer was a young, slim guy in a tipped-back homburg hat who Rocky knew only as Marvin – not a worker here, as far as Rocky knew he was some kind of professional gambler – and he was becoming watchful too. Rocky knew that Stan wasn't cheating. It was just that he was so damn smart. Stan said he liked games of bluff like poker, in fact, because unlike chess, say, there was no simple, logical way to get you through to victory from a given starting point; subtler qualities of the mind were needed.

But there was nothing subtle about the expression on the face of the guy sitting next to Stan, to his right, as yet again his chips were swept away to land up in front of Stan.

As Marvin cautiously began another hand, Rocky crouched down and plucked his friend's sleeve. 'Hey, buddy. Maybe we should get out of here.'

'What for?'

'Umm, you know. School stuff.'

'School's out today.'

That was true, the teacher had failed to turn up again, but these other characters wouldn't necessarily know that. Stan was supremely bright but capable of making basic mistakes in situations like this. 'Come on.' Rocky stood up. 'Cash in your chips.'

But the guy to the right reacted to that by grabbing Stan's arm with a fist like a claw hammer. 'You're not going anywhere, you little prick. Not with my dough in your back pocket.'

The other players froze. Rocky was relieved that there were no hands reaching under the table for concealed weapons; these were space industry workers, not movie gangsters. But one or two of the spectators on the fringe of the crowd stepped away from trouble with pops of displaced air, elusive flickers at the edge of Rocky's vision.

Rocky said, 'Let him go. Listen, he's one of you. He's an apprentice, like me. His parents work for LETC – both of them.'

'So maybe they taught him to work the cards, huh?'

The dealer, Marvin, held up his hands. 'Folks, please. We're just having a friendly game here.' He eyed Stan. '*I* know he's no cheat. He's too smart to cheat. And he's too smart to need to cheat. Face it, Alexei, he's just a better player than you. It happens.'

Somehow these bland words, blandly delivered, cooled the situation, Rocky saw. Marvin seemed to have a kind of natural authority, like an adult stepping into a circle of squabbling kids; you calmed down automatically. Rocky had observed that the Arbiters, local amateur peacekeepers, could be like that too.

But still the guy, Alexei, was steaming. 'He's a dumb punk kid is what he is.' He was still holding Stan's arm, and squeezing harder.

Stan, however smart, was small, dark, slim for his age, and he wouldn't be strong enough to break away. His teeth clenched as the grip became painful. Rocky held his breath. This could still end badly for Stan. He heard muttering about calling in an Arbiter.

But then somebody shouted out, 'Hey! They got a kobold! Over by the oh-two plant. Come see . . .'

The crowd around the table started to break up and make for the fresh morsel of entertainment. Marvin grabbed back his cards. 'Keep your chips, folks, you can settle up between yourselves when you're ready.'

Rocky took the chance to drag Stan's arm out of Alexei's grip, and pulled his friend to his feet. '*Now* let's get out of here.'

Even now Stan was grinning, though he winced as he massaged his arm. 'Not without my winnings.' He swept his chips into a pouch he carried under his Stepper box.

Marvin winked at him. 'Good luck with cashing them.'

Stan shrugged. 'There'll be other games. See you around.'

'Oh, you will,' Marvin said, sounding oddly enigmatic to Rocky's ears.

It turned out the kobold, a kind of twisted-up humanoid, had got itself trapped on the other side of the beanstalk facility, in the concrete shell of what was to be a liquid oxygen store. Following the crowd, Rocky and Stan jogged that way.

It was just after noon now, under a bright, washed-out Florida spring sky. If you didn't look too closely, Rocky thought, all you saw was people on a dirt plain roughly drained and cleared, surrounded pretty much by emptiness. But, rising from this desolate plain and up into the Florida sky, the spine of the beanstalk was already in place, a double thread electric blue and marked with flags, anchored to the uncompromising concrete block that was its temporary ground station: perfectly straight but at a distinct slant, rising until it was lost in the glare, heading for its orbital anchor.

Most stepwise Floridas were empty, at least in Low Earths like this, there being easier places in the footprint of the North American continent to kick-start a new colony. They weren't even particularly close to the coast, unlike Cape Canaveral on the Datum, which Rocky had visited once to see the shrunken space facility still launching comsats and weather satellites and such into a post-Yellowstone volcano-winter sky. But the geographic logic of the location was just the same on all the worlds. Florida was the lowest-latitude terrain in the footprint of the continental United States in thousands of worlds across the Long Earth, and for conventional space operations the closer to the equator you were the better, because of the boost you got from the Earth's spin.

And that applied, too, if you were building a ladder to space: the further south the better.

It really would be one enormous elevator system, an elevator that would lift you to orbit, and a hell of a lot cheaper to run and more reliable than the big old rocket boosters that even now were still flying out of Datum Canaveral. The whole thing had been under construction since Rocky and Stan had been eight years old, and the boys had met in the improvised schools they set up here for children of the workers, the 'stalk jacks'.

It was all ancient history to Rocky, who, like Stan, had been born in the very year Yellowstone blew. But he knew that this place, once a decent small town, had pretty much become a refugee camp, set up in haste in the days and weeks after the eruption, when folk had come flooding out of the Datum and overwhelmed the primitive communities of the Low Earths. Many of the refugees had been Datum urban types before the eruption and were pretty helpless out in the wilds, and they had just got stuck in the camps they had been put in. The camps, becoming permanent, had turned sour. 'Everybody became an expert at waiting in line,' his mother would say. So, after a few more years, along had come another government initiative, to turn such camps back into decent functioning towns – and that meant providing the people with work, such as this tremendous beanstalk construction, right here. In had come federal government officials, along with the prime contractor, the Long Earth Trading Company – LETC.

But in recent months the project had slowed down, for reasons beyond Rocky's primitive grasp of politics and economics. There had been lay-offs and slowdowns of the work schedules. For now, despite the existence of that line up to the sky, there was no flow of people and goods to and from space, as promised: nothing down here but this drained, trampled ground, with the blocky accommodation buildings, and the half-finished shells of factories and stores for materials and fuel and machinery, and the gantries for the conventional boosters that were still needed to complete the erection of the beanstalk. Today, nobody moved here save workers come to protest, or just with nowhere else to go since the latest shutdown.

The only excitement was the crowd that had gathered before the unfinished lox plant, drawn by the prospect of some spiteful fun. Rocky and Stan were closing on the plant now, and Rocky could see a knot of people, mostly men, gathered around *something*, a shambolic figure that flickered and returned, as if slightly out of focus in the bright sunlight: the kobold, trapped and frightened.

And, distracted by the commotion, Rocky had got separated from Stan. He could lay a decent bet where his friend was going to be found: where the trouble was.

Rocky ran forward more urgently, through the heat of the day.

The kobold was surrounded by a ring of men in LETC hard hats and orange coveralls. He kept trying to step away, but each time he vanished he came stumbling straight back, sometimes clutching his face or his belly. Evidently there were more workers in the neighbouring worlds to either stepwise side, ready to beat him up or steal his stuff to force him back.

The kobold was short, squat, heavily built, with triangular teeth that showed in his grins of terror. He had powerful-looking hands, and his bare feet ended in toes with claws; he looked like some kind of mole rebuilt to a human scale – and some said that was how the kobolds had once lived out in the Long Earth, ape-folk who had retreated underground. But today he wore grubby shorts and a kind of waistcoat and even a baseball cap, a dismal parody of human garb. And he had a belt slung over one shoulder like a sash, laden with knick-knacks that glistened and shone – bits of jewellery, plastic toys, sparkly gadgets. This was how the kobolds made their living, swapping stuff like this with humans, and trading it among themselves.

The kobold was a humanoid, evidently a relative of mankind whose ancestors had split off the main line about the time some uppity chimp had figured out that banging two rocks together was a good idea. Like other humanoids such as elves and trolls, the kobolds had evolved out there in the Long Earth. Unlike most of their cousins, however, the kobolds had continued to have some contact with humanity, and that had shaped them. They fed off scraps of human culture. They were more like magpies or jackdaws than human traders, it was said: more like kids swapping cards and game tokens in a playground, than like merchants working for profit. Yet people traded with them. And some of the kobolds, at least, were brave enough to come venturing deep into the Low Earths.

But something had gone wrong for this one. Maybe he'd said the wrong thing, made a bad trade. Maybe he'd just come up against another Alexei, Rocky thought, somebody bored by the lack of work and looking for a bit of fun, a diversion.

The mood still seemed playful enough. But Rocky saw a couple of young people, a man and a woman in the green uniform of Arbiters, move forward, evidently in anticipation of trouble.

Now one guy snatched the sash with the trade goods off the kobold's shoulder, draped it over his own, and paraded around, drawing laughs and catcalls from his buddies.

The kobold was mortified, and tried to grab the sash back. 'Mm-mine mine mine . . . C-cruel to poor Bob-Bob-mm . . . Mm-mine . . .'

The guy who'd robbed him faced him. 'Muh-muh-mine, Bob-Bob-Bob? Who says so?'

'Mm-mine . . . I tr-rrade . . . You want? Look, pretty mm-mirror, pretty jewel-ss . . .'

The guy held the sash out of the kobold's reach. 'Ooh, look at me, I'm Bob-Bob-Bob-Bob-Bob-Bob . . . Hey, Fred, what do you think? Maybe LETC should employ this guy.'

'Yeah, Mario, he's smarter than Jim Russo.'

'You'd make a damn fine CFO, Bob-Bob-Bob . . .'

And there was Stan, right in the middle of it all, just where Rocky knew he would be.

'Give that back.' Stan strode up to the worker, Mario, grabbed back the sash, and handed it to the kobold, who clutched it tight to his chest. Now Stan faced Mario. 'What are you doing here?' Stan turned to the crowd, whose noise was subsiding into a kind of confusion. 'What the hell are you *doing*, all of you?'

'Rocky.' Martha Berg was at Rocky's shoulder. Stan's mother was about forty, prematurely greying, careworn, wearing her own LETC coverall. 'I heard the commotion. I just knew it was Stan, I knew it.'

'You should have seen the poker game.'

'What poker game?'

'Never mind.'

'We have to get him out of there.'

Rocky feared she was right. But he also feared the consequences if they tried. 'Maybe it will blow over.'

'It doesn't look like it,' she said wearily.

Now Mario, who was twice Stan's size, shoved Stan's shoulder. 'What's your problem, you little snot? We wasn't hurting him. Just a slap to keep him here. A little fun, that's all.'

'He's just a damn kobold,' somebody called from the crowd.

Stan turned that way, fiery. 'Who said that? Just a kobold? He's not as smart as you are, so it's OK to pick on him, right?'

'No kobold is as smart as a human, dipstick.'

'Sure. So suppose somebody came along who was as categorically smarter than you, as you're smarter than Bob-Bob here. Would you say it was right for that person to humiliate you? Would you?' He faced Mario again. 'Here. Use me.'

'Huh?'

'I'm evidently not as smart as you either. Otherwise I wouldn't have walked into the middle of this, would I? So, go ahead. You've the right, according to you. What do you want to do, trip me up, strip me naked? Beat me to death?' He turned to the crowd. 'Come on – all of you, anyone. Who's going to be the first?'

For about one second, Rocky observed, his moral authority held, one slim young man facing the burly worker, and the crowd of his buddies. For one second Rocky thought he might get away with this.

And then a lump of concrete came whirling in from the crowd, missing Stan's head by inches. 'Get the little prick!'

There was a roar, and everybody seemed to surge forward.

Rocky lost sight of Martha, and was swept forward with the

rest. But he started to fight back, shoving and pushing his way towards Stan.

And suddenly those two Arbiters were at his side, flanking him, using their shoulders in a coordinated effort to bring him through the crush. In a moment they were over Stan, who was on the ground, having evidently taken a couple of punches, but grinning up at them.

The female Arbiter said to Rocky, 'You're his friend?'

'Yeah—'

'Get him out of here.'

Rocky reached down and grabbed Stan's hand.

But Stan, still grinning, said, 'Leave it to me.'

And for Rocky the world fell away – the sunlight, the pressing crowd, the smell of dust and wet concrete, as if he'd tumbled down a rabbit hole – as Stan dragged him stepwise.

13

RESPONDING TO ROBERTA Golding's summons, the four Next met in a farmhouse in another footprint of Miami, only a few worlds away from the LETC construction site. The house was just a few decades old yet long abandoned, and the marsh had already reclaimed the ground the vanished pioneers had roughly cleared. For Roberta Golding, at least it offered a welcome relief from the intensity of the sun.

Nobody knew they were here. The Next hid away, in the worlds of dim-bulb humanity.

They were due for a regular update meeting anyhow, which was why Roberta was in this part of the Long Earth, far from the Grange. But after the incident at the Bootstrap site with Stan Berg and the kobold, Melinda Bennett had requested an earlier session. Melinda was one of the two Arbiters who had come to the aid of Stan Berg and Rocky Lewis; the other, here too in his sweat-stained green uniform, was called Gerd Schulze.

The fourth person here today was Marvin Lovelace, the card sharp.

Marvin spoke first. 'He's obviously a candidate. The boy Stan Berg. Without even trying he was five, six, seven steps ahead of those construction workers in the game. With poker you need emotional intelligence, of course, you need to be able to read people. It was as if they were *showing* him their hands . . .'

He spoke in English, not quicktalk. They all did here. On Low

Earths, the crowded worlds close to the Datum, there was always a chance of some kind of eavesdropping. Even in a property like this, apparently abandoned, there could be a low-power cam left running by some opportunistic peeping tom, for instance. It was frustrating to talk so slowly, as if they were spelling out words with a baby's lettered wooden blocks. But they had to communicate somehow; they had to take a chance.

Gerd said now, 'He has emotional intelligence, maybe, but not maturity. He put himself at risk by charging into that crowd of bozos around the kobold.'

Roberta took off her spectacles and rubbed tired eyes. She was over thirty years old now; even among the Next, she reflected, maybe age was necessary for true wisdom. She remembered very well her own adolescence. She'd been only a little younger than Stan when she'd travelled on a Chinese twain into the far Long Earth, with all its wonders and horrors. Unable to look away – unable *not* to understand – she had cried herself to sleep, most nights. 'Are you mocking him, Gerd? Berg's instinct, however uneducated, may be better than yours. What was it you called the others – "bozos"?'

Marvin folded his arms. 'I reckon he was bluffing. Like in his poker. I think he knew he'd be saved.'

Melinda asked, 'Who by? Us?'

Marvin said, 'It's possible. Maybe he's guessed the true nature of the Arbiters – or at least has some unconscious suspicion about you.' The Arbiters, a purely voluntary force recruited from amongst themselves by the Next, worked to keep the peace on the Low Earths, in the general absence of police support after the post-Yellowstone implosion of Datum America. 'I sometimes think you're a bit too obvious, you guys in your green uniforms, wandering around the dim-bulb worlds, sorting things out.'

Gerd snorted. 'Whereas it's morally acceptable for you to fleece them at gambling games?'

Marvin held up his hands. 'I'm here to follow our consensus

aims, just like you. Even if it doesn't always seem wise to me. We went to the Grange in the first place as a refuge from these people, our mother culture, who put a bunch of Next kids in a high-tech concentration camp on Hawaii, and then considered bombing Happy Landings, our garden of Eden. Now here we are, out again, infiltrating their culture . . . Anyhow the dim-bulbs don't get suspicious about gambling. They almost *expect* you to be smarter than they are, almost expect you to cheat. High finance is the same, by the way.'

Which of course was why Marvin himself was a good agent, a good contact for recruitment. Next-candidate types like Stan were often drawn to gambling for the rare opportunities it offered in dim-bulb worlds to use their superior intellects to make some money. When they came, Marvin was in a prime site to spot them.

Roberta nodded. 'Your work's understood, Marvin. And appreciated. But you know as well as I do that the debate is fluid. Some say we shouldn't intervene at all, even in the most gross cases. And at the other extreme there is the Greening, the idea that we should work to restore humans to their wild state.' Which some Next theorists argued was something like humanity's Middle Stone Age, a pre-farming, pre-metals age of small wandering bands. All humans needed, some Next argued – all they needed to turn the Long Earth into a true Long Utopia – was a little gentle nudging from their intellectual superiors. Which, sceptics pointed out, when the cities broke up and the governments dissolved and humanity became a race of transient wanderers, would leave the Next in a position of permanent control . . .

Marvin folded his arms. 'So if we're unsure of our goals, why are we working on West 4 at all? Why the hell are we helping them build these big new space programmes? Some of them seem to be groping spontaneously, in fact, for something like the Greening. Look at the "combers". And you have workers out there in Miami 4 protesting because they think the slow pace of the project is the fault of their inadequate bosses. *We* know it's not. It's not even anything economic, financial, political. We know the problem is that human industrial society is softening at the edges. The lifestyle they call "comber" is just too tempting; especially after an accident or some such, you get swathes of workers just downing tools and walking away to go pick fruit. People don't *have* to work like this, and, increasingly, they just won't. So why are we here?'

Roberta sighed. 'Because these Low Earths still have large populations, after the Yellowstone emigrations. Declining, but still large. They *must* stay organized on large scales just to feed their own people. And because, for now, they *can* do this, and we can't. *We* need the benefits too.' The Next were still few in number, their direct technological capability limited. 'We rely on high-tech goods of all kinds. Frankly, we're parasitical on the Low Earth cultures for such goods. So, until we have a better solution of our own, we let this run – and encourage it, subtly.'

'Hmm,' said Marvin. 'You know, they tell a joke, the dim-bulbs. "Doctor, doctor, my brother-in-law thinks he's a tom cat." "Well," says the doc, "bring him in to see me and I'll cure him." "I can't," says the guy. "We need him to keep down the mice." That's what you're saying about the dim-bulbs. These guys are crazy, a pathology. It would be kinder to let them all wander off, back into the forest where they came from. But we won't let them be cured, because we need them to keep down the mice.' He laughed softly.

Gerd said, 'Well, we need to make a decision about this boy, Stan Berg. Whether or not he knows already what he is – and I have a feeling he does – we may need to get him out of here and to the Grange for his own protection.'

Roberta nodded. 'I agree. You're right. I'll break cover and talk to Stan and his family when he returns. Where did he go, by the way?'

Marvin shrugged, and the Arbiters looked blank.

14

A MONG HIS OTHER attributes, Stan was a much better stepper than Rocky, and as usual Rocky had found the latest plummet, across three worlds in a matter of seconds, hard to take.

He had landed in Miami West 1 doubled over and retching. At least there was nobody around to see it, even if they were standing in the heart of a sprawling development of vast concrete shells. This was a virtual-reality theatre – evidently, he saw from the signs, a conservation project of the post-Yellowstone Museum of the Datum movement.

Stan rubbed his back. 'You OK, buddy? Come on, let's get out of the sun.'

He led Rocky a couple of blocks – they saw nobody around – and pushed open a swing door into a cavernous empty space. Rocky glimpsed sheer concrete walls, roughly finished.

Then, without warning, the virtual-reality simulation kicked in. Suddenly it was as if he was outdoors again: he was in some dismal snow-bound city, under a leaden sky. An artificial wind blew in from somewhere, and it was *cold*. Like Stan, he was dressed only in light stepwise-Earth Florida-summer's-day gear; he was immediately shivering, and he wrapped his arms around his chest. 'Where the hell's this supposed to be? Some place on the Datum, right?'

'Yep. In England. You've heard of England? Welcome to the volcano winter. Come on, something to show you. Not far.' Stan hurried off through deserted streets.

Rocky, shivering like he'd break, had no choice but to follow.

They followed fading brown signs labelled 'Medieval City'. An outer belt of modern development – modern for pre-Yellowstone anyhow, all concrete and glass and houses in neat little rows, all abandoned, some burned out – gave way to an inner core of narrower streets, older buildings of stone and brick, and, towering over it all, a tremendous spire, slim, very tall, elegant, glimpsed here and there through gaps in the rows of roofs. The buildings here were mostly terraces, crowding the roads like rows of ageing teeth, and they had evidently been rebuilt and reused, some still residential but others converted into boarding houses or cafés or tourist-trap shops – and all of them were now boarded up and abandoned. There was a sense of great age, of generations having lived and died here, reworking the building stock over and over. It was all utterly alien to Rocky. Miami West 4, the community he'd grown up in, had few buildings older than *he* was.

They came into a kind of square, of ice-bound mud that might once have been grass-covered. And there before them, standing alone, topped by that great spire, was a cathedral, huge, its proportions distorted by their perspective from the ground – like a spaceship of stone, Rocky thought, that had just landed here.

Stan led him forward confidently. Set in a wall of elaborately carved stone was a heavy wooden door, which Stan pushed open; it was evidently unlocked. And then they were inside the cathedral. There was an immediate hush, a sense of even deeper age. Rocky had never been in such a building before in his life.

They walked down the cross-shaped building's long axis. Pillars of stone stood in tall rows, supporting arches which in turn held up a fantastically ornate roof. Rocky saw that the building itself was intact, more or less – even the great stained-glass windows were still complete – but the contents had been more or less stripped, leaving the long stone floor bare. Maybe the benches for the congregations that must once have gathered here had been taken for firewood. The whole thing must be built of nothing but stone and wood, Rocky thought, but it looked light as air.

Stan asked, 'You understand this is all a recent capture?'

'Sure.' That was the point of the Museum of the Datum movement, to preserve what was left of the cultural treasures of the mother world before they were lost in the post-Yellowstone abandonment. Portable treasures, art works for instance, were shipped stepwise, on people's backs or by twains, but buildings, whole city centres, could only be 'saved' as virtual-reality recordings.

Stan said, 'So you know where you are yet?'

'Disneyland?'

'Heretic. This is a place called Salisbury. Abandoned, like most of the rest of England. You can see the looters spared the cathedral, for reasons of their own. People do have values, even when they're hungry and cold.'

'*I'm* hungry and cold.'

The two of them sat on the floor by one wall, huddling for warmth. People had been building fires on the stone floor at the very heart of the old church, Rocky saw, where the long axis met the crosspiece, directly under the spire; the floor there was scorched, the ceiling stained with smoke.

'I guess you come here a lot,' Rocky said.

'How could I not? You have to go to the Datum for the really great old buildings, volcano winter or not. Some of the cathedrals and mosques and such are still in use over there. People go back to worship. In Barcelona, for instance, in Spain. The churches and mosques in Istanbul. This is my favourite, of all I've visited. All the better for being empty. It won't last for ever, though. That spire's just stone on a wooden frame. Somebody needs to keep it maintained.'

'Why do you care about these places, Stan? I thought you despised religion. I remember when that preacher came around the beanstalk site going on about the Pope. You made him cry!'

'I despise the religions we have, nothing but flummery and manipulation based on texts and materials so reworked over time they're all but meaningless. I despise the division religions bring; humans have enough problems without that. I despise con men like Father Melly. And yet, and yet . . . Don't you see it, Rock? Look at this place – imagine building *this* with nothing but thirteenth-century tools. Not only that, they kept on building it, generation after generation, lives of toil devoted to a single purpose. And look at what they made! Why, it was as ambitious in its day as a Linsay beanstalk is now. In a place like this you can reject the answers those builders accepted, you can even reject the questions they asked, but you have to cherish the urge to ask such sublime questions in the first place.'

Not for the first time, and surely not for the last, Rocky sensed a huge distance between himself and his lifelong friend – a distance that only seemed to be widening as they grew up. Yet he knew he could never abandon Stan. It wasn't just friendship, or loyalty, he was starting to realize. It was something more than that.

A kind of dazzling.

He blurted, 'Stan, sometimes you scare me.'

Stan looked at him, genuinely puzzled. 'Really? I don't mean to. I'm sorry. You're a good friend. But if you're scared, why are you here?'

Because I can't help it, was Rocky's only answer. 'Listen, I'm cold. Shall we get out of here?'

'In a while.' Stan stared up into the elegant spaces of the cathedral, his expression emptying, as if his mind was soaring up like a bird.

When they did step back home, they emerged into warm evening sunshine.

They strolled home; their families had neighbouring apartments in a rough dormitory development on the edge of the beanstalk facility. They reached Stan's home first – but Martha asked Rocky to come in for a moment.

Inside, sitting with Martha, was a woman, in her thirties maybe, slim, dark, grave, dressed in a kind of business suit. Rocky had no idea who she was.

Stan, though, seemed to recognize her. 'About time you showed up,' he said.

Rocky was baffled.

Martha's face was bleak. 'Rocky, this woman is called Roberta Golding. She is a Next. She says Stan is too. *He's* a Next, or they think so. And she's come here to take him away from me.'

15

'I ALWAYS KNEW he was special,' said Martha Berg. 'I suppose every mother thinks that. Even as a toddler, when he started to talk, he would gabble away.'

Roberta Golding nodded gravely. 'We call that quicktalk. All Next children do this naturally.'

They were sitting around a table in the small living room of Martha's house: Martha, this Roberta Golding woman, Stan – and Rocky, to whom the Next were not much more than a legend, a kind of horror story of the past, of smart kids the government had tried to lock up, or charismatic super-geniuses who had hijacked a US Navy twain and killed everybody. But this woman hadn't come for Rocky.

Stan was just smiling.

Martha went on, 'As he grew he was always running ahead of what his teachers planned for him. Fortunately that's not much of a problem here, because the schooling is so informal. Mostly Jez and I worked it out between us—'

'Jez, your husband.'

'He's aloft just now. I mean, up in the orbital anchor station of the tower. Takes days to get up and down, you know; even when work stops down *here* they're stuck up *there* . . .'

Roberta said, 'There's no rush. We don't have to make any decisions before you can speak to your husband.'

'Well, we kept his schooling going until he was beyond the both of us, and off on his own. There are pretty good online resources here. We just let him loose on that.'

Roberta glanced at Stan. 'I too grew up among humans, Stan. I know how frustrating it can be. How you have to keep yourself hidden.'

Martha said ruefully, 'Oh, he didn't do a lot of hiding.'

'But if he had grown up among the Next,' Roberta said softly, 'he would have been learning with others like himself – and in our community, the Grange, we adults learn from the children in their discovery of the world.' She eyed Stan. 'There is a whole universe of ideas to explore. The legacy we inherited from humanity is only the beginning, for us.'

Rocky blurted now, 'I hate the way you talk. We, you. Humanity, the Next. You look human enough to me. I'm sorry. I know it's not my business.'

Martha touched his arm. 'You're his friend. Of course it's your business.'

'But, in fact, *I am not human,* as you are,' Roberta said gently. 'Genetically we diverge. The structure of my brain is different from yours.' She smiled. 'The neurologists at the US Navy base at Hawaii, where the most intensive study of Next children was performed before the establishment of the Grange, were able to determine that much.'

'This Grange,' Martha said nervously. 'This is where you're proposing to take Stan. Where is it?'

'Far from here. Stepwise, I mean. We keep the location a secret. It was set up in the aftermath of an incident at a place called Happy Landings. A threat was made to destroy us. My kind. It could not have got us all, and the attempt was not made in the end; wiser heads prevailed. Nevertheless we heeded the warning. We have detached ourselves from the human world, for our safety, and yours.'

'But you're here now,' Rocky said. 'Acting undercover. Right?

Pretending you're something you're not. Like the Arbiters.' Who, Roberta had revealed, were Next agents too.

'I can't deny that. But we are here to study you, as well as help you. You are, after all, our precursors. And there has been no proper study of mankind.'

Martha said, a touch bitterly, 'You mean no study aside from what we did ourselves. Which doesn't count.'

'That is so. And we do try to help you, in various ways.'

Rocky found that disturbing. He was only sixteen; he knew he was ignorant, naive. But he wondered just how much influence a covert organization of super-intelligent post-humans might be having, working across the worlds of mankind.

'And,' Roberta said, 'we are looking for more of our own. Like you, Stan. Happy Landings was something of a forcing ground for the genetic development which led to our emergence: a peculiar community of humans and trolls thrown together, a product of the strange nature of the Long Earth. That was what created *us*. But now that genetic upgrading has spread through the rest of the population, and here and there, now and then, one of us will emerge among you.'

'Us and you, again,' Rocky said bitterly. 'Stan's a poppy growing in a weed patch, right?'

'Not at all,' she said blandly.

Martha said, 'And you're offering Stan a place with you in this – Grange?'

'We're offering him the chance to come visit us. See if he thinks he will be happy there.'

'Suppose he isn't,' Rocky said. 'Suppose he wants to come home. Will you let him?'

'Of course. It's not a prison, or—'

'But he'll know where you are. You said they already tried to blow you up once.'

Roberta said gently, 'Stan could not expose us without exposing himself. He's far too intelligent to do any such thing. Isn't that true, Stan?'

Stan hadn't spoken since first being introduced to Roberta. 'Talking to you is interesting. Like a chess game, almost. We can both see our way to the end game.'

She nodded, smiling. 'That is an acute perception. In a way it is as if we have less free will than these others. Because we can think our way through a given situation, discarding inappropriate alternatives.'

'*These others*,' Rocky said. 'You keep *saying* it.'

'But,' Roberta said to Stan, 'we do debate higher issues. Goals. Motivations. That's where our differences are expressed. At the level of strategy, not tactics.'

Stan nodded. 'And what is your strategy? What are your motivations? What do you intend for humanity?'

Martha said hotly, 'Isn't that up to us?'

'No, Mom,' Stan said evenly. 'Not with people like this in the world. You're no more in control of your own destiny than an elephant on a game reserve. That's a good analogy, isn't it?' he said, challenging Roberta. 'With you as the wardens.'

'It's not like that. At least, not all of us think that way. Certainly we want mankind to be . . . happy.'

'Happy? Wandering around without purpose, in a kind of garden, perfected by you. A Long Utopia. Is that your goal?'

'We don't have a goal,' Roberta said. 'At least, not an agreed one. We are developing our capabilities, exploring our own motivations. The debate on objectives continues. I invite you to join that debate. If you care about humanity as much as you seem to—'

'I need to think.' Stan stood, abruptly. 'Excuse me.' He stepped away.

When he'd gone, the room seemed empty.

Martha poured more iced tea. She said, 'He'll go with you. I don't have to be a super-brain to know that much. I know my son. He'll go, if only out of curiosity. But he'll come home again.'

'Perhaps,' said Roberta. 'But I think you should be prepared to lose him. I'm very sorry.'

Martha looked away, evidently unable to speak.

16

NELSON AZIKIWE HAD said, when offering to research Joshua's family, 'One never knows, when pulling such a thread, what might unravel.' Maybe, but it turned out to be a mighty stubborn thread.

It took months that stretched, surprisingly, to years – four years after the promise he'd made on Joshua's fiftieth birthday – before Nelson was able to make much progress with his search. His breakthrough came not through such networks as his online buddies the Quizmasters, but through his acquaintance with Lobsang – in fact, through an old friend of Sister Agnes, who heard through shared friends, she said, that Nelson was looking for information about 'London's scandalous past'.

For, to Nelson's surprise, his investigations had led him to that battered city.

Nelson met Miss Guinevere Perch in a Long Earth footprint of London. A couple of steps from the frozen Datum ruin, this new community was a tangle of hastily erected refugee camps cut into oak forest. A contemporary of Agnes, Miss Perch was in her nineties now, withered, birdlike, her hair a tangle, but with a beaming smile for visitors. She lived alone, though with daily assistance, in a house built in a fairly crude Low Earth colonial style. But she dressed richly, and in a room filled with exotic furniture a peripatetic butler served Nelson tea and cake.

Miss Perch gleefully showed Nelson images of the properties

she had once owned on the Datum, including a very expensive Georgian terrace house in central London. 'Handy for the House of Commons,' she said. And when she showed him glimpses of the exotic equipment she had kept in the basement of that terrace house, and outlined the activities that went on down there for the benefit of MPs and other parliamentarians – and a visitors' book, complete with covert photographic portraits, that spanned decades – he understood why she had got in touch with him. When it came to what was left of the British Establishment, even now, sixteen years after Yellowstone, Miss Guinevere Perch knew where the bodies were buried.

And with that power, she was able to help Nelson uncover some very private secrets indeed.

But as it turned out, when Nelson did begin to tug systematically on the thread of Joshua Valienté's origins, the story he unravelled went much deeper than the biography of Joshua's own father. It turned out to be a history, in fact, more than two centuries old . . .

From the stage door of the Victoria theatre and down Lambeth's crowded New Cut, the Great Elusivo – a.k.a. Luis Ramon Valienté, a.k.a. the Hon. Reginald Blythe, and a.k.a. a variety of other pseudonyms depending on circumstances – followed his mysterious interrogator, Oswald Hackett, towards the promised oyster-house.

The pavements of the New Cut, banks of a river of horse-drawn traffic, swarmed with people and their multifarious business. Of course they did at this time of a Saturday evening, in March of the year 1848, when the Surrey-side theatres opened their doors to let out the posh folk from the boxes, and the young costermongers swarmed out of the threepenny stalls. The shops were all open, the keepers in their doorways, the windows full of furniture or tools or second-hand clothes, or heaps of vegetables or cheese or eggs. But there was as much business being done from the stalls that crowded the street itself. The repetitive cries of the stall vendors or their boys rose up over the clatter of horses' hooves: 'Chestnuts, penny a scoop!' and 'Pies all 'ot!' and 'Yarmouth herrings three a penny!' Many of these voices were Irish; the destitute folk of that country had come to the city fleeing the famine, and were looked down on even by the poorest of the indigenous folk. More elaborate sermons came from the cheap Johns selling Sheffield-steel cutlery in their thick Yorkshire accents, and the patterers talking up their gaudy literature of gruesome crimes. Luis had to sidestep an old woman seated on a low stool, smoking a pipe, selling framed engravings of Queen Victoria, her Consort and her children from an upturned umbrella. The street entertainers were everywhere too, the ballad singers and the sword swallowers and fire eaters, an old blind woman playing a hurdy-gurdy, and one man with a tabletop display of mechanical figures from Austria, a princess dancing the polka, a trumpeting elephant, which held the attention of rapt street children . . .

Amid all this clamour, Luis kept his eye on the mysterious Hackett.

Luis was a quick study. Oswald Hackett was a powerfully built man in his thirties, some years older than Luis, dressed richly but soberly in a handsome-looking surtout, and walking with an expensive cane. In the light of the lamp by the stage door Luis had noticed that the skin of the hand holding that cane bore marks, scars made by chemicals perhaps. Was the fellow some kind of scholar, a scientist – a chemist? And educated by the sound of it; he had the slight bray, the elongated vowels, that Luis associated with a history shaped by Harrow and Oxford.

Right now the man looked somewhat sickened: pale, breathing hard as he marched along. But this March day was unseasonably warm, and the London air was a touch less sulphurous than usual – the reaction must be due to after-effects of the man's own disappearing act rather than to the climate. Still, Hackett kept pushing through the crowd, by an apparent effort of will.

'Further than I remembered to this oyster-house,' he said now, panting. 'Not used to these crowds; forgive my lack of breath. What a swarm this is – eh? As if London is one great decaying tree trunk through which the maggots and the weevils chew their way, selling bits of bark to each other for farthings . . . Ah, but I imagine you feel more at home than I do, Elusivo? After all it was on streets like this that you once scrambled to survive, did you not? Chewing your quid and watching out for the bobbies . . .'

Luis watched sweeper boys at a corner, competing to clean the path of grander folk passing to and from the theatres, some of them somersaulting or handstanding in hope of a tossed penny. He had the uncomfortable feeling that this Hackett knew far too much about him – about a life he would prefer to remain his own secret.

It was a sorry affair after all: his father a shopkeeper who had died poor, of consumption, his mother marrying again before dying herself in childbirth – and a stepfather who had never treated Luis with anything more than contempt, and had eventually thrown him out on the street. Luis was nine years old. Well, he had joined Hackett's 'maggots and weevils' of London to survive, at first sweeping the streets just like these boys he saw before him now, and using his unusual talent to get him out of scrapes – and, yes, away from the bobbies when he needed it. But then, aiming higher, he had developed a street act based on his disappearing tricks: popping out of existence behind a barrel, only to emerge from a doorway across the street. And that had got him noticed, and a job in the warmth of the Surrey-side theatres in variety shows or as an interval turn. All the while he had kept his secret: that his magic tricks weren't tricks at all – though if they weren't magic he wasn't sure what they were.

And now, it seemed, he had been noticed again.

There was no point beating about the bush, he decided. 'Never mind your oysters. So you can do *it* too, sir. I thought I was the only one . . . May I ask firstly what you call *it*? I do not like people having the better of me.'

'I have a name for *it*. But does a name matter? And as for you thinking that you are unique, all I can say, sir, is: so do most of the others. As has been true all the way back into deep history, probably. One of my own ancestors, or so the family story goes, was Hereward the Wake, and he was damned elusive too, wasn't he? Shall we prove it to each other?'

'Prove what?'

Hackett halted, glanced around, and led Luis into the shadow of an alley. 'What's your preference, Mr Valienté?'

'Preference?'

'Widdershins or deiseal?'

'I don't know what the devil— Oh.'

'There are always two directions in which to travel, aren't there?'

'I think of them as dexter or sinister.'

'Fair names. Of course we don't know which of our terms is congruent with t'other, do we?' He held out his cane – which Luis now recognized as a sword cane, containing a hidden weapon. Hackett said, 'Come – grasp the stick. Do me the honour of allowing me to take the lead. Widdershins for this first experiment, I think.'

Staring at the man, Luis considered. He had the feeling that his whole life hinged on this moment, the choice he took now. The chap could have no more on Luis than guesswork so far, guesses based on observing his stage show – it must be so, for Luis would surely have clocked the fellow if Hackett had followed him into the sinister forest to spy on him. Luis could still bluster this out. What could the man do, after all? He couldn't force Luis to cross over into the eerie silence of the widdershins woods . . .

On the other hand, of course, once they *had* crossed, and were out of sight of any bobbies, Luis might get the chance to silence the fellow for good and, simply, leave him there. To survive in London's demi-monde Luis had had to learn to be good with his fists from a young age. He was no killer, though he had before considered the possibility as a way of keeping his uncomfortable secret, *in extremis*. His life or Hackett's, that would be the choice. And yet, and yet . . .

His racing thoughts juddered to a halt. Here was another *like him*. Here was a fellow, educated enough by the look and sound of it, who might be able to *explain* this peculiar phenomenon which, it was true, Luis had always imagined was his and his alone, his peculiar gift and burden, a secret to be kept even from his own family.

Oswald Hackett grinned, studying him. Luis had the feeling that the man knew exactly what he was thinking, the choices he was weighing up.

Luis didn't trust this chap as far as he could throw him. But Luis had always been something of an opportunist; that feature had shaped the entire pattern of his life, his career. He would, he decided, see what the fellow had to say. If Luis didn't like what he learned, he could always slip away into shadows and anonymity, as he'd done several times in his life before – although it occurred to him that it mightn't be quite so easy to evade a man who could follow him even into dexter or sinister.

His choice made, without another word, he grasped the cane.

Hackett nodded. 'Good man.' He glanced about, evidently to make sure they were unobserved.

And, with the usual slight jolt to the Valienté gut, they were in the forest green.

Luis released the cane.

The trees here were oak, and not the wretched soot-coated specimens that populated the London parks but tall and handsome, like the columns in some great church, Luis often thought. The sky was bright and blue and not hidden from view by the city's pall, and it was a colder day here too. The city, that great reef of humanity with its buildings blackened by centuries of soot and smoke, did not exist *here* – if this dexter or sinister forest corresponded to the London Luis knew at all. The ground underfoot was firm and dry, as Luis knew well, for he popped over here several times a day in the course of his stage act. Not all of the terrain was so accommodating; much of the landscape hereabouts was a marsh through which a broad river and its tributaries washed: a version of the Thames perhaps, but untrammelled by humanity. Luis had to choose his theatres well for his performances. The stages he used needed to map over to higher terrain *here*, or at least dry land, for the punters might be confused by his magical reappearances if they always came accompanied by wet feet.

He became aware of Hackett, who was again doubled over, clutching his belly, breathing hard, looking pale. Luis had never made such a journey other than alone before, and now the presence of another in what Luis had come to think of as his own private refuge was something of a shock.

Hackett straightened with an effort, dug a paper packet from his waistcoat pocket, and gulped down a couple of pills. 'You don't suffer this?'

'What?'

'The nausea. Like a punch in the gut from some East End footpad.'

'Never had it.'

'Then you're blessed. And you saw I had a dose of it before, when I did my quick switch back and forth to show you my credentials.' Hackett straightened up and eyed him. 'I envy you, sir, you are evidently a more adept Waltzer than I am.'

'Waltzer?'

'It's my name for what we do – *this*. To Waltz. Don't you think the borrowing is appropriate? For we dance, you and I, as light on our feet as two German princelings, and skip to left and right, or in *some* direction, faster than the eye can follow. Waltz, do you see? Although I know the dance isn't so fashionable yet in the twopenny hops of Lambeth as it is in Windsor. And here we are, having Waltzed to the forest. Tell me, have you explored this – new world – to any extent?'

Luis shrugged. 'What for? There's nobody here.'

'No profit to be had, eh?'

'England's my world, sir. London.'

'And wherever you cross over, do you always find the forest?'

'Only ever tried it in London, and Kent, where I grew up. Yes, forest.'

'And the deiseal side?'

'The same.'

'Well, the forest is the thing, everywhere you go, in England at any rate. Some of my own ancestors – for the trait has been passed down the generations, and preserved in family legend, though *not* written down since one distant aunt was burned as a witch – some of 'em called themselves woodsmen, you know. One of 'em ran with Robin Hood. No wonder the Sheriff of Nottingham could never catch those outlaws.'

Luis snorted. 'Hood's a figure from story. A ballad.'

'If you say so. But tell me – if you do cross further, what then?'

That confused Luis. 'Don't know what you mean, sir.'

Hackett goggled at him. 'You're serious, aren't you? You've grown up able to take this first spin of the Waltz, but it has never occurred to you to take the second, or a third? To dance on, into yet another world, and another?'

Luis frowned. No, it had never occurred to him to try. 'To what end?'

Hackett shook his head. 'So you have no curiosity at all, not a grain of the explorer – why, Captain Cook must be turning in his grave to hear it. I did wonder if the stage name you chose reflects your true character. *Elusivo*, from elusive, or to elude – it comes from a Latin root meaning *to play*, you know.'

'Does it? Wasn't aware.'

'Sums you up, though, doesn't it?'

'Well, what of it? What is one to *do* with such a gift as this but to keep it hidden – to make a little profit – to play, if you like?'

'Oh, what an unimaginative chap you are, Valienté. I myself thought that way, as a boy, but grew out of it. And as I've been implying, many of my ancestors had better ideas. How about a spot of burglary? Or spying, or assassination, or . . .' Hackett stepped up to him boldly, all traces of his nausea gone. 'How about serving your country?'

An alarm like the whistle of a steam train went off in Luis's head. He extemporised. 'I've no idea what you mean.'

'Of course you haven't. Let me explain. But first – how about those oysters? Let's pop back and eat.'

The food at the oyster-house was indeed very fine, and Luis would have been happy to play along with shadier characters than Hackett for the benefit of a free meal.

Eating with a fellow always built up a certain degree of trust, Luis had observed before – especially if said fellow was doing the buying. They spoke of little as they ate, and by the time the empty shells had been stacked up and another round called for, they were, in a curious way, allies. Not friends exactly, but with a bond. Allies, each knowing that the other could disappear at any time, but each consoled by the fact that so could he.

Luis took a mouthful of porter and asked, 'So – the Waltzers. How many of us?'

'I know of fifteen,' said Hackett. 'Extant, that is, and then there are the records from the past, fragmentary as they necessarily are even within my own family, and fading into legend and outright spoofery the further back you look. We are rare, we Waltzers, Luis, as rare as a two-headed calf, and generally about as welcome. And often, I suspect, we don't breed true, so the talent must pop up and vanish again with the secret going to the grave with the bearer. Even so I assume there are many more in the world. Recently I found two in Margate, in the course of a brief holiday.'

'May I ask, a holiday from what, sir? I think I know all the escapologists and similar showmen in the city and I don't recognize you.'

119

Hackett cleared his throat. 'Well, I am no showman – not to denigrate your chosen course in life. I am in the fortunate position of having independent wealth. My father died when I was a nipper, but I inherited a decent trust fund on my majority – and then had the wit to invest a chunk of it in railway shares, and the fortune to pick the right stock.'

Luis said nothing, but cringed inwardly. His own father, by comparison, had backed the *wrong* horses in the mania of railway building that had followed the opening of the famous Liverpool & Manchester line, and had left his family destitute. He regarded Hackett bleakly. Fortune, he thought, follows the already fortunate.

'As to what I do with my time,' Hackett went on, 'I regard myself as a scholar, without affiliation to any particular body, though I have presented papers to the Royal Society and the Royal Institution among others. I have been particularly intrigued by the great treasury of information brought back by the bolder naturalists, from those who voyaged with Cook whom I mentioned, to more recent fellows like Darwin – have you read the volumes of his account of the voyage of the *Beagle*? Who knows how much, in the decades to come, we might not learn of the operation of the divine life-sustaining machine that is the Earth?

'And of course that scientific curiosity of mine has been turned on my own strange abilities, and those of my family and the rest of our scattered, furtive community. How has our peculiar faculty come about? What is it we do? *Where* are these enigmatic forests we visit? What is the meaning of it all? And what must we do with this strange gift? Tell me, Valienté, when did you first become aware of your own talent? Do you recall?'

'Vividly. I was being chased by a bull – it's not much of a story, to do with a couple of us scrumping apples where we shouldn't have been, I was no more than six – when suddenly I found myself, not in a farmer's field looking at a bull, but in a dense forest staring at something like a wild pig. Screamed the place down, then suddenly found myself *back*, but the bull had lost me. The whole episode had the quality of nightmare, and such I thought it was. Took me a while to find out how to do the thing purposefully.' But he had needed to develop his prowess when his stepfather had thrown him out, not many years after that incident of the apples – not that he intended to tell Hackett about that, if he didn't already know.

Hackett produced a pipe; he filled it, tamped it, lit it before speaking again. 'Six, eh? I was older – but then I suspect your talent is rather more developed than mine. I found it when I was about sixteen. I was at school, and in the arms of the headmaster's wife. I need not elaborate, but when it became necessary that I leave rapidly, and I found the window locked – well, I left anyhow, only to find no window and no headmaster, or wife, or school, or rugger field. Nothing but oak and ash trees, and swamp, and my own bewilderment.' He flicked an empty shell on the table between them. 'After that, I'm sorry to say, as an impudent young man I thought that the world was my oyster and I took what pearls I could find. Unlike you I was always impeded by the deuced nausea, but there are ways to combat that. As you might expect, no boudoir was secure. To the ladies of my acquaintance I was never less than a gentleman, but a persistent and rather omnipresent one. And of course money was no problem; no strongroom could exclude me.

'As I grew older I became sated, and I matured – and after one or two close shaves with various forms of authority I learned to become rather more discreet. There was one irate father with an antique of a blunderbuss . . . Then, of course, I came into money of my own, and as a man of affairs I became respectable. And terribly pompous probably, as most reformed rakes are – you can judge for yourself. But I never forgot my origins, if you like.'

'How do you find us? I mean those of us who can – um, Waltz.'

'Generally, just as I found you: hiding in the open. I admire your artistry, sir. Your tricks might *just* possibly be very clever illusions, they *could* be done by smoke and mirrors, or a bit of mesmerism, or some other subterfuge. You are smart enough to be extremely good but not impossibly good. Even a very observant and highly sceptical witness can go away from the show believing he has seen through your tricks, and feeling pleasingly self-satisfied as a result, while understanding nothing of the reality of your abilities. But I, who am like you, could see through the flummery.'

'And to what end do you seek us, sir?'

'Well, I could say that my ultimate goal – though it may sound a bit high-handed for a fellow with his chin greasy from Lambeth oysters – is to put our skills to constructive use. It is my intention, for the first time, presumably, in human history, to *organize* those of us with this faculty. To present a gift to Her Majesty and her government. To harness a talent that will ensure that Britain will continue to be the dominant power in this globe, as we have been since the downfall of the Corsican. And who could deny that that would be for the betterment of all mankind?'

Luis goggled at him. 'You're serious, aren't you? Well, sir, to raise but one objection, surely Prussia and France must have people with such powers as we possess?'

'The difference is, sir, *we* are British. This year, this spring, as you may know, all Europe is in a ferment of revolt – the Continent is a pit of medieval chaos. *We* are a rational nation. We are scientific. We are disciplined.'

'Really? What about the Chartists? And, you would go to the government? If we come out in the open at a time of such ferment, what's to stop them locking us up as dangerous lunatics and monsters – or, more likely, simply gunning us down where we stand?'

Hackett leaned closer, and spoke more softly, conspiratorially. 'The difference is, Luis, we will prove our worth. You mentioned the Chartists. Have you heard of the rally they're mounting next month on Kennington Common?'

17

THE CHARTISTS' DEMONSTRATION was planned for April 10.

Before the event, Luis took the trouble to find out something about the movement's aims and ambitions – as anonymously as he could, and mostly from the *Morning Chronicle*, which was a liberal and campaigning newspaper, copies of which were kept as props in the Victoria theatre. It was a difficult time for Britain, if you took the picture as a whole: the Irish starving, the Scots struggling to recover from the Highland Clearances of the century past, and considerable unrest among the urban poor in the industrial cities. There were riots in the mines, stories of weavers smashing their looms – and reports of 'Chartists' being arrested.

The Chartists were agitators for political reform, following the lead of proponents in the House of Commons itself. Luis learned they had had some successes, with parliamentary Acts to limit the use of children in the factories, for instance. But over the years there had been trouble with assemblies, demonstrations and strikes. Here and there troops had been called out, the Riot Act had been read, a few Chartist heads had been broken. Up to now the troubles had mostly been ignored by the political classes. As seen from London, the whole thing was just another symptom of the general awfulness of the northern industrial cities, which the old landed establishment affected to despise.

Luis himself had mostly ignored this too. Luis Ramon Valienté, alone since boyhood, concerned for only the integrity of his own skin, didn't see himself as part of a wider society at all. And besides, the disturbances had barely touched his own life. He could sympathize in the abstract with the plight of a child worked to a premature grave, but it was nothing to do with him.

Things were different now, however. This spring of 1848 was indeed a season of rebellion and uprising across Europe – even in such capitals as Berlin – and everywhere governments trembled and monarchies tottered. So far Britain had been free of such revolutions, but the continued flight of well-heeled refugees across the Channel was sending shudders down the spines of the wealthy and powerful. Riots even in London, in Trafalgar Square and elsewhere, had done nothing to calm nerves.

And now, in this ominous spring, the Chartists had called for a mass rally on Kennington Common, outside London. The ambition was to gather a throng a million strong and to march into the city. All this sounded an unlikely threat to Luis – surely it would blow over. This was poky, grimy old London, not some hotbed of ferment like Paris.

'Not a bit of it,' Hackett insisted. 'I have sources. The government is bringing regiments into town, the homes of ministers are being guarded, special constables are being recruited, the Royal Family are being removed from the capital, and so on and so forth. All under cover, of course – but I've seen one of the secret stashes of weapons they've prepared myself, at the Admiralty. They're determined this isn't to be the tipping point into a wider revolt. And that's where you and I come in, Valienté, my friend . . .'

His plan, it seemed, was for the two of them to infiltrate the mob, and to use their abilities to 'damp down the fire', as Hackett put it.

All this seemed alarmingly vague to Luis. What, were they to go slipping sidewise in the midst of a restless crowd of discontented unwashed being whipped up by political agitators? And besides, the whole scheme defied every instinct he'd developed over his lifetime to keep his 'Waltzing', as Hackett called it, a secret.

But his hesitation seemed to have been anticipated by Oswald Hackett, who began to speak with heavy emphasis about arrangements he'd made with certain special constables. These fellows had no idea what Hackett might be planning – Hackett had given only vague and mendacious hints that he and Luis were themselves agents of the government – but they'd agreed to work with Hackett, giving him the nod to identify certain ringleaders, foreign agitators and other troublemakers.

And Hackett gazed steadily at Luis as he spoke of those friends among the constables. His unspoken message could not have been clearer: *Run away, my lad, and these constables of mine will be down on you like a Lambeth rat on a bit of mouldy cheese.*

Luis saw, then, that he had no choice; he would have to go through with this farcical operation, striving to keep his own head intact in the process, and see what came of it next.

As it happened, on the morning of the great assembly it rained hard enough to drown more than a Lambeth rat, and spirits were thoroughly flattened.

A throng did turn up on the common at Kennington, but there was no million here as the Chartists had hoped for, there were mere thousands, ten thousand at most, Luis guessed. As well as the police they were faced by special constables guarding the bridges to the city, among them a goodly number of the rich and ministers of the government, Hackett said, volunteering in order to protect their own wealth and what they saw as the virtues of a constitution which needed no hasty reform, thank you. In the end the only outcome was the presentation of a comically inflated petition to the House of Commons – that, and a few scuffles and arrests. Luis thought the coffee-stall holders did a brisker business than the constables.

But still, in the midst of this relatively blood-free uprising, Hackett went to work with a will, and Luis had no choice but to follow him.

The plan was simple. A constable would point out a trouble-maker. Luis would Waltz to dexter or sinister, approach the suspect's position through the silence of the forest, spin back and grab him bodily – or occasionally her – lift him off his feet and Waltz one way or the other, and just dump the bewildered wretch amid the trees. No matter how hard they struggled when taken, the victims were always utterly baffled by their transition from one noisy world to the sylvan silence of another, and more often than not crippled by nausea too. Then it was a case of walk away a few yards and hop back into the melee; and, just in case anybody had seen the Great Elusivo pop mysteriously out of existence, Luis took care not to come back to the same spot and reinforce the impression.

At the end of the assembly, Hackett had told Luis, these temporary exiles would be rounded up from the forest, returned to Mother England and delivered into the arms of the constables.

'And,' Luis had said, 'if they blab about their experiences, about us—'

'Who to, the constables? Who's to believe an agitator spouting a lot of nonsense about trees and bogs in the middle of London? Especially if it's in French or German. Or even Gaelic – ha!'

'And if they come to some kind of harm—'

'What, if they get run down by a boar or swiped by a bear? Or, perhaps, the very act of being Waltzed over might kill 'em; some of my family legends hint at that possibility. Well, if so, nobody will grieve. Or even know. We'll leave 'em to a godless grave widdershins, and *au revoir.*'

In the end the work proved easy enough. Luis could look after himself in a fight, and the exertions of his illusion act had built up his bodily strength. The only cost to him was a few digs in the ribs, a kick on the shin, and one beauty of a black eye. Many of those identified for transportation were indeed foreign agitators, mostly French, and Luis was surprised at the extent to which the English movement had been infiltrated. He wondered if Hackett might after all have a point in his windy and unlikely scheme, if it all worked out so easily as this.

At one point, as he stood over yet another dizzy, nauseated Frenchie spewing out words faster than he spilled his guts – and, comically, wondering why his shoes were falling apart, their sole nails having been left behind in London (Luis himself always wore sewn-leather slippers) – Luis, taking a breather, caught the eye of another young man standing over his own doubled-up agitator. The man, tall, sinewy, grinned and waved. 'Mine's a Scotsman, would you believe? Pining for the Bonnie Prince. But earlier I grabbed a big Irish lad and I hoped it was Feargus O'Connor himself, but that mastermind of the Chartists eludes us . . .'

Until that moment Luis hadn't known that he and Hackett weren't alone here, working this crowd. But of course Hackett would recruit others – and of course he would keep it all a secret even from his allies, clutched close to his own chest.

Luis recovered his composure and called back, 'Mine's a French.'

'So I hear. Coarser language than you'll hear in the Marseilles docks, I'd warrant. Rather jolly fun, this, isn't it? Well, back to the grindstone; those agitators won't apprehend themselves – be seeing you!' He winked neatly out of existence.

So it was back to work for Luis too. At the end of the day he made off without incident.

And, to his blank astonishment, Oswald showed up that evening at Luis's theatre, and said that they had an appointment with royalty.

18

L UIS BORROWED A decent morning suit from his theatre manager. Hackett had stressed the need for confidentiality even now, so Luis pleaded attendance at a wedding. At that, he wondered if it might have been more convincing if he'd claimed he wanted the suit for an appearance before the magistrate.

Oswald Hackett, of course, looked peacock-magnificent as he gathered his small party at Charing Cross, where they would board landaus to take them to Windsor. *Small*: there were eight of them all told, eight Waltzers, all men, all about Hackett's age or younger. Luis had had no idea there were so many in Hackett's company. He recognized only one apart from Hackett himself: the tall, lithe-looking young man he'd bumped into in the forest.

There seemed no particular pattern to these fellows: some were short and others tall, some tough-looking and some not, some fair and some dark. Most looked as if they were of British stock, under-standably enough. Only Luis himself, with the Mediterranean roots of his family behind him, looked markedly less Anglo-Saxon. And all were well kitted out, though some, like Hackett, looked more comfortable in their finery. Luis guessed that some were from rather more privileged backgrounds than others.

Hackett didn't encourage conversation, and even suppressed introductions. He said sternly, 'You're not a bunch of new fags at some minor school. You're here to put yourself in the hands of Her Majesty, for the purpose of all manner of sly and covert affairs

– whatever my fertile imagination can dream up – and sly and covert it must be, given the nature of our shared talent. And in that case the less you know of each other the more effective you'll be. For if I don't know your name I can't betray you, can I? Which has been a lesson learned by rebels before, from our own Chartists, back through the French when they took agin their king, to the Americans when they turned on the English hand that fed 'em . . .'

Even so, as they boarded their coaches, that tall, skinny fellow made for Luis and slyly shook his hand. He looked about twenty-five, Luis's own age, and his grasp was stronger than Luis expected. 'The name's Fraser Burdon,' he said. 'Since we made our acquaintance already in the widdershins forest, there's nothing much for us to lose by swapping names, is there?'

Luis introduced himself, and in a quick conversation Burdon ascertained how Luis had been found by Hackett, and recruited.

Burdon said, 'As for me, I met the good Doctor up at Cambridge, where I'm pottering about in the natural sciences. Oswald was up there for a conference on the extinction of species, or some such – rocks are more my bag – and he spotted me "Waltzing", as he puts it, when I fell off a punt – sooner that than end up in the Cam; I never was much of a hand with the pole. I didn't want to get wet again, and I knew it was dry just there widdershins. Thought nobody was watching – careless, that. Still, here we are . . .'

Then they boarded the coach, with Hackett, and they didn't get the chance to speak again.

Windsor Castle seemed to Luis from without an intimidating pile, an excrescence of centuries of wealth heaped up on a core of medieval brutality. And when they were led into the sprawling walled compound through an entrance called the Norman Gate, and faced a mound of earth topped by the 'Round Tower', the interior struck him as gloomy and claustrophobic.

That sensation only got more pronounced as the party, passed

off from one flunkey to another, was led through a narrow doorway and deep into the interconnected buildings of the castle wards,
at first through grand passageways, but at last finishing up in a
remote, murky corner, where a trapdoor led to a staircase down
which they descended.

Then they were led by servants with oil lamps through another
warren of corridors and rooms, apparently entirely underground.
The chambers here were lined by shelves heaped with papers, and
with other items only dimly glimpsed as they walked on: hunting
trophies and stuffed animals, spears and drums, a kind of feathered
headdress. Luis, feeling increasingly enclosed and uncomfortable,
was aware that the servants who escorted them, despite their smart
appearance, were stationed front and back, and were all big, powerful men with plenty of room for weapons under their loose jackets.

'You are privileged, gentlemen,' Hackett said, his voice a respect-
ful whisper. 'This is a private royal vault. Here you've got the records
of many reigns, including the present one, and gifts from the colonies and other nations, and other assorted clutter. And it's down
here that Queen and Consort host their most private meetings.'

Fraser Burdon whispered to Luis, 'And perhaps it's appropriate that this should be the centre of the memory of the monarchy.
You know where we are, don't you? Under the original castle on
its motte, built by William himself after the Conquest. One of a
string of fortresses he established to keep a hold on London. Now
Windsor's the home to a young Queen and her growing brood, but
you can never forget that original purpose.'

Luis murmured back, 'I don't know about the history, but God, I
hate to be enclosed. I'm half tempted to Waltz out.'

Fraser looked at him strangely. 'But you can't. Not from down
here – not unless this was originally some natural cavern. You can't
Waltz out of a cellar, because there's earth or bedrock to either side,
widdershins or deiseal. Didn't you know that much? You really
haven't studied your own abilities very much, have you?'

This had never occurred to Luis, who rarely had cause to go far underground. He muttered defiantly, 'Well, I didn't know we were prepping for a test.'

At last they came to a better fitted chamber, with decent gaslights casting a clean glow over a smart but not ostentatious suite of furniture, a thick carpet, walls lined with bookshelves, and ceiling-to-floor mirrors that Luis guessed were intended to give an impression of space in this enclosed room. Open doors led to adjoining rooms. It was like the reception room of an unpretentious family of reasonable but not overwhelming means, Luis thought, based on his own limited experience of such places.

A small group of men were already in the room, mostly dark-suited, leaning on the mantel or sitting at their ease. The Waltzers stood in a rather self-conscious huddle on the carpet, but Oswald boldly struck a pose.

At length a major-domo type smoothly effected introductions, and as he did so Luis felt his own amazement grow. A man in his middle thirties, perhaps, stern, sharp-looking, in an anonymous suit, was named only as 'Mr Radcliffe'. Two burly butlerish fellows at the back of the room were not introduced, and Luis concluded they were either special constables or military men out of uniform, no doubt backed up by others elsewhere. But a grumpy-looking gentleman in his fifties who remained seated, rather rudely, with a sparse carapace of hair and bone-white mutton-chop whiskers, turned out to be none other than Lord John Russell, the Prime Minister.

And a handsome, well-built chap leaning casually against the mantel, in a crisp morning suit but with an intimidating set of whiskers of his own, was Albert, the Royal Consort.

The Great Elusivo had played some tough houses, but he felt utterly bewildered before this audience, even though Albert quickly insisted that no formality of behaviour was necessary. And he wondered whether somebody in the royal circle or the government

– perhaps this sternly watchful fellow Radcliffe – had thought through the consequences if any of the Waltzers had intended any harm to this royal personage. For, if they turned out to be dangerous, where better for such a meeting to take place than underground, from where, as Burdon had pointed out, none of them could Waltz away?

'Dr Hackett,' said the Prince. 'It is very good to see you again.' His accent was a crisp, heavy German.

Hackett answered proudly, 'Thank you, sir. Gentlemen, His Royal Highness has taken a keen interest in our – ah – novel proposal of service from the beginning. As I have described before, sir, the talent we share is just as I demonstrated to your assistant Mr Radcliffe that evening in Windsor Great Park some weeks ago. And now, during the Chartist Demonstration at Kennington, I hope we have shown its efficacy in practice. We – *move aside.* I could not tell you how we do it, any more, I dare say, than a newborn babe could explain to you how *he* took his first pace. We find ourselves in another place, a sort of forest. I've no idea what the significance of that is, which part of the world it might be – if it's our world at all. Perhaps we should send a naturalist to explore. Call for Mr Darwin!'

The Prince was gracious enough to laugh at this.

But the dour Radcliffe seemed to lack a sense of humour. 'Your flash doesn't impress. It is your utility in *this* world which is of interest to us, Dr Hackett.'

Flash – a bit of London street slang. The word jarred in this context, taking Luis by surprise. Perhaps there was more to this Radcliffe than there seemed – and, yes, an element of threat.

But Hackett was unperturbed. He said smoothly, 'Of course, of course. And you understand the principle of that utility, just as I demonstrated in the Great Park. I Waltz into the forest.' He took a pace to the left to demonstrate. 'Then I walk through that forest.' He took one pace forward, two.

As he approached Prince Albert, Luis saw how the butler types at the back of the room, and indeed Radcliffe, all stiffened, fully alert.

'And then I come back.' A pace to the right. 'Poof! I have disappeared, and reappeared out of thin air, *somewhere else*. Like a cheap stage illusion,' and he couldn't resist a wink at Luis. 'It is not just that I have been unobserved, you see. It is that I have, umm, *bypassed* any obstacle in this world – a wall, a line of troops, the hull of a bank strongroom. *That* is the secret of our utility to you.'

'You mention a bank,' said the Prince. 'It does appear that this faculty of yours would be of uncommon value to a thief.'

'True enough, sir. And maybe there are fellows out there in the world who would use this talent for such nefarious ends.'

Luis whispered to Fraser, 'He says it without blushing, despite what he's told us of his own rakish past!'

'There are, naturally, few authenticated accounts of the more honourable exploits of Waltzers like us in the past. I can only tell you of family traditions, passed down from father to son, though I do have some scraps of documentation in certain cases . . .'

Fraser whispered, 'And here comes Hereward the Wake again.'

But Hackett didn't go so far back this time. Instead he spoke of the Armada. 'Of course the court of Queen Elizabeth was replete with spies and agents. But my own distant ancestor did more than most to penetrate Philip's admiralty and return with plans of the invasion fleet. Elizabeth never knew of it, it's said, but *he* got his hand shaken by Sir Francis Drake. A few tens of years later another ancestor helped destabilize Cromwell and his Roundheads, for their godlessness made them prone to superstition, and they were bedazzled by a bit of fake haunting. Dash on another hundred years and a distant uncle was popping in and out of the camp of the Jacobite Pretender as he marched into England during the revolt of '45, getting up to all sorts of mischief. And I'll admit to a bit of work on the other side, when one of my great-great-aunts, of a colonial family, spied on Lord Cornwallis during the American war.'

He sounded to Luis like a patterer in the New Cut, and perhaps he was overdoing it. But he seemed to be holding Albert's attention.

'At any rate here we are, sir, at the beginning of your own long reign, ready to put our talents at your service. Call us your Knights, sir. The Knights of Discorporea!'

That seemed to amuse Albert. 'Though I own there was no such goddess.'

'Well, there damn well should have been!'

Albert nodded. 'I have consulted with Her Majesty on this. We are agreed that it is best that such a – unique – resource as you and your men comprise should be kept secret, within as tight a circle as possible.' He glanced at Russell, who glared back; the Prime Minister hadn't said a word, and was evidently resentful at wasting his time on a whim of the Prince, as Luis guessed he saw it. 'Of course,' Albert went on, 'your operations must be carefully controlled at all times.' And here he looked to Radcliffe. 'It does seem to me in fact that your greatest value may be in countering similar agencies operating for our rivals and enemies – for I don't imagine you would argue that such a talent as yours is an exclusively English trait, Dr Hackett?'

'Indeed not, sir, and you are wise to point that out.'

'But, yes, we do accept your offer of service. How could we refuse?' He paced, grave, thoughtful. 'I have a dream, you know, of unity in Europe and beyond – a brotherhood between the great powers, yes, even between Britain and Prussia. But in this year of petty rebellions many of my own relatives have been ousted from their thrones.' He glared at the Prime Minister. 'There are debates at the highest level of government about the destabilizing effects of Palmerston's foreign policy, but for me this also causes personal distress – distress for my family, and for my ideals. I believe, you see, that we must all, men of honour, serve as best we can. I had it in one of my addresses – perhaps you remember it, Russell? "I conceive it to be the duty of every educated person closely to watch and study the time in which he lives, and, as far as he is able—"'

A grumpy Russell finished for him, '"To add his humble mite of individual exercise to further the accomplishment of what he believes Providence to have ordained."'

'Well said, sir,' said Hackett, a mite toady-ish in Luis's opinion.

'And that, it seems to me, is precisely what you are endeavouring to do today.' Albert grinned, big, bewhiskered, magnificent. 'Go forth then, my Knights, in the name of the Queen, Saint George, and the goddess Discorporea!'

Luis and the rest burst into applause. No other response seemed appropriate.

'After all that I rather think some refreshment is called for,' said Albert. One of the flunkeys at the back of the room melted away. 'And as to your next mission, good Doctor,' Albert continued, putting his arm around Hackett's shoulders and walking with him, 'after your very effective work among the Chartist rabble . . .'

Fraser Burdon nudged Luis's elbow. 'Albert may be keen, but it looks like his missus is less so.' He pointed.

Luis turned, and saw through an open doorway a young woman in a white dress, book in hand, walking through an adjoining room. She struck Luis as quite pretty, though she was short and rather plump, her blue eyes a little too large, her chin a little weak. Still young, yet – if it was *her* – she had become Queen just a month after her eighteenth birthday, and had already borne six children. She glanced through the door at Albert's party – Luis would have sworn she looked straight into his own eyes – and then turned away, evidently disapproving, and hurried on out of his sight.

Fraser grinned. 'She looks just like she does on the stamps.'

As the Prince and Hackett talked, as more servants arrived with trays of drinks and rather stodgy-looking snacks, Luis was aware that Radcliffe stood stock still in the middle of the room, eyeing each of the 'Knights' in turn, as if memorizing every freckle on their faces.

19

Ben shrieked, 'Go away!'

'I'm afraid I can't do that, Ben,' Lobsang said calmly.

Agnes, sitting with her sewing basket, suppressed a sigh, and steeled herself not to intervene.

Lobsang was standing over Ben and the cat-litter box. 'You've done a good job with the litter, Ben. Shi-mi will appreciate it. But now you have to get washed because it will be time for supper soon, and I'm making mushroom soup. Look, there's the pan on the hearth. You like mushroom soup.'

'I hate 'shroom soup!'

'That's not what you said yesterday.'

'You're stupid.'

Lobsang laughed, as if the boy – now five years old, two years after their arrival here at New Springfield – had made a witty debating point. 'That's arguable.'

'You're also ugly. Ugly an' stupid.'

'*That* is a question of taste.'

'You're not my real Dad, you stupid!'

'Well, now, Ben, we've been through that—'

'Hate you, hate you!' Ben tipped up the plastic box so the litter spilled over the kitchen floor. Then he ran out into the stockaded yard, banging the screen door behind him.

Lobsang stood and stared after him, arms folded. Then he turned to Agnes. 'You could have helped.'

'I'm helping by not helping.'

'You're the one with experience of these creatures.'

'Children, Lobsang. They're called children.'

'Anybody who could raise Joshua Valienté to fully functioning adulthood – well, reasonably fully functioning – knows what they're doing. So, then – if my prosthetic limb was faulty, I'd call in a prosthetics expert. My relationship with Ben is evidently faulty. You're the expert.'

'And you're the one who wanted to be a father. Well, now's your chance.' She made shooing motions with her arms. 'Go ahead – father!'

He shook his head and spread his hands, the way she remembered he used to when she had made him sweep the leaves in his troll reserve back in the Low Earths, and she'd said he'd done a shoddy job and made him start over. 'But I don't know where to begin. He hates me.'

'No, he doesn't.'

'He said so!'

'He's five years old. He's trying to jab at you. He barely knows *what* he's saying.' She sighed. 'Look, Lobsang. Try to find out what's really bothering him. That's all the advice I'm going to give you.'

'But—'

She held up a finger. 'And if you try to drag me into this I'll leave the room. Might even have one of my naps.'

'Oh, yes,' he said bitterly, 'your *strategic* naps.'

'This is what you wanted,' she repeated. 'This is why we're here.'

Lobsang heaved a sigh. 'Well, I'd better get a broom to pick up this litter. At least I'm good at *that*.'

'Leave some for Ben to clean up. Just to make the point . . .'

Two years into their New Springfield experience, they were both still learning – just like, Agnes supposed, the Irwins and the Todds and the Bells and the Bambers and all the other folk who'd been here long before they showed up. But that was the plan. Lobsang, who had been observing the pioneering of the Long Earth for years, now wanted to try it out for himself, as 'George'.

Of course the New Springfielders had already achieved a lot. They knew about hygiene, for instance. They even made their own soap, from animal fat and potash from their charcoal burners. They had started making their own clothes as the stock they had brought from the Datum slowly wore out; they gathered hemp, flax, cotton, and wool from their own sheep and now Lobsang's, which they were learning to card, spin and weave. They even made foul-smelling candles from the fat of the pigs that had gone wild in the forest. And they were utterly at ease with the stepwise extensions of their world, their landscape – most of the time, in fact, unless there was a barn dance or a town meeting on, much of the population was worlds away from the old core of the founders' community. It was a way of relaxed, natural living in the Long Earth that Agnes had never witnessed before – and she imagined that the children growing up here, including Ben, would take it all utterly for granted.

In terms of their pioneering, they did cheat, as Agnes had slowly learned.

You saw few old folk, few very sick. They were lucky that one of the community, Bella Sarbrook, had some medical training, but when people got old, or seriously ill – or in one case when a couple had borne a disabled child – they tended to drift off back to the more sophisticated facilities of the Low Earths. Conversely the home-grown medicines and toiletries and stuff were supplemented by a trickle of produce from the Low Earths or Valhalla. Agnes didn't see anything wrong with that. As long as the Low Earth cities existed, why not use them?

Lobsang meanwhile was running experiments in farming. With the help of the neighbours he'd cleared some of the old fields the first settlers had laid out, and ploughed the land with his horses and cattle and some human labour, and had tried out his first crops: wheat in the lighter soil, oats and potatoes where the ground was heavier. The first wheat harvest, small as it was, had drawn curious volunteers, to reap with handheld sickles, to thresh and winnow. While not primarily here to farm themselves, the adults saw it all as good fun, and 'George's' small farm as a welcome addition to the education of their kids.

Of course it wasn't all newly invented. Lobsang was very impressed when Oliver Irwin showed 'George' a complete set of the Whole Earth Catalog, downloaded on to a wind-up e-reader. Lobsang had copied it into his own library, which was a row of mostly physical books kept in the gondola, including Defoe's *Robinson Crusoe*, Verne's *Mysterious Island*, Twain's *A Connecticut Yankee at the Court of King Arthur*, Stewart's *When Earth Abides*, Miller's *A Canticle for Leibowitz*, Dartnell's *The Knowledge*, and miniaturized bound magazine sets including early volumes of *Scientific American*, a pre-electronic *Encyclopedia Britannica*, even a facsimile of the first encyclopedia ever published, by Diderot in the seventeenth century. 'Encyclopedias are hedges against the fall of civilization,' Lobsang had said to Agnes, only slightly pompously. He seemed to have a long-term dream of building a civilization from scratch right here in the wilderness, like Verne's stranded travellers in *Mysterious Island*, all the way up to electricity generators and copper phone wires – and maybe going further, coming up with a kind of portable 'civilization kit' to give to the combers and their kind, to ensure the lessons painfully learned over ten thousand years of human progress weren't lost as humanity scattered across the Long Earth. Lobsang couldn't help but think big.

For now, however, he seemed content with the watermill he was planning down by the creek to grind his wheat. One step at a time.

Ben meanwhile had already started at the informal local school, hosted in the open air, or in one shelter or another, on one world or another. There were only a dozen kids, of all ages from four or five up to fifteen or sixteen. Marina Irwin, mother of Nikos, was the nearest thing to a head teacher, and she had them work and play together as a group, the older ones helping the little ones, and she drafted in adults to teach specific classes, two or three kids at a time. A lot of the focus was on practical skills, from how to pick wild mushrooms, and using the stars to find your way home in the dark, to weapons and hunting classes for the older kids. But there was culture: Marina had a copy of a complete Shakespeare that she made good use of.

As for the adult world, Agnes had soon learned there was no formal law out here. Nobody had a desire to refer disputes to the Datum US government, which in theory still operated its 'Aegis' policy, enforcing the laws of the US across all the nation's Long Earth footprints out to infinity. On the other hand there was no sign of the frontier justice you got in some remote communities. Many Corn Belt towns, for instance, had appointed sheriffs. Here, disputes were solved by mediation: by agreed compensation, with feasts that re-established friendships. None of that was as easy as it sounded, and it all required a hell of a lot of talking. But in such a small group the opposite to forgiveness and reconciliation was a long-standing feud, and nobody wanted that. People spent a *lot* of time talking through stuff out here – but then, they had the time to spare. And of course if the dispute couldn't be resolved one or other party could just step away. There would always be room for that final solution . . .

But right now, Agnes didn't want to leave.

Alone, she looked around, at this home they were fixing up. They'd got on with it quicker than she might have expected. This room, which Agnes called the parlour, had been done out by Lobsang like a small Buddhist temple, with a polished wooden floor, the walls coated with panels brought from the Low Earths and ornately decorated with red, gold, and splashes of green. All this was a long way from Agnes's own Catholic tradition, but she liked the sense of symmetry and order, the scent of incense, and the smile on the face of the statue of the Buddha – quite a contrast to the anguished expression of the crucified Christ. And little Ben liked the bright colours, which he said were 'Christmassy'.

They were happy here, Agnes decided. On balance. Life, as ever, was far from perfect. Sometimes all Agnes could see were the problems. But she had the wider perspective to see that overall, as best she could judge, the people here were getting it more right than wrong. Figuring out a new way of living, based on the long experience of mankind, and their own sturdy common sense. If this was why Sally Linsay had brought them here, it was a good choice.

The only problem was that Agnes was still having trouble sleeping.

She heard voices. Lobsang and Ben returning. She focused on her sewing.

20

IN THE COLD of Datum London, in dusty archives, in badly heated hotel rooms hunched over elderly tablets connected to an unstable web, Nelson Azikiwe continued to follow the tangled story of the Valienté family.

Followed it back more than two centuries, to 1852, and New Orleans . . .

Luis Valienté had never known a city like 'Orlins', as he heard the natives call it. But then, before his first entanglement with Oswald Hackett and his Knights of Discorporea four years ago, he had visited few cities away from his native London: Manchester where he had played a few shows before mobs of mill workers who made Lambeth's costermongers look like refined gentlemen, and Paris where he had wasted one particularly lavish booking fee on a week of rather bewildered holiday-making.

Now, in the August of 1852, as he and Oswald Hackett and Fraser Burdon strolled through the city, heading for their lodgings with their bits of luggage, he had trouble sorting out his impressions. The heat and the noise, the music and the smiling faces, the stink of the river and the sheer *chaos* of it all – as a dowdy Englishman he had never felt more out of place in his life.

'It is like Paris,' he said at last, reaching for one of the few comparison references he had available. 'In a way. Look at the architecture; some of it is quite elegant. Spacious and shady

– adapted to the climate, of course. And then there's all the French you hear.'

'To me it's more like London,' Burdon said. 'Take away the nice weather and ladle on a few centuries of soot, and you might have the East End.'

'Pah,' said Hackett, dismissive. 'To me the whole town is like one ongoing riot. The noise, the colour, the music that blares everywhere – if I could remember my Dante I would probably map it on to one circle of hell or another. One must always remember that none of this existed four hundred years ago. And this is slaving country, and never forget it – why, the largest slave market in America is here. A land of slave-holders and slave-hunters with their Bowie knives and their revolvers, and their bloodhounds and their scourging and their lynching.'

Burdon frowned. 'We don't need the piety, thank you, Hackett; we've had enough of that from the Prince these last four years. We're here, aren't we? We know the job – the mission, as ye call it. Let's stick to our purpose.'

'Yes,' Hackett said somewhat coldly, 'let's.'

They turned on to a grand and very lively street called the Vieux Carré, crowded with bars, hotels, cafés and establishments with less obvious identities which it seemed to Luis that Hackett knew rather too well. For all his pompous lecturing, Luis remembered what Hackett had told him of his rakish exploits as a young Waltzer. Hackett certainly had the look to fit in here; he was wearing a broadcloth coat, an embroidered waistcoat, a fine shirt, and a silk neckerchief. Fraser Burdon and Luis, both shabbily dressed by comparison, looked on rather enviously.

Luis was not very surprised when the establishment to which Hackett led them for their overnight lodging, on a slight rise at the heart of this district, turned out to be a bawdy house. It was something like a town house realized in an overwrought classical style

– and it was chock full of young women, remarkably beautiful in Luis's eyes, all elegantly dressed.

'My word!' said Burdon, staring around. 'It's like a display of exotic birds at Albert's blessed Exhibition.'

'But,' Hackett murmured, 'bawdy houses are often surprisingly sympathetic to the cause we serve today.'

He brought them into the presence of the madam of the house. Luis never learned her name. She was small, a little plump, her jet black hair streaked with grey and tied back neatly. Her complexion was dark; no doubt she was a product of the great mixing-up of peoples in this port – but aside from that, with her stature and her air of bossiness she reminded Luis uncomfortably of an older version of the Victoria he had glimpsed at Windsor.

She smiled at Hackett. 'You're the conductors, sir?'

'We are. And you have our passengers, with their tickets?'

'I do indeed. This way.'

Burdon cocked an eyebrow at this exchange. Both he and Luis by now recognized the peculiar jargon of the Underground Rail Road: a rail system that did not exist literally, but whose 'passengers' were escaping slaves.

The madam led them through gaudy reception halls. Luis never glimpsed the back rooms where the true and grubby trade of the place was transacted. The madam's own office was a kind of drawing room, not pretentiously decorated, but with a desk heaped with papers and studded with ink wells, a glass cabinet in one corner with a range of medicines – and, ominously, a rack of guns, from revolvers to hunting rifles, all looking well tended and no doubt loaded.

And a secret panel at the back of the office, opened by a catch worked by one of the madam's polished fingernails, revealed another room, lit by a single gas lamp, entirely enclosed. The madam allowed the three of them inside, then backed out gracefully, closing the door behind them.

Luis glanced around. After the brilliance of the day the gaslight seemed dim indeed. There were no other doors, no windows, no furniture. But he could guess why they were here. This entirely sealed-up room was a gateway to the widdershins world, a place through which Waltzers could pass without fear of observers.

Hackett grinned at them both. 'Leave your bags here; you'll not be needing them where we're going. I just want to make sure our precious cargo is safe, for we leave tonight, with our friends, on the *River Goddess* bound upstream for Memphis. All set? If you need a puking pill I've got some to spare. Widdershins we go. One, two, three—'

The site of this parallel New Orleans struck Luis as not much different from the regular version – given the absence of all the works of mankind, of course – and he wondered how dissimilar the details were of the braiding of the great river as it poured sluggishly across this flat, marshy landscape. But Luis's feet were dry, more or less; the slight rise on which the bawdy house stood evidently persisted here, a scrap of ground marginally higher and drier than the rest.

Still, they were all sweating immediately.

And Hackett slapped his neck. 'Got you, you swine! Further north of here, you know, there are all sorts of exotic beasts to be seen – and to run from. Giant camels, horses the size of big dogs, cave bears, lions: critters from which modern Americans have evidently been spared acquaintance by the veil of extinction. But here, nothing but mosquitoes, and they seem to persist everywhere. Oh, and alligators; don't go near the water.' He pointed west. 'There are our passengers.'

Luis saw what appeared to be an old army field tent, battered, roomy, its heavy canvas held in place with ropes and pitons driven into the soggy ground. A small fire smoked near an open doorflap, and shirts and trousers and greyed underwear were laid out on the spine of the tent, drying out after a washing.

And in the shade of a kind of porch, under a spread-out mosquito net, two men were sitting. They were both black. As the three Englishmen approached, one of them whipped aside the mosquito net, stood, and faced them armed with a kind of improvised club. The other, evidently older, stayed sitting, his back against a heap of blankets.

Hackett spread his hands. 'It's only me, Simon. Oswald Hackett at your service. Well, who else would it be? And these two fine fellows are here to help you make your journey north, beginning tonight.'

The younger man lowered the club and smiled. 'Mr Hackett. So good to see you again.'

Luis was surprised at the man's accent: well spoken, even refined, at least given Luis's limited experience of American intonation. But this man, Simon, had evidently been used brutally; one cheek bore an ugly-looking scar, badly stitched, and the opposite eye was closed by swollen flesh.

The older man, meanwhile, his hair and ragged beard streaked with grey, barely stirred.

There was a round of introductions. It turned out that Simon and the other man were grandson and grandfather respectively.

Hackett bent to speak to the old fellow, doffing his hat. 'And you, Abel. Do you remember me? I carried you over from New Orleans.'

'F'om tha' cat house,' Abel said. 'Haw haw! Shoulda lef' me there and the gels wudda finish' me off.'

'Then I came back with Simon . . . You remember?'

'Sho I 'member, Massa Hackett.'

'Please don't call me massa.'

'No, massa.'

'Come,' Simon said. 'Sit in the shade with us. We have root beer and I can brew a coffee . . .'

It was a strange gathering that they made in the shade of that antiquated tent, Luis thought, three Englishmen and two runaway slaves, drinking root beer and eating hard-tack biscuits – five men all alone in this widdershins world, he supposed, save for the cave bears and the dog-sized horses (which he wasn't entirely sure he believed in), and any other Waltzer who might be popping back and forth for his or her own purposes.

Hackett was quick to reassure the men that the plan he had made for their escape was still in place. 'We steam upstream as far as Memphis on the *Goddess*, and then change. At Cairo we change again and steam up the Ohio to Evansville, Louisville, Portsmouth. Then it's overland to Pittsburgh—'

Simon smiled. 'And across Mason and Dixon's Line to the free states.'

'And you're home and dry,' Hackett said.

'If all goes well.'

'Much can go wrong,' Hackett conceded. 'I wouldn't hide that from you. On the steamer you'll be huddled close to the boiler; it will be warm enough for you, and you'll be pitched about in the dark. And you may know that the slave-catchers nowadays have a way of smoking out the holds of boats like this, to be sure there are no stowaways. We have gear for you agin that threat – oilskin hoods, and wet towels for your mouths. But to ride a steamer is still better than walking all the way to the free states through this widdershins world, which is the only alternative. And we three will be with you all the way; we can always Waltz you out of trouble, wherever we are.'

Simon said, 'I could work in the open if you like. Pose as your servant. I can play the poor ignorant, like Grandfather. Roll my eyes and blubber for Jesus's mercy.'

'I've no doubt you can, and most convincingly. But you're runaways, Simon. And everyone knows how the Rail Road works; they'll be looking out for you all the way up the river. Why, given the Fugitive Slave Law the slave-catchers have the power to cross the Line itself, and the law says they're not to be impeded in their filthy work, even in free state territory. They even work in cities like Boston and Philadelphia, I'm told.'

'True, is true,' murmured the old man. 'Tha's why I'm a'goin' all'a way to Canada. Queen Victoria's Promised Land. Follow th' drinking gourd to th' North Star.'

Hackett nodded. 'That's it.' He glanced at Luis. 'The "drinking gourd" is the Big Dipper, which points to the pole star.'

'I'm a'goin' to shake the paw of th' British Lion, yes suh.'

'Yes, you are. But until we're home free you just stay out of sight as much as you can.'

Luis thought Simon, meanwhile, looked as nervous at the whole prospect as he might have been himself had their roles been reversed – as he had a right to be, of course.

Burdon said, 'Forgive me for saying this, Simon. You aren't quite—'

'What you expected?' Simon grinned easily, but showed cracked teeth. 'My background is somewhat unusual. Whether you judge that my subsequent experiences have been the worse for me because of that is up to you . . .' He sipped his coffee. 'As a little boy I was clever and good-looking – that's not bragging, consider it a fair description of the merchandise. I was befriended by the younger son of the master of the house – this was a cotton plantation in the wilds of Louisiana, with a hundred or so head of slaves – when you're children, you see, even such categories as slave and master blur into insignificance compared with the vividness of the game of the day. I was four years old.

'Well, when Alexander – the young master – began his schooling, he was something of a restless soul, and his father, observing I was bright and a calming influence on him, brought me into the house as a companion. Even by then I was aping the masters' speech, you see, and *they* would probably say "aping" is an appropriate term. But they dressed me up and encouraged me to speak well and mind my manners, and I became a study companion for Alexander – only at home, of course, never at school or beyond the bounds of the house. And in the process, naturally, I learned a good deal myself. I was brighter than Alexander but not markedly so; of course I knew not to outshine him overmuch in our shared work, but to let him think he could beat me at it – as often, indeed, he could. I was a happy child, sirs, unaware of my unholy indenture. It shames me to say that I was even unperturbed when my mother and my little brothers and sisters were sold on by the master – though later I would be enraged to learn from the other slaves that it was because my mother had refused the master's lustful designs.

'This went on as I grew up. Past the age of twelve or so Alexander was increasingly distracted by the company of his own sort, particularly the young ladies, but I was still useful as a companion at home. And I was given work around the house – and not just serving and cleaning and so on; past sixteen I was entrusted with some routine aspects of the plantation's accounts. It amused the master to have me wait at table for his fancier friends: a skinny slave who had the manners and the speech of an English lord, as he liked to boast, if inaccurately.'

He seemed nostalgic as he spoke of these times, though to be treated as a pet, a toy, however kindly, struck Luis as ghastly.

'Well, all things have their time. Alexander reached the age of eighteen and was sent off to a fancy college in New York. As for me, as I grew older I had no place in the household. A slave boy of twelve with fine manners is cute, but a man of twenty seems ever on the verge of insolence.'

Hackett said, 'And so he was turned out of the house. Just like that, after a lifetime of decent living, even if he was wholly owned. Cast down among the field hands.'

'You may imagine my fate,' Simon said, his eyes averted. 'To those men it was as if a white man had been cast among them. I was beaten, stripped, robbed of all I had, in the first hours. I fought back, oh, I fought back, but I was alone.'

'No,' Abel said now, stirring. 'Not 'lone. Had me, his gran'pappy. But his daddy dead. His mommy sol'. Other fam'ly kep' away. I fought 'em. Tha's my gran'chile, I told 'em. But I's old, suh, old and broken . . .'

'All of this I could have borne,' Simon said now, eyes closed, his voice steely. 'I would have grown stronger. I would have found my place. But then I learned that the master decided I was a trouble-maker – rather than the victim of the trouble, you see – and he intended to sell me on.' He opened his eyes and looked straight at Hackett. 'And that I could not bear, sir. I have seen the auction block – the slaves stripped naked male and female, grease rubbed into the skin to make it shine, the coarse inspection by the potential owners – the language of the stockyard.'

'You cun see why we's run,' Abel said.

Hackett grasped their hands, both of them; Luis thought he had tears in his eyes. 'Oh, I see it, sirs, I see it. And we will see you safe in the free states – where your learning and character, Simon, will be a boon, not a curse. Now, Burdon, Valienté – a word on tactics.'

He led the two of them outside. Luis found himself swatting mosquitoes immediately.

'Slavery!' Hackett began. 'What an institution. To own a human being from cradle to grave, to use as you wish – and then you own the children too, and the grandchildren off into perpetuity, like the offspring of some prize racehorse. I don't know which is the crueller – a life of grinding work, such as has broken poor Abel, or to be given a bit of kindness, a bit of civilization, then to have it arbitrarily swept away, like poor Simon.'

Burdon grunted. 'It's a devilish business either way if you're on the receiving end of it, and no wonder they will take such risks to escape it. Why, I've heard of fellows posting themselves to Philadelphia in boxes and crates! But let's not be too pious, Parson Hackett. After all, we British brought the institution to these shores.'

150

'Yes, but at least we're trying to put it right now, man. You know that Albert himself encourages us to work closely with the Underground Rail Road, even while the government has to turn a blind eye for fear of offending our American cousins. The slave-hunters with their whips and guns actually have the law on their side, of course, and a strong buck like Simon there might be worth a thousand dollars or more. Odd thing for a prince to be involved in, you might think – a secret network of safe houses and transport routes, and communication by nods and winks. But Albert did take great delight when freed slaves promenaded around his Exhibition, causing a few purple faces among the exhibitors from the American South!' He glanced over his shoulder. 'Which isn't to say that, while the assignment we're taking on is a noble one, it won't be difficult. You can see how we're fixed. Poor old Abel will be a burden. Whereas Simon—'

'Raised above his station,' Burdon said. 'He's going to be too clever by half, all the damn way to Pittsburgh.'

Hackett glared at him, disgusted. 'And is that how you think of him – even you? Well, thank God that in the free states there is a place even in America where a man like that can never be called "above his station".'

Now Simon called over, politely enough. 'Dr Hackett? My grand-father is asking for you. Wonders if Prince Albert has made any new speeches.'

'At once, at once.' And Hackett walked off to the tent.

Burdon growled to Luis, 'Well, I'll do my duty to Queen, country and my fellow man, and it pleases me to put one across those slave-catchers – though I'm getting deuced sick of Hackett. The man doesn't have a monopoly on conscience, y'know. But putting that aside, Valienté – what are your plans after this jaunt is done?'

Luis shrugged. 'Perhaps see more of America. First time I've travelled further than France.'

'How do you fancy making a bit of money? More than a bit, actually.'

Luis frowned. 'You're not talking about anything illegal, are you?'

'Of course not. Just listen. Even you must have heard of the Gold Rush. In the last few years half the population of this benighted young nation has scarpered for the hills of California, shovels in hand, drooling for gold.'

'And most of them have earned nothing but a ruined back, and poverty.'

'True enough. But a handful have become rich – very rich.'

Luis shrugged. 'Good luck to them. What's it to us? I'm no prospector.'

Burdon rolled his eyes. 'But I am. Studied rocks at college, remember? And besides, we don't need to be prospectors. Think about it, man. God! – why are we Waltzers always so blind to the possibilities before us? Suppose we picked one of those prospectors, one of the more successful fellows. We investigate his claim – study his reports, his maps. Even go see the shafts, the mine workings themselves, if we can get close enough. And then—'

Luis saw it in a flash. 'We step widdershins. And there's the same mine, the same seam—'

'As unworked as if America had never been peopled at all, and us with the maps in our hands. Of course there are practical difficulties, the worst being we can't carry iron-headed spades and picks across. But we can get around that. Why, we could just pick a site where we can pan it from the streams. And we'll have it all to ourselves, with none of the risks and uncertainties of prospecting, for all *that* will have been done for us. Now – tell me what's unethical.'

Luis had to grin. 'Feels like cheating, somehow.'

'I know! But it's not! Isn't it grand? We've spent four years already following Hackett around on these humanitarian chores of his. Don't you think, for all the risks we run on stunts like this, we deserve something more for ourselves than occasional pats on the head from old sausage-eater Albert? Not to mention the lingering suspicion that always hangs over us . . .'

Luis knew what he meant. He thought of Radcliffe, the secretive agent who was never far from Albert's side in their presence, and at their meetings with representatives of the government. While Albert, something of a visionary dreamer, enthused about the strange powers and benevolent deeds of 'my Knights', as he called them, others were evidently a good deal more suspicious of a bunch of such elusive characters, with access and influence in such high places. Maybe it was all too good to last; maybe it would end in tears for them, some day, and Luis, nearly thirty years old now, should think about his own future.

'I'll consider it,' he said.

Burdon slapped his own forehead. 'Ah, man! Don't consider, *do*.'

But Luis would not be swayed, not on the spur of the moment.

They returned to the tent, where Hackett, reading from a bit of paper, repeated in sonorous tones a speech of Albert's on slavery: '"I deeply regret that the benevolent and persevering exertion of England to abolish that atrocious traffic in human beings, at once the desolation of Africa and the blackest stain upon civilized Europe, has not as yet led to any satisfactory conclusion . . ."'

On old Abel this seemed to have the effect of an incantation. He grasped Simon's wrist with one arthritic hand. 'Simon, you listen to dem wuds. "De des'la-shun of Afric' . . . de blackes' stain." Don' you forget dem wuds, don't evvuh.'

21

THERE WAS SOMETHING wrong with the world.

Three years after her arrival here with Lobsang, Ben and Shi-mi, that was Agnes's definitive view of Earth West 1,217,756.

Oh, the people were fine. And it was the people who mattered in the end; Agnes had always known that, and the rest was just a backdrop.

But the world was weird.

Take the old Poulson place. In the beginning it had been Nikos Irwin, with his dog, who had spent his waking hours in that dilapidated swap house on the far side of Manning Hill. Nikos and his buddies seemed to be growing up now and losing interest, but their place was being taken by a new generation, including Ben and Nikos's little sister Lydia. Agnes had heard the lurid ghost stories, and dismissed them, but she could sense *something* odd every time she went down there, usually in search of Ben. Strange scents, elusive in the forest air. Once, a peculiar greenish light that had come emanating from the back of the house – only a glimpse, there and gone again. In Agnes's last incarnation, her own fatal illness had begun with a hard lump on her skin that didn't belong. The Poulson house was the same, she thought. It was a flaw, something wrong, something unwelcome, that didn't belong in this world. She hadn't yet decided to ban Ben from the place – she dreaded the battle that would follow if she tried – but she was moving towards it.

Above all, Agnes discovered, she hated not to be able to tell the time, house rules or not. Since she'd arrived she'd never felt as if she was sleeping properly here. The dawn always came *too early*, no matter what time of year it was. Sometimes she sensed that others had the same feeling, Marina Irwin for instance when she came round for morning coffee: a certain tiredness, a vagueness, muddled thinking. But without a decent watch Agnes couldn't tell if her sleep patterns actually were drifting, or by how much.

Even the animals seemed distressed. The furballs would emerge from their burrows and their holes in the trees at the wrong time. Sometimes the big birds would charge around the forest almost randomly, screeching like eagles.

She had considered asking Lobsang for access to her internal timers, or the clocks in the gondola. She kept putting it off; she felt as if that would be the beginning of the end, the fracturing of the dream.

Lobsang meanwhile wouldn't comment on any of this. Instead 'George' just kept his head down. He worked on his farm despite the vagaries of the weather, strengthened the stockade around their plot, fixed the roof of the house they were extending one room at a time, pulled weeds from his flower beds and cultivated his kitchen garden, and tended his animals and crops. He was sociable enough. He joined in the hunts. And, comically, he was trying to learn the fiddle so he could play at barn dances, filling the evening air on Manning Hill with a sound like an arthritic warthog.

Agnes supposed that in a way his behaviour represented a victory for her. He had revived her in the first place in order to provide a balance to his own tendencies towards omniscience and omnipotence. But now, and maybe it was typical of Lobsang and his obsessiveness to go to extremes, he'd abandoned his old self entirely and had devoted himself completely to this new life as 'George', rooted in the soil of a remote Earth.

And he resolutely refused to think about anomalies in the world.

Even the occasional flashes they saw on the face of the moon didn't distract him from his concentration on pioneering mundanity.

Well, that wasn't enough for Agnes, not any more. She decided to do something about it.

Shi-mi came to see her as she struggled with her gadgetry in the yard, in the lee of the house, away from the prevailing wind on this bright spring day. She'd taken a plastic funnel from her kitchen store, hung it from a bracket, filled it with fine sand from the bank of the creek, and allowed the sand to run out into a bucket. Now she was sitting on the ground and measuring her own pulse as the sand ran down.

If this world wouldn't allow clocks to work, she'd decided, she would damn well build her own. Never mind electronics, or even clockwork which was almost as much of a mystery to her. She'd gone back to basics.

The cat walked up somewhat stiffly, lay down beside her and inspected the rig. 'If I may ask, Agnes – what on Earth are you doing?'

'Can't you tell? I'm making an hourglass. And I'm missing Joshua. *He'd* put together something for me in a couple of hours, in a polished wooden case, probably . . .'

The cat licked her paws. 'There are a number of ways to tell the time. By a simple sundial for instance. Though that would take some weeks, at least, to calibrate.'

'I intend to do that too. But I want some other way, independent of the sun. I want to measure the length of the day. Shi-mi, I know this sounds dumb.'

'I travelled months on twains run by US Navy grunts. Believe me, nothing you say about mechanical matters will sound dumb to me. And I do know why you need to do this. We spoke of it before—'

'I think there's something wrong with time here,' Agnes blurted.

156

'The days are *too short* – or maybe too long. I don't know. All I *do* know is I'm having trouble sleeping, and always have had. And as all our watches and clocks are either back home in Madison West 5 or out of bounds—'

'My internal clocks are not accessible to me either.'

'—and I don't want to ask Lobsang because I think it would upset him if I started breaking the rules around here, I need to make some other kind of measurement. I figure that if I can measure an hour accurately, say, then I'll stay awake for a day and a night, from dawn to dawn, and just count the hours, count how often I have to empty the bucket. It's crude but better than nothing.'

'Noon to noon would be better. Easier to mark accurately. A sundial would help you with that. And it may be more precise to have smaller buckets, measuring half- or quarter-hours . . . Or you could use both, to cross-check the measurements. But how can you be sure your hourglass measures a true hour in the first place?'

'That's my problem, all right.' She showed the cat her wrist, her thumb pressed on a vein. 'My resting pulse has always been pretty steady, fifty beats a minute.'

'A strong heart.'

'Yes. I assume Lobsang will have replicated that when he, umm, remade me.'

'That is a very uncertain baseline.'

Agnes found it hard not to be sarcastic to a talking cat. 'I suppose you have a better way?'

'Yes. Build a pendulum.'

'A what?'

'A simple pendulum. A thread suspended from a beam, support-ing a weight. The length of the thread determines the period of the swing. A length of thirty-nine inches will give you a period of two seconds, almost exactly. That's if the pull of gravity here is the same as on the Datum, and when we arrived we measured that, among other parameters . . . A longer length would give you a longer period, more accuracy. You could use a reliable reference like that to build from. Make sand cups to measure a minute, combine them to get five minutes, thirty—'

Impulsively Agnes leaned over, cupped Shi-mi's face, and kissed the top of her head. 'Cat, you're a genius.'

But Shi-mi shrank back from her touch.

Agnes immediately forgot about her high school science experiments. Shi-mi had never reacted like that before, not ever. 'Shi-mi? What is it?' She picked the cat up, though Shi-mi wriggled in faint protest, and inspected her body, felt her limbs – and probed her belly, where she found hard masses. 'Are you ill?'

'I am old, Agnes,' the cat said, lying in her arms. 'Or so I have been programmed to become. My body swarms with nanotech agents, ageing me day by day. And because I am old I am ill. I suffer from a meticulously simulated arthritis, and various of my organs have problems. A remarkable feat of artifice.'

'Does it hurt?'

The cat said nothing.

'Well, would you like something to be done?' After only three years here, Agnes had not yet thought hard about her own future, the years when it would start to become odd if she did not show signs of age. She did know Lobsang had brought a suite of systems to allow them to adjust their appearance – but she also knew there were other options. 'You don't have to go through this. We could rebuild you. Fake your death. We could even call a twain and pretend it brought us another, younger cat.'

'No. I am myself,' Shi-mi said firmly. 'I have long memories. I was made by the Black Corporation as a mere technology demonstrator. But I sailed with Joshua and Lobsang on their first journey together, to the High Meggers and beyond. I travelled with Captain Maggie Kauffman to the ends of the Long Earth. In these last years I have been Ben's cat, nothing more, nothing less. I am not willing to discard all that.'

'You wouldn't have to. You'd still be yourself inside.'

The cat looked up at her, her peculiar LED-green eyes somewhat dimmed. 'I could not become some rowdy kitten and still be me. In any event there is no crisis, not yet, no decisions need be made. And I—'

But now Ben came running into the yard, and the conversation was ended.

Six years old, clothes scuffed, knees grubby, face a mud pack, hair a mess, Ben was a bundle of energy. He carried a basket of grapes. 'Agnes! Agnes! Look!' He held out his basket, and Agnes saw something gleam on his right arm, a kind of silver bracelet.

She put down the cat, carefully. 'What's that you've got there?'

'Grapes!'

'I can see that. On your arm.'

Hastily he hid the arm behind his back. 'Nothin'. Can I take the grapes in? Can I have some?'

'Come here, young man.' She held out her hand, palm up. 'Right hand please.'

Agnes's authoritative voice had been honed over two partial lifetimes dealing with children of all shapes, sizes and inner conditions, and Ben was nowhere near the most difficult she'd had to deal with. And now, clutching his grapes awkwardly, he walked up to Agnes and obediently stuck out his arm.

The bracelet was a little too big for him, and she slipped it off his wrist and over his hand easily. It was a simple loop of metal, evidently silver, evidently well made, and it was *heavy*; it had to be valuable. Price tags in dollars and cents didn't mean much here, but such items as this, usually brought out as heirlooms or tokens of weddings and whatnot, were prized.

Shi-mi murmured to her – too softly for the boy to hear; they still hadn't told Ben that Shi-mi was artificial. 'I've seen other children wearing such things. Rings, bangles.'

'I suppose I have too,' Agnes whispered back. 'I thought nothing of it.' She held out the bracelet. 'What do you make of it?'

Shi-mi licked it. 'High-grade silver,' she said. 'Very pure. Very finely manufactured, to very precise tolerances. This is machine-made; it didn't come out of some home workshop.'

'There's nothing like that here. The nearest to home-made jewellery we have are the reed brooches Bella Sarbrook makes in the fall.'

'Also no hallmark. So it doesn't appear to be of Datum or Low Earth origin either.'

'Then where—'

'Who ya talkin' to?'

'Nobody, honey. Just myself. Now, where did you get this, Ben? You're not in trouble. Just tell me. Was it the old Poulson place?'

'Uh huh.'

'Have you been down there again?'

'Uh huh,' he said reluctantly.

'In that cellar again no doubt. No wonder you're filthy. So who gave you this bracelet?'

'No one.'

'Then where did you get it?'

'Swap stuff.'

And Agnes's heart broke, just a little, for this was the first time she was aware of that Ben had deliberately lied to her. 'No, Ben. It wasn't in with the swap stuff. The swap stuff in that house is leaky saucepans and broken brooms and clothes people have grown out of. That's what the swap stuff is. Nobody puts lovely things like this in the swap stuff. So who gave it to you? Was it one of the other kids? Was it Nikos?' Her head spun briefly with ideas of theft, or some kind of cache left behind by the Poulsons, people she'd never met . . .

'Beetle man.'

The answer, totally unexpected, stunned her. 'What did you say?'

'Beetle man. He gave it. Nikos said it wasn't wrong.'

'Beetle man. What's the beetle man like?'

Ben grinned. 'Funny.'

She studied him, thinking hard. 'OK, Ben. Look, it's getting late. You run on in and wash your face now.' When he'd gone, she said to Shi-mi, 'When Lobsang comes in, he and I will be having a long chat. And tomorrow I'm going to the Poulson place myself. Without Ben, with Nikos. And with Lobsang, if I have to drag him by his prosthetic nose.' She tucked the bracelet into a pocket. Then she looked down, forcing a smile, and stroked Shi-mi's back. 'Now, shall we see how far we can get with this pendulum business? How long a string did you say – thirty-nine inches?'

22

I N THE MORNING Agnes left Ben playing with little Lydia in the care
of Marina Irwin.

Then Agnes, Lobsang and a shamefaced Nikos Irwin hiked across
Manning Hill to the old Poulson place. Nikos's dog Rio, elderly now
yet still puppyish, trotted alongside them, eager to explore, eager
to be involved. It was well after dawn on a relatively calm day; the
furball mammals had already finished their morning hunt, and
the forest was quiet in the lowland that sprawled below the hill.

'I can't believe you're involving me in this stuff,' Lobsang
grouched. 'I've got potatoes to top, beets to water—'

'What "stuff"?'

'Ben's a little boy, Agnes. Little boys go exploring. Worming their
way into things. Boys will be boys.'

'Oh, George—'

'Of course if they find some junk yard like this Poulson place
they're going to rummage through it.'

'George, Ben had a solid silver bracelet. If it was a bracelet at
all. If you ask around,' and since yesterday Agnes *had* been asking
around, 'half the kids in New Springfield are walking about with
such things. Every parent thinks it's just them. Everyone is a bit
embarrassed, I think, that their kid found such valuable stuff in the
Poulson place – stuff that's rightfully not theirs. Generally they kept
it quiet. Like you did until now, didn't you, Nikos?'

'Yes, ma'am.'

Lobsang said, 'You know, Agnes, people here are different from the urban types you and I are used to. They don't get to deal with strangers every day of their lives. They don't have cameras in their faces the whole time, a government taxing them, corporations endlessly modelling their behaviour so they can sell them stuff. Out here, you keep yourself to yourself.'

'Well, maybe. But, whatever the reason, nobody put together the pattern, did they? That these precious items are just flowing out of that ruined house like it's a closing-down sale in a jewellers' store. But *you* know the truth, don't you, Nikos?'

'Ma'am, the silver beetles are harmless—'

'Don't tell me,' Agnes said. 'We'll see for ourselves soon enough. But they're odd – yes? Something out of the ordinary. Out of place, even considering we're on a jungle world a million steps from the Datum.'

'Yes, ma'am.'

'And *you* took little kids down there, kids as young as Ben and your own sister.'

Nikos shrugged, uncomfortable, but with a trace of defiance. 'Yes, ma'am. But I've been going down there for years myself. They were safe with me. *I* was always safe.'

'He has a point, Agnes,' Lobsang said, annoyingly.

Agnes snapped, 'Tell me later when I figure out how much harm has been done.'

They came to the Poulson house, with its half-finished, broken-down stockade, the abandoned fields where saplings sprouted enthusiastically, and the house itself, whitewash peeling, an old swing on the porch choked by a vigorous vine. Only the door looked as if it had been recently used, some of the litter on the porch kicked aside to allow access.

Agnes asked, 'So, Nikos, do we go in the door?'

'You need to come round back.'

At the rear of the house was a pit, roughly dug into the thin strip of ground between the house itself and the stockade. It looked maybe eight feet deep. The ground around it was clear of the immature ferns that choked the rest of the area.

Lobsang looked into the pit. 'A cellar? But it's obviously unfinished. And there's a hole in the side wall.' He glanced at Nikos. 'Leading to what?'

'I thought you wanted me to show you, not tell you,' Nikos said with a trace of cheek. He turned to his dog. 'Rio, down. Rio – stay.' The dog, panting, curled up in a bit of shade, tongue out, watching the action. Nikos ruffled her head. 'She'll be asleep in a minute.' He slipped his pack off his back, opened it, and pulled out a smaller sack. It was lumpy, as if filled with rocks, and he tied this to his belt. Then he faced the adults. 'Ready?' He looked at Agnes. 'You're not scared, are you?'

'Don't get cocky,' Agnes said. 'Nikos, why don't you lead? I'll go second. George, you can be rear gunner.'

'Who put you in charge?'

'You did twenty years ago, when you brought me back,' she said softly, with an eye on Nikos. 'So, did you bring the flashlights?'

The passage down the sloping shaft that led from the 'cellar' was easy enough. In the years they'd been coming down here Nikos and his little buddies had dug in hand- and footholds.

But both Lobsang and Agnes were astonished when they climbed stiffly out of the shaft, and found themselves standing in a long, low chamber, lit only by their flashlights: a floor of trampled dirt, a smooth roof supported by pillars of rock or dirt. All this was evidently deep underground.

Agnes asked, 'What is this place?'

'I don't know,' Nikos said. 'Something to do with the silver beetles. I call it the Gallery. Because it's like a gallery in a big museum in a picture book my Mom used to read with me when I was little.'

He sounded different now, Agnes thought, in this echoing space, his face half-shadowed in the light of the flashes. Not so ashamed of the stunts he'd pulled. More like he was proud of what he'd found. Well, maybe he should be, she thought. She supposed he should have told people about this, but to have kept his nerve and go exploring in the first place was something.

'It's no gallery,' Lobsang said. 'Some kind of mine – and worked out, it looks like.' He splashed his light on the roof, the floor. 'An iron ore seam? This area's rich in ore, it's one reason New Springfield was planted here. But I'm not aware of any large-scale works here, apart from a few minor scrapes for the forges.'

'This is more than a minor scrape, George.'

'I can see that. So, Nikos, what about these silver beetles of yours?'

'Turn around,' said Nikos softly.

'What's that?'

'Turn around.'

Agnes and Lobsang turned, swinging their flashlights.

The beetle was here.

As their lights splashed on it, it unpeeled from the ground, standing on a cluster of hind limbs, its black carapace gleaming with silver insets, and semi-transparent sacs of some kind of gas clustered on its exposed, greenish underside. It was the size of a human.

And a kind of face, half-hidden behind a silver mask, swivelled to consider them.

Agnes was astounded, overwhelmed. Whatever she had been expecting it hadn't been something so utterly alien. She shrank back, would have fled if Lobsang had not held her.

'Stay calm, Agnes.'

'I am calm, Lob— George. I *am* calm. What the hell is it?'

Lobsang held his hands up to show they were empty, and carefully walked around the creature.

The beetle stood passively before Nikos, who had unwrapped his pack to reveal chunks of rock of various sorts, some hard like granite, some softer sandstone. Boy and beetle were a silent tableau while Lobsang inspected them.

'I've known people who've travelled to the ends of the Long Earth,' Lobsang said softly as he walked. 'I've travelled pretty far myself. But I never heard of anything like this.'

Nikos grinned. 'There's plenty more where he came from.'

'How do you know it's a he?'

'I don't imagine Nikos does, for sure,' Agnes said testily.

'Agnes – just tell me what you see.'

'Like an insect,' she said immediately. 'It *is* like a beetle. That black shell stuff that covers it looks segmented. I can't count how many legs it's got. Legs, or arms. Maybe it's more like a centipede?'

'I don't think it matches any class of creature known on Earth. Or on the Long Earth, in any working-out of terrestrial evolution. Not even the intelligent crustaceans Maggie Kauffman found during her journey of exploration aboard the *Armstrong II*.'

'Something new, then,' Agnes said.

'Or something *not from here.* Not from any Earth. Damn it,' he said with sudden petulance, 'I don't want this to be happening. I don't want *mystery.* I wish you hadn't brought me down here!'

'You don't wish that at all, George.'

He sighed. 'OK. What about the silver?'

Agnes looked closely. 'I see . . . belts. A kind of sash, slung across its upper body. Little studs that seem to be stuck in the, umm, carapace. Things like bangles on some of the limbs – just like the bracelet Ben came home with. And that mask, of course. The head, George. The head looks almost human, apart from the eye.'

'Eerie, isn't it? Probably a coincidence of form.'

His lecturing tone irritated her. 'Well, *you* don't know anything at all, George, not yet. But maybe Nikos does. Nikos, can you talk to this thing?'

'No,' Nikos said firmly. 'I've never heard them make a sound. Except for a kind of scraping when they walk. That's their armoured bodies, I reckon. Some of them fly. Their backs open up and wings unfold. When they fly, they kind of rustle.'

Somehow, illogically, that detail made Agnes shudder.

Nikos said, 'But you see more of that in the Planetarium. Not here.'

Lobsang said, 'The Planetarium? . . . Never mind. Tell us later. OK, you don't speak to them. So tell me what you're doing with those rocks.'

'I swap them for the silver things. The rings, the pendants. We pick up bits of rock from the ground, all around the forest, and we bring them here. If we're doing it properly we have to show them where we found the rocks on a map. I say *map*. It's just a kind of scribble I drew once.'

'You're swapping rock samples for silver artefacts?'

'I guess you could call it that.'

Agnes asked, 'If you can't speak to them, how did you work all this out? The whole idea of the trade.'

Nikos seemed irritated at having to be quizzed like this, in his own little empire. 'It took a *long* time. It started with a bit of quartz I had in my pocket, one of the first times. I just showed it to one of them. After that—'

'Never mind,' Lobsang said. 'Agnes, I guess the truth is nobody told this smart kid that communication between such divergent life forms was impossible, so he just went ahead and did it anyhow. But why would they want rock samples? Well, because they want to do some more mining, I guess. They need to study the landscape. But to what end? . . .'

'Show me,' Agnes said. 'Show me how you do your trade.'

Nikos shrugged. He just held out a bit of rock. Silvery limbs unfolded from the creature's belly, took the rock, and handed over a small silver artefact in return, like a pendant.

Agnes said, 'George, do you see that? The limbs. They're not just sleeved. Some of those arms are metal.'

167

'Mmm. Maybe that dark chitin-like carapace is actually artificial too. This thing could be some kind of cyborg. Half biological, half mechanical.'

'In that case,' Agnes said, 'it should feel right at home with us.'

Nikos glanced at her, puzzled by that.

Lobsang asked, 'Nikos, you say there are more of these creatures?'

'Masses. The first time I came down here the whole place was swarming. You don't see that so much now. I think maybe they'd nearly finished what they were doing down here.'

'OK. But you also see them in this place you call a planetarium, right?'

'I mean, it's not really a planetarium—'

Agnes asked, 'Another name from your mother's picture books?'

'Yeah. Seems kind of babyish now, I guess.'

'Never mind that,' Lobsang said. 'Can you show us?' He looked around. 'What, is it an adjoining chamber, another shaft?'

'Oh, no. You have to step there.'

Agnes recoiled as he said that, instinctively. 'That's impossible. Everybody knows that. You can't step out of an underground chamber, a mine, a cellar.' She thought of Joshua, who had taught her most of what she knew about stepping.

Nikos twisted his face. 'Well, it's a funny kind of step. I'll have to show you.'

Agnes glanced at Lobsang. 'You think we should follow? If *he's* survived it – and for all we know Ben too – I guess we can.'

Lobsang said pointedly, 'But we don't have our Stepper boxes with us, remember, Agnes. We weren't expecting to travel stepwise today.'

That was true, but they both knew, and Nikos didn't, that they had Stepper technology integrated into their bodies. Agnes even had a peculiar little hatch in the small of her back where she could insert a potato.

But Nikos said, utterly without fear, 'You won't need them. I've got my box on my belt.' He held out his hands. 'Come on. I'll take you.'

The beetle creature curled back to the ground, scuttled away with a scrape of chitin and metal on rock – and, as it receded into the shadows, Agnes thought she saw it wink out of existence. Maybe stepping was somehow possible down here, then.

She grabbed Nikos's right hand. 'Let's do it. What can possibly go wrong?'

Lobsang, more reluctantly, took the boy's left hand.

And—

The sky was orange-brown and crowded with stars, some of them big enough to show as discs, some tinged faintly green against the general background. A sun, fat and red, sat on the horizon, its hull fragmented by refraction. The ground was crowded with blisters, like domes, some low and close to the ground, some taller and bulging at the top, like mushrooms, almost like trees. Agnes saw something like a river, what might be a road alongside it.

It was all quite baffling. She took a deep breath. The air was thin and smelled of insects, like crushed cockroaches, metallic, sour.

And silver beetles crawled everywhere, along that riverside road, across the open spaces between the bubble-things. If the one they had encountered in the Gallery had crossed over with them, it was already lost in the crowd. None of them seemed to be paying any attention to a fifteen-year-old boy, and two androids masquerading as a farmer and his wife.

Nikos grinned. 'This is the Planetarium. Isn't it great?'

Agnes looked at him, and then down at herself. The strange light from the sky made the skin of her hands look orange, washed out the green dye of her shirt, the blue of her jeans. She didn't fit here, not at all. The strangeness seemed to descend on her, all at once. She couldn't handle it. She felt herself shivering.

Lobsang immediately hugged her. 'Calm, Agnes.'

'I didn't sign up for this, Lobsang,' she whispered, away from the boy.

'Well, it was your idea to come here.'

'Only because I thought Ben had been down here before us. Oh, God, *Ben*, he must have been terrified if he got this far . . .'

'I don't think he was. He kept coming back, didn't he?'

'Where *are* we, Lobsang? Some distant part of the Long Earth? Have we been through one of Sally Linsay's soft places?'

'I don't think any Earth ever had a sky like this. We're far from home.'

'How far? The Long Mars? Mars has an orange sky, doesn't it?'

'But not all those stars.'

'How did we *get* here? How could a step—'

'There have been rumours.'

'Of what?'

'Flaws in the Long Earth. Places where stepping a certain kind of way can take you – elsewhere. There were stories of Jokers with this sort of property – one, called the Cueball, Joshua and I discovered ourselves. Not that we stuck around to find out *how* strange it was.'

Yes, Agnes thought. This is a flaw. Not just the Poulson house, the hole in the ground. The whole of Earth West 1,217,756. Just as had been her intuition, almost from the beginning. A flaw, something that shouldn't be here. Somehow it was all connected. It had to be.

'Interesting,' Lobsang said.

She managed to laugh. 'What, one thing in particular as opposed to all the rest?'

'The sky. Those green-tinged stars. On one side of the sky, not the other. Now, why that odd asymmetry?'

'Oh, for God's sake.' She pushed away Lobsang's arm. Nikos was watching her; she felt embarrassed by the weakness she had shown. 'Take me home,' she said sternly.

*

At their cabin, Shi-mi was waiting for them by the door. She seemed to be bursting with news.

The cat said without hesitation, 'I was able to observe your experiments. The pendulum and the timer funnels and the sundial. I have come to a conclusion. I regret that the precision is uncertain—'

'That's OK,' Agnes said. 'Just tell me.'

'When we came here the day was twenty-four hours long. Just as on all the worlds of the Long Earth – well, almost all. I remember that well; I observed it myself. But now—' And she shuddered.

Agnes crouched down. 'Shi-mi, are you all right? Let me get you something.'

'No. Please, Agnes.' She opened her green eyes wide. '*Now*, according to your clocks, the day is shorter. *Twenty-three hours only*, plus a few minutes. You were right. You were right . . .'

Agnes stared at Lobsang. 'The silver beetles. The Planetarium. Now this, the world spinning faster on its damn axis. What does it mean, Lobsang?'

'I'll have to find out.' He sighed. 'So much for the homesteading.'

'To find out – what do you need to do that?'

'A twain,' he said. 'I need a twain, so I can see the whole world. And Joshua Valienté, Agnes. I need Joshua.'

23

For Nelson Azikiwe, patiently enquiring, the mysteries of the deeper history of Joshua Valienté and his family continued to unravel . . .

Luis Valienté never forgot his adventure with Abel and Simon, the runaway slaves, back in 1852. It was an incident that had made him proud to be British, and indeed to be a Waltzer, one of Oswald Hackett's Knights of Discorporea. A validation too, for the first time in his life, of what he *was*.

But as the years passed, he gradually became less and less entangled in the affairs of the Knights, and his life followed its own distinct path.

That path took a decisive turn thanks to his share in a fictitious Californian gold mine – all Fraser Burdon's doing, of course – a lode easily extracted thanks to their piggybacking on the results of some poor fellow's five years of prospecting in the true California. Luis marvelled at Fraser's ingenious cover-up of their strike's peculiar provenance. The mine, according to Fraser's account for the authorities, had supposedly been opened up by a 'distant cousin'. Its location had been 'lost', along with all documentation, in a botched robbery attempt when the 'cousin' had come into town and attempted to register his latest 'strike' . . . They got away with it. There were, it seemed, even wilder stories than that circulating in the strange subculture of the Gold Rush.

And suddenly Luis was rich.

Luis invested his gold money in the burgeoning field of steam engines, for, just as the railways were spreading their iron web around the world, so the oceans, the oldest transport highways of all, were being challenged by a new generation of ships driven by coal and steam, ever since the pioneering service of the *Great Western* from 1838. Unlike his father, Luis managed to invest well and wisely, on the whole – well enough that he could afford to dabble in another nostalgic passion, backing variety shows in the theatres of England.

He did learn that Burdon had sunk much of *his* money into armaments – a growing industry after decades of relative peace in Europe were ended by the brutal war in the Crimea. After that conflict, during his visits to London, Luis often noticed a veteran who had a pitch at a corner of the New Cut, a one-legged fellow who would ape army routines, marching and standing to attention and shouldering arms with his crutch. He wore a medal of some kind, and Luis wondered if he might have met the Queen herself, who had taken a great interest in the war, and had met the troops and handed out the gongs . . . Old folk would tell you there had been a flood of such figures a few decades back, after the war against Bonaparte. They had all died off since, but now there was a fresh crop.

Armaments! Burdon, he supposed, had always had an air of brutal realism about him that Luis lacked, for better or worse.

Not long after his American adventure Luis had married. His bride was a young woman who had once been a singer in the variety halls, and had flirted briefly but intensely with the Great Elusivo. 'Elusivo no more!' Hackett had joked, when acting as best man at the wedding. 'Now she's got you pinned down at last!'

The couple settled in a decent town house in Richmond, and raised a daughter who they christened Elspeth – 'Ella' to her father, in a nod to Luis's own 'elusive' past that was a secret even from his wife. Later came a son, Robert. As the children grew Luis kept an eye on them both, but to his relief neither showed signs of being a Waltzer, with none of the joys and complications such a condition might bring. The family lived modestly, quietly and respectably.

Luis noted the death of Prince Albert in 1861 – well, how could he not? The news dominated the nation. The Queen disappeared into mourning black, and all traces of the somewhat pretty if suspicious young woman Luis had once glimpsed in the vaults of Windsor Castle were extinguished. Luis did wonder how the passing of Albert, the great champion of the Knights of Discorporea, would affect their work. But truth be told, once he reached his own fortieth birthday in 1863, Luis heard little of whatever exploits the Knights were getting up to. His own increasing age made him that much less useful as an agent, of course. And Oswald Hackett had always had a secretive streak.

By the turn of the next decade – and while the British watched aghast as a newly unified Germany under its ferocious Chancellor Bismarck tore into France, advancing even to Paris – Luis's contact with the Knights had dwindled to the occasional, almost nostalgic, letter or visit.

So it was a surprise when Hackett called one day in the spring of 1871 and asked him to go to Berlin. He and Burdon were to make separate trips, he said, with instructions to visit particular locations, including government buildings and royal residences.

Luis was reluctant, but he was wary of angering Oswald Hackett. So he complied. He fulfilled his own mission without incident or alarm.

And it was a still greater surprise, a few weeks later, when he, Hackett and Fraser Burdon were all summoned once more to Windsor.

24

LUIS STAYED OVERNIGHT in a hotel on the Strand.

Restless, anxious, he was up before the dawn, long before his appointment with Hackett and Burdon. He made his way down to the river, where in the grey light the mudlarks dug for wood and coins and bits of coal: children and old women, up to their knees in cold river-bed ooze. And he saw the sewer hunters emerging from their tunnels with their hoes and poles, coated in filth, splitting whatever grimy haul they had retrieved from the muck. Even in the city streets there was activity at this hour, the bone grubbers sifting garbage for anything they could eat or wear or sell on. All these people were striving to be up before the competition, as if the city was a vast midden infested by human insects, just as Hackett had once said, rooting and sifting and consuming the slightest morsel they found.

By eight Luis had made his way to Charing Cross, where the others were waiting by the brougham that would take them to Windsor.

This time the three of them, all older – Oswald Hackett was in his late fifties now – were met only by the man they knew as Mr Radcliffe, with a few hefty flunkeys at hand.

This encounter took place with the four of them standing somewhat uneasily in a drawing room that Luis suspected was one of the castle's lesser chambers, deep in the bowels of the Conqueror's tower, but whose carpet alone had probably cost more than all his own holdings combined, and whose walls were adorned with black crape, in the funereal style Victoria had maintained since the death of the Consort. Just the four of them, save for 'servants' in suits who stood by the walls and doorways, looking to Luis's eye like nothing so much as Coldstream Guards playing at being butlers, and he imagined he wasn't far wrong.

Radcliffe too had aged, of course; he must be nearly sixty now, with a greying at the temples, a slight stoop to the posture. But his attention remained blade-like, his stare skewering. 'So, gentlemen,' he said. 'Once again we meet. No Prince this time, sadly.'

Burdon snorted. 'But maybe you'll have the Widow of Windsor serve us tea, what?'

Hackett glared at him.

Radcliffe's smile was the kind that did not extend above the line of his thin moustache. His advancing age had not mellowed him, evidently. 'You know why you are here – or I imagine you have guessed. You were all asked to go into the new Germany, and the heart of Berlin in particular. Now here you are with your reports. Would you care to accompany me to the archive? You'll recall it from your previous visit. The staircase down is just along the hall from here . . .'

Hackett would have followed, but Burdon grabbed his arm. Burdon said, 'Not this time, thanks. Gettin' a bit sensitive to being confined, in my old age.'

Hackett pulled away, eyes narrow, frowning. But Luis was surprised when, for the first time in Luis's memory, he deferred to Burdon's leadership.

Radcliffe affected mock surprise. 'You, Mr Burdon, the famous gold-miner of California, scared of a bit of shut-in? Surely not.'

'Occupational hazard. Well. *Are* you servin' us tea? Why not take it here?' He glanced around at the beefy servants. 'I imagine these fellows are discreet. There's no *reason* you want us down there, is there?'

Radcliffe gave way. He invited them to sit.

In short order a flunkey showed up with tea, another bulky fellow. As the man poured, Burdon murmured to Luis, 'I never thought to see such fine china handled by a gorilla's mitt like that.'

Now Radcliffe asked for their reports on Bismarck's Berlin.

When it was his turn Luis described the cover he'd devised. 'I posed as a theatrical entrepreneur, studying local acts with an eye to booking them for the English theatres. I took a room on the Unter den Linden, from where I had every excuse to stroll past the Prinz Carl Palace, and the ministries on the Wilhelmstrasse . . .' All this was by way of summary; they had all had to submit detailed written reports, including sketch maps. It had been enough for Luis to have inspected these great buildings from the outside; the others had Waltzed their way inside on more penetrating spying missions.

When they had all reported, Radcliffe nodded. 'Good, good. Now, I wonder if you have guessed why we have ordered such a mission. And why it had to be *you three*, the very apex of the pyramid of your Knights of Discorporea,' and he said the words as if they were ashes in his mouth.

'That's not hard to guess,' Hackett said sternly. 'I think you mean to strike at Bismarck himself.'

Luis was astonished by this allegation. But Radcliffe did not flinch.

And Hackett continued relentlessly, 'I can even guess at the logic.'

'Go on.'

'*To avert a European war*. We all remember the poor Prince with his dreams of unifying Europe under a drowsy dynasty – he married his and Victoria's eldest daughter to the crown prince of Prussia to achieve just that end. Well, that didn't wash with Bismarck. Now you have this tremendous brute of a German dog prowling around a European back yard that has been more or less at peace, as we all know, since the downfall of Napoleon. And in Bismarck you face a man ruthless and determined and of tremendous political and strategic skill—'

'Who might be the ruin of us all,' Radcliffe said, nodding. 'And who, as you say, has terminated a half-century of relative peace on continental Europe with a terrible war, and he and his successors might spark off more before the hash is settled. No, the man has to go before he does any more harm, and spends any more lives. Which is where you gentlemen take the stage.'

Hackett nodded thoughtfully. 'Well, this is a step up from the Underground Rail Road, and your petty bits of spying. Even compared to the time you had us go into Sebastopol during the siege.'

Luis raised his eyebrows; he hadn't heard of that one.

Burdon gave Radcliffe a mocking smile. 'But what exactly is it you would have us do? Abduction, assassination? Of the *German Chancellor*? Are you serious? Do you expect us to believe that Her Majesty's government would stoop to such a tactic? This isn't some Balkan principality, you know. And besides, such an act would probably destabilize all Europe and bring us to war even faster than Bismarck with all his scheming ever could.'

Radcliffe kept calm. 'It is the will of Her Majesty.'

'Phooey,' said Burdon. 'Produce her and let her tell us so herself.'

Hackett seemed appalled. 'Have some respect, man.'

Radcliffe stood. 'If only you would come to the archive, I could explain the scheme better. We have documentation – maps – reports – it is already an expensive and carefully considered operation.'

Burdon said, 'Determined to get us down in that hole in the ground, aren't you?'

Radcliffe took a breath. 'Also there is someone waiting to see you there. You met a prime minister once before, in Lord John Russell, many years ago. And now—'

Burdon laughed out loud. 'You expect us to believe that you

persuaded old Gladstone, not just to support your bonkers scheme, but to turn up in person and sit in some cellar waiting on the likes of us?'

Hackett seemed confused. 'It does sound rather unlikely, Mr Radcliffe. If you would care to clarify—'

But Burdon cut him off. He stood, facing Radcliffe. 'All *I* would care to clarify is that this meeting is over. Ta-ta, Radcliffe, and thanks for the tea. Now if you'll show us back to our brougham—'

'Now,' Radcliffe said softly.

Luis, still sitting, sensed rather than heard the massive form step up behind him. Then it was as if a thunderclap went off inside his head. He was aware of two, maybe three powerful men grabbing him and flinging him to the ground.

And he fell into the dark.

When he woke, he was in the well-remembered vault under Windsor Castle. Radcliffe, evidently, had got his way. And when he tried to move Luis discovered that his wrists and ankles were locked in shackles of heavy iron.

In the gas-lit gloom, just as before, here were the decent but not ostentatious furniture, the shelving with books and records, the doorways leading to further rooms crowded with gifts and gewgaws: the clutter of monarchy. It seemed just as it had been when Albert had leaned against the fireplace opposite, quoting his own speeches about duty, and Luis had thought he'd glimpsed Victoria hurrying by . . . All that, he realized, was nearly a quarter of a century ago.

But while the room hadn't changed, its human occupants had. Here was Radcliffe, standing before him with a cold smile. Luis, Burdon and Hackett, all of them struggling back to consciousness, shackled side by side in armchairs, each with a red-coated soldier at his back. There were more soldiers at the doors, by the walls, even in the rooms beyond.

As Luis moved his battered head the pain returned, a clamouring like gunfire. He bit his tongue to force himself not to cry out.

There was a nurse before him, a sweet-faced girl in a uniform. 'Drink this,' she said. She held up a cup of some liquid to his lips, warm and tasting of honey; he gulped it down greedily, and the pain in his head started to abate.

Hackett's face was ablaze with fury. 'You all right, Valienté?'

'Been better. Head still works.'

'Good man. Burdon?'

'Better than you'd think, old boy.'

Burdon seemed oddly at ease. But then, Luis reflected, he seemed to have been in control of events since they arrived here, more so than Hackett. Luis fervently hoped he still was – somehow.

Hackett looked up at the man standing before them. 'What's the meaning of this? What the deuce are you up to, Radcliffe?'

Burdon laughed. 'Yes, and where's Bill Gladstone? It was all a blind, wasn't it? The whole business of Bismarck – probably even our bogus trips to Berlin on government money – all a lure to get us into this trap.'

Radcliffe ignored him and studied Hackett. 'So, Dr Hackett, are you impressed with the way we took you down? I'm fly to the dodge, you see.'

More East End slang, Luis noticed.

'This is the way we've learned to tackle you Waltzers. Hit you with overwhelming force before you've got time to think about it, before you've time to slip away to whichever corner of hell you godless creatures visit when you're not here. And then, unconscious, bundle you up in a hole in the ground like this, where even you can't Waltz out – how do you put it? – either widdershins or deiseal. Efficient, ain't it? You won't give us the lucky dodge again. We've been practising, you see.'

Hackett glared at him. 'What the devil do you mean?'

And Burdon asked, more calmly, 'Practising on whom?'

'On more of your sort.' Radcliffe began to pace, calm, thoughtful. 'Here's what you fellows need to understand. Your day is done, you and your flash tricks. You were always something of an indulgence of the old Prince, God rest him. But once he had gone it was clear that Her Majesty had always found you rather repulsive. "More shadows than men," she said of you.

'Meanwhile I and many of my colleagues have always been suspicious of the power you wield, *and* the notion that it is only through your own good will that we can have any surety that you will not turn your powers against your own government. Why, every one of you when he's had the chance has used his talent to enrich himself, has he not? You, Burdon, with your phantom gold mine, and you needn't think we haven't unravelled the truth about that. You, Valienté, with your absurd act as the Great Elusivo.'

'What, are you a critic now? I got good notices in my time. Why, once in the *Observer*—'

'Even you, Hackett! Pious and pompous as you are now, you weren't so as a younger man, were you? I've a file on you as thick as my arm. No, you're too dangerous to be allowed to run around uncontrolled, d'ye see? And then there's the whiff of—' He sought the right word. 'The whiff of the *unnatural* about you. We're British, by God, a manly race. And we don't want your shifty, slippery sort pollutin' the blood, no matter how useful you may occasionally be – and, I'll grant you, you have been. Well, we've decided to bring you in – beginning with you three, among the first to present yourselves here all those years ago – what colossal arrogance you showed then! And now the first to be taken down.'

But not the last, Luis realized in a sudden panic, not the last. Now he feared for his family, for Ella and Robert.

Radcliffe said, 'And believe me, you'll never see daylight again. As you can see, we have learned how to deal with your kind.'

'By practising,' Burdon said. 'You told us that. Answer my question, then: on whom?'

'On whomever we could find. We've had the scientists working on it, chaps at the Royal Society, devising a programme of testing. Anybody we suspected might have your sort of faculty – the soldier who mysteriously dodged the bullets copped by everybody else in battle, the particularly prolific thief, the particularly persistent jailbreaker – that sort. And then we tested them to see if they could Waltz, or not.'

Hackett looked appalled. 'How, man?'

'By stressing them. Wall a man up in some sarcophagus. Set him in front of a firing squad. Chuck him in a cage and sink it in the Thames; if he can skip out he'll do so, you see. Mostly it fails – and, no, we didn't kill 'em all, but it's no waste if we had. One in a thousand, or less, showed signs of what *you* can do. And once they've stepped out you might think they'd be away scot free and beyond our reach, but many of 'em didn't even know they had the capability before being forced to use it – they had always just escaped unconsciously – and then almost all of 'em came right back again, and straight into the arms of my bonny lads in their red coats. Once we had 'em, it was down into a basement under the Royal Society for all of them. Very systematic people, these scientists. Very methodical. Although, if there's something in the brain that enables this Waltzing business, well, they ain't found it yet.'

'You're talking about vivisection,' Hackett said. 'You monster.'

Radcliffe bridled at that, and leaned over him. 'You're the monster, man! Not me! D'ye not even see *that* clearly?' He straightened up and resumed his pacing. 'What we have learned is how rare this ability of yours is. After all, the threat of violent death has been a common occurrence during human history; if Waltzing was any more prevalent you'd think we'd have noticed by now.

'Anyhow the government, as expressed through the rather discreet agency for which I work, has come to the decision that for the likes of you, *rare* isn't enough: *extinct* would be preferable. We're considering how to persuade friendly governments to come over to that way of thinking, and be done with you once and for all. Certainly once Britain is cleansed we'll be going out into the colonies with a similar programme.' He came to Luis, and looked him in the eyes, the mouth, as if inspecting a prize horse. 'We'll be merciful. No scragging for you, which is all you deserve.'

'"Scragging",' Luis reflected back. 'Come a long way, haven't you? But there are times when it slips, Radcliffe. Your mouth's like a Whitechapel sewer.'

Radcliffe curled his lip. 'Takes one to know one, Valienté. You'll even be comfortable for a while, you and your families, down here in the dark.' He straightened up. 'But when the last of you dies, in this cellar or another, that will be the end of it. So much for the Knights of Discorporea. Ha!'

'We'll see,' said Fraser Burdon.

'What's that?'

Burdon looked over at Hackett and Luis. 'Widdershins,' he said.

Hackett snapped, 'What? Impossible, man. We're in a damn cellar.'

Burdon shrugged, and his shackles rattled. 'Suit yourself. You with me, Luis? On my count. One, two—'

Luis, unbelieving, *Waltzed*—

And found himself in another hole in the ground, this one rough-walled, in a dark relieved only by the light of candles. But his shackles were gone – and so was his chair, and, emerging into thin air in a sitting posture, he fell back on to a rocky floor with a jolt hard enough to make his head throb anew.

He struggled to rise. 'Burdon? Hackett?'

'Valienté?' It was Hackett's voice; he must be as bewildered as Luis, and was ten years older too, but he had his customary tone of command. 'Just sit tight.' He held up a candle to reveal crudely cut walls all around, and what might be a wooden-lined shaft up to the surface. The two of them were alone in here. Hackett asked, 'Where the devil are we?'

And Luis laughed, and lay back on the cold ground. 'In a mine. I see it now – a mine cut by Burdon; we mined together in America, remember? We're in a shaft in a stepwise parallel of Windsor. *That's* how you Waltz out of a cellar. By staking out the ground in advance, and cutting a hole *in the precise same location widdershins.*'

'My God, you must be right. But Burdon must have planned this months, even years ahead! Knowing that some day he'd need it. What a suspicious mind the man must have.'

'He was right, though, wasn't he?'

'So he was . . . Where is he, by the way? Why's he not in here with us? Now I see I always underestimated him. Won't make *that* mistake again.'

There was a slight puff of air that made the candles flicker. Burdon stepped out of the shadows and walked forward into the candlelight.

Hackett demanded, 'What have you been up to, man? Why didn't you come over with us?'

'Well, I did. But once I was free of those iron shackles I took a few paces and went back.' He held up something, a blade, dripping dark. 'A detail I needed to tidy up.'

'Oh, Burdon,' Luis said, feeling oddly disappointed. 'You killed them?'

'Only that bastard Radcliffe. And he deserved it, don't you think? For what he did to those wretches in the coffins and the underwater cages. For what he intended to do to our families.'

'Our families,' Hackett said. 'We must get out of this cellar, walk somewhere we can Waltz back safely—'

'I've got the area signposted,' Burdon said. 'A one-to-one map. A bit rough but it will do.'

'Good man. We get back over. We get our families to safety. And then—'

'Yes?'

'And then we consider the future. For us, our families. And our "kind", as Mr Radcliffe called us.'

Luis thought he had never heard such a grim tone of voice from Hackett before. Yet he was right; the path ahead was clear – the only path they could take now. They must run to their families, and hide from the government's assassins.

Gingerly, in the flickering light of the candles, he got to his feet.

Nelson, having learned as much as he felt he needed to, went in search of Joshua.

But according to the most reliable source on Joshua's whereabouts, the Home in Madison, Joshua was gone, vanished once more into the deep Long Earth.

25

THE MAN STANDING at the door of the Berg house, here in Miami West 4, was aged maybe twenty-five – seven or eight years older than Rocky and Stan. He wore a battered wide-brimmed hat, leather jacket, scuffed jeans, heavy-duty moccasins. He had a pack on his back, and at his waist he carried a rolled-up whip, a Stepper box, and some kind of handgun. He looked ready for travel, Rocky Lewis thought immediately. Too ready, like a cartoon.

The guy stuck out his hand. 'I'm Jules van Herp. Born in Datum Quebec; my family evacuated because of Yellowstone when I was eight. Call me Jules.' He grinned at Rocky. 'So, you ready for the Grange?'

Rocky winced, and glanced around to see if they'd been over-heard. In the months since Stan had first been approached by Roberta Golding, the one thing that had been drummed into them was how secretive the Next were. You didn't even say the name of the Grange out loud. And now here was this clumsy character just blurting it out.

Stan emerged from the house, carrying a pack, blinking in the light. It was early morning here in West 4, and the sun was just rising beyond the thin sky-piercing thread of the space elevator. He stood by Rocky and inspected Jules van Herp. 'Well, you're not one of *them*,' Stan said dryly. 'Not with a dopy expression like that.'

'Oh, hell no. I just work for them. I'm here to help with your trip.'

Stan scowled at him. 'So if you're not a Next, what *are* you, Jules? A native bearer?'

Rocky winced again. For a young man who was increasingly thought of in these parts as a source of wisdom, Stan could be brutally cruel. But then, Rocky thought, they were both still just seventeen.

Jules did not seem offended, however. 'Just doing my job, and it's a job I enjoy. I'll take you to meet the others. Not far from here step-wise. I see you've got your pack. You won't need much once you're there, at the Grange. People always take more than they need, the first time. Some kind of comfort thing, I guess.'

Rocky asked, 'You've done this before? Taken people there?'

'A few times.' He glanced at his watch. 'We do need to move, however. You understand you'll be going through soft places?'

Rocky suppressed a shudder. 'So we've been told.'

Jules grinned easily. 'Don't sweat it, it's not so bad. Anyhow, you're safe in their hands.' His confidence in the Next seemed absolute, Rocky thought. 'But the soft places aren't like stepping. They're limited in space and time; you have to hit the right moment.'

'So we've appointments to keep.'

'That's it. Any more goodbyes you need to make?'

In fact, Rocky thought, as they'd waited for the Next to come take Stan away, it had been nothing but a long drawn-out goodbye for months.

'No,' Stan said simply. 'It's done. Let's get on with it.'

So, hastily, very early this September morning – and grumpily, with Rocky's head aching faintly from the last-night drinks party thrown by their buddies, who'd been told they were leaving to study beanstalk engineering techniques a couple of worlds away – with a stroke of their Stepper boxes they left Earth West 4 behind. Rocky watched the still incomplete space elevator vanish from his view, leaving the unspoiled sky of West 5.

Then, following Jules's lead, they stepped again, and again. Stan was a natural stepper, who only carried a box for cover. Rocky was a lot less capable, but Roberta Golding had supplied industrial-strength anti-nausea drugs, and these first steps, at least, weren't difficult.

It took only a few minutes to reach the West 10 footprint of Miami.

Here, Roberta Golding and Marvin Lovelace met them in the middle of a prairie; a scrap of shade from a clump of trees sheltered them from the light of an intense sun. Roberta wore her thick spectacles, and Marvin his card-sharp uniform of shades and small black homburg. They both wore nondescript travelling gear, and carried small packs.

Roberta smiled at them. 'Good morning. You're ready to go onwards?'

'I was expecting you,' Stan said to Roberta. 'But not him,' he jerked a thumb at Jules, 'or *him*,' and he pointed at Marvin.

Roberta laughed, good natured. 'Well, Jules is one of *you* who knows *us*, and who we can trust. He's here as kind of a middle-man who might be able to tell us if something goes wrong – better than you might be able to articulate for yourselves for now.'

Marvin grinned. 'And you know *me*, right? Good old Marvin, who saved you from getting beat up more than once for winning out fair and square over some stalk jack in the poker.'

'Anything we can do to help you feel grounded,' Roberta said. 'Which is why we encouraged you to bring a companion.'

'I've known Rock here all my life. He's like the brother I never wanted.'

That was classic Stan. Rocky smirked, and punched his arm.

Stan scowled. 'But it doesn't make me feel grounded to keep hearing all this talk of *us* and *them*.'

Roberta said evenly, 'This kind of reaction is common. It's possible for you to back out, at any stage. We will trust your discretion.'

Marvin nudged him. 'Come on, man. Don't bail now. Won't you always be curious about what you're missing?'

Stan shrugged. 'Fair point. Let's do this.'

'Good,' Roberta said firmly.

Rocky looked at Roberta dubiously. 'We're going through the soft places, right? What do we have to do?'

She smiled, evidently trying to be reassuring. 'Just hold my hand.'

They emerged in another prairie, with a subtly different ensemble of waist-high green plants, differently shaped trees – and, in the distance, a herd of tremendous beasts of some kind walking in the mist, dimly visible, like mountains on the move . . .

A passage through a soft place was *different*.

Regular stepping was like consciously striding from one stone in a stream to the next. Now Rocky felt as if he had fallen through some flaw in the world. He couldn't have described what he saw during the transition. But the vertiginous sense of falling was real enough, as was the bone-sucking chill he felt now, a harsh contrast to the warmth of the fall day on West 10.

To his shame, Rocky found he was still clinging to Roberta's hand, like a kid with his mother. He let go hastily.

'You have just travelled a thousand steps from West 10,' Roberta said. 'In fact a little more.'

Rocky asked, 'Which way did we come? East or West?'

'Does it matter? And we have moved geographically too; we are far from the footprint of Florida.' Roberta looked into their eyes. 'Are you both OK? The chill you feel is real; a soft-place transition extracts energy as a simple Linsay step does not, or not measurably. Also it will have felt as if you were in motion for some time. Seconds, perhaps longer; the feeling is subjective and varies between individuals. But in fact, if you had checked your watches, no physical time passes during the transition.'

'Teach me how to do this,' Stan said.

Roberta glanced uncertainly at Marvin, who shrugged.

Stan said, 'Look, you don't have a monopoly on soft places. I've heard of them before. Some humans who don't have the pretension to call themselves a separate species can find them too, right?'

'It is a question of training. Of mental discipline. You will not be ready until—'

'Just tell me.'

Roberta evidently wasn't used to being interrupted. But she said, 'It is all a question of imagination. Just as our hominid ancestors could look at a rock and picture the tool inside, so we can consider this world and imagine another. The more advanced the intellect, you see, the more detailed the visualization. And at last when the visualization is rich enough—'

'You step.'

'Yes. Into a world which, we think, crystallizes from a Platonic potential into the realm of the actual. It is just as in quantum mechanics – if two objects have a quantum description sufficiently precise, if their states are identical, they *are* the same object. To go further than simple Linsay stepping is essentially an application of higher mathematics . . . Oh, if only you could quicktalk! English is utterly inadequate, and *slow*. Like shouting poetry down a drainpipe. Stan, you may be able to learn.' But she glanced at Rocky, and her message was clear. *Not you.* 'Are you ready? We will make some stops – call them educational opportunities – before we reach our destination. Hold my hands, both of you . . .'

And Rocky, helpless, was hurled through another plummeting seven-league-boot leap.

26

THE AIRSHIP *SHILLELAGH* hovered over Manning Hill, over the Abrahams farmstead, tethered to the remains of the gondola which had delivered Lobsang, Agnes, a little boy and a cat to this world three years before. As Agnes strode up the hill, bearing a box of eggs – a souvenir of a coffee morning at the Irwins' – she realized that the twain had already been there a week. Agnes had become a lot more aware of the passage of time thanks to her clocks and calendars.

The battered old airship was a novelty, of course, in the sedate green world of New Springfield, and even after a week the children, and some adults too, still came to stare. Joshua Valienté had been introduced as a visitor, an old family friend, and nobody had questioned that simple cover story – even those few who had heard of this hero of the early days of stepping. And Joshua was generous with his time, as ever. After arriving in the airship he had given the local kids rides across the forest-choked landscape of Earth West 1,217,756. These kids thought nothing of stepping, nothing of the existence of the multiple worlds of the Long Earth – but few of them had ever got to see their home from the air.

Six-year-old Ben, of course, loved his Uncle Joshua. And Joshua made time too for Shi-mi, who had come hesitantly out to meet him when the airship first landed.

Well, Joshua had finally made it here. But he had taken some finding, after Agnes had sent the word out through Bill Chambers and the Sisters at the Home and other old friends. Since the final breakdown of his marriage Joshua had become more reclusive still, it seemed, spending even more of his time on his solitary 'sabbaticals', huddled in his Robinson Crusoe one-man stockades on remote worlds.

Agnes had been afraid of Joshua's reaction when he discovered Lobsang was still alive. In the event he just laughed. 'I knew it.'

Meanwhile the situation was becoming urgent.

For a world that had been sold to them as lacking pronounced seasons, there seemed to be a heck of a lot of weather. As the months they'd waited for Joshua had passed, there were more and more freak events: storms, droughts, howling winds – and, strangest of all, bizarre 'magnetic storms', as Lobsang called them, when auroras would flap in the sky like tremendous curtains, streaming north to south. Agnes had never heard of auroras at latitudes as low as this, not that she was any kind of expert. These storms had consequences. The furballs and their predators blundered about even more randomly than before. Maybe these creatures, like navigating birds, relied on a stable magnetic field for their sense of direction.

As for the people, the storms played hell with the few electronic gadgets they had that still worked. Agnes herself, of course, was a thing of clockwork and gears – that was how she thought of herself anyhow. When the storms came she fretted about how she, Lobsang and indeed Shi-mi might be affected. Lobsang told her not to worry; her innards were well shielded, and her substrates were biochemical rather than metal. Lobsang said that in fact they should be affected less than the standard-issue people around them, whose minds were also linked to their bodies through electromagnetic fields in their brains and nervous systems. That just made her more afraid for Ben, and his growing young body.

Well, Joshua was here now. And, a week after the arrival of the *Shillelagh*, he and Lobsang were ready to get to work.

*

Inside the house, Agnes found the two of them sitting at the kitchen table picking over beetle artefacts: silver bangles and pendants, what looked like a small Swiss army knife also wrought in silver, and a shard of smooth black material, curved, broken, like a piece of a smashed Easter egg.

Lobsang looked up. 'Ben's playing out back.'

'Good.' Agnes bustled around the kitchen, storing the eggs, preparing a fresh pot of coffee. 'I'll call him for lunch if he doesn't come in.'

Joshua said, 'Well, I guess we're about ready to go.'

'Go?'

'Go tour this world in the *Shillelagh*,' Lobsang said. 'Take a proper look at it, outside of this pinprick we inhabit.' He shook his greying head. 'It's amazing that we've done this, in retrospect. You and I, Agnes. Stepped into this one place, in a whole new world, with no real idea what's over the horizon.'

Joshua said, 'Well, that's how most people do it, Lobsang. First light tomorrow, as agreed?'

'Suits me,' Lobsang said. 'It won't take long to get ready. I've packed everything I'll need from our old gondola into the twain already.'

'Good,' Agnes said firmly. 'But what's all this junk on my kitchen table?'

'Samples,' Lobsang said, and he put his arms around the fragments, as if shielding them from her. 'We're trying to be scientific, if belatedly. These are beetle artefacts – given as gifts to the children – and a few scraps we collected from the Gallery, what appear to be detached limbs, even this shard of broken carapace. I was telling Joshua that I've put these through the mass spectrometer in the gondola.'

Joshua grinned. 'A backwoods pioneer with a mass spectrometer. You *are* a cheat, Lobsang.'

'But the only scientific equipment I have is what we brought to help service our android bodies – in my Frankenstein laboratory, as Agnes puts it. I had to adapt, improvise . . . The point is, from their isotopic composition I can tell that these things were made locally, from local substances. The silver was mined a few miles from here. The carapace shard is a kind of ceramic based on river-bed clay from Soulsby Creek. And so on.'

Agnes frowned. 'I thought you believed these creatures are alien. Not of Earth – of any Earth.'

'So I do. In form and function they just don't fit, in any version of the terrestrial tree of life. And, Agnes, I took Joshua through to the Planetarium. Whatever's going on there, *that's* surely a strong hint that these silver beetles have an extraterrestrial origin. But now that they're here they appear to be making more copies of themselves – breeding, you might call it – using local materials. Stuff from Earth, this Earth.'

Agnes said, 'What a cheek. This is our world, not theirs.'

'Quite.'

'So what does this all mean, Lobsang? What are these creatures up to? And how does it fit in with the days getting shorter?'

'That's what we mean to find out.'

'Well, something's wrong, that's for sure; this old planet's broken down and groaning . . .'

Joshua, who had known Agnes and her tastes all his life, grinned at that. Lobsang looked confused.

Ben's soft voice called from outside. 'George?'

Lobsang pushed back his chair and stood. 'I'll go see to him.'

Agnes said, 'Lunch will be ready soon.'

Joshua stood too. 'You need a hand, Agnes?'

She waved vaguely. 'If you like. I'm making chicken soup. Find what you can and improvise.'

He smiled, and began looking out ingredients and implements: vegetables, a chunk of goat's cheese, seasoning, a sharp knife and a chopping board.

'You always were a good cook,' Agnes said. 'Even when you were no older than Ben is now.' She looked sideways at him. 'And you are taking Lobsang's non-death well, I must say. I know you said you weren't too surprised, but . . .'

Joshua grunted. 'He's pulled a lot of stunts before. And I was half expecting a call.'

She glanced at him. 'Why? . . . Oh. You're talking about your headaches. The Silence, or the lack of it.'

Joshua had his own peculiar sensitivities to the condition of the Long Earth, it seemed, and had done since he was a boy. When the Sisters had seen him come home from his solo teenage jaunts in distress, they'd tried to tease out of him what he was sensing, feeling: trying to get the ineffable out of the most taciturn boy Agnes had ever met. He would speak of a Silence that wasn't a Silence, or of a sound that wasn't there, like an echo from distant mountains . . . He couldn't articulate what was evidently an uneasy sense of disturbance that sometimes translated into headaches, storm warnings in his own young head.

'Do you feel anything now? I mean, here?'

'Not specifically. It doesn't work like that, Agnes. *This* one's been coming for years, though. Noticed it before my fiftieth birthday, I remember.' He half-grinned. 'But when I sensed the thunder clouds gathering, I just knew Lobsang wouldn't let something as trivial as his own death get in the way of dealing with it.'

'He did need to recover, Joshua. He was reluctant, in fact, to face up to this business of the silver beetles. It's a distraction from his – humanity project.'

'But who else was capable of handling this situation?'

'Who else, indeed.'

'And it's a funny coincidence that, of all the possible locations in the Long Earth, he happens to be right on the spot where he's most needed. Don't you think?'

They were here because of Sally Linsay, of course. And Agnes thought back now to Sally's barely concealed amusement when she had brought them to this place. Had Sally *known*? . . . Just as Agnes had always suspected, had Sally been playing some kind of game of her own all the time?

Suddenly angry, she turned away. 'Whatever you say.'

'Agnes, you have any garlic?'

'There's some dried in the store. We've seeded it to grow wild but it hasn't taken yet . . .'

That evening they finished loading the *Shillelagh*. Lobsang and Joshua said their goodbyes to Ben, and Joshua made a gentle fuss of the cat.

The next day they rose at dawn. The boy was still asleep. Agnes, indoors, sitting with a coffee, heard a hiss of gas filling the buoyancy bags, and a whir of turbines. She went to a window, and saw the twain lift.

Soon the ship was lost in the immensity of the sky.

She went back to bed, though she knew she wouldn't be able to sleep again, in what was left of this truncated night.

27

THEY HEADED ROUGHLY south. Running at less than thirty miles per hour, Joshua figured it would take much of the day to reach the Atlantic coast, depending on the precise details of the local geography of this footprint of Maine. Joshua and Lobsang sat side by side in the ship's battered gondola, which was more like a travel trailer than the spacious liner-like elegance of the *Mark Twain*, the prototype airship aboard which, more than a quarter of a century before, the two of them had been the first to explore the reaches of the Long Earth, to the High Meggers and beyond.

And under the ship's prow endless forested landscapes washed by.

'Trees,' Joshua said thoughtfully. 'Lots and lots of trees. You know, the first thing I discovered on Step Day, when I took my own first step out of Datum Madison, out of the Home, was—'

'Trees.'

'Yeah. The Long Earth's big winner, trees.' The forest purred away below the twain. 'You say there are trolls here?'

'Oh, yes,' Lobsang said.

'Makes you think. To the trolls the Long Earth must appear as all one forest, a world wide and a million steps deep.'

'I think they are rather smarter than that, Joshua.'

'That Madison forest was mainly oak – nothing like this.'

'The Ice Belt worlds are a lot cooler than this,' Lobsang said. 'Here, it's trees from the poles to the equator.'

'You know that for sure, do you? You've seen it for yourself?'

'Well, you know that's not true. What I described to you is our best understanding of a typical member of this particular band of worlds.'

'OK. But *this* world evidently isn't so typical after all, is it? And here we are crawling around the globe like an ant on the rind of a pumpkin. I'm not sure what you're expecting to find.'

'Well, think about it, Joshua.' Lobsang looked up into a blue sky, an apparently serene sun. 'Even Agnes's sundials and pendulums have been enough to demonstrate that the spin of this particular Earth is speeding up. And it *is* just this one, by the way; I ran some checks in the stepwise neighbours, and they're unaffected . . .'

'Why do the New Springfielders stick around, then? Agnes says they go wandering stepwise anyhow. If the neighbouring worlds are still comfortable to live on – and I guess they must be getting steadily out of synch with *this* one as the days grow shorter . . .'

Lobsang smiled. 'But *this* is the centre, Joshua. This is their world, where the founders ended their trek. According to the records they stopped here because of a particularly rich seam of iron ore, not shared with neighbouring worlds, and I've a tentative theory that *that* is a by-product of this world's peculiar stepwise linkage . . .'

Joshua nodded. 'I get it. A pioneer's sheer stubbornness.'

'A stubbornness I feel I share – despite the magnitude of the storm that's breaking here.'

'Magnitude?'

'*If* this world really is speeding up its spin, that's a pretty large-scale effect. Already the planet's spin kinetic energy must have been upped by ten per cent.'

'Ten per cent? Wow. OK. So if it is these silver beetles who are somehow responsible—'

'It seems an unlikely coincidence if they're not.'

'Then they must be mounting some kind of global operation.'

'That's my theory,' Lobsang said. 'I figure we'll recognize it when we see it. Even from the perspective of an ant on a pumpkin rind.'

'Hmm. I'll tell you the first thing *I* noticed that was odd, Lobsang. *The moon.* On my very first night, something woke me. I looked out the window, there was the crescent moon – and I saw a flash, coming out of the dark side. Like something was being fired out. I figured I'd been disturbed by an earlier flash; this was a second one.'

'Joshua, you sleep lightly if a silent flash in the sky was enough to wake you.'

'I spend a lot of my time alone in the deep Long Earth, Lobsang. I've been living like that for decades now. Believe me, you sleep lightly, because sooner or later along will come an oddity that won't trouble to wake you before it eats you. Anomalies on the moon: you can't get much bigger than that, can you? But Agnes says she's been noticing these things since you arrived here – what, three years ago? And you took no notice.'

'I told you. I wasn't here for that, for astronomical-scale anomalies.'

'Even so, don't you think you took your eye off the ball? Lobsang, *the day here is too short.* There's something wrong with the moon . . . How much more obvious could it be?'

'What do you want me to say? I came here for Ben and Agnes. Anyhow we're here now, seeking answers.'

'OK. So we're looking for something big. Might take us a while to find it at this pace, even so.'

Lobsang dug into his pocket and held up a memory stick. 'Fear not. We have movies.'

'What you got?'

'The classics. *Blues Brothers. Contact. Galaxy Quest*—'

'Nothing with Julie Andrews?'

'Let it lie, Joshua.'

The forest rolled under the prow of the *Shillelagh*, apparently infinite, without interruption.

'So how about brunch?'

'Will you do the honours, Joshua? I took the liberty of loading aboard all the ingredients for clam chowder – we trade with a couple of communities at the coast, a few worlds over. I've no idea what the galley is like aboard this tub of yours.'

'I can play it like a fiddle. Happily not the way I've heard *you* play a fiddle . . .'

By late afternoon they were approaching the Atlantic coast. From high altitude they could already see the ocean, in the distance.

Joshua checked their latitude. All their instruments were inertial, based on dead-reckoning, and kept in heavily insulated cases; Lobsang had told Joshua that the many magnetic storms on this world screwed up most electronics. They were going to cross the coast, Joshua figured, somewhere over the footprint of Portland, Maine.

And beneath the ship's prow, Joshua thought the forest stock was changing. Perhaps there were tree species better adapted to the fresher air here, the salt breezes off the sea, a subtly different climate. It would be interesting to go down there, he thought, and sample the local wildlife, see if the populations of furball tree-dwellers and ground-burrowers, and the big birds and crocs that preyed on them, were any different from those around Lobsang's home in the denser forest. But it wasn't that kind of trip; they weren't looking on that kind of scale.

And as they neared the coast, the forest started to show extensive damage. From the air Joshua saw swathes of trees laid out flat, their great trunks lying parallel on the ground, as if combed. Elsewhere there were huge blackened scars, the relics of fires presumably sparked by lightning. The mark of strong winds, of storms.

Then, at the coast itself, Joshua saw a denuded coastal strip, like a beach, marked with black parallel lines: he thought the lines were sea wrack, driftwood, seaweed maybe. But as they descended for a closer look he realized that he had entirely misjudged the scale of what he was seeing. That 'beach' was maybe a mile deep, and the 'driftwood' was made up of whole trunks, complete root systems: thousands of mature trees uprooted as a child would pluck daisies, and flung down in rows.

Joshua, using binoculars, inspected fish-like forms, long dead: a shark, and what looked something like a fat seal, with stubby back legs. It was only when he saw that the shark was lying across a smashed tree trunk that he got an idea of its size.

'That thing's enormous.'

Lobsang grinned ruefully. 'This band of worlds has the largest sharks yet observed, anywhere in the Long Earth. No whales here; the sea mammals never grew so big.'

'Lobsang, you said you were looking for large-scale events. You got 'em. It's like the aftermath of a tsunami.'

'The coast was uninhabited; nobody to be harmed, nobody to witness it. But you understand that all this is a side-effect, Joshua. A by-product of the spin-up, the injection of all that rotational energy. The oceans slosh and so does the air. You get freak waves, storms. Far inland we've had some of the storms, but we weren't aware directly of the big waves.'

'Directly?'

'I have noticed earth tremors, coming more and more frequently. Others may have too, Agnes perhaps; we haven't discussed it. Well, you'd expect that. If this Earth is spinning faster its very crust must be distorting, the equatorial bulge increasing as the planet flattens out.'

'Do you measure the tremors? Since Yellowstone, everybody's a geologist, right?'

'Joshua,' Lobsang said patiently, 'we don't have any seismometers. Why would we bring a seismometer? As I keep telling you, I didn't come here to be a scientist. I came to *live*.'

'We'll need to get the scientists out here eventually, though. From the government, the Low Earth colleges.'

'If we can.'

'So which way now, Lobsang?'

'Let's stick to the coast. That's where the visible damage will be. For now the interior is sheltered, relatively, the continental forest protecting itself.'

'Fine. North? South?'

'South. If you were spinning up a world, you'd work at the equator, wouldn't you?'

'I don't know. I never thought about it. South it is.'

The controls of this airship were simple: a steering handle, a joystick; it was the work of a couple of minutes to set the course. Then Joshua yawned and stretched.

'Why don't you hit the sack for a few hours, Joshua? I don't need sleep, if I adjust my settings. You get some shut-eye; I'll play Robert the robot.'

'Who? Never mind. OK, Lobsang. Though I think I'll fix some supper first . . .'

Joshua slept well, waking long after dawn.

At a glance out of his window, all he saw at first was ocean and forested land, bathed in morning sunlight. Then he realized that the airship appeared to be circling, running in wide, gentle sweeps; he could see its shadow shift across the ground.

There must be something down there. Presumably nothing urgent, or Lobsang would have woken him.

He showered, shaved and dressed. He collapsed his bed back to a sofa, and folded away the partition that divided his cabin from the rest of the gondola. Passing through the small galley area he turned on the coffee perc and drank a slug of orange juice – except that it wasn't orange, not quite, but a compress from one of the many unfamiliar citrus types native to this band of worlds. Then, glass in hand, he joined Lobsang at the forward windows.

Still the *Shillelagh* banked and turned, and land and sea wheeled beneath.

'So,' Joshua said.

'I wanted you to see what's down there. But I wanted you to get your beauty sleep too, so I kept the ship running. I figured that shutting down the engines would alert your famous hair-trigger Daniel Boone senses—'

'All right, all right. You wanted me to see what?'

'Take a look. We're at the coast of New York State, or its footprint. Below us is Long Island. It's taken a battering from the storms and waves; its vegetation cover has been pretty much flattened.'

Joshua looked down at the island. A strip of silver, running east to west, lay across the scarred landscape.

At first glance it looked like a road to Joshua, or perhaps a rail track. It arced away to the west, running inland as far as he could see until it became a fine line, still dead straight, lost in the misty morning air. To the east, towards the sun, it strode across Long Island on slim pillars, and then on across the sea.

'Wow. That's what you wanted to show me. What's it for? It looks like a roadway. But I see no traffic.' Joshua imagined some immense invasion force falling from the sky, tank brigades sweeping along that mighty viaduct . . .

'Unknown, for now. I can make some guesses, but we need to see more. I do have some details. What it's made of, for instance – well, the outer surface at least; spectroscopy told me that. Steel. Nothing terribly exotic. No doubt built with materials mined here on this Earth, just as we saw the beginnings of back in New Springfield. And as to who made it—' Lobsang had a tablet, loaded with telescopic images. He showed this to Joshua now. 'It took me some time to find them. Not many of them about . . .'

In the magnified images Joshua saw silver beetles, a small party of them – five, six, seven. They hurried along the surface of the roadway – if it was a roadway – pausing every fifty yards or so to press what looked like instrument packages to the surface. Seen from a height they were very cockroach-like.

'So the beetles built this.'

'Evidently.'

'Are they testing it? Checking it out?'

'Something like that, I imagine.'

Joshua looked east again, towards the ocean. The viaduct stretched away, heading dead straight for the rising sun. 'I wonder what's supporting it out there. Beyond the continental shelf you'd need pretty long pillars.'

'Pontoons and anchors, perhaps?' Lobsang suggested. 'Like oil rigs. Joshua, that is one of many details to be determined.'

'Then what do we know?'

'That the viaduct extends at least from horizon to horizon, aligned precisely east to west – and that is east-west according to the Earth's rotation axis, not the magnetic compass directions. Given we have come across its span here, having essentially arrived at a random point—'

'Ah. You think it could go on for ever.'

'All around the Earth at this latitude, yes. Why not? Spanning the ocean to Europe and beyond, crossing the continental forests on great pillars. It would be interesting to see what allowance is made for the higher ground, such as the Appalachians to the west of here. Does it follow the contours? Or is it driven at a constant height through the mountains, with bridges and tunnels?'

'Well, we'll have to track it to know that.'

'And again, given we came across this so quickly, starting from our random origin, it's hard to believe this band is unique. The only one of its kind, happening to be at this particular latitude, so close to home? It's more likely there must be many mighty structures like this across the face of this world. I did tell you we'd find something large-scale, Joshua.'

'You weren't wrong.'

'And if this viaduct does girdle the planet – and if there are more like this – then the beetles must already be consuming the resources of this world at a prodigious rate. Somewhere there must be mines the size of small nations . . . This is a predation far worse than humanity ever inflicted on the resources of the Datum. It is – illogical – to feel ownership. To be territorial. In what sense does this world *belong* to humanity? There wasn't a soul here half a century ago, and even now only a few scattered communities at most. And yet—'

'And yet this Earth is more ours than theirs.'

'Yes, Joshua.'

'OK, Lobsang, we found this viaduct. What next?'

'We go on. See what else is out there.'

'Fine.' Joshua tapped a tablet to disengage the autopilot. 'I guess the basic question is, do we follow this viaduct, or not.'

Lobsang thought briefly. 'Not. I fully expect to find more viaducts of this kind; this one ought to be typical. We should look for them.'

'Fine. North, or south?'

'South. I still believe the main action must be at the equator . . .'

Under Joshua's guidance the *Shillelagh* turned its battered nose south, and the turbines once more bit into the air.

28

ONCE THE GREAT New York viaduct had passed beyond the horizon, there was no more sign of the silver beetles. Not for mile after mile, hour after hour.

Heading steadily south, they tracked the eastern coast of North America, which, as far as Joshua could tell from maps downloaded into Lobsang's tablets, more or less matched the geography of the Datum – minus the people, and plus a choking blanket of forest that in most places extended all the way to the sea. Lobsang claimed that in places he could see the forest colonizing the sea itself, with trees rooted in the tidal areas, like banyans. Inland too the character of the forest gradually changed. In the increasing warmth as they headed south, Joshua thought the forests looked lusher, richer, a more vibrant green, perhaps.

But they could see more evidence of disruption, more damage done by storms and freak waves. Even out to sea they peered down on the wave-smashed ruin of a coral reef.

For a late lunch, Joshua rustled up more clam chowder and served it with bread.

'You know, Lobsang, I've been with you over a week now and I still can't get over the fact that you faked your death. I always suspected you weren't entirely gone, but still . . . Even by the standards of your bizarro life, that's quite a stunt.'

'I didn't mean to deceive anyone. Especially not my friends. But it was not all artifice, not a simple lie. The aftermath of the confrontation with the Next *was* like a death to me. I, who had always regarded myself as the custodian of humanity, was *ignored*.'

Joshua grinned. 'Ouch. It's like that episode of classic *Trek* where the Greek gods lost their worshippers.'

'Joshua, I'm trying to describe my deepest existential crisis. Perhaps we could discuss *Star Trek* some other time.'

'Sorry.'

'I had a breakdown, Joshua. In a sense I *did* die, or part of me. And the surviving piece has become a pioneer. A farmer. Once I tried to apprehend the problems of all mankind. Now I am immersed in the particular. Or I was.' Lobsang sighed. 'And yet here I am. Agnes, my anchor, had me face up to my wider responsibilities.'

'And Sally Linsay.'

Lobsang looked at him sharply. 'Sally? What about her?'

'I talked this over with Agnes. Lobsang, you keep talking about coincidences, or the lack of them. Isn't it a coincidence that this crisis with the beetles has blown up slap bang in the world *you* happen to be homesteading?'

'I have wondered about that . . .'

'She set you up.'

'Who?'

'Sally, of course. You say you went to her for advice on a suitable world. And she brought you out here?'

'That's so.'

Joshua laughed. 'She *knew* there were problems here. Or she guessed it; her intuition about the Long Earth is pretty powerful. Remember how we first met her?' It had been on their first jaunt together into the deep Long Earth – on The Journey, as fanboy types now referred to it. 'There we were drifting through the High Meggers for the very first time, two bozos in a leaky prototype airship – and she'd *already* gotten wind of the crisis First Person Singular had caused, that massive stepwise disruption, and she was *waiting* for us. And now she's got hold of you and Agnes and dropped you right on top of this latest drama. That's why the world is blowing up under you, Lobsang. Sally made sure you were here when it did.'

Lobsang seemed angry. 'If that's true she should have consulted me.'

'Would you have gone to New Springfield if she had? You've just been telling me about your breakdown, about your need to escape. This was the only way she could swing it.'

Lobsang was silent, frozen.

Joshua sighed. 'You never guessed, did you? For all your world-spanning intellect, for all your experiments with human- ity, you're still horribly naive about people, aren't you, Lobsang?' He glanced out of the window, looking south, the Atlantic to his left-hand side, choppy and foam-capped, the storm-lashed forest to his right. 'No sign of any action down there. I think I'll take some exercise. There's a fold-out treadmill in back. Call me if anything changes.'

'Oh, I will,' said Lobsang stonily.

Joshua looked back with a grin. 'Poor old Lobsang. You want me to gather a few laurel leaves? It wouldn't hurt—'

'Go take your run, Valienté.'

29

WHEN AGNES WALKED slowly up the trail back to her homestead on Manning Hill, bearing a basket of mushrooms she'd picked by the river, Marina Irwin came out to meet her.

Agnes smiled warily. Marina didn't smile back, and Agnes might have expected that. This morning, with George/Lobsang away, Marina had agreed to watch Ben for a couple of hours. But the business of the Poulson house and Nikos had created some tension between the families. It was often this way, in Agnes's experience, when you had to speak to parents about their children.

It took a moment for Agnes to register that the expression on Marina's face was more serious than that.

She hurried forward. 'Is something wrong? Is it Ben?'

'No,' Marina said quickly. 'Not Ben. He's fine, he's napping. It's your cat, I'm afraid. It's Shi-mi.'

Agnes checked Ben, who was sleeping peacefully.

Then she looked for Shi-mi.

The cat was lying by the hearth. When Agnes arrived, Shi-mi tried to lift her head, but dropped back. 'Agnes,' she said, softly, scratchily. 'I couldn't reach my litter. I made a mess. I do apologize.'

Agnes ruffled the fur above Shi-mi's eyes. 'A quite convincing mess too.'

'My decline was sudden. An abrupt shut-down. I imagine the

process is realistic. Marina was very kind, but there was nothing she could do. I hope she is not distressed . . . Agnes?'

'I'm here, sweetheart.' The cat shuddered and yowled, and Agnes stroked her until she was still. 'We still have choices, Shi-mi. You know that. We can take you to the gondola, the workshop—'

'No. This is my place. I have lived here, these last years, as a true cat. People accept me. The mice fear me. I disdain the dogs. It is right that I, I . . . I-I-I-I—'

The sudden judder in her voice was mechanical, profoundly disturbing, an intrusion of artificiality – or in fact of reality, Agnes supposed. But she stroked Shi-mi's side until she was calm again.

Shi-mi said now, 'Agnes, say goodbye to Joshua for me. And Lobsang. And make sure you tell Maggie Kauffman what became of me. Tell her I expect Mac to crack a bottle of single malt – *Auld Lang Syne*, not the cheap stuff – in memory of a flea-bucket.'

'I will. You have always been a good friend, Shi-mi.'

'I am Ben's cat now. That's all I ever wanted to be, I've discovered. And I, I . . .' Her voice tailed off into a soft, quite convincing purr. Then, as Agnes stroked her, she shuddered once, and her eyes opened wide, and their soft green LED light faded to dark.

30

THE NEXT TIME he called a halt, Lobsang stopped the twain dead, in the middle of the night, without warning. In the pitch dark, as the engines shut down, Joshua woke immediately.

In shorts and a T-shirt he rolled out of bed, pushed out through the partition into the body of the gondola, and stumbled into the co-pilot's seat, beside Lobsang. A dashboard clock showed two a.m. The only internal light came from the control tablets, which under-lit Lobsang's face as he peered through the window. Outside, the moon, more than half full, was bright.

It was obvious why they had stopped.

Under the prow, looking south, Joshua saw ocean to his left-hand side, waves glistening like mercury in the moonlight. To the right lay land cloaked with forest green. And spanning the world from left to right, east to west, was another viaduct: slim, glistening in the moonlight, striding on confident pillars out of the ocean and across the land.

'Just like the last,' Lobsang said. 'I mean, the same dimensions, apparently the same material. The night is very clear. I can trace it all the way to the ocean horizon, as straight as I can measure.'

'Where are we?'

'About the latitude of South Carolina. Some five hundred miles south of the New York viaduct. Took us around eighteen hours to get here.'

'OK. So, Lobsang, if this is typical as you keep saying, if the whole world is girdled with these things – if they're all around five hundred miles apart—'

'There may be a couple of dozen of them. Of course the distribution may not be a simple spacing with distance, or latitude. We've no way of knowing, without a view from orbit.'

'This is just as you anticipated, it seems, Lobsang. Global. I wonder how long it took them to build all this.'

'We've no meaningful way to answer that question, Joshua. We don't know how long they've been here, on this world. Or how fast they work. I suspect they've accelerated their progress since they encountered us. Getting it done before we can react. But that's only a guess, for now.'

'OK. But *why*, Lobsang? What's it all for? A transport system? Rail lines? Are these aqueducts, like the Romans used to build?'

'I doubt it's anything so simple. I could make guesses, but it would not be constructive at this stage.'

Joshua studied him. His face, underlit by the tablets' glow, was even harder to read than usual. 'You sound subdued. Are even *you* in awe of what these beetles are building?'

There was no reply.

'So, what next?'

Lobsang said thoughtfully, 'We've come under no threat. The beetles must be aware of our movements; we passed over a work party, remember, on the New York viaduct. We are evidently irrelevant to them. And our findings cannot be lost, even if we do not return; I have already sent short-wave radio reports back to Agnes.'

'You think we should go on. All the way to the equator?'

'That's what I suggest.'

'Then let's do it.'

The airship forged on, tracking the North American east coast, heading steadily south.

It was evening of this third day of the journey when they came upon the next viaduct, another five hundred miles or so south. This one spanned Florida, at about the latitude of Miami.

They reached the next viaduct south, another five hundred miles or so, about midday of the next day. It cut across the ocean itself with no land in sight, to north or south. Under a cloudy noon sky, the viaduct was difficult to make out against the grey shoulder of the ocean.

'There's no Mexico here,' Joshua said, checking their position on a tablet map.

'Very observant.' Lobsang told Joshua that on this world – and on similar worlds in this band – Mesoamerica did not exist, as they knew it from the Datum. 'Here, the Pacific breaks through into the Gulf of Mexico. And if you were to cross the Atlantic you'd find the Mediterranean flowing through the Middle East into the Arabian Sea. So there is a continuous waterway running all the way around the planet, at about this latitude. As a result the global ocean currents are different. Once, long ago, it was like this on the Datum; the palaeontologists call it the Tethys Sea. In fact some Long Earth geographers call these worlds the Tethys Belt.'

'I guess that's one reason the world's warmer?'

'Yes. And if they've straddled the whole world with a viaduct at this latitude, the beetles must have mostly encountered ocean, on their way around. An incredible feat of engineering.'

Joshua said, 'And I used to think oil rigs out on the Gulf were impressive.'

'Onwards, Joshua?'

'Onwards, Lobsang.'

They came upon the next viaduct at dawn of the next day, the fifth of the journey. It clipped the northern coast of Venezuela – the northern shore of South America, which was, in this world, an island continent separate from the north.

They continued south, leaving the viaduct behind, crossing dense jungle, a green chaos beneath them.

Lobsang said, 'That forest is probably full of exotic animals of kinds nobody ever encountered before. An island world.'

'Leave it for your grandchildren to explore, Lobsang.'

On they sailed, heading deeper over the interior of the continent now, riding through another day and into the night. And at about midnight they came to yet another viaduct. This was the equator. Lobsang recommended they wait out the night to see it properly.

They came together at the windows at about six a.m., on the sixth day of their journey.

The airship drifted in the air directly over the viaduct. It ran, Joshua saw, almost parallel to the course of a tremendous river.

'That must be the local Amazon,' he said.

'Yes.'

'So now what? Do we descend? Down I'll go with an electronic parrot on my shoulder, just like old times?'

Lobsang forced a smile. 'We don't want to provoke any hostility. For now we wait.'

'For what?'

'Again, I suspect that when it comes, we won't be able to miss it.' He yawned and stretched, quite convincingly. 'Now might be a good time to make breakfast, Joshua. Anything but chowder . . .'

'Fair enough.' Joshua rummaged through the tiny galley. They had frozen meat and French fries, and energy to spare; he decided to make burgers. As he got to work he said, 'You know, I said it before, we're going to have to do this properly.'

'Properly?'

'A genuine global survey. Teams of scientists with seismometers and magnetometers and whatever. Geologists and climatologists to predict what's going to come next. Super-clocks, atomic or some such, to measure the spin-up of the world more accurately than dear Agnes with her pendulums.'

Lobsang grunted. 'And the President of the United States, to make a formal first contact and hand over a flag and a plaque? You're correct in principle, Joshua. It might not be so easy to assemble resources like that, not like it used to be. But we should try—'

A blinding light filled the cabin, a glare that shifted like a swinging searchlight beam. They both ducked, instinctively. It was as if some tremendous craft was flying over the airship.

Joshua dumped the food he was handling and ran forward to the window. He saw a fireball, burning and spitting, scrape its way across the pale equatorial sky, leaving behind a contrail of feathery white vapour. It was heading dead east, out towards the mouth of the Amazon and the ocean.

And now the sound hit them, a tremendous cracking boom that made the gondola shudder.

'My God.'

Lobsang was smiling grimly. 'I told you we couldn't miss it, when it came. How long have we been here? Six hours? There must be several passes like that per day.'

'What the hell *was* that?'

'At a first guess, I'd say it was probably a mass of moon rock, wrapped in some kind of electrically conductive shell. We've glimpsed operations on the moon before, remember. That rock must be one of a stream, pouring past the Earth, skimming the atmosphere. As they must have been for years now. This is how they're spinning up the Earth, Joshua. The beetles. With these latitude bands, and the hurtling space rocks. They turned this whole planet into a huge electrical motor. And they've only just begun.'

Joshua looked down at the green carpet of life below, the river, the blue morning sky: rich, ancient, stunningly beautiful. And unique, as was each of the worlds of the Long Earth. 'To what end?'

'To serve their own purposes. Will that food take long? We've learned all we need to learn, for now. Let's eat, and go home. We've got work to do. And, Joshua.'

'Yeah?'

'You might be right. Sally Linsay may have got us all involved in this in the first place. I think we might need her help to make an end of it.'

Joshua felt a peculiar, deep reluctance to respond. 'You know, Lobsang, it's twenty-seven years since the three of us first met, in the High Meggers, when you and I went sailing out on the *Mark Twain*. I feel like I keep being dragged back to reunions at a school I hated. You think we'll ever be rid of each other?'

'Not this side of the grave,' Lobsang said gloomily. 'You see, Joshua, there's something specific I need to ask of the two of you.'

Joshua touched his controls. The *Shillelagh* turned gracefully in the air and headed for home.

'What's that, Lobsang?'

'We need to get the band back together, Elwood. I need you to go find *me*.'

31

S TAN AND ROCKY weren't told where the home of the Next was.
When they got there, after passages through a *lot* of soft
places, and while their travelling companions exchanged bursts of
quicktalk, Rocky and Stan stood and looked around. Despite all
the mystery, the Grange seemed nondescript to Rocky. They had
emerged on the outskirts of a small township by a river: a few dozen
houses built of wood and mud brick and what looked like prefab-
ricated ceramic panels. Smoke rose up from chimney stacks. Just
houses, Rocky thought at first glance, perhaps a few small work-
shops, even barns, though he saw no domesticated animals. Beyond
the town a grassy plain stretched off to the horizon, where trees
crowded, a misty green mass. There were more such townships,
three, four, five, some blending into each other, off across the plain.
The sky was blue, the day warm – very warm, given they were at the
latitude of Valhalla, of Datum Chicago, so they were told.

Surely it was just another world, in the great stepwise necklace of
worlds that was the Long Earth.

'This could be anywhere,' Rocky said.

'No church,' Stan murmured.

Rocky looked again; he was right. 'What about it?'

'Every other place you go. Every *human* place. There's a church,
or a mosque, or a synagogue, or a temple. And no town hall either.
Humans always build town halls. Americans anyhow.'

Rocky shrugged. 'Maybe the Next just don't like town halls.'

'Or *clothes*? . . .'

A small group of people came by, a variety of ages; evidently they'd been down to that river, swimming, fishing maybe, and now were on their way back into town, for their skin was glistening wet. And they were showing a *lot* of that skin. They wore variants of moccasins on their feet, and belts hung with tools, twine and other oddments. Not much else. And no adornments, Rocky managed to notice as he stared, no jewellery or pendants; even their hair was cut neatly but with no sense of styling.

When they saw the boys staring, the group, young men and women alike, shared bursts of quicktalk, and turned away, laughing.

Marvin was grinning. 'Put your eyes back in their sockets. You'll get used to it.'

'I seriously doubt that,' Rocky said.

The little group of travellers broke up. As Roberta and Jules made off for destinations of their own, Marvin led the boys to a small house on the outskirts of the township. 'This is a place I share with a few others. It's not *mine*. You'll get the idea, we don't really own stuff here. I'll go bunk down elsewhere for now. You're going to need a private space, time alone. Time to decompress. You especially, Rocky.'

'I can see that.'

'But you too, Stan, you'll have a lot to take in. There's food in there. Dried meat, fruit, coffee. Go to the river for water, it's clean. You can build a fire. There's blankets, clothes that ought to fit if you need them. By which I mean, cover-up clothes like you're used to. You're in Rome, but you don't need to do as the Romans do. Get some rest. I'll come by in the morning.' He glanced at them. 'You won't be disturbed. People will leave you alone.'

Rocky said, 'Why? Good manners?'

Stan cocked an eyebrow at him. 'Not that. You don't pat the head of a stray dog, do you?'

Marvin said tiredly, 'Make up your own mind. See you in the morning. Oh, one thing. I wouldn't recommend trying to step away. The only way out of here is via soft places. The worlds to either stepwise side are *much* less hospitable . . .'

The cabin turned out to be cramped, functional, neat, clean, with no decoration whatsoever. Stan dumped his bag, and went straight out 'to explore', he said. He didn't pause to ask if Rocky wanted to come.

Rocky set the fire, put on some coffee, unpacked his own bag, laying out his stuff. He found the routine comforting.

He made one trip out of the cabin, to fetch water from the river in a couple of pails. He came across another group of people in the water, in the warmth of evening, a little further downstream. Laughing, playing, they could have been kids skinny-dipping anywhere. A part of him longed to join in. But when he heard the high-speed gabble of their quicktalk, he turned away.

Back in the cabin he made up a bed from a heap of blankets and turned in early. He didn't expect to sleep well. He dug out his e-reader, a precious item brought out of the Datum by his parents when they'd first moved out to West 4, and, by candlelight, flicked through some comics.

He was surprised to find himself being shaken awake by Stan. Suddenly it was morning.

Stan asked, 'You OK?'

'I slept like a baby, I guess. You?'

'Me too.' Stan shrugged. 'I think maybe they put something in the food.'

'I didn't eat any food.'

'Or the coffee. Something to keep us savage apes quiet.' He looked restless. 'Listen, let's get cleaned up. I bet you Roberta's here any minute.'

Rocky was just putting his e-reader outside the cabin door, to allow it to charge up through its small solar panel, when Roberta did indeed show up. To Rocky's relief, though she was dressed much as had been the people he'd encountered yesterday, she at least wasn't showing much flesh, wearing a kind of shift under a loose sleeveless jacket full of pockets.

She smiled. 'Ready? Good morning, boys. Come on, let's walk.'

Rocky asked, 'Where are we going?'

'Well, I want to give you a flavour of how we live here. I thought we'd start at the school.'

Stan shrugged, indifferent, as he closed the cabin door behind him.

As they walked she went on, 'Lesson one, by the way. We dress for practicality, not for show. This jacket I'm wearing, as you'll see, does feature arguably the single most useful invention human beings ever came up with: pockets. Otherwise we wear only what we need, what is comfortable, generally as little as possible. You can tell we don't go much for surface appearances.'

Stan grinned at that. 'I think she's telling you that the Next don't get horny in the presence of skin.'

'Not quite that,' Roberta said patiently enough. 'Sex is very important to us. It binds us together, just as it did our ancestors. We're just not – obsessed by it. It's the way a child's behaviour may be controlled by mild hunger, say, which an adult can easily put aside. Besides, there is a different balance in the Next cortex, it seems, away from shallow visual stimuli towards an appreciation of the deeper content. *Looking* doesn't excite us so much. There are downsides. We don't appreciate visual art, as you do. We under-stand it – we just aren't moved by it.'

That shocked Rocky, and he thought of the comics on his e-reader. 'You have no art?'

'Not visual art, not primarily. Nor do we appreciate fiction – story-telling. We seem to lack the capacity to immerse ourselves in the imaginary.'

Stan grinned. 'I think she's being polite, Rocky. She doesn't "lack the capacity" to do anything. She means, you humans "lack the capacity" to resist the hypnotic wiles of a story-teller.'

'If you wish. We do appreciate music – especially elegant, structured, mathematical music. But we do have bodies, you know. We dance, we sing; we need that. And you don't play a Bach fugue at a line dance.'

Rocky said pragmatically, 'Well, you can only get away with dressing like that if you've got the climate for it.'

'That's true, and we do have the climate here. Which is why those who live here chose it, a world of this particular band, this temperate, seasonless location.'

Rocky frowned. 'You say, "those who live here". Don't *you* live here?'

'Not me, sadly. I grew up in human communities. I'm drawn back there, for better or worse. And that's where I'm valuable, where my vocation lies, as a sort of interface. A bridge.' She smiled. 'You're probably too young to remember. Once I worked in the White House, as an adviser to the President. But this *is* home for me. The only place I'm truly safe, for one thing.'

Stan looked around. 'I see grass. A few wildflowers. Those trees, in the distance. No animals yet.'

'You're thinking you could work out where you are in the Long Earth by classifying the flora and fauna? Don't be fooled.'

Rocky said, 'What is this, a Joker?'

Stan shook his head. 'I think she's saying they engineered it. This location, somehow. Imported samples of different biotas. Something like that?'

Roberta shrugged away the question. 'That's all irrelevant.'

They passed a party digging out what looked like a drainage ditch, down towards the river. Grimy, sweating, working hard: at first Rocky had the uncomfortable idea that these might be humans – ordinary people, like him – somehow pressed into labouring for these superhumans with their semi-nudity and their lofty taste in music. But as they passed he heard snatches of quicktalk.

'I know what you're thinking,' Roberta said. 'How does the work get done? In a town full of geniuses, who decides who sweeps the street or empties the cess pit?'

'No,' Stan said. 'You just do it. No mystery.'

Rocky frowned. 'Well, it's a mystery to me.'

Roberta said, 'I think Stan understands this, intuitively. We just get it done. When we see a problem, such as the allocation of basic work, we see further than you; we see all the way to a solution, immediately. The work must be done – this ditch must be dug. Some are better equipped for such work. There can be no argument about that. And then that necessary solution mandates our necessary actions. The only discussion is the immediately practical: is it to be my turn today, or yours? Do you see?

'Newcomers often ask about our governance systems. Do we have councils, leaders? Mayors, presidents, kings? We are still few enough that most of us can gather in one place to discuss significant issues. Again, the solution to a problem is usually obvious to all, the actions circumscribed by necessity. We run our affairs based on *reason*, you see, rather than *opinion*. That is, not on guesses based on too few facts. It is only loftier questions of philosophy, if you like, that divide us, where the goals are not clear, even not easily formulated.'

Rocky felt like defending his own kind – if he really was a different kind from these aloof characters. 'People must cheat. You must have crooks.'

'Of course they do,' Stan said. 'Game theory mandates it. No matter what system you have, a small proportion of cheats can always prosper.'

Roberta said, 'We tolerate the cheats. Few succeed, actually. Remember that each of us can see the other's moves clearly – it is as if you tried to cheat in a game open to all the players, like chess. It's possible, but very difficult. And if an individual's actions become excessive, social pressure is usually enough to correct the situation. We do have criminals, Rocky – only a handful, our numbers are small. We call them "ill", and treat them accordingly.'

Stan said, 'Maybe. But the very first Next individual most people heard of back on the Datum was called David. *He* was a criminal. Hijacked a military twain, killed most of the crew, got rescued by another twain, tried again. Next criminals are attracted to the human worlds, are they, Roberta?'

'We are aware of such issues, and deal with them—'

'Is it possible that the *only* Next that humans encounter out there in their own worlds are all criminals or insane?'

Rocky thought Roberta kept her temper remarkably well, after days of travelling with Stan, of goading like this. Maybe *that* was an authentic sign of superior intellect.

She said, 'You should not rush to judgement. Now, the school . . .'

The 'school' was centred on a small building, but most of the teaching seemed to be done in the open air – if you could call it teaching.

Out in a yard fenced off by a rope, there were maybe thirty kids, Rocky thought, of all ages from toddlers up to fourteen or fifteen. They sat in groups talking, or they played at games, running, counting, clapping. Some laboured at what looked like actual school work, writing, assembling puzzles, working with tablets – no drawing, he noticed. All of this was laced by their usual high-speed quick-talk, a sound that merged into a kind of white noise for Rocky. The few adults here moved amongst the children, watching, listening, sometimes quietly talking among themselves, a few making notes on pads and tablets.

A child fell and scraped her knee, and started to cry, a very human sound. She was scooped up by a woman and taken indoors.

'It's like no classroom I was ever in,' Rocky said.

Stan said enviously, 'Yeah, but I wish I had been. All this freedom.'

Roberta said, 'Most of the supervisors are family members. But our families aren't like yours. Our numbers are still few, and our relationships are fluid as a logical consequence. We don't have marriages so much as shifting alliances for child-rearing; we are trying to maximize the diversity of our gene pool. A kind of shifting polygamy.'

Rocky frowned. '"Maximize the diversity"? What about falling in love?'

Stan just laughed. 'Ha ha. Rocky wants to fall in *lo-ove*.' Classic Stan. 'But it's just another human illusion, my friend. Like fine art and religion. We've all been wasting our time for ten thousand years.'

Roberta said, 'Stan, it's suggested that when you join us you should spend some time working in the school.'

'For the first time since you came to fetch me out of West 4 I feel flattered. You think I've got something to give as a teacher, do you?'

She smiled back. 'You don't understand. These people aren't here to teach. Oh, they supervise, these are small children after all. But really they are here to listen.

'We are a new kind, you see, Stan. Our intelligence is in a category above that of humanity, the old variety. Yet we *know* very little – not much more than humanity had discovered for itself, and even that was riddled with flaws, misconceptions and sheer dreaming. And we aren't like humanity with its rich ancient culture stored in the fabric of a civilization outside our own heads: the books, the buildings, the sheer accumulation of inventions. *We* have nothing like that. Not yet.

'And so we find we can learn from the play of even the youngest children, who arrive in this world fresh, free of the limitations and misconceptions we inherited from humanity. We may garner from their play anything from a new design of spanner to a new, intuitive approach to transfinite mathematics. Even the babies, even the toddlers, when they "learn" to speak, invent their own vocabulary, their own grammar, even their own mathematics. We don't teach the children so much as learn from them.'

All this seemed chilling to Rocky. 'But from what you say, they don't draw pictures for Mom to stick on the fridge door. They don't have stories before bedtime.'

Roberta nodded. 'You see that as a loss. I don't blame you; I grew up in the human world too. They *are* little children. They do play silly run-around games and take naps. And we have trolls, here in this world. Maybe you heard their call in the night. We bring in the trolls in the evenings. They snuggle. Help the children sleep.'

Rocky asked, 'Why do they need help sleeping?'

Roberta glanced at him. 'They are extremely bright children, Rocky. At a very young age they gain an awareness of the fragility of life, of their own vulnerability. Human children, I think, believe they are immortal. Whereas our children—'

'Ah,' said Stan. 'No illusions. And they can't be distracted by accounts of heaven and the afterlife, or other fairy stories.'

'I learned this lesson myself, at a young age.' She briefly closed her eyes.

Rocky asked, 'Don't you have any religion? None at all?'

'Not yet,' she said. 'Come. Let's walk on.'

They hadn't gone much further when a group went by, quick-talking noisily, carrying picnic lunches, towels, tablets and pads of paper, heading out of town. Some of the party nodded to Roberta as they passed, and glanced at Rocky and Stan incuriously. They were mostly young, but there were a couple of women who might have been about fifty, Rocky thought. The presence of the older people made him realize how rare they were here; there couldn't be many folk over mid-twenties. It was a young community.

Roberta pointed at one of the older women. '*Her* name is Stella Welch. One of the brightest of the pre-emergence generation. She once worked as a relationship counsellor on the Datum, would you believe? She'd been thrown out of university – she was studying mathematics at Stanford, but the regular academic institutions of humanity couldn't cope with her. Now, here, she's become one of our leading thinkers on cosmological evolution. Before we found her, she worked out most of her ideas in private, on scraps of paper—'

'Einstein in the patent office,' Stan said. 'Figuring out relativity in his spare time.'

'That's right. I told you that where we have disagreements, Stan, is at the apex of our philosophies – the levels of goals, ultimate objectives. I think we all agree that the purpose of intelligence is to apprehend the world. But how to achieve that apprehension? Some, like Stella, think big. She wants us to understand the cosmos on the largest of scales – and, perhaps, some day, participate in its evolution. But others disagree. We have a philosopher, you might call him a poet, who has styled himself "Celandine".'

'Like the flower,' said Rocky.

'That's it. Strictly speaking the lesser celandine, a beautiful little wildflower, the spring messenger. Wordsworth admired it, yet it was treated as an invasive species in North America. Well, so it was, I suppose. Celandine, *our* Celandine, argues that all that is essential of our reality can be reached through the contemplation of a single flower: the mathematics of its diploid and tetraploid forms, the way its small face presses to the sunlight. Celandine says we should reach for the numinous, you see, not through the infinite but through the infinitesimal. You must meet him.'

'Oh, we must,' said Stan, straight-faced.

Rocky asked, 'So where are they going, the cosmologist lady and her friends, with their swimming costumes and all?'

Roberta smiled. 'We have a hot spring about a mile north of here. You might call the meeting they'll have a seminar. Or you might call it a hot tub party. If you're prissy you might call it an orgy.'

Rocky said, 'If I went with *them* I don't think I'd get much cosmology done.'

'I told you,' Roberta said. 'We enjoy sex. We do use sex socially . . . Right now there's a fierce debate going on over esoteric interpretations of some of the fluctuations in the radiation that's been detected coming out of the massive black hole at the centre of the Galaxy, and that's what Stella's group are going to debate. Passions among us can get just as stirred up by academic arguments as amongst you, you know. But it's a lot less easy to fall out if you're sitting in a hot tub grooming your opponent.'

'Grooming!' Stan laughed. 'Good word. Like the bonobo chimps.'

She nodded. 'You see, you do understand. Stan, you *will* come here, you know. You will accept your place here.'

Rocky said hotly, 'You can't give him orders like that.'

'But I'm not,' she said gently. 'Rocky, remember what I told you about how we lack free will, by your standards? Because often we can *see* what needs to be done, and have no choice but to do it. So it is with you, Stan. I'm sure you can *see* that your place is here, with us. It's just a question of where you fit in.'

But Stan seemed distracted and didn't reply.

'Hey,' Rocky said. 'There's our buddy Jules.'

Jules van Herp looked grimy, hot, but he was wearing Next clothing, as Rocky had come to recognize it: a loose waistcoat, some kind of loincloth, a belt with straps for tools. 'Been digging that drainage ditch,' he said to Roberta.

'No wonder you're sweating.'

'I like to join in.'

Roberta said, not unkindly, 'I'm sure everybody appreciates your contribution.'

Jules looked pathetically pleased. He spoke in a gabbling burst, and Rocky realized that he was, incredibly, attempting quicktalk, or imitating it.

Stan stared at him, as if disgusted. 'Hey, Rocky. Remember that kobold that hangs around the plant sometimes?'

'Bob-Bob.'

'Yeah. Grinning and mugging, trading his bits of tat. Trying desperately to be a human, a person. Never ever going to *be* one.' He stared at Jules. 'Remind you of anyone?'

Jules seemed upset, but he didn't reply. He looked to Roberta, as if she would make it right for him.

Rocky said, 'Hey, that's harsh, man—'

'Is it?' Stan turned on Roberta.

Something in him seemed to have snapped, Rocky thought. Roberta recoiled from his sudden anger.

Stan said, 'So is *this* the outcome of your great Next experiment? Humans like Jules here, reduced to performing tricks for your approval, all their dignity gone? Your own lost children, crying without comfort in the dark?' He glared around at the Grange, as if in disgust. 'Is *this* the best you can do?'

Roberta snapped, 'Your remarks are inappropriate. A dozen years ago the Next were scattered, stigmatized, locked up in human institutions. Now we are together, proud, growing strong, confident. You will learn, with us. Great minds think alike—'

'Hmm,' Stan said. 'You ever read Tom Paine?'

'Of course—'

'*The Rights of Man*, 1792. "I do not believe that any two men, on what are called doctrinal points, think alike who think at all. It is only those who have not thought that appear to agree." I'm with good old dim-bulb Tom Paine, not you. I humbly disagree with you – hell, no, I don't feel humble at all.' He looked at Rocky. 'I'm out of here. You coming?' He held out his hand.

Rocky was taken aback. 'But we only got here a day ago.'

'So what? I'm a Next, remember. A quick study. And I learned all I needed to know.'

'You *can't* leave,' Roberta said now. 'It's impossible, unless one of us takes you.'

Stan grinned. 'You know that's not true. Not any more. And you always knew I wouldn't stay here. Like you said, we super-minds can see all the way to the end game, right? So if you're as smart as you say you are—'

Rocky, ever practical, asked, 'What about our stuff?'

'Screw it. I'll buy you new jockey shorts. You coming or not?'

'Hell, yes.' And he grabbed Stan's hand.

Roberta made to get hold of them. 'Wait – you can't—'

But Stan could.

32

Earth West 389,413.

Joshua's first impression was that this world, towards the outer Western edge of the Corn Belt, was unimpressive. A little drier than most of its neighbours, maybe, the forest more sparse, the grasslands thinner. No animals in sight; he saw none of the big herd beasts that characterized such worlds.

And yet somebody had come here, to this world, to build a home.

Deep in the heart of a stepwise Kansas, by a sluggish river, a sturdy log cabin stood back from the flood plain. Joshua, watching from cover from a couple of hundred yards away, could see how a nearby forest clump had been cut for timber. Fields had been marked out and roughly fenced. There was a wood store, a hen house, what looked like the beginnings of a forge. There was even a garden, contained by a picket fence, where flowers grew this summer's day. All of this was surrounded by a neat stockade to keep out predators, and to contain any stock animals. Joshua was impressed. Yet it struck him that one couple could have built all this, given time and determination.

But the hen house was broken open now. Whatever animals had been kept here, goats or pigs or sheep, were gone, slaughtered or driven off. The fields were overgrown, the potatoes needed earthing, even the flowers were growing wild.

The house, though, was not empty. And Joshua, peering through his lightweight binoculars, thought he saw a face staring out of one window, a man's face, roughly shaven, fearful. The face disappeared, the man ducking back.

Whoever he was, it was obvious why he was afraid, and who he was afraid of. For Sally Linsay was here.

It was the spring of 2058. Since his airship tour of beetle-world with Lobsang it had taken Joshua nearly half a year to track her down.

He found her settled on a bluff to the west, overlooking the farmhouse.

Joshua approached her small camp, whistling softly. The tune was called 'Harpoon of Love', a fragment of their shared past that she might recognize. Then he walked into her field of view, with his hands up.

At least she didn't gun him down immediately. When she recognized him she turned her back and returned to her scrutiny of the farmhouse, squatting easily, her rifle of aluminium and bronze and ceramic in her lap.

'Took me months to find you,' he called as he walked up.

She shrugged.

When he got to the top of the bluff he found Sally sitting beside a deep-dug hearth laden with ash, a hearth evidently repeatedly used. Bones were heaped neatly, testifying to the many small animals who had given their lives here to keep her alive. And there was a pail of water, presumably fetched from the stream below. Even clothes, washed, spread over the rock, drying in the dusty sunlight.

He said, 'You've been here a while, right? A regular home from home.'

'What do you want, Joshua?'

'What the hell are you doing here, Sally?'

'Tell me what you want. Or just go, I don't care.'

'I'm here because of Lobsang.'

She didn't take her eyes off the farmhouse below. Her hair was

brushed back tightly from her lean face, giving her an intense, predatory look; the wrinkles around her eyes were deep. She was over
sixty years old now, he reminded himself.

She said, 'What about Lobsang?'

'He needs us. You. He said you'd probably be expecting the call.'

'Would I? Why so?'

'Because you took him and Agnes to New Springfield in the first
place. You set him up. So he says. Now he says you owe him.'

'I don't owe anybody anything. I never did.'

Joshua sighed. 'Well, he's giving up playing happy families with
Agnes. Now he wants us to do something for him. "I need you to go
find me," he said. He wants himself back. The old Lobsang.'

'Isn't that impossible? When he "died", he burned out all his iterations, so I was told. All his backup stores, in space, stepwise. Even
those probes he had out in the far solar system, the Oort cloud.'

'There's one copy he couldn't reach. You know the one I mean.
From The Journey.'

'Ah. Yes, of course. The ambulant unit we left behind to converse
with First Person Singular, at the shore of a desolate sea, more than
two million worlds out ... God, that's nearly thirty years ago.'

'Maybe even then he was thinking of it as an ultimate backup.
And now he wants it back. One more journey, you and me. Just like
the old days.'

She grunted. 'You and I don't have "old days", Valienté. How *did*
you find me?'

'Come on, Sally. You always did leave a breadcrumb trail. You
want to be found, just in case ... This time I started at Jansson's
grave, in Madison. The flowers you left there—'

'I don't need to hear about your brilliant detective work.'

'Also there have been rumours, of the setup you've got yourself trapped in here. This stake-out. You know how it is. Combers
spread gossip like a contagion. And you've been here a long time.'

'The bad guys are trapped, in that farmhouse. *I'm* not trapped.'

He kicked at the heap of animal bones. 'Oh, really?' He squatted down beside her, opened his pack and pulled out a plastic bottle of water and a strip of jerky. Sally refused the water but took a bite of jerky. 'It's impressive you've managed to pin this place down alone like this, for so long. But you need to hunt, collect water. And sleep. Even Sally Linsay needs to sleep.'

She shrugged. 'I mix up my hours. No set routine, so they never know where I am.' She lifted the rifle and without warning cracked off a shot; Joshua, looking down, saw splinters fly up from the porch of the farmhouse. 'Even when I sleep I set up automatic fire, random timing.' She slapped the rifle. 'This is one smart gadget. Sure they could rush me. I'd get some of them, but the rest could reach me. They haven't the guts. If they had any guts they wouldn't be here in the first place.'

'Who are they?'

'What do names matter, out here? It's what they've done that counts.'

'How many?'

'Five. All male. I think they're related, a father with sons, or maybe cousins. A pack of them.'

'Why don't they just step out of there?'

'Because I went in and smashed their Stepper boxes.'

'Tell me why you're here. What these guys did.'

'Look at the place,' she said bitterly. 'You can figure it out for yourself.'

'The pioneers. Just one couple?'

'Yeah. I found a journal that the bad guys threw out the door, with other trash. They grew up on the Datum, survived Yellowstone, ended up in a Low Earth refugee camp – that's where they met – and spent the next few years watching their parents cough their lungs up from the ash. When they were free of that they came out here, with all their parents' savings used up on a twain delivery of the tools they needed, a few chickens, a pregnant sow. They hammered together their farmhouse, planted their crops and their flowers, raised their pigs and their chickens. She got pregnant. They always hoped others might follow, that some kind of township would grow up here.'

'But these characters showed up first.'

'Joshua, they'd done everything right. They had a stockade, they had a cellar as protection against stepping raids. None of it was any use, not against enough force, not against men like these who will use that force without hesitation. They might have had a chance, a window, if they'd just gunned down these guys as soon as they showed up here. But good people always hesitate. Stupid, stupid.

'I figured out some of what happened. They killed the husband immediately. When I found the place a few days later the woman was still alive. You can imagine. She was pregnant, Joshua. I tried a raid of my own, hoping to get her out. They killed her pretty quick, hoping to get rid of a witness, I guess. And then—'

'And then you took your position up here. And, what? You've contained them ever since?'

'It will take them a while to starve. I drove off the animals in the stockade, but there's plenty of dry store in there, salted meat. The farmsteaders were careful to guard against a bad season. And there's a water supply, a clay pipe from the river. I haven't been able to cut that, there's not enough cover for me to reach it.'

'You're hoping that the hunger will drive them out.'

'No. I'm hoping they'll starve to death, and save me the trouble.' She said this levelly, glaring down at the house. 'Or maybe they'll kill each other. I hear arguments sometimes. Even a gunshot, once, inside the house. They've been calmer since the corn liquor ran out.'

Joshua studied her. 'You won't kill them yourself. Right? I mean you could. You could step in there and blaze away. You could torch the house. You'll let them die this indirect way, but—'

'I don't kill, Joshua. I *have* killed.'

He knew this about her.

She said, unprompted, 'Sometimes it's necessary. But it's not a policy.'

'Why not?'

She didn't take her eyes off the farmhouse. 'Because I don't trust myself. Because once I start, I may not stop. At times I feel *rage*...

'People like this, Joshua, they're the worst of mankind. Predators. Parasites, preying on the labour of others. Consuming decent lives for the sake of a few hours' fun. How many times have this band pulled a stunt like this before? Because, believe me, it looks to me like they're practised at it. And they foul up the Long Earth, the way humans were doing on their own planet long before. You want to know how I found this set-up? From the trolls.'

'What trolls? . . . Oh.' He realized that he hadn't heard a note of a troll-call, sighted a single one of the otherwise ubiquitous human-oids, since arriving in this world.

'I go where the trolls *aren't*. That's how I know how to find trouble, humans screwing up the place even more than usual.' She blinked, shook her head. 'When I was on Mars I had a long talk about this, with Frank Wood, the astronaut guy – remember him? He accused me of being the conscience of the Long Earth. Not what I want to be called, but it made me think.'

'After you told him where to shove it, no doubt.'

'When I find something like this – I can't stand it, Joshua. I can't stand by and let this happen.'

'Yet you're reluctant to kill. Not in cold blood.' He thought he understood. 'And so you're stuck, aren't you? You're caught between conflicting impulses – to destroy these bandits on the one hand, not to kill on the other. Just as you're contradictory about conceal-ment; you hide yourself away, but leave clues so you can be found. You're like a computer program stuck in a loop. Lobsang would understand.'

'So go get him and have him spell me on the stake-out.'

He laughed. 'I've a better idea. You've got me to help you now.

Suppose I go fetch a twain. A military ship. The US Navy is still running patrols out of their base on Datum Hawaii. The Navy isn't what it was, but they'd bring home perps like this for justice.'

She snorted.

'Come on, Sally. This isn't the Old West. You've got a live crime scene here. You're a witness to much of it, forensics will establish the rest. That's your way out. You stay here, keep them kettled. I'll go find a Long Mississippi waystation and send a message. Then I'll come straight back, and I'll stay with you until this is resolved. OK?'

She said nothing.

He sighed, stretched out on the rock, sipped more water. 'Look, take your time deciding. I'm not going anywhere today, I'm bushed anyhow.'

She looked down at him with the thinly veiled contempt that had always, somehow, characterized their relationship, across nearly three decades. She said, 'Oh, make yourself at home. Well. What shall we talk about? I know. How about you tell me what Nelson Azikiwe found out about your father?'

He squinted up at her. 'Of course you'd know about that.'

'You know me, Joshua. I know everything. I was there, remember. I know you went cry-babying to him about Daddy on your fiftieth, after I left you with him. Midlife-crisis cliché or what?'

'I just wanted to know who my father was. Is that so wrong? Turned out to be a good question. It took years for Nelson to nail it down, mostly because much of it is ancient history, pre-digital. He had to go hunting in person around archives on the Datum, those that survived.' He glanced at her. 'He found out a lot about my family. *And yours*, if you want to know.' That got her attention. 'Nelson wouldn't even let me help pay his expenses and stuff. I think he enjoys the hunt. Solving puzzles . . .'

'Just cut to the chase, Joshua. Did you meet dear old Dad, or not?'

He sat up and faced her. 'Yes.'

33

It had been earlier that year, the early spring of 2058, when Nelson Azikiwe had called Joshua from Datum London, where, he said, the last piece of the puzzle had turned up.

So Joshua went to meet him.

It wasn't safe to just step into London any more. You couldn't rely on ground levels; the continuing post-volcanic winter had left the city ice-choked, and thanks to clogged drains much of it was flooded. You had to come into the Datum elsewhere, and travel across geographically. As it turned out, the nearest to London Joshua could reach by a stepwise twain ride was Madrid, eight hundred miles to the south.

The Spanish capital was prospering, relatively. The shifting climate bands had turned central Spain temperate, and Madrid was now much as northern France had once been; wheat fields flourished where olive trees had grown sparsely. Most of the world's great cities, Joshua guessed, anywhere north of here, were worse off.

After a night in a shabby suburban hotel, Joshua made his way north by train, on the main line through Zaragoza and Barcelona, across the snow-clad Pyrenees to Toulouse, and then further north through France.

Paris was a tough stop: a Parisian spring was now like the worst of a Wisconsin winter. The city seemed to be functioning, with a few diehards going about their business, but in the Champs-Élysées, wide and deserted, the silhouettes of vanished crowds had been painted on boarded-up store windows, a wistful echo of vanished times. Joshua, in the day he spent waiting for his onward transport, found the emptiness eerie.

From here the way into London was by a twain, with engines protected against lingering Yellowstone ash – even after all this time the flight of jet aircraft was still severely curtailed. So Joshua flew over an English Channel where icebergs crowded what had once been one of the busiest stretches of water in the world.

From the air southern England looked as ice-bound as northern France, London a heap of abandoned buildings rising from snow banks and frozen flood plains. The Thames was a stripe of silver snaking through the city, long frozen solid; Joshua glimpsed what looked like skidoos skimming along the ice. As the twain passed over the city Joshua made out young pine trees growing sturdily in the parks, and whole districts that looked as if they had been burned out. The daylight was already fading, and Joshua could see the effects of power shortages, all too familiar now wherever you came from: districts blacked out, tower blocks that looked abandoned completely.

The twain at last descended over Trafalgar Square.

Joshua checked into one of the few hotels still operating, a fading, half-boarded-up pile on the Strand. Nelson had arranged this, as well as the various permits Joshua needed to move around London. There were no working elevators, and in his room door an old electronic key system had been drilled out and replaced with what looked like a Victorian-era lock and key. Inside the room was a notice about the hours when the power was most likely to be available. The central-heating radiator was lukewarm to the touch, and the wind whistled through a cracked window.

That evening, bundled in Arctic clothing, Joshua went for a walk.

The West End, what of it was still accessible above the risen river, was uneasy, shabby, the theatres and shops mostly boarded up. Joshua guessed that Datum London must, like most high-latitude cities, be mostly supported by its footprints in neighbouring stepwise Earths. But in the shop windows of Oxford Street there was some local produce: Canada geese and rabbits, hunted in the wintry Home Counties.

There wasn't much traffic, on roads that seemed too wide: some folk on bicycles, a couple of police cars. Joshua spotted a red London bus fitted with a gasifier unit. The few people out in the streets wore facemasks to guard against lingering volcano ash. Even so the air didn't seem as bad as it might have been before Yellowstone; at least the fumes from millions of internal combustion engines had gone, to be replaced by a sootier smog from wood-burning fires.

Joshua glimpsed one police action taking place in a side road, a tough and brutal raid in which step-equipped officers swarmed out of nowhere, hammering their suspects with overwhelming force.

Back in his hotel room Joshua spent the hours before sleep scanning TV news channels and a partially functioning web service, trying to get a sense of a world he rarely visited. Datum Earth wasn't recovering any that he could see. The news channels, underfunded and competing for sensationalist stories, told lurid tales of wars in the Middle East, brushfire battles over water in central Asia.

There was one peculiar item about the satellites in space. Over time many of these had fallen silent, and were one by one being dragged down into the Earth's atmosphere by friction with the air, where they burned up. The International Space Station had been the latest casualty. Long abandoned – the last crew had come back to Earth just days after Yellowstone – there had, at last, been no more propellant to sustain its orbit. The news report said that people had come stepping back to the Datum, to the track of the station, just to see it fall. Joshua saw sketchy images from handheld cameras of streaky fire in the sky.

He flicked through the channels until he found a recording of a soccer match: Liverpool versus AC Milan, a recording from a vanished, more colourful age. There was something else Step Day and Yellowstone had ruined, he thought sourly: organized sport. Still, the game was an exciting one.

Joshua dozed off with the match still unfolding on his tablet. He slept uneasily, immersed in the pressure of too many minds.

In the morning he went back to Trafalgar Square. And here Nelson Azikiwe met him, appropriately enough at the foot of Nelson's Column.

Nelson was bundled up in furs like a bear. 'The headquarters of the Royal Society is just a short walk from here. Carlton House Terrace.'

They set off through the frozen streets.

'I did have to make a special request to get into this archive, and have it opened for your visit.'

'I appreciate all this. But I hope you're not spending too much, Nelson.'

'Oh, good Lord, no, don't worry about that. I have a connection in the office of the Archbishop of Canterbury, and *he* has connections everywhere else. Also, ask your mentor Sister Agnes about Miss Guinevere Perch some time. Besides, some of Lobsang's own researches gave me a good steer. And there's always the thrill of the chase! You know me, Joshua. And wait until you see what I've discovered . . . So what do you make of London?'

'Kind of surprised it's still functioning at all.'

'Well, nothing is as it was, Joshua. Most people who live here now work for the government, or one of its contractors. The main task is simply to keep the city alive, to preserve its architectural and other treasures. And then there are others who have chosen not to leave their homes, and survive as best they can. London, in fact, is slowly reverting back to a state your own ancestors might have recognized.'

'My ancestors?'

Nelson smiled enigmatically. 'You'll see. Ah – here we are . . .'

The frontage of the Royal Society was relatively modest, Joshua thought. In a front yard enclosed by railings, a narrow track had been blasted clear, and they walked between walls of dirty snow and ice heaped feet high. A London copper in thick winter gear nodded as Nelson produced a pass of some kind, and allowed them through the door.

In the unheated reception area the tattered remnants of posters for long-ago conferences still stood on stands, and the marble floor shone, frosted over with old ice. The only light came from the windows, and from a few electric lamps connected by insulated cables to a generator that chugged in the distance.

Nelson, carrying a battery lantern, led Joshua deeper into the building, and down a broad staircase. 'Watch your step. Supposedly they keep this clear of ice, but . . .'

Another doorway, another stair downward, and they reached a corridor, much more cramped, darker yet, along which Nelson strode confidently, though he studied a map he drew from his coat pocket.

'What is this place, Nelson?'

'Why, it's the Royal Society's archive. Their *secret* archive.'

The anonymous door at which they finally stopped was labelled obscurely: ARCHIVE ROOM 5/1/14 R.S. PARA. The door itself was sticky but opened with a push. Within, Nelson flicked a light switch to no avail, tutted, and held up his lantern. Joshua saw rows of shelves heaped with dusty documents, in file boxes, folders, even a few scrolls.

Nelson led Joshua into the room. 'Of course the Society was always ferociously rationalist, but among the wags on the governing council this room is known as the Reliquary. Where the Catholics keep the bones of their saints, you see? *This* is where they kept the stuff that never quite fit the prevailing world view – and stuff that had some bearing on national security.'

They reached a table on which a file box lay open, containing a book, a single volume. Nelson looked at Joshua, evidently expecting some reaction.

'Nelson, I asked you to find my father. All this—'

'To understand the present, Joshua, you must learn about the past. And that's especially true when it comes to a family history as tangled and as deep as yours. I told you that Lobsang's work gave me a steer. Why, he's been looking for evidence of natural steppers practically since Step Day itself.'

'That's Lobsang for you. He was always quick off the mark.' Joshua rummaged through his memory. 'He told me about some of it. Percy Blakeney. Thomas the Rhymer. Some kind of small-time thief called the Passover—'

'His agents found traces of him in Somerset, yes. And some of the individuals Lobsang identified led me, one way or another, to the conspiracy.'

'Conspiracy?'

'Joshua, I found roots of all this going back to the nineteenth century. There was an incident in 1871 when the official organization, such as it was, was terminated.'

'What organization?'

'Steppers, Joshua. A kind of league of natural steppers. At that time they called themselves the Knights of Discorporea. They'd been operating for some decades before they were shut down. The surviving records were judged to be of scientific interest and were stuffed down here rather than being destroyed – luckily for us. But there was one more significant meeting, in 1895. And that's where the modern world was shaped – and your own life.

'All of *that* explains why your father did what he did. Doesn't justify it, doesn't excuse it, and there can be no forgiveness for the way he abandoned your mother. But it does explain it. I will tell you all you want to know – well, all I can – but I wanted you to see this final piece of the jigsaw for yourself.'

'I don't understand any of this, Nelson.'

'Read this.' And he tapped the volume on the table.

Joshua pulled off his gloves and, reluctantly, picked up the book. Leather-bound and with smooth, creamy paper within, it must have been expensive once. He opened the cover to reveal a page bearing an inscription in an elegant but hard-to-decipher copper-plate handwriting. He read the inscription, and his breath, which had been frosting in the cold air, caught in his throat.

MY ELUSIVE LIFE
BEING A FULL ACCOUNT
BY
LUIS R. VALIENTÉ, ESQ.
FOR THE BENEFIT OF MY BELOVED FAMILY

'Take your time,' Nelson said. 'We can stay here as long as you need.'

34

T HE CARD, INVITING Luis to lunch at the Drunken Clam in Lambeth, was dated the previous day – October 15 1895 – and was anonymous, signed only as by a 'fellow traveller'.

Of course it was from Oswald Hackett. Even a quarter-century after that fateful encounter with Radcliffe in the dungeons of Windsor Castle, no matter how he had hidden his past – even to the extent of changing the family name – Luis had always known that Hackett would be able to find him, that such a summons would come. That his past would catch up with him some day.

And of course he felt compelled to attend.

It wasn't hard to get away. Since the death of his wife Luis had lived alone, and his son and daughter, both grown, had long flown the nest, Ella to a comfortable marriage, Robert to take up engineering for which he showed an unusual aptitude, marrying somewhat later in his life. So Luis travelled to London by train from Bristol, where his financial interest in various steamship companies was based – controlled by means of a layer of company holdings under a false identity, and with no trail back to initial investments under his own name before Radcliffe's attempted entrapment of the Waltzers in 1871.

Indeed, Hackett had insisted that their birth names should not be used at this meeting. Luis had even considered going in disguise, cropping his whiskers or shaving his head or some such, but when he contemplated the prospect it seemed an absurdity for a man in his seventies. No, he was going to London for lunch with old friends at the Drunken Clam, and he'd defy any man who challenged him otherwise.

And if Radcliffe's successors caught up with him at last, then to the devil with it all, for he'd had enough of skulking.

His train was delayed.

And then, once he'd arrived in London, he couldn't resist a stroll around some of his old haunts. Oxford Street was now a grand thoroughfare lined with fine, spacious shops; Fleet Street a medieval alley chock full of traffic; Covent Garden Market crowded with more than a thousand donkey barrows, he estimated, and women with loads balanced precariously on their heads, its cobbles slick with crushed leaves; and at last Lambeth's New Cut itself, with the costermongers in their corduroy clothing, and soldiers strolling with uniforms casually unbuttoned, and coachmen in their livery and tradesmen in their frock coats, the street packed as ever with stalls and vendors of fried fish and hot potatoes, and beggars and entertainers, even street mummers – and, yes, with shoeless children, as much as it had ever been – as if the great reforms of the age, in education and public health and trade unionism, had been but fantasies.

Distracted by all this, he was a little late getting to the oyster-house.

The other two were here before him, and they stood to greet him. Both had aged well enough, Luis supposed. Fraser Burdon, who was about Luis's age, was as whip-thin and fit-looking as ever, with a leathery tan that told of years spent in warmer climes. Oswald Hackett was a decade older, in his eighties now, and it showed; Hackett had fattened up, was as bald as an egg, and could stand only with a stick, but he lumbered to his feet to shake Luis's hand.

Then they sat. Luis observed two books sitting on the table before

Hackett, one an academic tome he recognized, the other a novel he did not, with a fawn cloth-bound cover featuring a sketch of an idealized sphinx.

A waitress briskly took their order.

Hackett grinned, showing bad teeth. 'Let's introduce ourselves, gentlemen. Maybe we ought to write our "names" down; at our age it's going to be easy to forget. And by Christ, sometimes I forget who I *was* . . . My name is Richard Foyle.'

'Woodrow Boyd,' said Burdon. His accent had a new twang to it, and Luis studied him curiously; maybe he had moved away from the old country – permanently to America, perhaps?

Hackett prompted Luis. 'And you, sir?'

'John Smith,' said Luis.

Hackett snorted laughter. 'Oh, for God's sake, man, you almost *deserve* to be hanging by your thumbs in some cellar under Whitehall. Now, I know you both have children, Mr Smith and Mr Boyd. What have you told them of your, ah, past indiscretions?'

Luis said softly, 'I took each of mine aside at their age of majority and told them the lot. Seemed to me the best way to equip them to protect themselves in future, and their own children who may be blessed with our strange faculty – or cursed. As to the name, it's not an issue for Ella, who's married now. Robert, though, insisted on reverting to the old family name. Proud of the family origins, he says. The young! What can one do? In any case I have a close friend, a lawyer; we cooked up a story about an adoption, and so that's all above board.'

Burdon said, 'But it leaves you damned exposed, man. *If* anybody's still on our tail after all these years, which I doubt. I'd condemn you if not for the fact that my middle 'un is going down the precise same route. There'll always be Burdons.' He turned to Hackett. 'It's probably a risk for us to be gathering here in London – indeed, in one of your old haunts, if I remember your anecdotes correctly. Maybe you should get to the point.'

Hackett said, 'Let's get to the oysters first, for here they come . . .'

The service in the Clam was as brisk and friendly as ever, Luis thought, and the oysters just as relishable, even if, half a century later, the prices would have shocked the Great Elusivo.

Burdon, however, tried one and all but spat it out. 'My God. How can you eat these things? As if the Thames is one great mucky spittoon and I just took a mouthful of phlegm.' He tapped Hackett's book. 'This is a volume of Darwin's *Origin of Species*, is it not?'

'Yes, and it's a first edition, man, so keep your greasy fingers off.'

'If Darwin were here I'd demand to know what theory of "natural selection" can possibly have produced something as ugly and as useless as an oyster.'

Luis laughed. 'I dare say he'd have an answer.'

Hackett grunted. 'And I'd invite Darwin to speculate on our own peculiar condition – and our future. I have followed his work since his accounts of the voyage of the *Beagle*, you know. Saw the man speak a couple of times, but never met him. It's to my regret now that I didn't approach him when I had the chance; he died a dozen years back – or was it more? But in a way it was his ideas that made me resolve to bring us together again – the three of us, the first of the Knights. And the last, I fear, for I've found no recent trace of the others with whom we worked. We need a way forward – for ourselves and our descendants. *We* three may go to the grave skulking like whipped dogs, but that's not good enough for our children – for, believe me, some of 'em are going to inherit our uncomfortable, umm, faculties, just as you say, "Mr Smith". And what's to become of *them*, eh? What are we to do for them?'

'Nothing,' Burdon said. 'For we'll be long in our blessed graves. Let the future take care of itself.'

Luis said, 'But it's thirty years or more since *Origin of Species* was published. What is it that's prompted you to call us together now, Hackett?'

Hackett actually clipped him around the back of the head for that indiscretion. 'Good question, "Mr Smith". The answer lies in the pages of *this* little book.'

The second tome on the table by his plate was a novel. '*The Time Machine*,' Luis read from the spine.

'By some chap who writes for the magazines. Calls it a "scientific romance". The book's a sort of fairy story about Darwin's scheme of selection. Or a nightmare. It shows a future in which mankind changes, evolves – bifurcates – over a span of hundreds of thousands of years. Becoming something quite different from the modern stock.' He searched their faces. 'D'ye see? That's one root of my idea, my scheme. The other comes from dear old Grandpa Darwin, and if you've ever read his book, which I'm sure you haven't, you'd know that an early part of it, and a deuced long section it is and written in a rather lifeless tone, is all about pigeons.'

'Pigeons?'

'The breeding of fancy pigeons for particular traits. That's the key to his argument, you see. Just as a man will breed his pigeons or his dogs for colour or body shape or whatnot by consciously matching up the types he wants to promote, so nature, all *uncon*-sciously, selectively shapes its stock of animals and plants using the blunt scalpels of hunger, a lack of room to live, changes in the weather, and extinction.'

'You've lost me,' Luis admitted cheerfully. 'Our oysters have gone extinct, by the bye. Shall I order another round?'

Burdon ignored him. 'You haven't lost *me*, "Foyle".' He leaned forward and lowered his voice. 'You're talking about cross-breeding our children, aren't you? The way a man breeds his horses.'

At that word, *cross-breeds*, Luis saw it, all of a sudden, and forgot about the oysters. 'My God, man. How can you conceive of such a thing?'

Hackett sneered. 'Thank you, Lord, for blessing me with compan-ions of such small imagination! Forget horse breeders and pigeon fanciers. Think of arranged marriages. Haven't our own aristocracy been pairing off their sprogs for generations? Not to mention the royalty. And I know for a fact, "Smith", that the new mercantile rich you associate with are doing exactly the same thing now, purely to keep the wealth in a closed circle of families. All I'm suggesting is – let's do the same. For our own protection, our families'. And,' he added more ominously, 'to improve the blood.'

Burdon said heavily, 'You'd better tell us exactly what you propose.'

'Simple enough. We establish an organization – a Fund, let's call it, to be handled anonymously by one of the better banks – no, more than one, let's spread the risk across institutions, indeed across nations – umm, "Mr Boyd", you may be able to handle the American end. Now let's suppose you have a grandson of marriage-able age, "Smith".'

'Actually I do have a grandson.'

'Good. While you, "Boyd", might have a spare granddaughter of similar age. The Fund keeps a list of our families and others, the births and deaths and so forth – all quite above board, with opera-tives who have no idea of the true purpose. But when two eligible candidates pop up in the fullness of time, they are – approached.'

Burdon said, 'Approached?'

'It might work this way. Letters arrive, from a nominated bank. A meeting is arranged between the two youngsters. Each is told that if they would consider a liaison, then a gift would be available – call it a grant. We'd have to consider the wording; the only stipulation would be the birth of a sprog, of course, which is the point of the exercise. Perhaps there would be a sweetener to make the meeting in the first place: fifty per cent of the balance might be paid up at the marriage, and a further fifty per on the occasion of the first litter. But if the youngsters don't hit it off, they can walk away with no harm done. D'ye see? There's no compulsion, no hardship – everybody wins, including a young couple with an unexpectedly good start in life.'

Luis grunted. 'How much of a "good start"?'

Hackett shrugged. 'That's to be decided between us. A thousand pounds, perhaps.'

Luis, who had started out earning shillings in flea-pit theatres, was nothing if not careful with his money. 'A thousand pounds? Are you mad?'

'Certainly not,' Hackett growled, 'and ye needn't pretend, either of you, that we haven't the resources between us to establish a fund healthy enough to generate such sums through the interest paid. And it needn't just be the three of us.' He produced a piece of paper, tucked into the endpapers of *The Time Machine*. 'I've done some research – well, I've had plenty of time to do it, and the resources, and don't ask me how. Beyond those I contacted like you two, there is a slew of families like ours, their histories studded with Waltzers, or possibilities anyhow, like true pearls on a paste necklace.'

Luis scanned the paper, which was a simple list of surnames. *Blakeney. Burdon. Hackett. Orgill. Tallis. Tallyman. Valienté . . .*

'You need to be careful with that,' Burdon murmured.

Hackett nodded and tucked the paper away. 'You understand that we are strengthening the blood, increasing the chances of the faculty emerging in a given generation. Many species respond quickly to such domestication. I suspect Darwin would predict that the results ought to be visible in a very few generations. A century or so, perhaps.'

Luis said, 'And when said cross-breeds produce a Waltzer child to order – what then? What's to become of it? It will be in danger of just such a risk as we have faced in the course of our own lives – suspicion and persecution, especially if, despite appearances, the successors of Radcliffe are still on our elderly tails.'

Hackett nodded. 'It's a fair question. Initially there would need to be some way of keeping tabs, an agency on hand to advise the bewildered young parents of toddler Jimmy when he starts popping out of existence.'

'But the need for that would fade with time, I imagine,' Burdon said. 'The more Waltzers there are, the more the families will *know*. Because Uncle Jerome or Aunt Ginnie will have had just the same peculiar trait.'

'That's the idea. So what do you think?'

Burdon said softly, 'You've always thought big, "Foyle". All the way back to the days of Albert and his Knights. But this is a stretch, even for you. To manipulate the generations – to try to shape the future, centuries ahead—'

Luis tried to take all this in. 'To change the very flavour of mankind itself. What arrogance, sir!'

Hackett flared, 'Arrogance? But what is the choice? To leave our descendants unprotected, to be picked off for their magical ability by these – others? An ability with the capacity for so much good – have you forgotten the Underground Rail Road?' He tapped the cloth-bound cover of the novel. 'And besides, as this tome shows us, the future will shape mankind willy-nilly if *we* don't, like it or not.

'But the oneness of humanity will be gone, it's true. "We are living at a period of the most wonderful transition, one which tends rapidly to accomplish that great end to which all history points – I mean, of course, the realization of the unity of mankind."' He studied their faces. 'You recognize that quote?'

'Albert,' Luis said. 'I bought his *Golden Precepts* after his death.'

'Well, that fine dream is bogus. The coming war with Germany, and it's inevitable, you know, will see to that. But after the flags are folded there will be a deeper divergence than any between nations. For we, we humans, will become *two* kinds, at least – d'ye see? There'll be the old sort, Radcliffe and his crew, *Homo sapiens sedentarius*. And then among 'em will arise the new sort, us – *Homo sapiens transversus*. That's the best I can do with my schoolboy Latin; let Darwin's successors sort it out. And in a century or two, *if* we do this, our new kind will flood this good Earth – and those green forest worlds into which we Waltz, I dare say. And then, who knows what the future will hold? Eh? What's it to be? It's that or the subjugation we saw with poor Abel on the Mississippi. Subjugation, or glory.' He studied their faces, a very old man, determined, intent. 'Are you with me? Are you?'

35

'YOU CAN GUESS the rest,' Nelson told Joshua, deep in the hidden basement of the Royal Society, both of them huddled in the cold over Luis's handwritten journal. 'Hackett's programme of inbreeding worked, and very quickly.

'Within decades there was an explosion of natural steppers in the human population. That's what I infer from the available evidence anyhow. Surely many of those steppers disappeared into the Long Earth, lost to some accident or other – or just seeking places to hide. It would have been interesting to study Happy Landings, before it was destroyed. See if there was any upsurge in the number of drifters turning up there.'

Joshua thought back. That remote colony, ultimately the source of the genetic upgrading that resulted in the emergence of the Next, had been a kind of natural sink of steppers, a well that all the soft places led to. 'Yeah. I do remember folk from there saying that in recent times they had come under more pressure. Too many people coming in, the ancient balance with their troll population lost. But it wasn't the kind of place to keep proper records, was it?'

'No. And meanwhile those steppers who remained close to the Datum would have been secretive. Surely the lesson of what became of the Knights of Discorporea wouldn't have been lost. But no secret is easy to keep.' He let that hang.

Joshua sighed. 'Don't tease me, Nelson. You've found a few stories, haven't you?'

'Not all of it conclusive. For instance – have you heard of the Angel of Mons?'

'No. Should I?'

'Maybe not. The Great War, 1914. British soldiers in the trenches spread stories of mysterious figures who would appear and vanish again, helping the wounded. Some said they were the ghosts of English archers from the Battle of Agincourt, centuries earlier.'

'Hmm. Whereas in fact they were my great-great-uncles?'

'That's the idea.' He opened a notebook and checked an entry. 'The official line is that it all came from a bit of fiction by a Welsh writer called Arthur Machen. Which was a very effective cover-up, for the time. In the 1940s, during the next war, I believe there must have been steppers aiding elements of the Home Guard, the volun-teer army who were preparing to resist a Nazi invasion of England. I saw a version of a memoir by Tom Witringham, from which some pages had been excised – Witringham set up guerrilla-war training for selected Home Guard units. There could easily have been useful refuges in the stepwise worlds, resistance hideouts, caches of food, explosives, you name it – everything but guns and ammo because of the steel . . .'

The story went on, in Britain at least reflecting the changing concerns of national history.

'In the 1950s, Cold War spies. James Bond with a step ability, Joshua! In the 1970s, it looks as if they were infiltrating the unions and the IRA—'

'This all seems very virtuous.'

'Oh, I've no doubt there was the usual streak of jewel thieves, peeping toms and other rascals. With time I may be able to pin down more from police records. And this is only the British connection – well, the whole inbreeding conspiracy did start here – but clearly there were elements overseas too, especially in America. We know that from what you've told me of Sally Linsay's family history . . .'

36

SALLY WAS HUNCHED over her bronze rifle, peering down at the farmhouse. 'I know some of this. My father was never a stepper himself. But he married into a family of steppers.'

'I remember how you told me that as a kid you used to take your father over into stepwise Wyoming, where he had his workshop. Nelson said your mother came from an Irish offshoot of the Hackett clan.'

'My father loved my mother. I guess he still does love her memory, for all his other faults. And he was fascinated by stepping, even though he was no stepper himself. He studied the phenomenon scientifically, eventually dreamed up the Stepper box. But he hated my mother's family – the "old-country clan", he called them – with their letters and phone calls. You see, before she met my father, there had been some family pressure on my mother to "marry the right sort". I always thought it was to do with money. Well, that was the story they told us kids at the time. I never knew different, until now. Never knew they were *breeding steppers*. My father never told me. Even though we went all the way to Mars and back together! I suppose it never occurred to him to confide in me. Knowing him, it wouldn't.'

'I never heard from any Fund when I was growing up,' Joshua said. 'I suppose the Sisters would have kept them away from me, even if they found me. And they never put pressure on you?'

'They may have tried, but if so they could never find me. I stepped away from Datum Madison a year after Step Day, and I never came back again. Not long enough to be tracked down by that shadowy coven, anyhow. Of course my father got his revenge on them, with Step Day. After that almost anybody could step, with a Stepper box costing a few bucks, and that blew their nasty little conspiracy wide open.' She looked at him sharply. 'Anyhow, what about your father? Did Nelson find him in the end? That was the point of the exercise.'

He took a breath. 'Yes, Nelson found him, Sally. Through the Fund's records. He's in a retirement home in New York, West 5. Originally from the Bronx – he's Irish American.'

'Heart-warming. Less of the stalling, Valienté. Spill the beans.'

'He's – ordinary. He's called Freddie. Freddie Burdon. You know I grew up using my mother's name. Of course the Home had no records of my father.'

'Burdon. Another genetic legacy of the Discorporea days, then.'

'Yes, but he never stepped, not before Step Day. I guess he carried the gene, though. He's seventy-four years old now; he was only eighteen when I was born – seventeen when I was conceived. Just a kid, for God's sake . . .'

37

'OF COURSE I remember your mother.' Freddie Burdon had a broad Bronx accent. *Ya madd-ah.* 'Of course I remember Maria. Who wouldn't? Whaddya think I am, a monster? . . .' And his speech broke up into coughing.

He looked older than his age, Joshua thought. Old, shrunken over an imploded chest, face angular and bony. He was like a sick bird. His skin tones were grey. Even his clothes, a worn jacket and trousers, looked grey, as if stained with ash. He claimed that his emphysema was a legacy of heroic volunteer work he'd done in the aftermath of Yellowstone, helping the victims escape, even though he'd already been in his fifties then. Joshua suspected that was bullshit, that smoking had done the damage; even now Freddie's fingers were stained nicotine yellow.

They were in a charity home, a big boxy construction of timber and concrete typical of a Low Earth footprint city. Outside, the air of this version of Brooklyn was faintly smoggy, like a memory of how its Datum parent had once been.

Freddie looked dwarfed, out of place and out of time. He was lucky, Joshua thought, to have finished up in a refuge like this. Joshua made a silent resolution to pump some money into the place, but out of his father's sight, and out of his reach.

Freddie, Joshua learned, had trained as an electrician but had never got a qualification. He'd drifted from job to job, spiralling down as he'd aged. He'd never had family – not after Maria – and had never accumulated money.

'Of course I remember Maria,' Freddie said again. 'Look, I was no stepper. Even with a box, when I tried it, I puked my guts up. But I had the genes – didn't I? And so did your mother. And look what we made.' He coughed again, but grinned, a ghoulish expression. 'The great Joshua Valienté! The world's most famous stepper! Only good damn thing I ever did was you, son.'

'How did you find my mother?'

'Well, they sent me the name, an address.'

'"They"?'

'A bunch of bankers representing the families. The Fund, you know. And there was a cheque inside that first letter, with a promise of more if I went to see her, if we got to know each other, if we married, if we had a kid. A regular instalment plan. But it wasn't, you know, *compulsory*. Just a kind of suggestion. And the money wasn't that much, looking back. If I'd ever had any money I probably would have turned it down.'

'But you had no money.'

Freddie grinned wider. 'Not then, not now. So I thought, what's there to lose? At least I can go meet the girl. You have to understand she was only fourteen then; this was in the nature of setting up a long-term relationship between us. So I pocketed the dough and headed over to Madison, Wisconsin, and looked for the family. Only to find—'

'She'd run away.'

'Yeah.' He coughed, hawked, and spat into a handkerchief. 'She'd had some version of the same letter. Wasn't happy at home anyhow, and now there was this pressure to hook up with some stranger. Only fourteen. Well, I tracked her down.' He tapped his forehead. 'See, I'm no stepping superhero like you, but I had a brain on me then. She was in this home for kids—'

'On Allied Drive.'

'Was it? Can't remember. I do remember those nuns. I asked for Maria. Said I was a cousin. Well, I was, wasn't I? They didn't trust me further than I could spit. Don't blame them, looking back; I was seventeen years old and a piece of work, you know what I'm saying? I might have given up.'

'If not for the money.'

'If not for that. Then I saw her coming back from school, that was what did it for me. God, she was beautiful. *You* got your looks from my side, God have mercy on you. Well, I wasn't going to give up after that. I found a way to get to her.'

'How?'

'Bribed a cleaner. It all became a scandal when—'

'I know. Freddie, she was only fourteen.'

'Yeah, mister high and mighty? Well, I was only seventeen, so there. Look, Joshua – you want me to tell you it was love at first sight? All I know is we liked each other, and I took her out a couple of times, she found a way to sneak out.' He submitted to another coughing spasm. 'We were just kids, OK? But I made her laugh, and she was rebellious and as cute as hell. We had fun, that's all. At first. Though the nuns gave her a tough time.'

'But you had the letter from the Fund in your pocket. Did you think you were *entitled* to her? This beautiful kid? That you had some kind of rights over her?'

'No! It wasn't like that. Christ, you should have been there. Look,' and he seemed embarrassed, he leaned forward and whispered, 'we never went past first base, OK? Until one night—'

'Do I want to hear this, Freddie?'

He shrugged his hunched shoulders. 'You came to me, remember. It was a summer night, 2001. She was looking her best. She had this cute pink angora sweater, and I remember she always wore this dumb little monkey bracelet that her mother had once given her. And I had a bottle of Jack Daniel's I'd lifted—'

'Oh, Christ, Freddie.'

'What do you want me to tell you? It was *ordinary*. Just a fumble. We were drunk, we went too far. *Ordinary*. Sorry if that's not what you want to hear.' He leaned closer, and Joshua could smell the cigarette smoke on his breath. 'And I know it was illegal, but I never forced her. OK? I was stupid, not bad.'

'So she got pregnant.'

'Caught first time. Just our luck.'

'And you ran out?'

Freddie spread his hands. 'What would you have had me do? I couldn't support her, let alone a kid. Even if it had been legal. I was a kid myself. Yeah, I ran. I figured those nuns would look after her better than I ever could.'

'Not well enough,' Joshua said grimly.

Freddie looked at him. 'So that's it. That's the story, the top and bottom. I was just a kid, and I lived a whole life since then. If you want me to tell you I never loved again, I'd be lying. But I never forgot her, Joshua. Hurt me years later when the Fund told me she'd died.'

'You never came to find me, did you?'

He laughed sourly. 'Yeah. *That* would have gone down well. So now you found me. Now what?'

Joshua thought that over for a long moment. Then he stood. 'I guess our business is done.'

'Oh, is it? You think you got "closure" now?' He made quote marks in the air with his fingers, to Joshua a very old-fashioned gesture highlighting an old-fashioned word. 'Hey, where you going? Will you come see me again?'

Joshua considered that. 'Maybe.'

'Listen,' Freddie called after him. 'I know you're disappointed. Whatever you expected of me, good or bad, I've always been that, at heart. *Disappointing*. But I'll tell you something, Joshua. You never knew about me, but I knew about you. Followed you in the papers, and online. How could I not? After Step Day and all. Maybe I never came to see you. But I never asked you for money, did I, Joshua? And I'll tell you something else. I never went back to the families for the money they owed. I mean, for fulfilling the contract, for knocking Maria up. That was the point of it all, wasn't it? I never asked for that money, Joshua. Even though I was owed. That's got to count for something, hasn't it? Even though I was owed!'

Sally said, 'And that was it?'

'That was it.'

'Have you been to see him again?'

Joshua shrugged. 'I guess I will, when this latest Lobsang business has blown over.'

'Just an ordinary guy, huh.'

'Yeah. Not some demonic seducer. And not much older than me, though he looked it. That was the strangest thing. Didn't feel like he was a father at all. We were just two old men together. Well, I got that monkey off my back, I guess.'

'You atoned with your father, Joshua. Important step on your spiritual journey as a mythic hero.'

He squinted up at her. 'You laughing at me?'

'Me? Never. And I guess that whatever you say about Hackett and his cronies, they achieved what they set out to achieve. They changed the genetic composition of mankind. They changed the world, the whole future.'

'And screwed up our lives in the process.'

'True,' she said. 'So what now?'

'So now we eat, sleep – or at least I do – and in the morning I go call the cops. And then we go find Grandpa Lobsang.' He studied her. 'Deal?'

She closed her eyes, cradling her rifle. Then she said, 'Deal.'

38

NEW SPRINGFIELD COMMUNITY meetings were generally well attended. In a place where you had to make your own entertainment, people turned up, even if just in hope of seeing some fireworks. People would come drifting in from their stepwise lodges, the population slowly gathering. But this particular meeting was going to be fractious. Agnes knew it.

It was taking place outside the Irwins' principal home, a sprawl of tepees and tents, just over the Soulsby Creek ford from Manning Hill. Everybody was here, sitting on the grass or on chairs hauled over. Oliver Irwin was standing there like he was chairing the meeting – well, in a way, so he was – with Marina sitting at his feet, and Lydia curled up against her, and Nikos with the elderly Rio a huge sleepy lump at his side. There were Angie and Nell Clayton, and the elegant, elderly Bells with the grandchildren they cared for, and the cheerful Bambers, who always looked like they'd just crawled out of the swamp they made their living from. Lobsang and Agnes and seven-year-old Ben sat quietly to one side on a log, keeping a low profile, and Agnes hoped fervently they would continue to do so.

All around them the blustery wind blew, and there was the usual stink of sulphur in the air, commonplace now, and somewhere sheep bleated miserably. Even the trees of the endless native forest were dying back. It wasn't a happy day, it didn't feel right. But then, Agnes reflected sadly, it hadn't felt right here for months, if not years.

And over all their heads hovered the massive bulk of a twain: a military airship, the USS *Brian Cowley*.

The ship hung silent, its turbines idle, the great hull held in place by mooring ropes anchored to the ground. You couldn't help but be intimidated by the huge ceramic armour plates of its underbelly with their weapons pods and spy-hole observation ports, or by the row of spruce military officers on the ground, who had come down from the ship to tell the folks of New Springfield that they were going to have to leave their home.

Agnes's fears were fulfilled. From the beginning the meeting didn't go well.

At Oliver's invitation the ship's captain, called Nathan Boss, a stiff-looking forty-something, stood up to make his pitch. 'If you'll just let me go through the logic of what we're trying to do here—'

Somebody yelled, 'Don't go *through* anything. Just go *away!*'

Catcalls and laughter. That was fair enough, Agnes thought. These people had come out to this world precisely to get away from having smart men in uniforms tell them what to do.

'We're here to help you,' Captain Boss tried now. 'We came here with a team of scientists to study what's going on here, in this world. And I brought with me a letter passed on from my own command chain – in fact there is a note for you from President Starling himself—'

'That crook!'

'*I* didn't vote for him.'

'The President says that the whole of the extended stepwise nation is with you at this difficult time. We only want to help you—'

'Then shift that ship and quit blocking the light on my beets!'

More laughter.

Lobsang leaned over to Agnes. 'Ironically, it's obvious why they're so crabby.'

'Of course it is. Nobody's getting any decent sleep.'

And they hadn't for a long time. In the months since Lobsang's airship jaunt to the south with Joshua, things had worsened dramatically. The length of a day was now down, incredibly, to just twenty hours. Not only that, according to Lobsang who was now measuring such things for himself, the spin-up of the world seemed to be accelerating further.

The nights went by too fast, and it was as if they were all permanently sleep-deprived, or jet-lagged. Of course you could just step away to the neighbouring worlds if you sought a normal day-night sequence – worlds where, bizarrely, sunrise and sunset were drifting out of synch with the home world. But, Agnes had seen it for herself, the more the day here shrank in length, the more people came back to their homes, night after night, as if defying reality, and their own weakness.

'Stubbornness,' Agnes said now. 'Sheer, dogged, Yankee stubbornness. Ain't no clattering sci-fi monster of a silver beetle going to drive me out of *my* home.' For it seemed obvious to everybody that the strange creatures who shared this world must somehow be responsible for the other odd phenomena; you didn't need to see Lobsang's global system of metal viaducts to understand that. 'And the more jet-lagged we get the more stubborn we become.'

'True, perhaps. And this world *is* the one the founders chose – this is where they have the bulk of their iron tools, for one thing, even if they were drawn here to an ore seam the beetles' actions may have created. Why should they give all that up? But that doesn't mean we shouldn't listen to the advice of the Captain here and his crew. I mean, they did bring a properly equipped science team.'

'But the Navy wouldn't even be here if you hadn't called them in, Lobsang.'

'Somebody had to. I'm concerned, Agnes. Not just for us, not just for this town . . .'

Agnes glanced down at Ben, who was trying to work a handmade wooden yoyo. He wore a beetle-silver bangle on his wrist, as did most of the kids in this town. And he looked tired, snappy, irrit-able, just like the rest. She grabbed Lobsang's hand, synthetic flesh on synthetic flesh, but it felt like a human contact, warm, strong. 'Look, Lobsang, Oliver Irwin is the mayor of this dump, in all but name. You played your part; you brought in the Navy. Now let Oliver do the talking. Let these others sort it out. *Don't be Lobsang.* Be George. Be ordinary. Be Ben's dad. That's why we came here, remember. It's best if everybody figures this out for themselves – makes their own decision about their lives, rather than have *you* make it for them.'

He took a deep breath, 'I'll try, Agnes. I will try.'

Captain Boss, visibly frustrated by his reception, yielded the floor to one of his officers, a woman, late forties, slim, dark, crisp-looking.

'My name's Margarita Jha. Commander, USN. I'm the chief science officer on this vessel, the *Cowley*. As the Captain indicated we have on board a slew of specialists, civilian and military, come to study the strange phenomena that are afflicting your world here. Their team leader is Dr Ken Bowring of the US Geological Survey, whose speciality is seismology. We also have meteorologists, ocean-ographers, you name it. We even have an anthropologist with an attachment to the SETI Institute, that's the Search for Extraterrestrial Intelligence, come to study your, ah, unwelcome neighbours . . .'

Jha spoke well and fluently, and was listened to politely in return. She had an air of command her captain rather lacked, Agnes thought.

'But,' Jha said, 'my own specialty is biology. That's where I started. And as a biologist I have to tell you that, unfortunately for you, and your kids, your animals, your crops – indeed, for all the living things native to this particular stepwise Earth – now that the spin-up has reached a period of twenty hours or so, we've passed a fundamental limit.

'You *can't* adapt to a day of that length, or shorter, and nor can other living things. Experiments connected to the space programme have shown this; twenty or twenty-one hours is the minimum length of day we can withstand.' She counted the points off on her fingers.

'I'm talking about your chickens not laying properly. The critters you call furballs, who come hunting at dawn – you must have seen them staggering around as if they're drunk or high, at all the wrong times of the day, and then the poor little beasts get snapped up by the big birds and other predators, as long as *they* are awake and functioning. The flowering plants can't track the sun. Even the trees are suffering, in the long run. Your world has an intricate ecology, just as we find everywhere on the Long Earth, and a beautiful one – but that ecology is dependent on a twenty-four-hour daily cycle. I'm afraid we're predicting a significant die-back, and soon. And that's even before you start to talk about the effects of the volcanism that's breaking out, the fires, the ash clouds suppressing the temperatures, the toxic gases you can *smell* – we all remember Yellowstone, don't we? Ken Bowring will tell you about that.

'Folks, it's not just your lives that have been disrupted. We're talking about a peculiar kind of extinction event on this world. And it's your great misfortune that your township has been caught up in it.'

Captain Boss stepped forward. 'Thank you, Commander. Admirably clear. Any questions?'

Oliver Irwin was still standing. He glanced around at his neighbours. 'I'm sure I can speak for all of us. What are we going to do about this, Captain?' He looked up at the military airship. 'What are *you* going to do about it?'

'Well,' Boss said, 'in the long term we intend to continue to study this phenomenon, or this group of related phenomena, as best we can. But in the short term we're going to have to lift you off this rock, and take you, your children, and all your goods, somewhere safe. I know you have stepwise lodges, but I understand this particular world was the centre, for you. We'll take you wherever you want to go.' He added with a forced smile, 'Look, we won't leave anyone behind. Your pets – even your farm animals will be saved. The twain is a big ship.'

Oliver stiffened, and the townsfolk muttered.

Agnes groaned. 'That young man just does not get it.'

Oliver Irwin said, 'Sir – Captain Boss – let me tell you this. This isn't a "rock". Or a "centre". This is our home. And when I ask you what you're going to do about it, I don't want to hear you say we need to run and hide.' A rumble of approval from his neighbours. 'We're not quitters. We're Americans. We're pioneers. That's why we're here. That's why we're going to *stay* here. And if you can't help us,' to yells of approval, 'then please do what Al Todd asked you to do, and get that big ship of yours out of the light of his beets.'

'Darn right!'

'Well said, Oliver.'

Boss looked helplessly at Jha.

The science officer stepped forward again. 'We do sympathize, sir. Really. The US Navy isn't fond of quitting either. But we don't even know what we're dealing with here—'

'It's those darn silver beetles,' said Angie Clayton. 'That's obvious enough.'

Boss said, 'But we hardly know anything about them. You know that we've taken the *Cowley* on a tour. We spanned much of the continent, this footprint of North America. The creatures you call the beetles are building – something. Like immense road systems. What we don't know is why they're doing all this. What the purpose of their network is. And unless we can figure out at least that much—'

Lobsang sighed.

Agnes plucked his sleeve. 'Lobsang. *No.*'

'—then we can't even predict what comes next—'

'I must speak up,' Lobsang murmured.

'George wouldn't. Sit still.'

'—we don't have any kind of handle on any of this—'

'But I do,' Lobsang announced. He rose to his feet, grave.

Agnes covered her face with her hands. Oliver stared. Ben looked bewildered.

Captain Boss glanced over. 'I'm sorry, Mr – Abrahams, was it?'

'George Abrahams. I do know what the beetles are constructing. It's a Dyson motor.'

'A what?'

'Maybe you'd better let me speak to your science people.' And Lobsang walked past Oliver Irwin, towards the crew, as if taking over. Just as Agnes had dreaded.

Al Todd got to his feet and pointed. 'Yeah, you do that, Abrahams, you big shot! I always thought there was something not right about you. All our troubles started the day you showed up here. Maybe you should hitch a ride on this Navy tub right back out of here!'

The meeting started to break up, the mood frustrated and angry.

Ben stared up at Agnes, wide-eyed. 'Agnes? Does Mr Todd mean it?'

'No, Ben. He's just upset, is all. He doesn't mean anything. Now you come with me while George is busy, those chickens won't feed themselves . . .'

39

'DYSON? YOU MEAN Freeman Dyson?' The man was asking the question even as he shook Lobsang's hand.

'Manners, Dr Bowring,' Jha murmured. 'Introductions first. Mr Abrahams—'

'Actually I'm a doctor also.'

'I apologize. Dr George Abrahams, meet Ken Bowring, US Geological Survey. As I said back there Dr Bowring is the team leader of our civilian science cadre.'

'Freeman Dyson, though. That's who you meant, isn't it? Come, walk with me, sir, please. I'd like to show you the data we're assembling, the interpretations we're making.'

Margarita Jha didn't know what to make of this man Abrahams. He was tall, slim, a little elderly for an early generation of such a new community, perhaps. But there was something about him that didn't quite fit. His accent was basically east coast American, she thought, but not quite pitched right, as if he was forcing it. His handsome but rather unremarkable face seemed expressionless – or rather, it was as if the expressions followed the emotional trigger by a perceptible interval, as if they required some conscious impulse. Maybe this guy Abrahams was just an eccentric. Mankind, splintered across the Long Earth, had begun to diverge, culturally, religiously, even ethnically, and in all that room it seemed to her that what she would once have called 'eccentrics' were becoming the norm. But even so, Abrahams puzzled her.

'So,' said Bowring, 'you're a doctor of—'

'Engineering. My doctoral research was in communication with trolls. I was sponsored by Douglas Black.'

'Fascinating, fascinating,' Bowring said, distracted. 'With the collapse of the old Datum academic institutions, we must rely increasingly on the generosity of figures like Black to fund our research. Still, the work gets done. You know Black himself?'

'I've met him. Before he became a recluse. Or so it's said . . .'

Jha, and others of the crew, had been involved in another twain mission that had taken Black, in secret and at his own request, to a refuge much further away than either Bowring or Abrahams imagined, probably. She kept her counsel.

They came to the rough work station Bowring and his team had set up, in the shadow of the twain hovering above. Trestle tables were laden with tablets and heaps of paper, meteorological charts, maps; there were samples too of the local flora and fauna. All this was a pale imitation of the more extensive science suite up on the twain itself.

Bowring said now, 'It's certainly a pleasure to find you here, Dr Abrahams. Coming in cold to a situation like this, there's only so much progress we can make in a fixed time. No offence to the people here; your neighbours seem a smart, decent, very fine bunch of people. But to have had a scientifically educated man on the spot for some years—'

'I understand.'

'Tell me about a "Dyson motor".'

'Do you have a map of the world? Or any kind of global view . . .'

The Navy crew had toured the continent in the twain, and had sent up sounding-rockets for a higher-altitude view. There was even a clutch of simple orbiting satellites, though they had yet to complete a full planetary survey. There were various ways of viewing the result; they had maps on paper, electronic images, photographic surveys. Jha's favourite was a globe you could handle:

a basketball borrowed from the crew on to which a projected photographic mosaic had been glued. It looked pretty much like a globe of any stepwise Earth, save for a peculiar local readjustment of the continents: that gap between South and North America, the global seaway that ran from the Atlantic coast through the Mediterranean and out through Arabia to the south. That and the ubiquitous green of forests that stretched all the way to the polar regions, north and south.

But on this globe there were also false-colour markings of anomalies. Lurid orange bands around the coasts of the continents showed tsunami damage. Peculiar fractures circled the Pacific, divided the Atlantic lengthways, and spanned the southern oceans from northeast Africa south and east towards Australasia: the planet looked like a cracked vase, Jha thought. The cracks were huge tectonic flaws, bands of volcanoes and quakes. And most striking of all were the spidery bands of silver that followed the equator, and the lines of latitude to north and south.

Abrahams picked up the basketball and traced the silver lines with a finger. 'I have seen some of these. I took my own twain journey to the south; I saw enough for me to infer the rest. You'll be able to look it up for yourself. Freeman Dyson was a twentieth-century engineer who thought big. He worked on Project Orion, on how to use military-specification H-bombs to drive a spacecraft. And he came up with at least one conceptual scheme of how to spin up a world.' He pointed to the latitudinal bands. 'You wrap the world in conducting straps, and run an electrical current through them to generate a shaped magnetic field around the planet, a field shaped like a toroid, a doughnut. You have another electric current running pole to pole through the planet, and you close the loop with an arc through the magnetosphere. That causes the auroras we've been seeing from the ground. And then you throw in a stream of spacecraft, starting in high orbits and spiralling down through the toroidal field.'

'Spacecraft?'

'They need only be simple. Massive, but simple. Lumps of moon rock, for example, wrapped in some kind of conducting blanket. On my own twain journey, we reached the equator. I saw such rocks in the sky. You must have too.'

'Yes. We've also been observing the moon, from where projectiles of that type are evidently being launched.'

'And have been for years – since my wife and I first arrived here. The physics is trivial. The flyby rocks come in, they are dragged by the Earth's new magnetic field, and, thus coupled, they pull at the Earth. Each rock speeds up the planet's spin, just by a fraction. Then, when they reach their lowest orbit, they start to push *against* the planet's magnetic field to spiral back out of there again – and, again, they give the planet another minute shove. Theoretically, it's as if the Earth has been made the armature of a huge electric motor.' He looked at their faces, seeking understanding.

Jha said, 'I think I get it. Metaphorically anyhow. I have a daughter. When she was little, in the park in our home town back on West 5, there was a roundabout, a simple thing, a wooden disc with hand rails spinning on a pivot. The kids liked to run by it; each one grabbed a rail and let it go, and with every tug the roundabout spun a little faster.'

'That's the idea.'

Bowring sucked his teeth. 'So the world's spinning faster. What about the conservation of momentum? Where's the extra spin coming from?'

'I don't have the facilities to observe properly,' Abrahams said. 'Perhaps you do. It appears that the flyby objects stream off towards the sun. There they are probably deflected at closest approach by a gravitational assist – or maybe they use solar sails – and that way they harvest angular momentum from the sun, and return for another pass. It's a slow process for an individual rock; it must take months or years to make a full orbit, from Earth to sun and back again. But with a stream of such rocks the accelerating effect becomes continuous.'

'So let's see if I've got this straight,' Jha said. 'The latitude bands, the magnetic field they create, are ways of coupling these flyby rocks to the Earth. But what's really happening is that through the rock stream some of the sun's spin is being transferred to the Earth.'

'The sun's angular momentum, yes. And its angular kinetic energy.'

'Yeah. A hell of a lot of energy,' Bowring said dubiously.

Abrahams smiled wistfully. 'That depends on your perspective. Suppose you doubled this Earth's spin rate – brought the day down to twelve hours. You'd need four times its original angular energy. But to top up the spin to that rate would take just *thirty minutes* of the sun's total fusion-energy output. It's a lot to us, but if you can tap a source as vast as the sun . . .'

Bowring said grimly, 'Well, the damage is being done. Dr Abrahams, I'm sure you can imagine the kind of effects the spin-up is having on this world as a whole. Every Earth is essentially a ball of liquid: the iron core and the mantle. The solid crust is only a fine rind laid over that liquid interior. Under the continents the crust is maybe sixty miles thick, compared with the Earth's radius of four *thousand* miles. It's as if the Earth is a big round crème brûlée.

'Because of its spin – I mean its regular, standard-issue twenty-four-hour spin – *every* Earth is deformed, flattened slightly, not quite a sphere, bulging at the equator. Normally this isn't a problem. And the natural state of things is actually for the spin to be changing anyhow, slowing very gradually over geological time. The solid crust has the chance to adjust to the changes of deformation.

'That's not the case here. In the few years since the spin-up has begun, the crust's deformation, at the equator at least, has increased by around eight miles. That might not sound much, but the ocean-floor crust is only about three miles thick. And so—'

Abrahams traced the jagged lines that spanned and circled the oceans on the basketball globe. 'Fractures in the sea bed.'

'I'm afraid so. There are natural faults where the sea floor is spreading, such as down the spine of the Atlantic, and where the oceanic tectonic plates butt up against the continents, such as around the coasts of the Pacific. Now these faults are cracking, opening up, and you get quakes and volcanism. If they're underwater, you can get tremendous tsunamis that batter the coastal areas—'

'The smell of sulphur in the air.' Abrahams smiled sadly. 'The aroma of Yellowstone. Wonderful sunsets. Symptoms of a world coming apart at the seams. And bad news for anybody like me, who only came here looking for a spot of quiet farming.'

Bowring looked impatient, uncomfortable. 'I must keep stressing that this is still largely guesswork. Extrapolation. We have so little data . . . This is not the Datum, which is, or anyhow was before Yellowstone, saturated by survey gear of all kinds. Networks of seismometers, for instance. I myself worked at the Large Aperture Seismic Array in Montana, an exquisite instrument. And of course the climate was monitored by ships, planes, satellites, as well as weather stations with a global coverage. Here we have only our one observation platform in the *Cowley*, a few pinprick settlements like yours, Dr Abrahams – forgive me – and a handful of observations from the instruments we can emplace. We need gravimeters to measure the planetary morphological distortion, line-of-sight lasers to measure the distortion directly.'

Jha said, 'I know you're doing your best, Ken. As we all are.'

Bowring grunted, visibly unhappy. 'At least we *can* do something. I myself was trained up properly, before Yellowstone. But the Datum science institutions have never recovered from the volcano. The next generation of scientists will be amateurs, if that. *Then* we'd have no hope of understanding something like this at all.'

'So,' said Abrahams, 'we've talked about the what. Have you got any closer to understanding why this is happening?'

'Well, we're asking the question, at least. Come see . . .'

274

The silver beetle was, self-evidently, dead.

It lay on its back on a table, the gas pods removed from its green underbelly, its sections of silvery armour carefully detached and laid aside, its carapace of what looked like black ceramic sliced through and peeled back to expose a greenish, pulpy mass within.

'I have to emphasize we didn't kill this thing,' Bowring said. 'We found this corpse—'

'Or this inert unit,' Jha corrected him. 'There's no consensus yet over whether these creatures are alive or not.'

'Very well. We found him in the big exhausted mine working you call the Gallery. Evidently inactive. We've no idea what happened to him, or even how long he's been there; we've no idea how processes of decay work with these creatures.'

'Or even if he's a he,' Jha said dryly.

'True enough. It's hard not to anthropomorphize. Especially when you see one standing upright, with that eerie mask-like face turned to you.'

'You settlers call them "beetles",' Jha said to Abrahams. 'I've heard the scientists call them "assemblers". The marines under our Colonel Wang are calling them "bugs".'

'But we don't know what they call themselves because they won't talk to us,' Bowring said, sounding exasperated. 'We believe they are capable of communication, Dr Abrahams. Well, that must be true for them to be able to accomplish such complex feats of engineering as the viaducts. We believe they are individuals; they exhibit individualistic behaviour – such as the first ones discovered by the children here, who began trading rock samples for bits of beetle jewellery. You could regard that as a kind of preliminary communication, if you like. Pre-symbolic. You could even see it as a kind of play.'

'Play?' Abrahams mused. 'I hadn't thought of that.'

'Play, yes. Their assaying of this world has evidently been very extensive, and it's hard to imagine a few random ore samples given them by uneducated kids can be of any real value. It's a chink of hope we might somehow get through to them. And that they're not *evil*. Not if they can be playful.'

'Hmm,' Abrahams said. 'Even the conquistadors loved their children, Dr Bowring. Even the Nazis, probably.'

'True enough. Anyhow that's as far as we've got. We have one of the SETI crowd here who's been trying to get them to recognize prime numbers in symbols, heaps of stones. You know the kind of thing: mathematics is supposedly the universal language. The beetles just walk away.'

Abrahams laughed. '*I'd* walk away if you started counting out prime numbers to me. How boring . . .'

Jha leaned over the beetle on its table, a facemask over her mouth. The dissection had progressed a lot since Jha had last seen the specimen, but in the body's interior she made out nothing but a kind of spongy mass, undifferentiated. 'I'm just a lowly plant biologist, but even I can see we're lacking in internal structure here. No obvious organs, no skeleton.'

Bowring shrugged. 'We think the ceramic shell acts as a kind of exoskeleton, to support the weight. And there is a *lot* of weight; that spongy stuff is very high density. We've run various scans – MRI, sonar. There is structure in there, but it's a kind of network with identifiable nodes, not a collection of organs like the human. The same kind of structure extends to the head, which seems to be more a sensor pod than a brain pan.' He glanced at Abrahams. 'Which could be significant. The human skull has grown over our evolutionary history, but even so there's only so much room in there – and cerebral functionality has to share space with extensive areas devoted to sight processing, for instance.'

'Hmm,' Abrahams said. 'Whereas if these creatures have their brains in their stomachs, so to speak—'

'Room to grow. And if they are potentially very smart, they're also very capable. Take a look at this.' Bowring picked up a tablet, which showed an image of a bug's manipulator arm. He swiped the image to magnify a section.

Jha saw that the 'limbs' terminated with splits, into twig-like appendages like fingers. But the 'fingers' bifurcated too, into still finer manipulators.

'It goes on down to the nano scale,' Bowring said. 'We think these creatures could manipulate molecules.'

Abrahams said, 'You call it a "creature". We return to the point. Is it a creature, though? Is it biological?'

'As Commander Jha said, opinion is divided on that. Animal or robot? My own theory, for what it's worth, is that this is some kind of very advanced cyborg. And a very *old* design, to the point where the technology and the biology have merged, seamlessly. The manipulator substructures certainly look engineered. On the other hand the basic body plan looks like a throwback to some biological origin, to me. I mean, it's not efficient. Why not have the whole body as a kind of modular robot? That way you could split off substructures, merge whole bodies to form larger structures . . . Certainly the capability to engineer on a molecular scale and upward gives them enormous manipulative power. Dr Abrahams, I think a beetle could make anything from almost any ingredient, given the right elemental composition.'

'Including a copy of itself?'

'Yes. We know these things have – reproduced.'

'Using locally sourced materials – beetles grown from the substance of this world. I found that out myself. This is a von Neumann replicator, then. A machine capable of reproducing.'

'Among other capabilities, yes. And when they combine they are clearly capable of tremendous feats, like their globe-spanning viaducts.'

'But these creatures don't come from Earth at all,' Abrahams said. 'I mean, from any of the worlds of the Long Earth.'

'Right,' Bowring said grimly. 'And of course our best evidence for an extraterrestrial origin—'

'Is the Planetarium.'

And to get there, to travel from the mundanity of New Springfield into the utterly unknown, the highly trained and heavily armed crew of a Navy twain had to submit to being stepped over hand in hand by local children, just as had Lobsang and Agnes from the beginning. Children who had figured out how to do this by themselves years ago.

40

MARGARITA JHA HAD stood beneath this alien sky several times since the twain's arrival here at New Springfield. She'd never got used to it, and never expected to. The party of marines and scientists who were working here in the Planetarium, at a small base camp of tents and trestle tables – and a gun emplacement – were a welcome dose of the mundane. There was even a place for the local kids, the vital stepping link, with food and drink and books to read, even toys.

Once the party had stepped through, Colonel Jennifer Wang, who was in charge here, approached Jha with a brisk nod. Wang, the commander of the *Cowley*'s small marine detachment, wore body armour and a facemask, though nobody had any proof that the latter was necessary; the Planetarium air was benign. 'Commander Jha.'

'All seems quiet.'

'Yes, ma'am, just another routine day here at Bug Central. Bugs doing their bug stuff and leaving us alone. Step easy, Commander.'

'Thank you, Colonel.' As routine an exchange as they'd ever had, Jha thought. She'd known Wang for a long time, in fact, since they'd shipped together as junior officers on the *Benjamin Franklin* under Maggie Kauffman many years ago.

And yet – look where they were! You couldn't escape the thought: what if the gossamer bridge they had just crossed to get here vanished as suddenly as, presumably, it had appeared? But here were these marines in this extraordinary place, and the young scientists from the *Cowley* doing their jobs, joshing and complaining about the food as if they were in some training camp in a Low Earth Iowa. Of course the local kids weren't troubled at all. Jha suppressed her own gloomy speculations. What else could you do?

She went to rejoin Abrahams and Bowring, who were peering up at the crowded sky.

Bowring said, 'It's clear this world doesn't *belong*. Not in this chain of worlds, our Long Earth. We're a little light on mathematicians in this expedition,' he said ruefully. 'Damn brain-boxes tend not to travel well. But those we do have are suggesting we're seeing some kind of flaw in the Long Earth. I mean, its structure in higher dimensions.'

'It has to be something like that,' Abrahams said.

'I'm afraid we have no kind of handle on that yet, on how this could happen – or how to fix it. We're going to need somebody a lot smarter than us to figure that out.'

'Indeed,' Abrahams said dryly. 'But there's no evidence that the beetles can step, is there? I mean, aside from the unique step that takes them from Gallery to Planetarium.'

'None at all,' said Jha severely. 'But we're keeping an eye on that. The Captain's posted sentries in neighbouring worlds, stepwise. It seems that a handful of these bugs leaked into New Springfield from – someplace else. Well, from *this* place, wherever this is. The point is, now they're using the resources of New Springfield's Earth to breed like rats in a granary. We do not *want* these bugs to step over into another Long Earth world and start all over again. And, worse yet, spreading even further.'

'A wise precaution.'

Bowring said, 'But we are making some progress with our observations.' He pointed at the sky, the crowding discs of the stars. Many of them were too bright to look at directly, like fine needles in the eye if you stared. 'Evidently this is a world inside a globular cluster, a dense cloud of stars. The density tails off if you look through the crowd and further out. Clusters are big balls of stars, quite compact, and most of them orbit the centre of the Galaxy, each travelling as one big mass.'

'But which cluster?' Jha asked. 'Have you made any progress with that?'

'Actually, yes,' he said with a grin. 'Clusters differ in their age, their metallicity, their size, and we can measure such parameters. We *think* this is a globular cluster called M15 in our catalogues. Thirty thousand light years from Earth – well, that's about as far away as the centre of the Galaxy. Very old but pretty big, a hundred thousand stars crammed into a space less than a couple of hundred light years across. The astronomers we have on board are pretty excited, actually. There's believed to be a big black hole lurking at the centre of this cluster – a mash-up of dead old stars, I guess. They're thrilled to be up close and personal with such a thing.'

'But black holes aren't what we're here to study,' Jha said reprovingly. 'We're primarily studying the assemblers. Whatever they seem to be doing on this world.'

'"Doing on this world",' Abrahams repeated. 'They're clearly not native to Earth. You don't think they're native here either?'

Bowring shrugged. 'Hard to be definitive, we've so little evidence. But, those bubbles you see?' He gestured around the landscape. 'Sacs of air everywhere. They look biological, like flotation sacs on seaweed – much larger of course—'

'Yes.'

'The gaseous contents of the sacs match the contents of the bags you see attached to individual beetles. And they all contain a subtly different suite of gases from the local atmosphere – which itself isn't far from Earthlike, which is why it's breathable for us. In the sacs there's more carbon dioxide, more sulphur compounds and so on. Rather like a dilute industrial smog, from the peak days of the Datum.'

'Terraforming,' Jha said. Suddenly she saw it. 'You think the bugs are manufacturing a different atmosphere. They aren't native to this world. They're terraforming it.'

Bowring pursed his lips. 'Well, that's the wrong word. Not making it like the Earth, as we would . . . Delivering conditions that suit them, presumably. *Xenoforming* – perhaps that's a better term. They came to this world to make it like their own.' He looked around, pulling a face. 'Look at them swarming everywhere. They take the stuff of this world, and are making it into copies of themselves. How disgusting – what *greed*.'

'Perhaps,' Abrahams said. 'But we aren't so holy. The European explorers imported their own farm animals, their vermin, even their song birds to the Americas, to Australasia. What have the Europeans done save convert a significant fraction of those continents' biomass into hundreds of millions of copies of themselves? Just like the beetles. If by a rather low-tech method.'

'They are disturbingly like us, then,' Bowring said.

Jha asked, 'So if they aren't from this world, then where?'

'Well, I can only speculate.'

Jha sighed. 'I have a feeling we don't have time to get everything peer-reviewed, Dr Bowring. Speculate away.'

'I think they crossed space, to this world. As opposed to stepping here. They are interstellar travellers. Look up there.' He pointed to his left, at the sky. 'It may or may not be visible to your eyes – it isn't to mine, but the youngsters can see it, and the spectrometers show it clearly. The stars in *that* direction, many of them, have a greenish tinge.'

'Dyson spheres,' Abrahams said immediately. 'Or some kind of clouds, at least. Another of Freeman Dyson's big ideas: stars surrounded by life-filled artefacts. Silver beetles, spreading across the stars.'

'Yes. They are expansionist. Colonizers, as humans have always been. That's what we *see* up there, visible in the very sky, a grand, expanding wave of them, coming from somewhere in *that* direction, to your left, which is to the periphery of the cluster. I suppose it's possible they didn't originate in this cluster at all. But they are certainly spreading through it.

'This particular world, the local star, must be somewhere close to the wavefront. Because in *that* direction,' he pointed to his right, 'we see no green stars.'

'OK,' Abrahams said. 'But they didn't cross space to get to New Springfield.'

'No. They stepped there, as we did. I suspect they just stumbled through some kind of warped stepping process into the Gallery, and found themselves on that particular Earth – and they're treating it quite differently. With the big spin-up, rather than a replacement of the air and what-not, as they're doing here.'

'Why the difference?'

'I do have some ideas about that.' Bowring pointed directly above his head. 'Up *there*, at the edge of the colonization wavefront, we see something else, orbiting the stars. Neither the usual cosmic furniture, the planets and the asteroids of a virgin system, nor the green that characterizes the beetles' colonization push. We see another kind of cloud, orbiting some of those stars. Big chunks, irregularly shaped.'

Abrahams whistled.

'Purposeful destruction?' Jha asked, wondering.

'If I were not a respectable scientist I would be prepared to speculate that there, at least, somebody is fighting back, against the beetles' expansion. And that may be why we find so much activity by the beetles, just now, in the New Springfield Earth. It's no coincidence. *It's because they encountered us.* They have learned to anticipate resistance. And so they accelerated whatever programme of work they had, in order to get it done before we have a chance to fight back, to stop them.

'As to what that programme is, as I said, at New Springfield they seem to have adopted a different strategy. They aren't xenoforming that world. But what?'

'I think I know,' Abrahams said. 'Dyson didn't conceive of his spin motor as an end in itself. He was thinking of how to build his great spheres, artefacts that could enclose a whole star.'

'Ah,' said Bowring. 'And the only way you can get enough matter to do that—'

'Is to dismantle a planet.'

'*Dismantle.*' That mundane word shocked Jha. 'How could you do that? . . . Oh.'

Abrahams said grimly, 'By spinning it up, faster and faster, until—'

'Yes.' Jha took a breath. 'I need to talk to the Captain.'

Abrahams said, 'And I need to talk to my wife.'

41

Professor Emeritus Wotan Ulm, of the University of Oxford East 5, author of the bestselling if controversial memoir *Peer Reviewers and Other Idiots: A Life In Academia*, had consented to give a recorded lecture on von Neumann replicators to be carried as briefing material on the US Navy twain USS *Brian Cowley*.

'. . . Is this thing on, Jocasta? What do you mean, your name's not Jocasta? Young lady, I am seventy-eight years old, my childhood home is under ten metres of ice, and I haven't got time for *your* nonsense. Eh? What green light? Ah . . .

'Von Neumann replicators, then. Like a super matter printer – a printer that could produce another matter printer. A machine that can make a copy of itself. Much like yourself, Jocasta! What could we do with such a technology?

'How about colonizing the Galaxy?

'In the last century, in a more innocent age of happy memory, the physicist Frank Tipler proposed a way we humans could colonize the stars, and cheaply into the bargain. Tipler's scheme assumed nothing much beyond the slower-than-light transport methods we can easily envisage today. Just as in our exploration of the solar system, we would begin with unmanned probes. The first wave would be slow, no faster than we could afford.

'But the probes would be self-replicating, you see: capable of constructing anything, given raw materials, including copies of themselves. And that's the clever bit. Earlier the great physicist John von Neumann had shown that such machines are theoretically possible – and, after all, human beings are capable of replication with very little training . . . Have I made that joke already, Jocasta? Oh, very well. I'm seventy-eight, you know.

'Now, when such a probe arrived at its target, it would settle down, look around a bit, perhaps grow a few human colonists from some seed bank – you know the kind of thing – and then, crucially, start to build copies of itself, a new generation of probes that will move on, further and deeper into the Galaxy, in search of homes of their own.

'We can expect the migration to continue, in all directions outward from the Earth, pretty relentlessly once it has started. And the process would be self-financing, and *that* would have been music to the ears of every money-grubbing university administrator with whom it has been my misfortune to lock horns. That's because the new colonies would be built from local resources, requiring nothing of Earth. *We* must invest merely in the cost of the initial generation of probes.

'But there's a trap.

'Suppose we start colonizing the stars, after the manner of Tipler. Earth is suddenly the centre of a growing sphere of colonization – a sphere whose volume has to keep increasing, if a constant growth rate is to be achieved. The leading edge, the colonizing wave, has to sweep on faster and faster, eating up worlds and stars and moving on to the next, because of the pressure from behind . . .

'Imagine then a Tipler wave of replicating robots swarming across the Galaxy, turning fallow star systems into copies of themselves, working feverishly just to keep up with the pace of expansion. Even if such a probe arrived in an inhabited system it must immediately crush any native life, transforming all in its path into more copies of itself. It would have no choice; it would have no time to do otherwise, to maintain the momentum of the expansion.

'Is this infeasible, technologically? Not at all. *We* could almost build such things.

'Would it be unethical to unleash such a compound-interest horror on the rest of the universe? Most people would think so, but don't ask a banker.

'Is this what the colonists on that godforsaken High Meggers world seem to have discovered in their hole in the ground? A Tipler wavefront? Sounds like it, doesn't it? . . .

'What's that, Jocasta? What should be done about New Springfield? Well, I should build a very, very high wall around these fellows, metaphorically speaking.

'Now then, is that enough? I am seventy-eight years old, you know . . .'

42

AGNES WAS SUSPICIOUS as soon as Lobsang said he had a plan.
'A plan? A plan to do what? Lobsang, you already blew our cover, all but, by standing up in front of those Navy officers and taking over the meeting.'

'I don't think it matters. The universe isn't giving me any choice, Agnes.'

'Oh, don't get pompous. Do you imagine the universe cares about *you*? Look, Lobsang, think about it—'

'What is there to think about? Who are these beetles, these bugs, to fall on a world and consume it for their own purposes – everything it was, everything it could have been, gone in a flash, just to fuel another minute stage of their own endless expansion?'

'Hm. I'd say you have a point if it wasn't for the fact that that's what humanity has always done, as you've lectured me about many times.'

'That's true. But now *we're* in the path of the juggernaut. And there are evidently people, minds of some sort, fighting back in the Planetarium sky. Are they not right to resist? Should we not at least try as well?'

Agnes shook her head. 'Maybe. Maybe not. I just don't see why it has to be *you*. And besides, how can we fight back against creatures who can modify whole worlds?'

'An inferior technology might be able to strike a blow against a superior, given boldness and the advantage of surprise. Consider

Captain Cook,' he said. 'The Hawaiians killed him, when he landed on their islands.'

'Much good it did the Hawaiians in the long run.'

'Agnes, I don't think I can save this world. But perhaps I can stop the beetles spreading further, from threatening more of the worlds of mankind. But I'll need help.'

'You've already sent Sally and Joshua on some kind of mission, I know that.' Not that Agnes was sure what that quest was about.

'Yes. But even if they succeed in their quest I don't think it's going to be enough.'

'Then what? Who else do you want?'

He said simply, 'The Next.'

43

As for Joshua and Sally:
Hand in hand, they emerged from their fall through the latest soft place, the latest flaw in the great tangled structure that was the Long Earth. Joshua found himself standing on red, gritty earth, by the shore of a body of water, a turbid grey sea, or lake maybe. *Standing*: in fact he immediately crumpled over, all the energy sucked out of him. And he was suffused by a cold deep in the core of his body, as if he was suffering from hypothermia, even though the air here was warm, if dry, salty. Squatting on his haunches he wrapped his arms around his body and tried to still the shivering by main force.

This was the after-effect of passing through soft places. Joshua, having travelled on and off with Sally for many years by now, knew that she had grown up with a knowledge of the soft places, and a basically subconscious ability to detect and use them. His own best mental image was that the Long Earth was like a necklace of worlds, spread out in some higher order of reality, along which he could step one by one, in one direction or another, which had arbitrarily been labelled 'West' and 'East'. But, it seemed, that necklace wasn't a simple string but looped back over itself, intersecting itself in knots and cuts. So, if you could locate it correctly, a soft place could take you on a seven-league-boot step across a far stepwise distance in the Long Earth, and if you worked it right a long way geographically too. Damn useful if you knew how to use them. Damn interesting for the theoreticians too. And damn tough for any but the very best steppers.

He'd get over this; he'd been through it before. But the older you got, the harder it felt. And every damn time, these days, the stump of his left arm, under the prosthetic hand, ached like hell.

Sally, meanwhile, was already at work. She had dumped her pack on the ground, pulled out a kind of trenching tool, and started to dig a hole. She had always been tougher than Joshua physically, and even though he had been a poster boy for stepping for forty years, with her mastery of the soft places Sally had always been far more at home in the Long Earth than he was. But he could see that their journey had affected even her too, and she moved stiffly as she dug.

He asked, 'What the hell are you doing?'

'Checking we're not on an island.'

'An island? I thought we came looking for Lobsang, not for islands.'

'We are. You can make yourself useful, if you like. Go take a look at what's over that ridge.'

'What ridge?'

She ignored the question.

When he felt able he stood up, dropped his own pack beside Sally's, and looked around. This shallow beach did indeed lead up to a ridge, maybe a remnant of eroded, wind-sculpted dunes.

He walked that way.

The sand under his feet was fine, almost dusty, and very dry. But it let his boots sink in with every pace, using up even more of his energy. They seemed to be well above the high water mark at least, hence the dry sand. But there was no sign of life on this beach, he noticed, no worm casts, seaweed, shells, no wading birds, no crabs working the water that pooled nearer the edge of the sea. No driftwood either, and he wondered how they were going to build a fire.

The sun was high in a milky, washed-out sky. The only sounds were the soft lap of the waves, and the scrape of Sally's trenching tool. A lifeless world.

His legs were aching and he was panting by the time he reached the summit of the ridge. Up here he found himself looking over an almost flat, red-brown landscape, the horizontal broken by tired-looking remnants of hills on the horizon. The only colours were the pale grey-green of what looked like lichen on the rocks, and a purplish smear on the crust of a mud pool a little further inland. There wasn't a scrap of vegetation anywhere – though he did see the grey-blue of a stream, or river, maybe half a mile away, running down to its own rendezvous with the sea. So there was fresh water to be had, at least.

In his time he'd travelled far across the Long Earth, but he'd rarely seen a less promising landscape. However, the air was free of mist, and he could see dry land all the way to the horizon in every direction. He was not on an island, unless it was a pretty gigantic one.

He returned to Sally and reported in.

'Good,' she said. She sat back, scraped sand from her bare arms, and swigged water from a plastic bottle. She'd dug a respectable arm's length into the dirt. 'And I think I dug far enough down to prove there's no carapace lurking down there. At least the work warmed me up.'

Carapace? 'Why are you so concerned we're not on an island?' After all these years Joshua still got annoyed when she was being cryptic. 'Where are we, Sally?'

She closed her eyes. 'I memorized the precise number. Earth West 174,827,918.'

'Shit. A hundred and seventy-five *million*?'

'That's according to the catalogue compiled by the *Armstrong II*, the Navy airship that came this way more than a decade ago. Believe the number or not. Some people think the Long Earth gets – chaotic – over large enough scales, and simple numbering doesn't work any more. Hardly matters if it does, does it? As long as you know where you're going.'

'As you do, evidently. But even so, Sally, I never came remotely so far before.'

'I know.'

'Which is why I feel so beat up?'

'You got it.'

'And you think we'll find Lobsang here?' Meaning the ambulant unit that they had left behind on Earth West 2,000,000 plus, twenty-eight years ago, as it had departed with an entity that had called itself First Person Singular.

'I know we will,' she said with her usual strained patience. 'Which is why I brought you here.'

'Fine. So what now? I guess I could go fetch some fresh water. There's a stream just over thataway.'

'You do that.'

'I don't see any wood for a fire.'

'The nights aren't cold. Also there are no roaming critters to be kept away. Not on the continental land anyhow. A lean-to and our survival blankets will be enough.'

'I guess there's no hunting to be done. No fish to be fished from that ocean.'

She shrugged. 'We can survive on our rations for a few days, Joshua. We could process bacterial slime if we had to. But we won't be here long – just as long as it takes to find Lobsang – or for him to find us.'

'And how do we go about that?'

'It's all in hand, Joshua.' She reached into her pack and pulled out a small radio transmitter set. 'Short-wave radio. Our signals will bounce around the planet. Lobsang will hear. Go fill up the water bottles. I'll let you set up the antenna if you like, it's a fold-up kit. I know how you boys like your gadgets . . .'

But Joshua had stopped listening.

The sea was no longer featureless. Suddenly, it seemed, there *was* an island, not far off shore, a shield of green and yellow on the breast of the grey water. He pointed. 'How did I miss *that*?'

Sally murmured, 'Don't beat yourself up. It wasn't there before.'

Belatedly Joshua thought to rummage in his pack for his binoculars.

On the island, through the glasses, he saw a suite of life quite unlike anything that characterized the mainland as far as he'd seen. Beyond a fringe of what looked like beach, there were forest clumps, and animals moving – what looked like horses, but small, almost dog-sized. Even the seawater by the shore was mildly turbulent, evidently full of life.

And this 'island' had a wake.

Sally was watching him. 'You understand what you're seeing?'

'Sure.' He grinned; he couldn't help it. 'It's just as Nelson Azikiwe described. He said Lobsang took him to see a creature like this, off the coast of New Zealand but a lot closer to home, something like seven hundred thousand worlds out.'

'Lobsang called *that* one Second Person Singular. It was actually a lot more typical of its class of creatures than the one we encountered, the one who called herself *First* Person Singular. The one that *liked* you.'

Only because Joshua, somehow, with his odd, almost troll-like sensitivity to the presence of other minds, had been able to sense her thoughts, even across the great span of the Long Earth. Thoughts that to him had been like the clanging of some great gong, echoing from beyond the horizon: thoughts full of bafflement and loneliness. And she, in turn, it seemed, had sensed his presence too.

'First Person Singular wasn't normal,' Sally said. 'She was the one gone wrong. Hence the mutual attraction between you, no doubt. Lobsang called the class of these beasts Traversers.'

'And this is why we came here . . . Sally. Something's happening.'

All around the living island the water was bubbling, growing more turbulent. Joshua saw that its profile was diminishing, almost as if the island was collapsing on itself, and the trees that sprouted from the rocks and earth that had collected on the back of this mobile creature shook and shuddered.

'It's *sinking*,' Joshua said.

'Yep. Submerging again. It's what it does. Keep watching . . .'

Now, Joshua saw through his binoculars, flaps opened up on the island ground – flaps of some crusty material, big, irregular, hinged by some kind of muscle, like a clam's shell. The shy little horses bolted for the flaps and dived down through them without hesitation, disappearing from Joshua's view into the body of the island beast. The flaps closed tight, just as the waves lapped over their position.

And then the island simply sank, its apparently rocky 'shore', the trees, its cargo of plants and animals, slipping under the waves until only a patch of disturbed water remained, swirling like a feeble whirlpool, with nothing but a few leaves left scattered on the water surface.

'Just as Nelson described,' Joshua said. 'I hardly believed it.'

'Now do you see why I wanted to make sure *we* weren't on an island? This world is the origin, Joshua. Where the Traversers came from. Actually the *Armstrong* crew understood what they saw here pretty well, they'd read the accounts of the journey of the *Mark Twain*, and they got it about right in their reports . . .'

The *Armstrong*'s science team had observed biological complexity in this world and its neighbours. There was more than just lichen and bacterial slime here, if you looked for it. But that complexity was not expressed as on the Datum, organized into plants ranging from blades of grass up to sequoia trees, or animals from the smallest amphibians up through horses and humans and elephants and blue whales. Here the complexity was at a global level – almost. As if the evolution of life had skipped a step and gone straight from green slime to Gaia.

Here, in the lakes and oceans, compound organisms swam: each like a tremendous Portuguese man o' war, microbial swarms linked into huge protean life forms. They were living islands. And, as the *Armstrong* crew had observed, those compound organisms often enveloped animals within their structures – animals, however, like the miniature horses and other creatures Joshua saw now, that were *not* native to this world, but had been collected from elsewhere.

'Lobsang may understand it better by now,' Sally said. 'I guess he ought to, after all this time.'

'So we're on the home world of the Traversers. Why?'

'Because this is where Lobsang must be. The last time we saw him, at the end of The Journey, he was disappearing into the sunset on the back of First Person Singular, the mightiest Traverser of all. Where else would he be?'

Joshua lowered his binoculars. 'So now what?'

'So now we set up our radio, and make ourselves comfortable, and wait. Come on, Joshua, a life alone in the High Meggers has always involved a lot of waiting around. You want to play with my antenna kit, or not?'

So they got down to pioneering, in perhaps the most desolate landscape Joshua had ever visited. 'A world like a sensory deprivation tank,' he told Sally after a couple of days. The only excitement came from what he thought might be glimpses of the Traverser, but they all turned out to be illusory, after that first visit, just the shadows of clouds on the grey sea.

Until their fifth day on the beach, when the Traverser returned.

And somehow Joshua was not at all surprised when those carapace flaps cracked, and after the usual horse-like creatures emerged to gambol in the sun – and deer-like creatures, and bear-like and dog-like creatures, and animals that looked like mashed-up, misshapen combinations of all these familiar forms, even things like small stegosaurs – after all of them, an ambulant unit came walking calmly up into the light, as if climbing a stair. The human-shaped machine was quite nude, a walking statue, and yet even from here Joshua could see evidence of damage: one arm was missing entirely.

'You two,' the unit said mildly, calling across the water. 'Of course it would be you two.'

'Play time's over, Lobsang,' Sally said, and Joshua thought there was a note of genuine sadness in her voice.

44

H E SAT WITH them, in their rough camp on the desolate beach.
He even accepted a share of their rations. Sally handed him
chocolate, and a tin mug of coffee brewed on their small solar-
powered stove.

'Mm, chocolate,' he said, biting into a bar he held in his left hand.
His right arm was missing from the shoulder. 'You know me, Joshua.
I always did relish my food. At least this version of me; I can't speak
of my subsequent iterations, and it has been twenty-eight years
since I last participated in a synching. Even during the voyage of
the *Mark Twain*—'

'Clam chowder and oysters Kilpatrick,' Joshua said.

Sally snorted. 'The good old days in the Bluesmobile. After thirty
years apart, you two haven't changed.'

Lobsang said, 'These days, mostly I draw my energy directly from
the sunlight.' He stood and turned, and Joshua saw a silvery panel
glisten on his back, reaching down to the top of his buttocks: a
solar-cell array. 'I bask like a plant.'

There had been other modifications, Joshua had the chance to see
now, aside from that missing arm. The naked body was quite hair-
less, lacking even eyebrows. In places the skin seemed to have been
patched; Joshua saw no seams, but there were swathes of a subtly
different shade from the general pale brown tan. And *the genitalia
had gone*, to be replaced by a rather gruesome metallic plug in the
groin: a simple release valve, it seemed.

Lobsang said, 'I do need solid sustenance, of course. Organic biochemistry to support my gel substrate. I can consume bacterial scrapes, algae. Some of the Traversers on this world bear fruit trees, even root plants. And at times the Traversers allow me to consume the flesh of their deceased animal specimens, if it is suitable – if the death is the result of an accident, perhaps, if the meat is not corrupted.'

Joshua said, 'Bacon?'

'On good days.'

Sally said, 'Lobsang, your arm . . .'

Joshua said, 'Yeah. But it's not his missing *arm* that's drawing my attention.'

Lobsang grinned. 'Makes you wince, does it, Joshua?' He reached down to his groin and casually pulled out the plug.

Joshua felt a sympathetic twinge in his own groin. 'Please.'

'I had suffered damage in the course of our journey, you'll recall. Notably when we fell into the Gap. And in the years after you left me with First Person Singular, time took its toll; this unit was never meant to be able to sustain itself without workshop maintenance, not for a period of decades. I sacrificed the arm, and other organs,' he said, winking at Joshua, 'for spare parts. I doubt I could pass as a human again. But then, I did not imagine I would ever need to.'

'Well, I'm glad you survived,' Joshua said.

'Me too,' Sally said grudgingly. 'Though not surprised.'

'Thank you for your good wishes. And now you come seeking me out.'

'Lobsang asked us to,' Joshua said. 'I mean the one who replaced you, who assembled himself from the iterations, the backups you left behind.'

'There's much I can deduce, by your very presence. Something has happened.'

Joshua said gently, 'You could say that.'

'Are the odds against us? Is the situation grim?'

'You could put it like that,' Sally said. 'Although that sounds like a line from a movie. You two will never grow up, will you?'

Joshua dug in his pocket, and produced a memory pod, a small capsule. 'He – Lobsang – gave me this. He says it contains the briefing you'll need.'

Lobsang nodded, his eyes closed. 'I will come with you nonetheless, of course, regardless of the contents of the briefing; I must trust my own judgement – *his* judgement.' He glanced at Sally. 'You travelled through a soft-place network?'

'Of course. And we'll go back that way, if you can take it.'

'I don't have a choice, do I? Can you give me a few hours, before we leave? After so long – it will take me some time to say goodbye to my life here. I have learned a lot, of course, but there is much I've yet to understand. The Traversers evolved here, in this band of worlds, but they roam the Long Earth, though few seem to come as far as the Datum.'

'Some sure do,' Joshua said with a grin. And he told Lobsang how a later edition of himself had found a Traverser, which *that* Lobsang had called Second Person Singular, which seemed to have wandered so far down the Long Earth that it may even have strayed into the oceans of the Datum itself – for it had collected people.

Lobsang made an odd gesture, as if he was trying to clap with one hand. 'Whole families, living in the belly of the whale. How wonderful. But of course humans fit the sampling strategy. There seems to be a certain selectivity about the creatures the Traversers want. The animals are all of a characteristic size, within one or two orders of magnitude of a human, or a troll. No tiny rodents – though some of those seem to smuggle themselves on board even so. No pliosaurs or whales, at the other end of the size scale. Their sampling is careful and selective, and ought to do no harm to the populations they are taking from. First Person Singular, by the way, was an exception, a sport. She became not a sample-taker but a destroyer. She took it *all*, a motile extinction event, purposeful, sentient, devouring whole biospheres—'

'Until she could go no further,' Joshua said, remembering. '*Samples. Select.* You make it sound like there's some purpose behind it all. But what purpose? To create a zoo? An ark?'

'Or a biological collection, like Darwin on the *Beagle*? I suspect if I knew the answer to that, Joshua, I would know very much more about the greater mysteries of our existence. And I suspect that the deeper question is not what that purpose is – but who *intervened* in these creatures' evolution to give them that purpose.'

Joshua puzzled over that. 'Good one. Textbook enigmatic, Lobsang.'

Sally stood up. 'While you two pick up your bromance, I'm going for a walk.'

Lobsang's face was distorted, lopsided. Joshua, watching with fascinated horror, saw that he was trying to smile. 'Lobsang, you look like a stroke victim.'

'Sorry. I had no mirrors. I will practise. I wouldn't want to scare anybody.'

'No,' Joshua said carefully. 'Especially not your son.'

He took that bit of news calmly, nodding, his expression blank. 'I have been a busy chap, haven't I? I don't think a simple synch will be enough this time.'

'I wouldn't think so, Lobsang.'

'Shall we walk?'

So Lobsang completed his preparations, and they left for home.

But by the time Joshua, Sally and Lobsang had completed the long stepwise journey back to New Springfield, the situation there had got a whole lot worse.

45

THE GLOBAL EXPEDITION was Captain Boss's idea. He would select a diverse group with broad experience and opinions, load them aboard the *Cowley*, and take them on a brief tour of this suffering world, before coming to a final decision on what to do about the problem of the silver beetles. Joshua thought this Navy captain was either showing a democratic instinct or indecision, depending on your point of view.

So the party gathered outside New Springfield, ready to board the great craft over their heads, enduring an awkward wait for the elevator cage to descend.

Joshua looked around. Alongside himself and Sally, still newcomers to this battered world, here were the science people from the twain crew and its civilian passengers. Agnes stood between *two* versions of Lobsang, the sombre elderly-gentleman pioneer edition and the battered robot explorer, eerily alike yet unalike. The Irwins, colonials from New Springfield, were here as representatives of their neighbours, who were still stubbornly sitting it out in their lodges on stepwise worlds. The Irwins were very obviously trying not to stare at the ambulant units – they'd only recently learned the truth about their animatronic neighbours.

The newly arrived Lobsang, dressed in a nondescript Navy coverall, was easily distinguished from his twin, at least. For the sake of those who had to look on him, the more obvious flaws in this Lobsang's visible skin had been roughly patched – but he was still lacking that arm, and one sleeve was neatly sewn flat. Of those present only George, Agnes, Joshua and Sally knew that the right arm wasn't all this ambulant unit was missing. For Joshua the worst moments had come when the two ambulants had swapped data, at the beginning. They would clasp hands, or stare into each other's eyes, and Joshua imagined streams of data pouring from their gel-based processing cores through the medium of their touching palms, or chattering in sparks of light between their eyes, as they synched their understanding.

And, to complete the group, here was a young man in a homburg hat who called himself simply Marvin, standing beside a middle-aged woman, brisk, sturdy, competent-looking, named Stella Welch. Dressed simply, plainly spoken, these were representatives of the Next, somehow summoned by Lobsang. They looked very ordinary to Joshua, but then he'd only met immature Next before, like Paul Spencer Wagoner. The sun cream, dark glasses and floppy hats they all had to wear out in the open – the extreme winds had thrown water vapour high into the stratosphere and broken down the ozone layer – did nothing to add to the authority of the Next.

'I imagined Vulcans,' Joshua admitted to Sally.

She rolled her eyes. 'Look at us. What a crew. Three androids, the egghead science types, two blank-eyed brainiacs, two bewildered Mom-and-Pop homesteaders – and two lifelong misfits in me and thee, Joshua.'

Agnes said dryly, 'It's like a Traveling Wilburys reunion tour.'

That made 'George' laugh.

His one-armed twin 'Lobsang', though, looked puzzled. That was another difference between them. Maybe his knowledge of late-twentieth-century rock bands, always an essential around Sister Agnes, had eroded away during his decades with the Traversers. Indeed this long-lost copy of Lobsang had been staggered to meet Agnes in the first place, and even more so to discover why his successors had had her reincarnated. The Lobsangs had diverged, interestingly.

The Irwins glanced over, as if offended by the laughter, as well they might be. Agnes had told Joshua something of how it had been when 'George' had finally revealed his and Agnes's true nature. All Agnes could do was apologize to the neighbours she had deceived – and who now kept their kids away from her as if she was about to turn Terminator.

And then there was Ben. As far as Joshua could see Agnes and Lobsang were putting the boy through a process of slow, gentle revelation. It was never going to be easy. Of course this day, the day of truth, had to come for their adopted son sometime. But now it was forced on them, in the middle of a wider crisis.

Yes, this twain certainly had a motley and divided crew, Joshua thought. But who else was there to do this? Who was better qualified to handle the problem?

And the reality of the problem was not in doubt. Even as they stood here, the morning sun, a mother-of-pearl disc sporadically visible in the ash-laden air, seemed to Joshua to *move* perceptibly, the shadows it cast shifting like an accelerated movie of a sundial. The various timers the ship's science teams had set up confirmed that the rotation of this world had in the last few months sped up to an astounding twelve hours – half the original day. Even the two Lobsangs had given up trying to estimate the energy that was pouring down from the sky, had given up trying to predict the end point.

At last the elevator cage arrived. They gave a ragged cheer.

Joshua Valienté was no fan of enclosure, and he was certainly no friend of the US military.

But it was a relief, this day in early January of 2059, to ride up from the ground of New Springfield at last, to get out of the stinging sunlight and be enclosed in the sterile, womb-like interior of the USS *Brian Cowley*. Joshua breathed deeply of clean, recycled, humidified, filtered air, air that smelled of nothing but electronics, carpets, and military-issue boot polish – air that did *not* smell of death, of ash and sulphur and rot and the smoke of burned forests, air that did not make your lungs ache, for the world outside was even losing its oxygen to the continent-wide fires.

The twain itself was interesting to Joshua, a veteran of such vessels. The 'gondola' of this *Armstrong*-class ship, though the crew called its habitable compartment by that name, wasn't a gondola at all but entirely contained within the body of the thousand-foot-long lift envelope, with observation galleries around the ship's equator leading back from the bridge at the very prow.

The civilian party from Springfield were brought to one such gallery now, led by Margarita Jha, the ship's science officer. Waiting for them here was Ken Bowring. The burly seismologist seemed to be enjoying this experience far too much, Joshua thought. A yeoman, a smart young man, passed among them with trays of coffee, soft drinks, water.

Distant turbines hummed, the great ship shuddered slightly as if coming fully awake, and they were lifted smoothly into the air.

'Anchors aweigh, then,' Agnes murmured, peering out of the window.

The Irwins, Oliver and Marina, went to stand together close to one of the big viewing windows, peering out into the smoky air.

Ken Bowring stepped forward. 'I do understand how you feel,' he said to the Irwins. 'But look how much has changed, in the years since the bugs started their spin-up. You can see how much damage has been done, even right here.' He pointed. 'The basic features of the landscape are still there, of course, and they still bear the names you gave them. Manning Hill, Soulsby Creek. There's the old Poulson house, as you call it . . .' The Poulson house, the beetles' portal, was now the centre of an intensively observed, heavily guarded military compound, where science crews kept watch day and night on this flaw in the world. 'But look over where Waldron Wood used to be.' The slab of dense forest beyond the creek to the north was gone now, a burned-out ruin.

The settlement was quickly lost in the greying forest as the ship lifted higher and sailed smoothly through the sky, heading north-east.

Oliver Irwin said gloomily, 'Everything's dying, isn't it? And what isn't dying is burning. Or both.'

Bowring said, 'Pretty much. The serious die-back began, just as we predicted, when the local day dropped below twenty hours or so. This is a world of forest, and all those dead trees are very combustible.'

Margarita Jha, spruce in her Navy uniform, said now, 'Funnily enough, you know, Ken, as the spin-up approached the current twelve hours, we saw something of a tentative recovery of the wild-life. The local critters seemed to be able to adapt somewhat, treating two half-days as a single day, if you see what I mean. The same for some of the flowering plants. We observed a similar effect at sixteen hours, though clearly the resonance wasn't so simple.'

'Interesting,' Bowring said. 'There's probably a paper in that—'

'You're so damn *cold*.' That was Marina Irwin, her words blurted out. 'That's our home out there. A world is dying. And you call it "interesting".'

Marvin and Stella Welch, the two Next, reacted to that. They turned to each other and exchanged a short burst of their strange, incomprehensible quicktalk. Joshua was reminded of the high-speed data exchanges as the two copies of Lobsang had synched.

Lobsang, the Traverser-world version, spoke now. 'You must not condemn the scientists for their attempts at detachment. There appears to be nothing we can do to save this world. We must try to ensure that the beetles' activities do not spread *beyond* this Earth. And we can best do that by studying these phenomena, by observing, analysing, speculating.'

'You're right to pick us up on our tone, though,' Bowring said to Marina. 'I apologize. I didn't mean any disrespect.'

'And in fact the best way to honour this dying world is to cherish it in its mortal agony.'

Sally pulled a face at Joshua. 'Strikes me that *this* Lobsang's time in the wilderness has burned all the fun out of him, and left behind all the bits I could never stand. All that cosmic destiny stuff. Pompous ass.'

Joshua shrugged. 'Lobsang is Lobsang.'

They rose now into a layer of murky grey air, so that their view of the fire-scarred green below was obscured. Joshua heard the engines' tone shift, adjusting.

Bowring said, 'We're rising into a layer of volcanic ash. The air's full of it now.'

Jha said, 'There's no need to be concerned about the ship. Since Yellowstone all Navy twain engines have been fitted with ash filters. We could fly in this crap for weeks.'

Bowring said, 'We calculate that the bulge at the equator is now around fifty miles, which is the thickness of the crust under the continents. So now we're seeing quakes, volcanoes, on land as well as under the sea.' He grinned ruefully. 'Oddly enough the local version of Yellowstone hasn't gone up, not yet. But the San Andreas gave way on a massive scale, and the Cascades are letting rip—'

Oliver asked, 'How far is this all going to go?'

'Well, we can't tell. This isn't some natural phenomenon we're studying. Everything we observe is a consequence of the purposeful action of these creatures, the beetles. And the end state of this world will be determined, not simply by natural processes we can predict, but by the beetles' intentions.'

Marina snapped, 'But what do you think those intentions are? *You're* supposed to be the experts. You must have some ideas. Do we just watch as they smash everything up?'

Ken Bowring reached over and touched her arm. 'We have tried, to *do* something. At New York. We're going there; you'll see. But you might not find it much consolation.' He spoke more widely. 'Folks, we'll take our time on this trip. We'll be monitoring, surveying as we go, but not setting down unless absolutely necessary. We expect to be over the New York City footprint in twelve hours, no earlier – that is, about this time "tomorrow", given the truncation of this world's day.'

Jha gave them a professional smile. 'Which makes my announcement of a cocktail reception in the Captain's cabin at sundown seem a little flat, because that's just four hours away. In the meantime, please make yourselves at home. The yeoman will show you to the cabins we've allotted you. You may stay here, or visit the science areas, but please don't wander around without an escort. If you need anything just ask any of the crew . . .'

'Christ,' Sally snarled. 'A cocktail reception. What is this, the Love Boat?'

Joshua said, 'Come on, Sally. Relax for once. Even you can't step away from mid-air. Have a bath. Drink a cocktail.'

She glared at him. 'Maybe I'll make a cocktail of your face, Valienté. Hey, you, Ensign Crusher! You have a gym on this tub? I feel like pumping some iron . . .'

46

THE SHORT DAY ended quickly.

When the dark came, Joshua skipped the cocktails and tried to nap. But everything felt wrong, out of step.

Before the dawn, still in the dark, he returned to the observation lounge. A group had gathered before the window, George and Lobsang, Agnes, and the two Next, Marvin and Stella Welch. Or perhaps they'd just stayed here.

Stella smiled at Joshua. 'Restless, your friend Sally, isn't she?'

'You got that right. Always been the same. But then she grew up stepping.'

'Yes. With a remarkable native ability.'

Joshua looked at Stella curiously. Somehow he hadn't expected the Next to be interested in any of the individual people around them – the non-Next, the 'dim-bulbs', as Paul Spencer Wagoner and his buddies had always called them. Next always seemed far more interested in each other. Yet here these two were.

As if reflecting that thought, George said now, 'It's good of you to have come here. It was my idea to summon you.'

Joshua had been surprised about that, considering how Lobsang seemed to feel about the Next's supposed abandonment of him. Maybe he wanted to use this situation to make some kind of contact. But his argument had been strong, as he'd explained it to Joshua. 'What if these silver beetles do find a way to spread across the Long Earth? The Next, as inhabitants of the Long Earth, are just as vulnerable to the consequences as the rest of us . . .' Of course the Next had come.

But Joshua was curious. 'How *did* you summon them, umm, George?'

'I just spread the word. I posted news on Low Earth sites. Sent messages to locations associated with the Next – for example the naval base on Hawaii where several of the Next children were held for studying. Nelson helped with that. Oh, and I also used the prison facility where the ringleader of the rogue group who hijacked the airship *Armstrong* is still being held – David?' He turned to Marvin and Stella. 'I suspected I only had to raise awareness of this issue and you would notice. For, although you claim to have withdrawn to your enclave hidden somewhere in the Long Earth – and I myself was responsible for sealing off Happy Landings to help cover that trail – I never had any doubt that you would keep watch over the human worlds. How could you not?'

Stella said, 'Of course it is in our interests too to resolve this situation safely. But, as far as I know, this issue of the silver beetles is the first time any human agency has actively asked us to intervene, to help.'

The older Lobsang grinned, and Joshua saw that his control of his facial expressions had improved drastically in the time since he and Sally had brought this unit home. He said, 'Of course it is ironic that your first call from humans should be from an individual whose own humanity has always been in question. Whose nature has, in fact, been tested in law.'

Stella nodded. 'I agree, that is fascinating. Your extraordinary story, Lobsang, George – your claims of reincarnation—'

George said, 'In the end the legal verdict contained some wisdom. If an entity is *capable* of pleading for the right to exist, then it surely *has* that right. Humans may be a lot dumber than you – why, they're a lot dumber than *me*—'

'But they are capable of wisdom,' Stella said. 'Oh, yes, we know. Many of the Next owe their lives to that very fact.'

Lobsang glanced at George. 'You must not think that we two are identical. My *brother* and I. Our experiences are quite different. With First Person Singular I have contemplated the very large, the infinite. Whereas you—'

George sighed. 'At New Springfield I have explored the viewpoint of a single individual. A human. It's what I wanted, what I designed myself to be. But I knew that this crisis with the beetles required a superhuman perspective. It demanded the old Lobsang. And so I called for you, fortuitously a survivor of earlier iterations.'

'It was wise,' Lobsang said.

Stella said, 'We have similar philosophical divergences among our thinkers in the Grange. Some – like me – consider the grand scheme, the bigger picture. The destiny of life in the universe. Whereas others focus on the small, the infinitesimal. We have a man who has named himself Celandine—'

Marvin clapped George on the back. 'There you go. You think the way we do. I heard you saying you were distressed when the Next cleared out of the human worlds without bringing you along. But perhaps you have some of the Next in you after all.'

And George smiled at this praise, almost shyly.

'Oh, I can't stand this,' Agnes muttered, and she stalked away.

George, talking to the Next, didn't even seem to notice she'd gone.

Joshua hurried after her.

'Agnes? You OK?'

'Oh, what do you think, Joshua? Look at him lapping up the praise from those creepy brain-boxes. This is what Lobsang *is*, in the end. Or what he always wanted. The machine that would be God. If he can't rule in heaven alone, then at least he can be part of the pantheon – so he thinks. And he's forgotten all about being human, which is what he *said* he wanted.'

'But that's why he brought *you* back—'

'Bah. Oh, forget about me, Joshua. What about Ben? He's the one who counts – *he's* the one who will be hurt if he loses his father.' She faced him. 'You're the first to know. We're splitting up. Me and George. When this latest crisis is over.'

That dismayed him, and he let it show. 'That's truly sad, Agnes. I mean, it's not George's fault he ended up sitting on top of the biggest current crisis in the Long Earth.' No, he reflected, if it was anybody's fault it was Sally Linsay's, who'd led Lobsang here. In her subtle, offhand, indirect way, maybe Sally was turning out to be central to this whole situation . . . He tried to focus on Agnes. 'Where will you go? Back to Madison?'

'I don't think so. I'll find a new place to settle, a home to build, and I'll live my life as mother to Ben. Which is all I want now.'

'You say I'm the first to know about this. Does George know, yet?'

'Since I only just decided – no, not yet. Give me a chance to tell him myself.'

Joshua said, 'I know you, Agnes. I know damn well there's no point suggesting you think it over. Because you won't change your mind, will you?'

'Never found the need to before. Don't intend to start now.' She stood for one moment more, as if reluctant to leave Joshua's side. Then she smiled sadly at him, and walked out of the gallery.

47

J OSHUA DIDN'T MANAGE to sleep any more during the remains of the brief 'night'. He washed, shaved, forced down some breakfast. He felt oddly groggy when he arrived back at the observation gallery, in the sudden dawn.

The two Next were already here, along with the Irwins, and Agnes standing uncomfortably between Lobsang and George. Margarita Jha came to join them. Only Sally was missing, which was typical of her. Maybe she had found a way off the ship after all.

And Joshua wondered too if Agnes had broken her news to George yet. Maybe not. Clearly George was in his element here, side by side with the Next facing a major crisis; Agnes was probably kind enough to let him have his moment.

Looking down, he saw that the airship had made its appointment. The landscape below was familiar from his own visit here with Lobsang. There was the profile of Long Island, there the churning Atlantic – and there was the tremendous viaduct constructed by the beetles, just as before, striding across the land and out to sea.

Ken Bowring joined them, wearing dark glasses. 'Quite a sight, isn't it, Mr Valienté? George Abrahams told us about the trip you made here, showed us the records. Has much changed?'

'If you saw our records you'll know. Last time around, Long Island still had some forest. Now . . .'

Now the island was bare rock. Joshua imagined tremendous waves battering at coastal provinces like this, stripping them of vegetation cover, every living thing, even the topsoil ripped off. The viaduct itself was just as it had been before. But there was something new, a circular feature directly under the viaduct, dug into the rocky ground – like a crater, perhaps. Its floor glistened, like glass.

Bowring was staring down grimly.

Joshua said, 'You OK?'

Bowring grinned, a forced expression. 'One too many cocktails with the Captain last night – hell, it was only a few hours ago, the damn nights aren't long enough to sleep off a hangover. But this—' He waved a hand at the scene below.

He didn't need to say it: overwhelming. 'I know,' Joshua said. 'But what's that scar? The circular feature.'

'That's what I want to know,' said Marina Irwin.

Ken Bowring said, 'Marina, you asked yesterday if we've been doing anything about this situation. Well, we have tried. Scientifically, we've tried to understand the beetles, to communicate with them.'

'In search of a weapon to use against them,' Joshua guessed.

Bowring said bluntly, 'Shoot a gun at one of the damn things and the round just bounces off its hide. Or it absorbs the slug and becomes that bit stronger.'

Jha said, 'I know it sounds brutal, but I think our commanders hoped we'd find some kind of bioweapon. We've come up with nothing so far. And besides, these are cyborgs, a fusion of life and machine; even if we attacked the biology we're not sure if that would actually stop them.'

George said, 'And the scar below?'

Jha said, 'When we failed to make a dent in the bugs themselves, we tried attacking their works. These viaducts. We tried a whole series of demolition tactics—'

'Cut to the chase,' Oliver Irwin said. 'You used a nuke, didn't you?'

Jha nodded. 'A tactical weapon. Only a few multiples of the

Hiroshima bomb, in energy. Well, we cut the viaduct! Right where you see the scar. We had a party *that* night.'

'But,' Bowring said, 'within forty-eight hours the damn beetles had built the thing back again. As you can see. The bugs at ground zero must have been destroyed. But for the survivors the fall-out – the radiation – doesn't seem to affect them. And as far as we can tell the incident made no difference to the spin-up process.' He glared down at the viaduct. 'You have to remember that these structures girdle the planet. We have a lot of nukes – including many that have been converted to steppable materials.' He grimaced. 'Just in case we ever needed to fight a Long Earth nuclear war. Maybe with some kind of concerted effort we could disrupt them, slow them down. But at what cost? This Earth turned into a nuclear wasteland, on top of its other problems? And we couldn't eliminate all the beetles anyhow.'

Marina looked horrified. 'We can't stop them, then.'

Jha said evenly, 'Not on this world, no. They've simply ignored everything we've tried to do to them, just as they ignored every contact we attempted.'

Marina said, 'So are we just going to give up?'

Now Stella Welch, the Next woman, shared a brief exchange of quicktalk with Marvin, and stepped forward. 'It's time for us to be open with you. You have called on us for help, and you were wise to do so. Yes, Marina, we have to give up this world. We can't destroy the beetles. But we *must* protect the rest of the Long Earth from these creatures. The threat of their spreading is great.'

'All this talk,' Marina said, anxious, angry. 'What are we going to *do*?'

Welch faced her. 'We think we have a way. *We must seal off this world.* Make it impossible to step into, or out of. We have been study-ing the phenomenon of the Long Earth. Stepping itself. We believe it may be possible to do this. There will be costs – for us, as well as for you, whose home this was.'

Marvin frowned at her. 'Costs for us? We haven't discussed this. *You're thinking of Stan Berg*, aren't you?'

Marina asked, 'Who?'

Stella ignored her. 'Yes, Marvin, it may be necessary to use him. *He may be the strongest of all of us.* As demonstrated by the facility in exploiting soft places that he seemed to develop simply by observing us. If he can be brought here—'

'You want me to arrange for him to be collected?'

'I think that would be wise.'

Joshua had no idea who this Stan Berg was, but he already felt sorry for him. 'What "costs"? Of what kind?'

Stella looked at him gravely. 'The world must be closed, you see—'

'From the inside,' Marvin said.

Ken Bowring gaped, and took off his sunglasses. 'This is the first I've heard of this. From the inside? The inside of what?'

Stella and Marvin exchanged a look. 'It is difficult to explain without the mathematics,' Stella said.

Joshua said, 'I think they're saying that whoever does this, whoever saves the Long Earth, will be laying down their life.'

There was a shocked silence.

Then George stepped forward. 'We asked you here to help us, and now we must trust you. And we will. What can we do to assist you?'

Stella glanced at Joshua. 'First of all – could you please persuade Sally Linsay to talk to us?'

48

As it turned out, as Rocky eventually came to figure it, by the time the Next came to 'collect' him, Stan had started to whip up so much trouble at Miami West 4 that there were all kinds of people who would have been glad to see the back of him regardless.

On the very day the Next came for him, in fact, Stan was preaching. Then again, most days he was preaching now, since coming back from the Grange with a head full of new ideas.

In the heavy afternoon sunlight of a late spring day, in this footprint of Miami – at the foot of the space elevator, an eggshell-blue thread that connected Earth to sky – Stan sat on the roof of a low concrete bunker and looked out over his fellow stalk jacks, a hundred or so of them gathered before him. And the crowd was in turn being surveyed by uniformed state cops, company security guys, and presumably by other agencies undercover. Ready for the trouble which seemed to be attracted to Stan.

And Stan Berg said, '*Apprehend. Be humble in the face of the universe. Do good.* Eleven words. Three rules. There endeth the sermon for the day, unless you want to hear a few lame gags . . .'
Laughter.

Even Rocky, at the back of the group, could hear him clearly. Aged just nineteen, Stan had developed a way of projecting his voice.

Rocky stood here with three women. Roberta Golding, the enigmatic Next woman who had escorted them to the Grange. Melinda Bennett, the young Arbiter, who had revealed herself to

Rocky as a Next on his return, living quietly among 'ordinary' people, just as quietly intervening to help keep the peace – or, if you listened to Stan, to anaesthetize mankind into passivity. And Martha, Stan's mother, listening to her son preaching, who quite clearly did not want to be here, and yet just as clearly could not bear to be anywhere else.

This was a meal break before the evening shift, and Stan had attracted a good crowd. Stan himself looked totally at ease as he took a bite of his sandwich, and a sip of alcohol-free beer. He said now, 'You know, I never did like numbers much.'

That raised a chuckle from his fellow workers, who knew Stan was one of the brightest in the pool and had forever been turning down training chances in favour of staying with these people, the stalk jacks, his friends – friends who were increasingly his followers.

'Oh, I was *good* at the numbers. Wouldn't deny that. I could count to three before I was, well, three.' He pulled a face. 'Which confused me. But round about then I figured that I mostly didn't need the numbers that go much *beyond* three. There was only one of me, two of my parents, together we made three.' He looked down at his lunch. 'I got three sandwiches here, three beers. I guess I'll be needing the john three times during the shift.' He looked around with a grin. 'And I've been figuring, if I was to ask somebody smart, I mean *really* smart, what life was all about – how I was to live it – I think I'd measure that smartness, not by how many words he or she spouted, not by how many books he or she had written—'

He picked up a book now from his pile of stuff. Rocky recognized a battered old copy of Spinoza's *Ethics*. Stan threw it out into the crowd, and people jumped to grab it.

'No,' Stan said, 'I'd think they were smarter the more they boiled down their wisdom. The closer they got to the number three – to three simple rules of thumb, if you like. Who needs more than three? Such as.' He held up his left thumb. 'Rule of the First

Thumb. *Apprehend.* Which is a nice word if you roll it around your mouth. *Apprehend.*

'It doesn't just mean "understand", although it includes that meaning, fully. It means you should face the truth of the world – not let yourself be fooled by how you'd like it to be. You should try to be fully aware of the richness of reality, of the mixed-up complexity of all the processes going right back to the birth of the stars that have produced you and the world you live in, and this very moment . . .

'And you need to apprehend other people too, as best you can.' He gazed out at upturned faces. 'Even those close to you. *Especially* those close to you. "You cannot love what you do not know." That's from an old religious teacher, some saint or other. That makes sense, doesn't it?'

'I grok you!' somebody called, to general laughter.

Stan grinned back. '*That's* catchier. And here's another way of saying this. *Be here now.* Which is the title of an Oasis album.'

One of the senior engineers, an elderly British guy, raised a solitary whoop in response. 'Gone but not forgotten, Stan!'

'*Be here now.* If you have a god, then consider that every moment you're alive and aware in this glorious world is a moment of awareness of that god – and to live in that moment is the only way you *can* be aware of your god . . .'

Melinda murmured, 'Now he almost sounds like Celandine.'

Martha said fiercely, 'But there's also some Spinoza in there, I think. For all you brainiacs dismiss the work of mere humans. Also the rationalist atheists who said our ethics must be drawn from human experience . . . I've tried to study this stuff. So I could find ways to talk to my son. Did you see who caught the book, by the way?'

Rocky had. 'Mo Morris.' One of the innermost group Stan called his 'buddies', and some of the jealous outsiders referred to as 'superfans' – if not by some more pejorative term – and who Martha called the 'misfits'. Mostly young, mostly male, they were odd, needy characters, at least in Martha's view, for whom Stan's sudden charisma, revealed when he got back from the Grange, filled a hole in their lives they'd barely even known existed. Now here they were, lapping up every word, recording Stan on their phones and tablets, or just slavishly writing down every word he uttered, every lame joke. Certainly none of them had hung around with Stan *before* his secret journey. They were a growing flock from which Rocky, his oldest friend, the only one around him now aside from his mother who'd really known him *before*, was increasingly excluded.

And yet Rocky couldn't walk away, any more than Martha could. For Rocky feared for Stan's safety.

Stan was still talking. 'And you know what I'd expect this smart person to say to me next?' He stuck up the thumb on his right hand now. 'The Rule of the Second Thumb. *Be humble in the face of the universe.* Of course if they were that humble they wouldn't be laying down the law in the first place. *Be humble.* You got to be aware of your limits, right?' He glanced up at the space elevator. 'We all have meaningful jobs on this thing. But you do what you can do. Unless you can solve fourth-order differential equations you ain't going to be much help in the design office, are you?'

'I bet you could solve them, Stan,' called up one of the buddies.

Stan shrugged. 'Not beyond third-order. I told you I can only count up to three.'

Laughter.

'*Be humble.* Some of you are paramedics, first responders. The first thing they teach any medic is *do no harm.* Isn't that right? Help if you can, but at least don't make things worse in your ignorance. But to accept that limit you need to *know* your ignorance. Here we are building this mighty monument. We know what it's designed to do, we've all seen the projections and the business models: the fruits of the sky brought down to this Earth. But none of us *knows* what effects it's going to have, not in the short, medium or long term. We live in a reality that's not just complicated, it's chaotic. Unstable.

So, *be humble in the face of the universe.* Know the limits of what you can achieve, what you can know. And in a chaotic universe, at least don't snafu stuff even more than it already is snafued . . .' He raised an arm and mimed flicking his middle finger at the cable. 'You know, I have this fantasy that if I touch this big guitar string just right I could set up this huge oscillation . . . That's one small pluck for a man, one giant twang for mankind—' Hastily he stuck his hand in his pocket. 'Best not take the chance!'

More laughter.

Roberta tapped Melinda's arm. 'That's getting a response from the agitators.'

This was Melinda's and Roberta's term for a wider circle of 'friends' of Stan's. Mostly older than the misfits, many of them blue-collar workers, men and women, they were union leaders, organizers, campaigners – some of them even disaffected middle management. From their circle had come the leaders of the most damaging down-tools strike the beanstalk project on this world had seen so far. They seemed to want to use Stan and his gatherings as a focus for discontent with LETC, the other contractors and the government.

Melinda murmured, 'All Stan's talk of hubris, of overreach. That's been a common thread in their own talk. It's a theme they can use to challenge the position of their corporate and political masters.'

Roberta nodded. 'Stan may also have been unwise to speak of bringing the beanstalk down. Even to raise such an idea, however playfully, will ring alarm bells with the security agencies.'

Martha glared at the agitators, who were smiling and nodding at each other as Stan spoke. 'Look at them. Such *hard* people. Troublemakers with their own agenda. I know that. And the cops know it from the way they keep an eye on them.' She sighed. 'If only Stan knew it too. He's so innocent, for all his brains.'

Rocky knew there were real tensions here in Miami West 4, and had been long before Stan had begun his self-appointed mission. The beanstalk project was falling well behind schedule, and was eating its investors' money. The problem had always been keeping hold of the workers. This was after all the Long Earth, and even Florida West 4 was pretty empty and wild and exotic. In the heads of the young elevator workers, old dreams were forever being subverted by the new. All of which forced the management to try to tie down their workers with restrictive contracts, or to reward them handsomely to keep them on side – which, of course, gave leverage to those who sought more.

Meanwhile the Next, as represented by Roberta and Melinda, had their own concerns about Stan and his message, and as he spoke on Rocky heard Melinda and Roberta exchange short bursts of quicktalk.

'But you see,' Stan said now, 'I would want to ask this hypothetical person advising me to be a bit more active. *Apprehend. Be humble in the face of the universe.* Well, I could sit on my butt and manage that.' He glanced around, as if in surprise to find himself still on his concrete plinth. 'In fact I *am* sitting on my butt, but that's by the bye. I think they'd sum up the rest something like this, with the Rule of the Third Thumb.' He looked down at his own two thumbs. 'Now, you see, I haven't really thought this through. Because I ain't *got* a third thumb.' He looked down at his crotch, innocently. 'Of course I could improvise.'

One of the buddies called, 'Not with your mom standing in front of you, you won't!'

Rocky saw Martha's glare at that. She hated to be referred to by any of this bunch of inadequates, as she called them.

'OK,' Stan said, with a grin. 'Take the third thumb as read. What's important is the rule, which is: *Do good.*' He looked down at his mother now. 'That sounds a little bland, right? Kind of Mom-and-Pop instructions for when you're about seven years old. But the question is, *how* should you do good? After all the right path isn't always clear – everybody knows that, you face dilemmas about that every day.

'Well, if you're faced with some situation, some dilemma, remember the other rules of thumb. *Apprehend*. Try to understand the problem, the people involved, as much as you can. *Be humble in the face of the universe*. Make sure you don't screw things up further, at least.

'But you can do more. Do the good that's in front of you. If somebody's hurting, or about to be hurt, try to save them. Figure out who's vulnerable, in any situation. Who's got no power, no choice? It's a good bet that you won't go wrong if you help *them*. Even so, there may be situations where that's not clear. So there's a much older rule I came across, which some call – or versions of it – the Golden Rule: do as you would be done by. Would you want *this* done to you? Would you want to be *saved* from this situation? If so, do it. If you're not sure, don't.' He shrugged. 'You're not going to get it right every time. It's *impossible* to get it right every time. We live in a chaotic universe, remember? Be humble. But I figure it's worth *trying* to get it more right than wrong . . .'

People started asking questions now.

Melinda sighed, listening absently. 'Hear that? Some of them call him "Master". Others are writing it all down. I think we just heard the Sermon Under the Beanstalk, delivered by a messiah called Stan.'

Martha almost snarled, 'He's just a kid.'

Roberta said gently, 'With respect, Mrs Berg, I don't think that's fair. His message is simple but contains great depth – a depth which I am sure will be revealed by contemplation and exegesis in the months and years to come. *Apprehend*: one could take that as a mandate to achieve full awareness, indeed full self-awareness. To master the passions, for example – not to eliminate them, but to ensure they don't control you. *Be humble in the face of the universe*: hidden in there may be a mandate for our management of the world, of all the worlds. We should embrace diversity, for example, for we can never know the consequences of our interventions in a maximally complex system like a biosphere.' She glanced at Martha.

'You've said you are not religious. You did not raise Stan in that tradition. His sermon sounded free of religion, humanist, perhaps even atheist. Yet buried deep in its implications there was even a guide as to how to approach God – any god, or gods. *Consider that every moment you're alive and aware in this glorious world is a moment of awareness of that god – and to live in that moment is the only way you can be aware of your god* . . . That's the basis of a creed that even the Next could embrace. And all of it packed into just eleven words, delivered by a man just nineteen years old.' With liquid-bright eyes she looked around, at the crowd, the young man on the plinth. 'This is not a trivial moment. This is the birth of a movement. Potentially a religion. A new force in the affairs of humanity.'

Rocky felt his temper flare. 'By which you mean, dim-bulb humanity. It wouldn't be the first time we "dim-bulbs" have dreamed up a new religion, even without your help.'

Roberta said, 'But, you see, the problem is these "rules" of Stan's *have come from a Next*, not a dim-bulb. For that's what Stan is, whether he wants to admit it to himself or not – for all he's rejected our own tentative thinking so far. He's trying to build a bridge between Next and humanity, clearly. But his teaching could be profoundly destabilizing.'

'Good,' Rocky snarled.

Melinda frowned. 'You need to keep your voice down.'

'In fact, Rocky, I need you to come with us.' A woman's voice, speaking quietly.

Rocky turned, startled. Standing there was a woman Rocky didn't recognize: late middle-aged, in traveller's gear, with greying blonde hair under a sun-bleached hat, she was stern, silent, intimidating.

Roberta nodded. 'It is time, then. We need you to help us save him, Rocky. And to get him out of here.'

'Save Stan?' Rocky asked wildly. 'Save him from what?' He turned on the middle-aged woman. 'And what the hell do *you* want?'

She looked like she wanted nothing more than to just light out of here. And yet she held his gaze. She said, 'I'm one of you – not a Next. And I hate this as much as you're going to. But I came to help convince you they're right, Rocky. And you, Martha. Stan must come with us, for he has a duty to perform. In a place called New Springfield.' She smiled, oddly sadly, wistfully. 'He's going to be a hero, Rocky. I'll tell you as much as I understand myself, I promise.'

This was the beginning. When Rocky began to learn for the first time that the Next intended to take Stan away from this place. And that they needed Rocky to help.

'Who *are* you?'

'My name is Sally Linsay.'

49

ROCKY, INCREASINGLY APPREHENSIVE, was taken, with Sally and Roberta, to the local corporate headquarters of the Long Earth Trading Company.

From the outside the LETC HQ was nothing exciting, a single-storey block of timber and concrete – like a Cape Canaveral bunker, built for safety as with all human-habitable structures anywhere near the beanstalk site. But its pale concrete walls bore the LETC name and logo picked out in chrome: a line of stylized figures carrying a huge tree trunk on their shoulders, crossing between shadowy stepwise worlds. This was how the company had started out, hauling Long Earth timber to the Datum on human backs. Now it was building a space elevator.

Once inside, Rocky was led to a kind of conference room, with a big, slanting picture window facing the construction site, the beanstalk itself. Massive metal blinds were poised to roll down over the windows in case of any disaster.

Sally Linsay, still wearing her traveller's hat, grinned at Rocky and sat down. 'Come on, kid, you sit by me. You want some water?'

'What are we doing in here?'

Roberta said, 'Mr Russo of LETC loaned us the facility, so we could talk in private, about our plan – about Stan. And without surveillance.'

'What does Mr Russo care?'

'Frankly, Rocky – and I'm sure you know this already – the corporation don't want him around here. He's too much trouble. And so when Sally Linsay and I turned up saying we wanted to take him away—'

Sally glared at her. 'We never met before today, before we were both sent here. But I know you. Roberta Golding. Originally from Happy Landings. Just fifteen, you were the only western student to travel with the Chinese on that mission to Earth East Twenty Million. Before Yellowstone you were invited to the White House as some kind of intern, and next thing you know you're a guest on the President's Science Advisory Council. And since then—'

'Since then,' Roberta said, 'I have joined my own people. No, Sally, we never met before. But we did work together before, through Joshua Valienté. Saving hundreds of Next children from their internment on Hawaii. Whatever you think of us, we will always be grateful to you for that.'

Sally didn't look to Rocky like she did gratitude very well. 'And here we are working together again. Funny old world.'

'But you understand why, Sally,' Roberta said. '*You* have from the beginning, more clearly than any of us. That's why you sent Lobsang to New Springfield. You sensed something wrong there. And why you offered to help now—'

'You say he's a problem.' Rocky glared at Roberta. 'Stan. For you maybe, for LETC. He's no problem for me.'

'But he *is* your problem, Rocky,' Roberta said gently. 'I know it. I've seen you with him, remember. You're the same age. You've known him since childhood. You came all the way to the Grange with him, and back. And you've stuck with him, while this – circus – has blown up around him and his teachings, and his other old friends have faded away. That's true, isn't it?'

'Only his mother, and me. Even his father won't see him any more.'

'For you it's personal. And that's why you're here, why we need your help. You want to protect him – I can see that – from these acolytes who are attracted to him, who want to use him for their own purposes.'

Sally snorted. 'Just as *you* want to use him, for *your* purposes.'

Roberta showed no irritation. 'What we want above all is for Stan to find his true destiny. That's the best way we can help him. And that is *not* by letting him rabble-rouse the workers here. The authorities are growing concerned about the situation here, Rocky. I mean the government, state and federal. Homelands Security. Also the police. Here you have an agitator threatening the stability of the industrial operation, and the security of the high-energy, high-risk facility at the centre of it – not to mention jeopardizing the tax revenues to be garnered from it, now and in the future. If LETC has him shipped out of here they'll find a sympathetic ear in government.'

Sally said, '"A sympathetic ear." What the hell does that mean? All the kid's doing is talking. What happened to free speech in this country?'

Roberta smiled. 'Some would say it got repealed when President Cowley came to power.' She turned to Rocky. 'But all these author-ities do have a point. You have to understand. Stan is still only nineteen. Suppose he were to continue down this path, as he matures further? He is no ordinary preacher; he is a Next. Human culture may not be – ready – for his message. Surely you can imagine the damage he could do—'

'Yeah, you trotted out that line before,' Sally said coldly. 'But I'm starting to suspect you Next have another agenda in play here, don't you? Stan Berg thinks we should work together. You brainiacs, us dim-bulbs. He says we share a deeper common humanity, and together we should build on that. What a naive young man he is,' she said, her voice dripping with sarcasm. 'What a challenge to your pride—'

Rocky blurted, 'I can see what you're really doing here. All of you.' They broke off and looked at him. '*You all want rid of him.* The company, so they can build their beanstalk. The government, so he stops stirring people up. You Next, so he stops driving us out of your control. You're ganging up on him, combining your interests, getting him out of the way. It *suits* you all to get rid of him, whatever is going on in this distant place, in New Springfield. And you want *me* to help you take him away?'

Sally covered Rocky's hand with hers, an unexpected touch of humanity. 'It's not just that, Rocky. Yes – all these characters want to see him out of the way. It's how prophets are usually treated, after all. But there's a kernel of truth under the manipulation. We really do need him.'

'*We?*'

'All of mankind.' She smiled, a twisted grin. 'Both flavours.' She glanced at Roberta. 'No more arguments, no more manipulation, no more justification. Let's just tell him.'

And so Sally and Roberta, slowly, steadily, with no dramatics or visual aids, tried to tell Rocky the story of Earth West 1,217,756, of New Springfield. And of the creatures called silver beetles, and what they were doing to that world – and of the threat they might pose to the whole Long Earth, and a scattered mankind.

When it was done, Rocky felt overwhelmed. 'I don't see how Stan can help you with this. What's he going to do, preach at these – beetles?'

Roberta said now, 'Rocky, you'll have to trust us.'

'Trust you? I don't trust any of you Next.' He faced Sally. 'But *you*. If I ask you straight questions, will you tell me the truth?'

She nodded gravely. 'If I can.'

'Is this necessary, really? Does this – closing up – have to be done?'

'Yes. Yes, I believe it does.'

'Does it have to be Stan? Why?'

Sally spread her hands. 'It's hard to explain. A sufficiently advanced stepper isn't just a traveller. He, she, interacts with the way the Long Earth itself is put together . . . And Stan is the most advanced stepper I ever came across. It's as if he *understands* the Long Earth better than anybody before or since. And that's what makes him so powerful.'

Roberta said with dogged patience, 'It's all theory, frankly. One point, however, is that Sally here is going to have to work with him on this. Coach him.'

Sally grunted. 'More like, we'll be learning together . . .'

'Why not just ask for his help? Why this press-ganging?'

There was an awkward silence. Sally said at last, 'Because, Rocky, we can't afford for him to refuse.'

'And if Stan does this – *if I give Stan up to you* – will he survive?'

Sally sighed. 'No,' she said. 'No, he won't survive.'

Rocky tried to take it all in. 'Will he be alone?'

'No,' Sally said firmly. 'I can promise you that. Personally.' And she took hold of Rocky's hand.

50

THEY WASTED NO time. If it had to be done, they'd decided, it was best done immediately.

It was evening when they got back to the elevator base site. Stan was still on his plinth, with his followers and some of the other workers. His sermon had triggered a bull session that looked like it could go on all night, Sally thought.

Rocky made his way through the crowd towards Stan.

Sally stood back, with Roberta Golding and Stan's mother.

'Good,' Roberta said, watching. 'Rocky's doing well. Nice and calm. Just a friend coming to bring Stan home to his family. Not like an arrest at all . . .'

Martha said dully, 'The way Rocky's chatting to the followers as he passes – you'd never know what's in his soul. He always was a good friend to Stan. But he's going to have to carry this with him, the memory of what he's doing, for the rest of his life, isn't he?'

Impulsively, Roberta hugged her. 'I guess there's no greater price a friend can pay.'

Rocky reached Stan. He grinned, accepted a bottle of beer, and pointed to Stan's mother at the back of the crush. Stan shrugged, looking like he was apologizing to his fan club. Then he picked up his jacket and began to make his way out of the peaceable crowd, Rocky's arm around his shoulders, with no resistance from his followers.

Roberta murmured, 'I once told you that you'd lose him, Martha. One way or another. At least this is a good way, a positive way—'

'No,' Martha snarled. 'There is no good way.' And before the boys got back through the crowd, she broke away from the women and hurried off.

51

O N Earth West 1,217,756, the end game was close, everybody said.

Joshua could sense it. If you stood out in the open on this world, under the streaming sky, you could *feel* the shuddering of the planet as more and more energy was poured into it by the beetles' globe-spanning motor. And you could *see* the quickening spin in the almost perceptible shifting of the shadows, on the rare occasions when the sun was visible through the cloud.

As seen from orbit by the small observation satellites thrown up by the *Cowley*, the spinning world now looked like Jupiter or Saturn, striped with horizontal bands of cloud. Two-hundred-miles-per-hour hurricanes stalked the oceans and spilled on to the land, battering the already devastated coastal regions. Inland the cores of the once-global forests still stoutly resisted the storms, but only a handful of the furball mammals, living underground or deep in the trunks of trees, had recently been seen.

The day was reduced to less than eight hours. As estimated by Ken Bowring and Margarita Jha of the *Cowley*, this world's rotational energy had increased nine-fold, gravity at the equator was down three per cent, and the planet's flattening as it spun up was now causing crustal distortions of a couple of hundred kilometres – far more than the maximum thickness of the crust itself. Joshua couldn't believe such numbers. And it was getting worse. Lobsang and George guessed that the beetles' coupling of Earth to sun was being enhanced by some means more advanced than the obvious Dyson-motor latitudinal viaducts and streaming moon rocks – some means of transferring huge quantities of spin energy and momentum that human observers were not equipped to recognize ... But there was no time left to learn.

Joshua, however, didn't need science measurements to apprehend the unfolding tragedy here. And it seemed to him that the ultimate possibility was at last being taken seriously, among the scientists and military people, Lobsang and his Next allies. The possibility that the goal of the beetles was not the transformation of this world into some new form, but its destruction.

And that made the final decision, about whether to go ahead with the operation the military people had come to call the Cauterizing, an easy one to make.

Team Stan, as the boy himself had called them – Stan, George and Sally – gathered in the lee of Manning Hill, on the north-western periphery. On the summit of the hill still stood the wind-smashed remains of the home George and Agnes had lived in with their adopted son.

The townsfolk had long gone, the Irwins and the Bambers and the Todds and the Claytons and the rest, gone with their dreams, off to build a new home someplace else. Nikos Irwin, who with his dog Rio had first encountered the beetles in their mine working, had gone with his family – but Rio had died a few months back, and left her bones in the ground of this doomed Earth. It was less easy to be sure that the rest of this planet was empty of people too. Before the weather had closed in the *Cowley* had undertaken spiralling tours of the North American continent, broadcasting warnings, setting up automated radio stations; there was even a comsat flung into orbit, similarly blasting out instructions to step away – as if, Joshua supposed, anybody still struggling to hang on to this spinning-top of a world needed to be told. Well, if anybody stayed for the end game it was their decision, their responsibility; they must be able to guess what was coming.

Whereas Lobsang – George Abrahams, Agnes's husband – Sally Linsay, and young Stan Berg, who were staying for the end, didn't need to guess. They would get to see it for themselves.

The final round of goodbyes was ghastly.

Joshua watched Stan Berg, wearing robust military-specification survival gear that almost fit him, trying to deal with his mother Martha, and Roberta Golding, the enigmatic Next woman who seemed so drawn to him. Stan for his part seemed more concerned for Rocky Lewis, the boyhood friend who everybody muttered had 'betrayed' Stan.

'You won't be forgotten,' Rocky said thickly, his guilt obvious.

Stan grinned. 'You betcha. Have a drink on me with the stalk jacks under that freakin' space cable.'

'We'll remember you. Everything you said and did – you had so little time – we'll remember it all, and pass it on.'

'Just clean up my jokes, will ya?'

Rocky's face worked. 'Stan, I—'

Stan grabbed him, hugged him close, patted his back. 'Don't say it. You did what you had to do. You did what was *right.*'

'Not everybody sees it that way.'

'What matters more, what I say or what they say? And I say it's OK. You remember that.' He released Rocky.

Now it was his mother's turn. Unlike Rocky she did not submit to the hug Stan offered. Joshua thought she blazed with anger, a fire visible in her face, her posture. Maybe it was a way of staving off the loss. Stan's father, Jez, wasn't here at all; he'd never followed Stan to this place, his Golgotha.

'Mom, I—'

'Don't say it. You've said enough. All your *words.* That's what they used to take you away from me. First those losers and chancers who surrounded you in Miami. They're already turning you into a cult, you and your foolishness. A cult and a corporation. Do you know they already registered your image rights? That's the kind of people *they* are. And now this.' She turned and glared at Roberta. 'These people with their manipulation and their fancy theorizing.'

'Mom, it's not just theorizing. I've been through it myself, the arguments. I think they're right about what's going to become of this world. The Cauterizing might work.'

'*I don't care.* Nothing justifies this, for me—' Something seemed to break in her. She turned and blundered away.

Stan pursued her. 'Mom. Mom! . . .'

Now Agnes came to Joshua, arm in arm with George, the homely elderly-appearing ambulant who had been her husband here – the copy of Lobsang who was going to be left behind here, in New Springfield, with Stan. Agnes was still wearing her pioneer gear, the uniform she had adopted on coming here to build a home on this doomed planet.

Agnes took Joshua's hand. 'It's going to be a long ride home, isn't it? You, me, Martha, Rocky. The other survivors of all this. It's Rocky I feel for the most.'

'Well, that's you, Agnes. Always drawn to the damaged children.'

'Isn't that a good instinct? Believe me, the damage that's already been done to that boy will haunt him through his life. Even after his death he'll probably be vilified for his betrayal. There are precedents, you know.' She turned reluctantly to George, still clinging to his arm. 'But you – *must* you stay?'

He smiled, an elderly, elegant, kindly gentleman, wearing scuffed, sturdy frontier clothes, like Agnes's. 'Well, we've been through this, Agnes. I can't take part in the Cauterizing itself. But I, with my long-lost brother, did contribute a great deal to the theory – to the mathematics. And since the operation is largely mathematical, I can lend a great deal of support to—'

'It doesn't have to be *you*. You have a spare.' And Agnes glanced over at the second copy of Lobsang, the ambulant unit from the world of the Traversers. He, it, wore a modest coverall, that one sleeve sewn up. He stood apart from the group, utterly still, statue-like, younger in appearance than George, his face empty of expression. 'He knows everything you do.'

'Yet we're not identical, and never can be.'

'*Why* stay? For the science? You'll be trapped behind the Cauterizing. You'll never be able to report back. Never be able to synch, to download your memories into those big banks at your transEarth Institute or—'

'There may be a way, some day. Why, Stella Welch and the *Cowley* science staff have seeded this world with probes and data-gathering equipment, with the same reservations in mind. You may as well measure what you can, even if you're not sure you can retrieve the data. And besides—' For a moment, a very human resentment twisted his artificial face. He said more thickly, 'Agnes, *this was our world*. My world, my home, with you. Now it is threatened with destruction. I will be the only one of us homesteaders who can be present. I am not the man I was before I came here with you, Agnes. I have invested much of myself in this place – as did we all, the Irwins and the rest, the Poulsons before them. I must see this. I must remember. As best I can.'

Agnes took his hands in hers. 'What about all you "invested" in Ben? You should have seen him when I left him, an eight-year-old boy alone in a cabin on a military airship, crying his heart out.'

'There's nothing more I could do for him. Nothing more I could say.'

Joshua said, 'At least you'll be out of reach of the prosecutors, after you've once again saved civilization as we know it.'

George grinned. 'Even now, old-movie gags, Joshua?'

Joshua, giving in to an impulse, went over to the ambulant and hugged him. 'In spite of everything I'll miss you.'

'Please, Joshua. Not in front of the Next.'

Agnes snapped, 'Oh, you're impossible, the pair of you.'

George glanced now at his Navy-issue watch, its presence on his wrist a symbol of a definitive break from the timeless ethos of New Springfield. 'Please excuse me, there are final preparations . . .' Gently he disengaged his arm from Agnes's. 'We'll still have time before you go.' He walked away.

Joshua put his arm around Agnes's shoulders. 'I'm sorry.'

'Don't be,' she said evenly. 'It's typical of Lobsang that as soon as I decide I'm leaving him, he leaves me. But the truth is I lost him the day the *Cowley* came, and he took it on himself to speak up for the community. Or maybe when the problems with this world became too obvious to ignore. Or maybe I never had him at all – thanks to Sally Linsay, who planted us on this doomed world in the first place, and I'm damn sure she knew what she was doing.'

Joshua shrugged. 'She may have felt she had no choice. That's what the Next say. They can see their way through to an optimal end to the game, and so have no choice about how to play it. I sometimes think there's something of the Next in Sally. If she glimpsed this end-game all the way back then, if she sensed something wrong here, well, she was right, wasn't she? And if that's true, she's paying the price herself.'

'Good,' Agnes said with almost a snarl, and Joshua was taken aback. 'There,' she said more calmly. 'I got that out of my system. Now I can forgive her . . . And here she comes, right on cue. I'll give you some time together.' Agnes squeezed Joshua's hand, and walked away after George, without another glance at Sally.

Joshua and Sally faced each other. As ever she wore her travelling gear, her shapeless hat, her sleeveless jacket with all the pockets, her pack on her back, ready to move.

'So this is it,' Joshua said.

'I guess.'

'You really have to stay?'

She shrugged. 'Stan has the raw ability, but I'm the more

338

experienced stepper. They need me to help him.' She seemed calm, accepting. 'I always suspected it would finish up like this.'

He looked inside himself. 'After all we've been through together, I don't know what I feel.'

'Then stop picking the scab,' she said sternly.

'It seems like yesterday when we first met.'

'When *I* found *you*.'

'In our flying penis, as you called our airship. In the High Meggers. You and your pet dinosaurs basking in the sun.'

'Ancient history.'

'We had lunch. Fresh-caught oysters on an open fire, on that distant beach.'

'I guess I'm heading for another kind of beach now, Joshua.'

'What about your father?'

'Still alive, as far as I know. Made a fortune out of his patents on the beanstalk tech we brought back from Mars.'

Joshua frowned. 'I meant, why isn't he here? Does he *know*? About this, about you? Did you try to contact him?'

She shrugged. 'He'll know all about it. He always did know everything. If he wanted to be here, he would be.'

'But did you try—'

'Leave it, Joshua. My business. As for you, remember me to Helen. That little mouse.'

'She was always wary of you, you know.'

'Of course she was. To her, I was a symbol of the side of you she could never reach, and she knew it. She was good for you, Joshua. But we make our own choices.'

'I guess that's true. But I take it that right now *you* have no choice—'

'Not with this. I never did have. Not from the first moment I heard about the problems on this world.'

'And you brought Lobsang here. What *did* you hear? How?'

But Sally, who had always been immersed in her own networks

of information spanning the Long Earth, had never answered questions like that, and didn't now.

'Anyhow, because of that, I'm going to lose you,' he said gently.

She grinned. 'Don't go soft on me now, Valienté.'

'Sally—'

'Be seeing you.'

And she disappeared, vanishing stepwise, as precociously and abruptly as she had always done, from their very first meeting on the beach with the oysters and the dinosaurs.

52

IN THE RUINS of New Springfield, when the *Cowley* and its passengers had stepped away at last, the three left behind stood alone.

Sally took a deep breath. 'It's amazing how different a world feels when you're alone in it. Refreshing.'

Lobsang – the replicant formerly known as George Abrahams – grunted. 'You're turning into Joshua.'

'I'll take that as an insult.'

'Well, I think it's a relief,' said Stan Berg. 'That it's done, at last. The goodbyes. Now we can get on with the job.' His voice was flat, his face expressionless.

Sally exchanged a glance with Lobsang. Suddenly this man, this boy – this super-intellect of the Next, this prophet, this mother's son – seemed very young indeed. Young and scared. And he had a right to be, Sally thought. Yet, despite his youth, he had taken on this responsibility, and faced the tears of his mother, because he had seen the danger, presumably, more clearly than any of them. That was the curse of Next intelligence: you had no comforting delusions.

She said, 'Come on. Let's get done what we stayed here to do. Where shall we go? I guess we could be anywhere, on this broken planet.'

Stan looked around. 'Top of the hill?'

Lobsang smiled. 'Where my home is, or was, what's left of it. Suits me, so long as we don't get blown off.'

The climb up Manning Hill wasn't steep, but difficult in a wind that hit them harder the more exposed they were. At the summit, Sally could see the foundations of the Abrahams house, the pits they had dug for sewage and storage, the lines of postholes outlining abandoned fields. But little was left of the farmstead but scattered debris, wind-smashed, the labour of years erased.

Looking down from here, Sally could still see the basic layout of the landscape Lobsang and Agnes had lived in, the forest, the creek that had drawn the settlers to this place. But now the creek was brown, turbid with washed-down mud, and the forest was dying back, scarred by fires, battered by the wind, wrecked by the touchdown of twisters. Hundred-year-old trunks lay scattered like spilled matchsticks.

And already the sun was setting behind the racing clouds, another of this world's truncated days coming to an end.

She grabbed her companions' hands firmly. The three of them stood close together, holding hands in a ring, face to face on this desolate hill, resisting the gusty wind. They had to shout to make themselves heard.

Lobsang said, '*When shall we three meet again?*'

Sally grinned. '*In thunder, lightning, or in rain?*'

'*When the hurlyburly's done, when the battle's lost and won . . .*' Stan blinked a squall of rain out of his eyes. 'Don't look at me like that. We had good schools in Miami West 4. It wasn't all stalk jack engineering.'

'Well, the quote's apt given the weather,' Lobsang said. 'And it is a battle. A battle we already lost. But maybe we can win the war, the war for the Long Earth, with this single strike.' He looked in their faces. 'Just so we're all on the same song sheet: the projections of the spin-up have been uncertain for a while. In the last few days the rate of energy increase has gone super-exponential. Hard to model, to predict. We told our families we might have weeks left. But that was for their comfort, yes?'

Stan nodded. 'I know. What's the latest guess?'

'Not weeks. *Hours.* A couple of local days, if we're lucky.'

'It makes no difference,' Stan said, with an authority that belied his years. 'But we need to get the Cauterizing done before we run out of time.'

Sally squeezed his hand harder. 'So how do we do it, Lobsang?'

'Stella Welch and I have gone through it . . . Let's be clear where we are. This world has become, presumably by some higher-dimensional accident, a point of intersection of our Long Earth, our chain of worlds, with another chain. Another Long world. A chain to which the world we call the Planetarium belongs.'

Stan said, 'Like two necklaces crossing. Tangling up.'

'That's it. Visualize that. It's important that you visualize . . . Step along one axis, East or West, and you follow the track of the Long Earth. Step another way, North or South, and you follow the Long Planetarium, as the beetles seem to have done. So the connectivity of the Long Earth is unusual here. Broken. What we want to do now is *change* that connectivity, make it the way we want it. Visualize it. Imagine what you're going to do, Stan . . .'

Stan closed his eyes. 'You could pinch the necklace of worlds, the Long Earth. Knot the thread so one pearl is cut out of the chain, the pearl that's tangled up with the Planetarium necklace. Detach this world from the Long Earth necklace completely . . .'

'Yes. Think about that. A simple repair job. Picture it. You too, Sally. Stepping has always been a mental faculty. Even the act of creating a Stepper box is a kind of mandala, a kind of autohypnosis, a way to unlock a potential in us that already exists. To step is a feat of the imagination – one must be able to visualize another world, in a sense, in sufficient detail, to reach it. A very fine description – so fine that the description *becomes* the object, just as quantum physics is essentially about information—'

'Lobsang,' Sally warned. 'Less of the techno-babble.'

'Yes, yes. I apologize. But you must see that to talk this through is an essential part of the process. For you, Sally, it is like reaching for a soft place. A different kind of flaw in our own Long Earth's connectivity, where the loop of worlds crosses over itself. I've seen you search for such places. You look inwards as much as outwards. You position your body . . .'

Sally tried to imagine that, tried to imagine reaching for a soft place now. Sometimes you could *see* them, see a shimmer in low sunlight, often at liminal places, places of borders – between water and land, perhaps, a shore, a river bank; at dawn or sunset, the border between day and night. And now, on this world, she had reached her own ultimate border, between reality and unreality, existence and non-existence. Life and death.

'We are reaching for a soft place,' Lobsang said, steadily, hypnotically, as if reciting a prayer. 'Or perhaps we are creating one . . . A *permanent* soft place, a tunnel, a bypass, that will cut out this world permanently, welding together the worlds to East and West, to either side. It is almost as if we are persuading everybody who comes after us that this flawed world is *not here* any more, that there is nothing between the worlds to West and East.' He closed his eyes. 'We are changing the linkage of the Long Earth, in this one place, for ever . . .'

Falling.

Sally staggered. Suddenly she felt very cold, colder even than the wind's chill, as if she had fallen through a soft place, the longest fall she'd ever known.

And Stan cried out. He released their hands and toppled back, stiff as a cut-down tree, landing on his back in the grass. He began to twitch, convulse, and spittle flecked his open mouth. Lobsang hurried to his side.

As Lobsang tended to Stan, battered by the wind, Sally tried experimentally to step out of here. *She couldn't.* It was as if she were confined between two walls to either side that she could not see, walls of glass. For her, a natural stepper, it was a strange, unnatural feeling.

'We did it, Lobsang,' she said, wondering. 'The Cauterizing.'

'*He* did it, mostly. With your help.'

'What does it mean, Lobsang? For the future. If Stan here is typical, and not some kind of super-powered freak. If the Next can take apart and reconstruct the Long Earth itself – what will they do with such powers?'

'That's no longer our concern,' he said sternly. 'Give me a hand here.' He'd got Stan turned over on his side, in the recovery position, but the boy was still fitting. 'I have a med kit in my pack. Then we're going to need to get into shelter . . .'

She hurried down the hill, in search of the med kit.

53

I N THE LEE of the hill, in a sturdily constructed lean-to – a last gift of the crew of the *Cowley* – the three of them spent an uneasy four-hour 'night'.

They ate, wrapped in survival blankets. None of them slept. The air felt increasingly warm, smoky, ash-laden, like the air of the Datum just after Yellowstone, Sally thought. And the noise was continuous now, the rush of the wind, a rolling thunder, like the sound of distant artillery.

Stan recovered quickly from his fit, especially once Lobsang/ George had administered a bowl of Agnes's chicken soup. He chose not to describe what had gone on in his head at the moment of the Cauterizing, and the others didn't press him. Another issue, Sally thought, for a future none of them was going to see.

The morning came with a dawn as abrupt as a thrown switch.

That and a savage earth tremor, a drop that felt like they were on some vast elevator that had just slipped its cable a couple of feet, Sally thought.

The *Cowley* crew had left a small science station. Lobsang consulted this as they drank coffee from a flask.

'Incredible,' he said. '"Today" will be less than six hours long, day and night. The rotational energy of this Earth has roughly *doubled* in the last twelve hours. You have to hand it to those beetles. It took them a long time to build this vast machine, this interplanetary motor. But now that it's up and running, energy and momentum are just pouring down from the sky. And here's what it's doing.' He opened a tablet which showed a mosaic of global images, taken from space. 'These are coming from the small satellites the *Cowley* crew put into orbit, before they left . . .'

Sally looked closer to see. Under its new latitudinal bands of cloud, the face of this Earth in outline was much as it had always been, the school-atlas shapes of the continents, the blue-grey of the oceans. But a network of jagged red lines spread over the interior of the continents, and glowed under the oceans, although thick banks of steam obscured much of the view over the water. 'It's like a bowl full of lava, that somebody dropped on the floor and cracked.'

'That's not a bad analogy,' Lobsang said. His finger traced the glowing flaws scribbled across the face of North America. 'The planet's crust is just a fine shell around a ball of liquid rock and metal. Now that shell is breaking open. You can see the boundaries between geological provinces, faults opening up – cracks between the tectonic plates.' He pointed to a livid blemish in the west. '*That* is the local Yellowstone; it went up at last. But soon even the continental plates themselves will start to crumble. They must. The planet's deformation has become so severe that at the equator the mantle itself is rising to the surface now.' He rubbed his face. 'We may not see it all. All the crap that's pouring into the air – why, the volcanic debris alone may block radio signals from the satellites.'

Sally said, 'Listen, we should eat while we've got the chance – and not just Agnes's soup.' She rummaged through their supplies, bequeathed by the *Cowley*.

Stan was staring at the images. 'They're going to finish this. They really are going to take this Earth apart altogether, aren't they? It seems such a waste.'

'The beetles wouldn't say that,' Lobsang said. '*They* believe they're improving the neighbourhood.'

Sally laid out food packets. 'Well, we have beef, chicken, bread, salad stuff. I wonder if they packed any mustard?'

Stan said, 'But why would the beetles do this? What's the point? I thought the theory was these beetles are colonizers.'

'That's how it looked from the world we called the Planetarium,' Lobsang said. 'Which they appeared to be terraforming, to their requirements. But we also saw evidence of conflict, in the sky of the star cluster. A war in heaven. Evidently their colonizing wave is being opposed. But *here*, by coming stepwise to this Earth, the beetles suddenly found themselves in an empty world – empty of their competitors at any rate – and under an open, empty sky. In such a situation the optimal strategy, for aggressive colonizers, must be—'

'Like a dandelion,' Sally said, seeing it suddenly. 'Or a puffball fungus. To colonize all the empty space, as widely as possible, as fast as possible, before anybody else gets a chance. And that means sending seeds off in all directions, as many as you can.'

'Ah.' Stan closed his eyes. 'I understand. They take apart the whole Earth. They capture the dispersed mass, turn it into—'

'Copies of themselves, probably,' Lobsang said. 'The numbers are staggering. If they turned this whole world into a horde of beetles, each of which weighs as much as an adult human, say, then there could be as many as ten billion *trillion* of them, scattering in all directions. Far more beetles than there are stars in the Galaxy.'

Stan said, 'And each one, in principle, capable of landing on a virgin world, and replicating away until it's achieved the same damn thing again.'

'All of which is why we needed to ensure the beetles didn't spread into the Long Earth stepwise, that we contained them here. Otherwise—'

Sally smiled. 'Otherwise, in a few years, the worlds of the Long Earth would be going up like a string of firecrackers, one by one.' She mimed explosions with her fingers. 'Poom! Poom! Poom! . . . And from each contaminated world the beetles will spread out to infect an entire Galaxy.'

Stan shook his head. 'You know, I told my followers that above all they should do no harm. This world was inhabited, with a freight of life of its own, unique, irreplaceable. What kind of being would *do* this?'

'Creatures like humans,' Sally said bluntly. 'That's all. I don't imagine you ever saw much of the Datum – of the mess we made of that, in the end.'

'Humans also built cathedrals,' Stan said softly.

Lobsang said, 'Even with the beetles it might not be as black and white as that. There may have been a more innocent motive at the beginning, a drive for peaceful colonization. Perhaps these beetles are descended from units which – mutated. Went rogue. Maybe a programmed drive to be *efficient*, not to be wasteful of the resources they accessed, morphed into a commandment to use up *all* the resources in reach. Well, the places they transform will be tidy, but it will be the tidiness of death, of sterility. After all they don't seem to be intrinsically evil; they even seem to have *played* with the children of New Springfield. It's just that they got out of control.'

'Garbage,' Sally said. 'You're overthinking it, Lobsang. The beetles are just like us, and that's that.' She held out a plastic plate heaped with sandwiches. 'Chicken or beef?'

Lobsang tentatively took a chicken. 'There's one option I need to inform you about,' he said. 'Before I have to use it.'

Sally, suspicious, glared at him. 'Even now, you've got a stunt to pull, Lobsang?'

He pointed to the sky. 'I could upload myself to one of the *Cowley*'s satellites. Transfer my seat of consciousness from this ambulant unit into space. Where it might survive even the final destruction of the planet—'

'Do it,' Stan said.

'It would mean abandoning the two of you.'

'To a last few minutes of fire and brimstone?' Sally said. 'So what? I agree, Lobsang. Keep observing for as long as you can. That's why we came here.'

'And if you ever get the chance,' Stan said, 'tell somebody.'

Lobsang nodded. 'I'll make it so.'

Stan said, 'But if you're leaving early, Lobsang—'

'Yes?'

'Can I have that last chicken sandwich?'

54

I N THE NEXT brief night Sally actually managed to sleep a little, her thin survival blanket over her body, her head on her backpack.

She was woken by her own coughing. Smoke in the air, tickling her throat. She opened her eyes. Lying on her side, under her blanket, she was facing out of the little camp, and looking at the trunk of a long-dead tree, wrapped in an equally dead strangler fig.

But there was movement inside the fig, in its shadows, dimly visible in the dawn light. A small face poked out of the lattice of wood, a long snout, big eyes. It seemed to study her, as if she might be a threat, or an opportunity. Then the creature scuttled out into the open. It wasn't much bigger than a mouse, with smooth brown fur, but with big, powerful back legs, like a miniature kangaroo. It sniffed, looked around – froze – and then leapt into the air, clopping its jaws closed around some insect, and landed and scuttled back into the shadows.

Lobsang touched her shoulder. 'One last dawn. One last chance for the furballs to hunt.'

Still lying under her blanket she said, 'All coming to an end today, then.'

'I'm afraid so—'

The ground lurched, and Sally, lying there, felt herself being *lifted up.* As if she was a child in a stepwise footprint of Wyoming, and her father had scooped her up in his arms. The rise went on for seconds, pinning her to the ground. Then, just as suddenly, it stopped, she gasped, and the land *fell*, surely through several feet. She landed hard on her back.

'Up you get.' Lobsang stood over her, hand outstretched.

Feeling very elderly, Sally accepted the help. But then she pushed her feet into her boots, grabbed her pack, her multi-pocketed jacket and her hat, and was ready for action once more.

Stan was already on his feet, grinning. 'The end credits.'

'I think so,' Lobsang said.

'I don't suppose there's any point asking what's for breakfast?'

Sally smiled. 'It's your show, Stan. Where do you want to be?'

He pointed upwards. 'Top of Manning Hill again. We may as well get the best view we can.'

'Good,' said Lobsang. 'I'll lead the way, I know the trail. But watch out for fissures. And if there's another tremor like that big one, throw yourself flat . . .'

The view from the top of the hill was obscured by drifting smoke. Overhead, clouds streamed like a speeded-up movie effect. From up here Sally could see that the remaining buildings of New Springfield were shattered now, heaps of splintered timber, and along the line of Soulsby Creek a deep fissure had opened, revealing the glow of lava. The spilled water hissed and boiled.

Lobsang said, 'Look at that. *Our* place was destroyed early, by the winds at the top of this hill. Now the rest of the town has gone.'

'Shaken to pieces,' Sally said. 'I'm sorry, Lobsang – George.'

He shrugged.

'Fire,' said Stan. He pointed. 'There, there, there . . .'

Whole swathes of the continent-spanning forest must be alight now. Sally saw how the fire was spreading, the trunks of mature trees going up with whooshes, like splinters of kindling. In one place she thought she saw movement, heavy animals on the move. Those big birds the colonists had spoken of, presumably. They'd survived this much, then.

She pointed this out to Lobsang. 'But there's nowhere for them to flee.'

'No. The fire's spreading. Joining up. When it surrounds this hilltop we'll be trapped—'

'I suspect that will be academic, Lobsang.'

There was a tremendous groan from deep within the hillside, as if the rock itself was stressed beyond endurance. Again the ground lurched, dropping this time, and Sally stumbled, almost fell. Even when the drop was over the ground continued to shudder.

'Down,' Stan shouted. 'Let's sit down. That way at least we can't be thrown over.'

They hurried to comply, sitting in their tight witches' circle, on the shaking ground, holding hands firmly. Sally watched the clouds washing past the sun. She was convinced she could see the sun itself shift across the sky, visibly, so fast was the world's rotation now.

'One hour,' Lobsang called.

'What?'

'When the day is reduced to a single hour. That's when the rocks at the equator will be moving so fast they'll effectively be in orbit, and the air will start leaking away – the final break-up will begin.'

'But we won't get to see that,' Sally said. She squeezed Stan's hand. 'Not long now.'

'Good,' he said fiercely.

'You have no regrets?'

'I'm dying young,' he said, his face screwed up against the dust-laden wind. 'I didn't get the chance to say all I needed to say. I hope that my words will do no harm, in the future. I needed more time.' He shook his head. 'But I also needed to be *here* ...'

Lobsang was staring. '*Chak pa!*'

Sally looked over his shoulder. She saw that as the tremors worsened, swathes of landscape at the bottom of the hill were breaking up, almost liquefying, and the surviving forest was *sinking*, square-mile chunks of it vanishing from sight in clouds of dust, as if it was falling through wet cardboard. The noise was all around them now, the howling wind, the roar of the fires, the rush of huge masses on the move. She remembered the little furball living in the fig, and she hoped it had had time to enjoy its last meal, had got back to its young before the end.

Stan looked at Sally. He had to shout to make himself heard. 'What did Lobsang say?'

She grinned, remembering a voyage through the Gap, long ago. 'Tibetan swearing, I think. Is that right, Lobsang? Lobsang?'

Lobsang was sitting stock still, as if hypnotized.

Sally grabbed his chin, pulled his head to face her. His eyes, an old man's rheumy eyes nested in wrinkles, were blank, vague, as if he had succumbed at last to Long Earth Syndrome. 'Go,' she yelled. 'Go! Before you lose yourself. Now!' She slapped his face as hard as she could.

'Ow!' He raised his hand to his cheek. Then he grinned at her. 'Good luck, Sally Linsay. It's been a privilege.'

His eyes rolled back, and he tumbled stiffly over, a puppet with its strings cut.

And the ground dropped from beneath her.

Not by a few feet this time. It dropped out of reach, *gone*. For a heartbeat she still had hold of Stan's hand. But he was torn from her grip, and they were whirled apart.

Then she was falling in mid-air, in the smoke and the ash, as if she were a moth over a campfire. The ground below was gone altogether. Her world was three-dimensional now, with only fire under her, and gushes of steam and white-hot sprays of what must be liquid rock, and around her trees and chunks of cooler rock falling as she was, and above her clouds that boiled. She was tiny, a mote in this immensity. But she had her hat jammed on her head, her pack on her back. And she saw, in the last instant, a human figure: Stan, it must be, flying as she was, and he was waving his arms and legs, starfishing in the air.

She thought back on her life, all that had happened to her, all she had seen, all she had done. She was Sally Linsay, pioneer of the Long Earth *and* the Long Mars, and she'd never planned to die in her bed. What a way to finish. Falling in the hot air, she yelled in exultation—

Flame licked. The moth was consumed.

55

ON ANOTHER WORLD, under a different sky – in another universe, whose distance from the Datum, the Earth of mankind, was nevertheless counted in the mundanity of human steps – Joshua Valienté lay beside his own fire.

And he gasped, suddenly feeling hollow, as if he'd been punched in the stomach.

56

WHEN LOBSANG HAD first met Joshua, he had downloaded a node of his consciousness into a soft drinks machine. It had been a playful gesture, a practical joke. Why not pull such stunts, if you could? But Lobsang had been young then. Comparatively.

The experience of having his mind housed in this small automated spacecraft was not unlike being stuck inside that vending machine.

The satellite, launched from the long-gone *Brian Cowley*, was no larger than a basketball, with very limited manoeuvring and self-repair capabilities. Lobsang felt tiny, diminished, crippled. But the craft was studded with sensors, its hull glistened with lenses, and small, wispy antennas were fixed to struts extended from its flanks.

And through these lenses and sensors, Lobsang was able to witness the death throes of a world.

This probe had been in synchronous orbit, more than twenty thousand miles high, and from out here Lobsang could see it all: a whole hemisphere at a glance, the planet like a dish held at arm's length. The blanket of air was stained by smoke and steam. Immense auroral displays cupped the world at north and south poles, and Lobsang speculated about a tremendous distortion of the planetary magnetic field as it collapsed. Storms swirled, giant weather systems white and purple and sparking with lightning, lashing the turbulent oceans and pouring on to the land. Still Lobsang could make out the forms of the continents, just – he saw the Americas, North and South, sweep across the face of the globe as the world turned through its final, desperately accelerated rotations. But increasingly there was little difference between land and sea, for rivers of molten rock ran brightly along the spreading fractures of the ocean floors, and filled the tremendous crevices that were opening up on the continents. Briefly Lobsang was reminded of spacecraft views of Io, innermost moon of Jupiter, a world tormented into unending volcanism by its primary's mighty tides.

But Earth was evolving quickly, and even that comparison was soon lost. With startling speed the continents *dissolved*, as if fifty-mile-thick granite was no more than a mere skim being burned away by the red-white heat of the interior. Now Lobsang saw raft-like fragments of landscapes rotate, tip up, even grind against each other in collisions that threw up immense mountain ranges that could survive only minutes. Surely, already, nothing could be left alive down there: nothing left of Stan and Sally.

And still the spin-up continued. He could see the growing obliquity of the world as a whole now; the planet seemed to soften, its surface stretching, accommodating. It seemed to him that a new transient geography was forming on the exposed mantle, with rivers of hotter material erupting from the interior and running across the marginally cooler surface, rivers that washed away the last scraps of solid crust. There was even a kind of weather as vast clouds of plasma broke through the surface and spread glowing tendrils across the planet's face.

Now a new phase began. What looked like a kind of tornado opened up on the equator, directly below Lobsang's position, a swirling mass with a darker centre – a centre that exploded with stupendous force, spraying fragments out into the dissipating atmosphere. It was a volcano, a massive outlet of mantle energies, on whose flanks even Yellowstone would have been no more than a glowing speck. Looking to the planet's horizon Lobsang saw more such giant features in profile, blisters visibly rising about the world's distorted curve, all around the equator. And from this angle Lobsang could see huge bolides thrown out, masses of glowing rock rising above the horizon, for a few moments still falling back to the sea of molten silicate below. But then came one tremendous eruption, and a spray of bolides escaped from the world altogether and sailed off into space, spinning and cooling. Significant chunks of the Earth, already being lost to space.

Now he saw evidence of the beetles, for the first time. What looked like tremendous filmy butterflies, with wings of net that must be hundreds of kilometres across, came sailing down from higher orbit to drift through the gathering ring of cooling rock fragments around the equator, scooping them up. A cynical harvest was beginning.

The world's shape seemed to deform visibly now. The poles must be sinking at hundreds of miles per hour, the equator distorting at a similar rate, and the big volcanoes became mouths that vomited material continuously into space. The surface was featureless, almost, save for the equatorial volcanic wounds. The world was a drop of liquid, with an almost abstract beauty, Lobsang thought.

Then there was a kind of pause, as if the planet was drawing breath.

And the surface seemed to lift off, all at once, like a tremendous global eruption. Vast amounts of material, a spray of shining rock and clouds of plasma, lifted high into space, some of it flowing in great currents in the sky, perhaps shaped by the remnant magnetic field. Lobsang saw a brighter, inner light – the light of the core itself, perhaps, a mass of compressed liquid iron the size of the moon – shining through the disrupted outer layers, casting straight-line shadows hundreds of miles long.

The net-ships of the beetles fed eagerly.

And as the mass of the Earth dispersed, its gravity field gently began to loose its hold on Lobsang's vessel, a tiny, unnoticed cork bobbing on the surface of a turbulent cosmic sea, drifting away.

With the wreckage of Earth receding, Lobsang turned his mind to the future. His own future.

He took an inventory of his ship's systems. This was a hardy little craft; as long as it didn't get swept up by the beetles itself, it would survive the death of the world. As well as a robust inner power supply it had solar-cell wings to be unfolded, and an ion rocket for manoeuvring: a rocket that would deliver a small but persistent push that could, in time, take him anywhere.

And, he discovered, the craft had a limited but functional self-repair capability. Even a small matter printer. This was no silver beetle, but the probe could manufacture spare parts to maintain itself, even manipulate its environment. He could last indefinitely, as long as he could reach a source of raw materials. He could even build himself a new body.

Where to go, though, to find those raw materials? Off on a comet, perhaps? Or further out into the dark, where ice worlds swarmed far beyond the planets? And if he *could* get out there, he would not be helpless; there was no end of things he could do. But there was plenty of time for that.

Plenty of time, too, to reflect on what he had seen. All he had left behind.

He felt a sharp stab of loss, as if Ben's face had materialized before him. But the choice was made, and it had been the right one. He had his memories, of Selena Jones, of Joshua – of Agnes, of Ben, of their home. And he had plenty of time to deal with a cosmos full of the silver beetles who had destroyed everything he cared about.

He fired the small rocket. The tiny ship slowly drifted away from the ruin of the Earth, away from the feeding frenzy of the beetles, towards the cool spaces beyond. He had plans to make, places to go.

And he smiled.

Just like before, Agnes. Soon, once again, I'll be in with the Oort cloud.

Acknowledgements

We're very grateful to our good friend Jacqueline Simpson for tracking down the source of Stan Berg's quotation in Chapter 48 – 'You cannot love what you do not know' – which comes from the first paragraph of the thirty-seventh sermon on *The Song of Songs* by St Bernard of Clairvaux.

All errors and inaccuracies are of course our sole responsibility.

T.P.
S.B.
December 2014, Datum Earth

BOOKS BY TERRY PRATCHETT

The Discworld® series

———————— Other books about Discworld ————————

THE PRATCHETT PORTFOLIO
(with Paul Kidby)

THE DISCWORLD ALMANAK
(with Bernard Pearson)

THE UNSEEN UNIVERSITY CUT-OUT BOOK
(with Alan Batley and Bernard Pearson)

WHERE'S MY COW?
(illustrated by Melvyn Grant)

THE ART OF DISCWORLD
(with Paul Kidby)

THE WIT AND WISDOM OF DISCWORLD
(compiled by Stephen Briggs)

THE FOLKLORE OF DISCWORLD
(with Jacqueline Simpson)

THE WORLD OF POO
(with the Discworld Emporium)

MRS BRADSHAW'S HANDBOOK
(with the Discworld Emporium)

THE COMPLEAT ANKH-MORPORK
(with the Discworld Emporium)

THE STREETS OF ANKH-MORPORK
(with Stephen Briggs, painted by Stephen Player)

THE DISCWORLD MAPP
(with Stephen Briggs, painted by Stephen Player)

A TOURIST GUIDE TO LANCRE –
A DISCWORLD MAPP
(with Stephen Briggs, illustrated by Paul Kidby)

DEATH'S DOMAIN
(with Paul Kidby)

A complete list of Terry Pratchett ebooks and audio books as well
as other books based on the Discworld series – illustrated screenplays,
graphic novels, comics and plays – can be found on

www.terrypratchett.co.uk

Shorter Writing

A BLINK OF THE SCREEN
A SLIP OF THE KEYBOARD

Non-Discworld books

THE DARK SIDE OF THE SUN
STRATA
THE UNADULTERATED CAT (illustrated by Gray Jolliffe)
GOOD OMENS (with Neil Gaiman)

With Stephen Baxter

THE LONG EARTH
THE LONG WAR
THE LONG MARS
THE LONG UTOPIA

Non-Discworld novels for young adults

THE CARPET PEOPLE
TRUCKERS
DIGGERS
WINGS
ONLY YOU CAN SAVE MANKIND
JOHNNY AND THE DEAD
JOHNNY AND THE BOMB
NATION
DODGER
DODGER'S GUIDE TO LONDON
DRAGONS AT CRUMBLING CASTLE

BOOKS BY STEPHEN BAXTER

Proxima

PROXIMA
ULTIMA

Northland

STONE SPRING
BRONZE SUMMER
IRON WINTER

Flood

FLOOD
ARK

Time's Tapestry

EMPEROR
CONQUEROR
NAVIGATOR
WEAVER

Destiny's Children

COALESCENT
EXULTANT
TRANSCENDENT
RESPLENDENT

A Time Odyssey

TIME'S EYE (with Arthur C. Clarke)
SUNSTORM (with Arthur C. Clarke)
FIRSTBORN (with Arthur C. Clarke)